SNEAKER WORLD

A DAMAGED PO$$E NOVEL

B.R. SNOW

Copyright © 2012 B.R. Snow
ISBN: 978-0984967537

Website: www.brsnow.net/
Twitter: @BernSnow
Facebook: facebook.com/bernsnow

Other Books by B.R. Snow

The Damaged Po$$e Series

- American Midnight

- Larrikin Gene

- Sneaker World

- Summerman

- The Duplicates   (*Coming Summer of 2016*)

Other books

- Divorce Hotel

- Either Ore

To Laurie

For all the obvious reasons.
As well as others not quite as apparent.

Greetings fellow Po$$e members.

And welcome to Sneaker World.

There's an old joke, although some maintain that the story is more accurately described as folklore, about a tribe of pygmies called the Fucarwee who live in complete isolation on a remote tropical island surrounded by a magnificent rainforest. Legend has it that the name of their tribe derives from their daily ritual of walking around their small village staring up from the dense foliage that blocks most of the sunlight and muttering to themselves, "where the fucarwee...where the fucarwee?"

However, this is not the story of the tribe you are about to meet.

But as I reflect on some of the other characters you will encounter as you navigate through the narrative about to unfold, it should become apparent that many of them are asking themselves that very question.

And if they are not, perhaps they should be.

Because the longer I remain on this planet that, of late, seems to be spinning faster than the scientists would have us believe, combined with what we see and learn about who does what to whom and when, I've truly become convinced of one thing:

There's a little bit of Fucarwee in all of us.

And if there isn't, you just haven't been paying attention.

Enjoy the ride and, as always, try to minimize the damage.

Be well.

PS - Murray says hi.

1

Summerman lowered the book and squinted, his left hand shielding his eyes from the late afternoon sun. He looked past the small man grudgingly inching his way out from water's edge and the two hundred pound dog woofing at him to hurry up.

Past the handful of swimmers and would-be surfers.

Past, after pausing to admire the skinny dipping woman's endless dolphin impression, all other distractions until his narrowed eyes came to rest on the horizon where the axis of sky and ocean met and merged.

Summerman smiled. Yes, life on this side could be very good.

"Damn it, Murray. Knock it off."

Summerman's gaze left the horizon, and he watched Merlin continue his cautious, off-shore adventure. Merlin's exploration had ended knee-high, but Murray wasn't satisfied with the effort. Summerman laughed as he watched the massive dog nudge Merlin forward. It wasn't a fair fight.

"I said knock it off, Murray."

The dog woofed loudly, spotted Dolphin Girl, and swam towards her.

"Well done, Murray," Summerman said. "You get Dolphin Girl. I get the phobic."

"Hey, Summerman. Check this out." Merlin was staring down through the clear water and meticulously shuffling through the white sand. "Look at this fish."

Summerman dropped his elbows in the sand to prop himself up for a better view and immediately regretted the decision. He winced against the heat and decided to try a lotus position from the safety of his beach towel. He poked his chest with a finger and watched as the skin changed from a luscious pink to white, to dark purple, then back to pink.

"Medium rare," he said, pulling on a shirt.

"Excuse me, sir. Did you order two Screaming Meemies?"

1

"I did indeed." Summerman squinted up at the young man holding a tray. Summerman beamed back at the huge smile he was getting from the waiter and guessed his age somewhere around twenty-five. He put his height somewhere around four and a half feet.

"Hey, Summerman. You gotta see this fish." Merlin refocused his stare beneath the surface.

"Enjoy your fish, Merlin. I'll stick with the Screaming Meemies."

"I'm not kidding. It's amazing. It's orange and black with green antennas sticking out the side of his head. And it's trying to nibble my toes."

"This is not good," the waiter said. He knelt down in the sand and set the tray aside. "You must tell your friend to get out of the water."

"Tell him to get out?" Summerman laughed as he watched Merlin. "It's taken me three days just to get him in that far. He wouldn't even shower the first two days until he'd tested the water for bacteria." He glanced up at the waiter. "He's such a baby."

"No, I am serious," the waiter said, staring at Merlin. "That fish is very dangerous."

Summerman stood and squinted at the fish that was now slowly circling Merlin's legs. Merlin transfixed, shuffled in a small circle to maintain eye contact. His movements only served to make the fish circle faster.

"That little thing?" Summerman said. "How dangerous could it be?"

The waiter began reciting.

"Sharp teeth resulting in hundreds of bites like paper cuts."

"Paper cuts? Man, I hate those." Summerman poked his forearm with a finger. "I'm fried."

"Severe spasms sometimes followed by total paralysis. If left untreated, death is also a possibility."

"Really?" Summerman leaned forward to get a better view of the fish. "That little bugger?"

"Believe me; it is very dangerous. The locals call him, the Revenge of Shiva."

"Shiva. Like the Hindu goddess?"

2

"Yes. Now please tell your friend to slowly get out of the water."

Summerman stood up and walked the short distance to water's edge.

"Hey, Merlin."

"Yeah," Merlin said, not taking his eyes off the fish that had come to rest on the top of his left foot. "Man, is this the coolest thing or what?"

"Why don't you get out? Your Screaming Meemie is getting warm."

"In a minute."

The waiter joined Summerman at the edge of the water and called to Merlin. "

You may not have a minute, sir."

Merlin stared at the waiter and then glanced at Summerman. "Who's the Smurf?"

"I am only someone who cares about your best interest, sir. You must immediately remove yourself from the water. But do so very slowly."

Merlin froze and stared at Summerman. "What's going on?"

Summerman took a long slurp of his drink and shrugged his shoulders. "Well, you see, Merlin. Apparently, there might be a bit of a problem with that fish."

"Problem?" Merlin increasingly agitated, glanced down at the fish, then back at the two men standing on the shore. "I don't see any problem. It's resting on my foot. In fact, I think he's, yes, it's tickling the top of my foot."

"Oh, no," the waiter said.

Fear began to override Merlin's curiosity.

"Oh, no what?"

"That's not a tickle. He's preparing to strike."

"Preparing to strike?" Merlin laughed. "Gee, for a minute there I was beginning to worry. Ooh, the big bad fish is going to strike." Merlin wiggled his big toe at the fish. "Ooh, death by fish tickle."

The late afternoon air was pierced by the screams of a man in excruciating pain. One hundred feet offshore, four buzzed resort guests froze as they mulled the possibilities.

"Uh-oh. I hear screams. Shark?"

"Here? No way, dude. We're too close to shore."

3

"Are you sure?"

"Of course, I'm sure. The beach is right over there."

"No, you idiot. About the shark."

"What shark? Oh. Yeah, I'm sure. Sharks hunt in cold water."

"Are you sure?"

"You're swimming ten feet away. You tell me."

"What?"

"About the water. It's warm. Right?"

"Yeah. It's perfect."

"Well, there you go. Problem solved."

"Cool."

An empty beer can floating in the water, grazed one of the swimmer's legs.

"Shark!"

"Where?"

"My leg!"

The swimmers churned their way back to shore and spent the rest of their day in safer waters; the swim-up bar in the middle of the resort's pool.

Murray recognized the scream and immediately swam in Merlin's direction. Dolphin Girl glided her way through the waves as she followed Murray back towards shore.

Merlin fell back into the water, and his left foot broke the surface and hung suspended. He twitched violently against the backdrop of the setting sun. Summerman and the waiter raced into the water and dragged the spasmodic Merlin by the shoulders to dry land.

"Get…this…thing off…me."

Summerman watched as the waiter covered Merlin with a beach towel. The fish's antennas whirred, and it chomped harder on Merlin's left toe.

"S-s-sonofabitch," Merlin screamed.

His body racked with convulsions as the screams echoed against the distant rainforest that filled the center of the island.

"Here." The waiter handed Summerman a bar rag. "Put that in his mouth."

"Will that help?" Summerman said.

"No, but he's scaring the guests."

Summerman nodded and stuffed half the towel in Merlin's mouth. His muffled screams continued.

"Wait here. I'll be right back. And don't let him move." The waiter sprinted towards the resort.

"Mmmm…mmm…fu…kkkaa." Merlin howled and shook like a vibrating bed.

"Hang in there, Merlin. Help is on the way."

Summerman patted Merlin's head as he struggled to hold him still.

"Ggg…gget…th…the…ffff."

Summerman leaned in closer and cocked his head.

"I'm going to need some clarification here, Merlin."

"Ggg…gggg…fffu,"

Summerman removed the bar rag from Merlin's mouth.

"Yeeeeeeeeooooooowwww!"

Wincing, Summerman tried to stuff the rag back in Merlin's mouth. Merlin wasn't playing.

"Open," Summerman said. "Open your mouth. C'mon. Don't be such a baby."

Merlin violently shook his head.

"C'mon, Merlin. Open your mouth."

Merlin slowly maneuvered his quivering right hand and extended his middle finger.

"That's not very nice." Summerman struggled to hold Merlin more or less stationary on the sand. "C'mon, open up."

Merlin shook his head but changed his mind when the fish tightened his grip. His eyes rolled back in his head as his mouth opened.

Summerman stuffed the bar rag back in place.

"Good boy."

He brushed the sand off his hands and turned his attention to the fish that had managed to wedge most of Merlin's big toe between its razor sharp rows of teeth.

Merlin's convulsions increased as whatever toxins the fish was pumping into his body continued to head north. Summerman leaned forward to examine the fish. Both bright green antennas spun rapidly on their axis and, despite being deprived of its requisite salt water, the fish showed no signs of loosening its grip. Like a dog playing tuggy with a sweat sock, it held on even as its body flapped back and forth in the breeze.

A small group of onlookers arrived and kept a safe distance as they watched the proceedings. The waiter emerged from the pack carrying a small leather pouch. He raced across the sand and slid on his knees through the sand. He came to a stop near Merlin's foot and looked up at Summerman.

"Try to hold him still."

The waiter dug through the pouch.

"Easy for you to say," Summerman said, ducking away from Merlin's wildly swinging leg.

"Just grab his leg and hold it down." The waiter reached into the pouch and removed a pinch of paste stinking of dead fish.

Summerman wretched at the smell but wrapped both arms around Merlin's leg. Seizing his opportunity, the waiter reached for the fish and pushed the paste into its eyes. Immediately, the fish stopped flopping and appeared to gag. The waiter placed a small amount of the paste around the fish's mouth. The fish released its grip and spent the next several seconds gagging and trying to get the taste out of its mouth. Taking his cue, the waiter grabbed the fish by the tail and hurled it over his shoulder where it landed with a soft splash. The fish spent several moments catching its breath, then disappeared from sight.

"You put it back?"

The waiter glanced at the incredulous Summerman and shrugged. "They're sacred."

"Well, that makes perfect sense." Summerman shook his head and refocused his attention on Merlin's steak tartare toe. "Man, that's gotta hurt."

Merlin's muffled screams confirmed Summerman's suspicion. The waiter reached into the pouch and extracted a small handful of another stinking paste. He carefully applied it to Merlin's toe and built a large poultice. The waiter sat back on the sand and admired his handiwork. "He'll be fine." The waiter brushed sand off his serving jacket.

"When?"

"Eventually."

Summerman removed the bar rag from Merlin's mouth and leaned in.

6

"How you doin, little buddy?"

"F-f-fucking hurts."

"I'll bet," Summerman said. He sniffed the air and laughed. "Man, you stink."

"F-f-finding this f-f-funny?"

Summerman used the bar rag to wipe away Merlin's drool and sat down in the sand.

"Well, you have to admit, it's something you don't see every day."

"You and your tropical holiday. We could have gone to Paris."

"When Doc calls, we come running, remember?"

"F-f-fuck him."

Summerman wiped Merlin's brow with the bar rag. Murray dashed across the beach, stopped next to Merlin and Summerman and shook vigorously.

"Jesus, Murray. You couldn't have done that when you got out of the water?"

Murray woofed and splayed out in the sand in front of Merlin's bandaged foot. He sniffed several times and sneezed. He padded across the sand and stretched out on a towel underneath his sun umbrella.

"Your dog?"

Summerman nodded at the waiter.

"That's Murray."

The waiter stared at Murray and tentatively extended a hand. "He looks like a tiger. Does he bite?"

"Only if he hears somebody calling him a tiger."

The waiter took a few steps back as he continued to stare as the massive animal. The crowd of onlookers began to disperse in the general direction of the resort as the Happy Hour bell clanged. A sunburned boy stayed behind and stared at Merlin as devoured a large ice cream cone that was dripping onto his protruding stomach.

"What are you looking at? You f-f-fat little f-f-fuck."

"Merlin," Summerman said. "What's the matter with you?"

"Well, he is a f-f-fat fuck."

The young boy stopped licking his cone and glared at Merlin. He swung a chubby leg and followed through with a swift kick to the injured foot. He resumed eating and waddled off. Merlin screamed and groaned his way through another round of body spasms.

"You deserved that," Summerman said. "What on earth has gotten into you?"

"Don't worry," the waiter said. "It's just another side effect of the fish poison. It's quite common for victims to express verbally whatever thought comes into their mind. I believe in the west you call it Tourette's. It will pass as the toxins work their way through the system."

"I don't have Tourette's, shrimp." Merlin struggled to a sitting position. "What are you, f-f-four-foot-four?"

"Four-six," the waiter said, ignoring the insult.

"Excuse me. I hate to intrude, but I couldn't help but notice that paste you applied seemed to begin working immediately."

All three men turned in the direction of the melodic voice tinged with a French accent. Dolphin Girl, clad only in a bright yellow sarong loosely tied around the waist, was standing a few feet away casually combing the salt out of her long, jet black hair. Up close, she was even more impressive.

"I'm so glad I don't have Tourette's right now," the waiter whispered.

"You got that right," Summerman whispered back. "I'd be in a whole bunch of trouble."

"Great tits," Merlin said, staring up from the sand at the statuesque woman.

The woman blushed and folded her arms over her chest.

Summerman stared down in disbelief at his diminutive friend, a card carrying asexual who viewed sex the way others would a root canal.

"Thanks, I guess. I hope my appearance isn't making any of you uncomfortable."

"No, no, no," Summerman said. "Not at all."

The woman smiled and closed her eyes and enjoyed the cool breeze washing over her. "I just love feeling the sun and wind against my skin." She opened her eyes and knelt down next to Murray, who was stretched out on his towel. "What a magnificent animal."

8

Knowing a good thing when he saw it, Murray rolled over and offered his belly to the woman. She accepted the invitation and scratched vigorously.

"I'll take some of that." Merlin lay down on his back and waited.

"Merlin. Jesus, what is wrong with you?" Summerman turned towards the woman. "That's Murray." He nodded his head at Merlin. "I have no idea who that is."

"Murray," she said. "You like that, don't you?"

Summerman scanned her browned skin from head to toe. The combination of genetics and swimming had created the perfect female form. That form, combined with the jet black hair that ended near the top of her legs along with her emerald green eyes, was leaving him speechless. Unfortunately, it was having exactly the opposite effect on Merlin.

"Do you shave or wax?"

"Merlin," Summerman said. "Stop it."

Summerman turned to the woman. "I apologize for my friend. He's had a rather bad experience, and he's just not himself."

"Yes, I understand that the bite of the Revenge of Shiva can be quite devastating. Potentially fatal if left untreated. That's why I'm so intrigued by the poultice you used."

The waiter, unable to maintain eye contact, shuffled his feet in the sand. "It's just an old family recipe."

The woman smiled at him.

"I see. Would you mind if I took a closer look?"

"I guess not," the waiter said.

"Knock yourself out," Merlin said.

She dropped to her knees on the sand with her back towards Merlin and leaned forward to examine the poultice. Summerman gasped and looked down at his injured companion.

"Merlin...," Summerman said, his voice rising in warning.

Merlin swallowed hard and propped himself up in the sand on both elbows. He glanced at Summerman and then refocused on the woman who continued to examine his toe.

"It's quite amazing," the woman said not looking up. "Remarkable texture. Yet incredibly firm."

"Thanks. I thought you'd never notice," Merlin said.

"And when I blow on it, it seems to harden faster."

9

The woman turned her head and looked at Merlin. "Can you feel that?"

"Oh, yeah. M-m-major wood," Merlin said, gasping through clenched teeth.

The woman gently brushed Merlin's calf with her fingers.

"How about this? Any sign of paralysis or can you feel my fingers?"

"Not sure," Merlin said. "Maybe a little higher."

The woman focused on her analysis, continued to work her way up Merlin's leg with gentle strokes. She paused at mid-thigh to check in again.

"How about that? Can you feel that?"

Merlin swallowed hard. "Maybe."

"Hmmm," she said. "Paralysis and numbness are supposed to arrive within minutes of the bite. But in your case, the paste appears to be counteracting the toxin. Are you sure you can't feel my fingers?"

Merlin bit through his lip and tasted blood.

"Not sure. Need doggie. Woof."

Murray cocked his head and barked once.

She eyed Merlin suspiciously and used both hands to squeeze his upper thigh.

"Maybe a bit more pressure."

His eyes rolled back in his head as she squeezed. Merlin moaned and arched his back.

"Okay, I get it," she said. "You're a little faker aren't you?"

"I'm going to need some clarification here," Merlin said.

The woman smiled and gave his leg a long, hard clinical squeeze. Merlin exhaled slowly then swallowed.

"Well, we certainly aren't having any problems with blood flow, are we?"

She stood and brushed sand off her arms. She turned to the waiter.

"If you don't mind, I'd like to talk some more with you at some point."

"I guess that would be okay," the waiter said.

"Great," she said. "Maybe I'll see all of you at dinner later." She looked down at Merlin. "I hope you feel better."

"I don't think that's possible," Merlin said.

10

She smiled and waved and casually strolled towards the resort. All three continued to stare at her until she disappeared from view.

"Wow, she's something," Summerman said.

He turned his attention to the waiter.

"You have my undying gratitude for saving my friend's life. By the way, I'm Summerman."

He extended his hand and shared a firm but strange handshake with the waiter.

"I'm Bantu. It's nice to meet you, and it was my pleasure."

Merlin climbed to his feet and limped over to the waiter and extended his hand.

"I'm Merlin."

"Nice to meet you, Merlin."

Merlin stared down at the young man's right hand he was holding. The thumb was in its normal position, but the other four fingers appeared stuck together.

Merlin stared at the waiter.

"Webbed fingers?"

"No, stitched."

2

Genevieve strolled towards the resort, stopping to buy a frosty Taj Mahal from one of the staff who worked the beach outside the resort.

"Where you keep money?"

"Just charge it to my room, please." Genevieve retied the sarong around her chest. She drained a third of the icy beer with one swallow and departed with a wave.

She entered the resort compound, flanked on one side by the immense swimming pool populated by a handful of guests on the precipice of an alcohol and sun-fueled nap. Waving to a small group of admirers she had acquired, she headed down the long patio that flanked the pool and eventually led to the hotel lobby. She retrieved her room key at the front desk along with a stack of messages. She glanced at the source and crumpled them into a ball. She tossed them into a nearby wastebasket and swayed down a long, open-air corridor covered by a thatched roof. Upon arriving at her bungalow, a name that failed to describe the comfort and opulence that awaited her, she opened the door and was greeted by the sound of a ringing phone.

Genevieve closed the door, removed her sarong and stared at the phone. She waited until the caller lost patience and then crossed to the mirror that filled one side of the room to begin her examination. She knew that her current routine was not sustainable, but each day in this paradise would remain filled with sun, sand, and surf. She moved closer to the mirror and examined her face.

"Thirty-nine and holding. You're hanging in there, girl," She frowned. "But this too shall pass." She allowed herself a moment of self-pity and then focused on her hair. Soon she abandoned her attempt to get her fingers through the tangled, salt-encrusted mass and headed to the bathroom. Genevieve began filling the Jacuzzi with hot water and a diverse collection of scented oils and bath bubbles. She stepped into the shower and spent several minutes washing and conditioning her hair. Satisfied that it would recover from the abuse, she turned off the shower, wrapped her luxurious lengths in a towel, and eased her way into the Jacuzzi. As the water reached mid-calf, she paused and waited for her body to relax against the heat. With her towel doing double-duty as a pillow, she sank into the tub, closed her eyes and inhaled. A combination of lavender and rosemary surrounded her, and she reached for the light switch. Now cocooned by the hot, fragrant water and darkness, she closed her eyes and slipped away from the outside world.

Her serenity was destroyed by the ringing that echoed off Italian tile. She opened her eyes in the dark but did not move, hopeful that the intruder would go away. A third ring, then two more reverberated through the bathroom.

"Merde." She flipped on the light and squinted against the brightness. She removed the towel from her head and grabbed the nearby phone. "Goodbye, perfect day." She took a deep breath and cooed into the phone. "This is Genevieve. Oh, hi. How are you?"

She sat up in the tub and massaged her neck with her free hand.

"Yes, I got your messages. I was planning on calling you a bit later. Figured you were in meetings. Today? I've been out…prospecting."

Holding the phone between her ear and shoulder, Genevieve grabbed a comb and began working it through her hair using long, slow strokes.

"Uh-huh. Yes, I know it's been a week, but this is not a place where you just walk in and start exploring. Besides, I haven't seen any signs of life anywhere outside the resort."

She put the phone down on the edge of the tub and picked at a reluctant strand of hair.

"Not that I've been anywhere outside the resort." She returned the phone to her ear. "What? I didn't say anything…I'm telling you, it's just not that easy to do…Yes, of course, unless that person is you. Well, not everyone is like you. That's why you are who you are, right?"

She smiled and checked her arms for sun damage.

"No, I am not being a smart ass. Look, I think I may have had a breakthrough this afternoon. No, I don't want to talk about it over the phone. You never know who might be listening. Uh-huh…uh-huh…yeah. Well, I'm thinking it's probably going to take at least another…month."

13

Genevieve jerked the phone away from her ear and listened at arm's length for the next several seconds.

"Are you finished? You don't have to be such a bastard. Look, you knew when you hired me that the bulk of my research would involve field work. Yes, we did have a nice time that night. No, I don't regret it."

She shook her head at herself in the mirror.

"But we both knew I would be spending a lot of time on the road."

Genevieve switched the phone to her other ear and slid deeper into the water.

"Well, I'm sorry," she said. "This is what I do. And I take my work very seriously. Plus, I want to make sure you get full value out of this contract. Uh-huh…yes, I know…yes…yes…yes. I know but Jesus Christ, Bent…sorry…Bentley…Jesus, all right. Sir Bentley. When you hired me, you didn't think it was going to be all champagne and blowjobs did you?"

Genevieve waited for a response.

"Did you?"

She drummed her nails along the edge of the tub. The rapid clacking sound reminded her of a miniature cowboy riding his horse into the sunset.

"Well, did you?" she said. "Good answer."

She rubbed her eyes and yawned.

"What's that? What am I wearing right now? Please, not now, Bent. I've had a very long day. Plus, I was exploring a mangrove swamp, I'm caked in mud and crocodile shit. I smell like a four day old dead fish that's been baking in the sun. I've got some skin rash that looks like it might be contagious….What's that? You have to run? Okay, I'll talk with you soon. What's that? Soon. Bye."

Genevieve hung up the phone and turned on the Jacuzzi jets. She turned off the light, repositioned the towel, and leaned her head back. She felt the water rushing up and around her thighs and sighed. Closing her eyes, she tried to drive the phone call out of her head.

"That's what you get for banging a billionaire,"

Sufficiently self-chastised, she laughed. The cumulative effect of the hot sun and cool water fueled by the two beers she'd guzzled took over. The jetting hot water began to coalesce in her upper

14

thighs, and she repositioned herself. Soon her throaty purr blended perfectly with the Jacuzzi's.

3

Sir Bentley Carruthers, billionaire, sneaker magnate, and exploiter of the poor on four continents, tossed his phone in the general direction of his assistant and harrumphed his way back into the leather chair behind his immense teak desk.

"Did you manage to reach her, Sir?"

Bentley examined the ornate fountain pen he had received from the White House as a thank you for his efforts on behalf of some endangered owl he wouldn't recognize if it bit him. Or maybe it was an eagle. Annoyed, he looked up at his assistant who hovered nearby.

"Gene, this thing doesn't work." Sir Bentley tossed the pen onto the desk.

"It needs to be loaded, Sir. I'll take care of it."

"You'd think for a million bucks they could at least put some goddamn ink in the thing."

"Most inconsiderate of them, Sir."

"Indeed." Sir Bentley rolled his shirtsleeves down and inserted gold cufflinks. "Now what did you just ask me?"

"I was asking if you managed to get in contact with your advance scout."

"Advance scout? Jesus, Gene. We're not making a western here. Yes, I just spoke with her. Nothing to report as of yet, but she thinks she might be on the verge of a breakthrough."

Sir Bentley, deep in thought, tapped the Owl pen on his desk.

"You seem troubled, Sir."

"I'm just anxious to get this one off the ground."

"Well, in all fairness to you, sir, the exploitation of indigenous people sitting on a goldmine of tribal medicines requires careful planning and execution."

Sir Bentley nodded in agreement.

"Very true. But let's not use the term exploitation. It tends to conjure negative impressions. Let's stick with, the necessary

16

commercialization of underutilized and valuable indigenous resources capable of providing enormous benefits to mankind."

"Well put, Sir."

"Indeed. And if those pygmies don't know the value of what they're sitting on in the first place, I don't feel compelled to enlighten them."

"Of course not, Sir. You snooze, you lose, right?"

"Indeed. A rather proletarian description, but accurate nonetheless."

"What if they offer some form of resistance?"

Sir Bentley scoffed and leaned back in his chair. "Sticks and stones make break my bones, but guns and missiles set the tone."

"Oh, that's good, Sir."

"Indeed. Don't worry. If they do offer any resistance, I'm fully prepared to deal with that as well. We need to get over there soon."

Gene forced a smile.

"I see."

"You're not pleased with my selection of her to lead this effort are you?"

"Permission to be frank, Sir?"

"Granted."

"I'm just not sure that when she learns about the details of what we're trying to accomplish here, Sir, she will have the requisite skill set and personal attributes. In all honesty, I must say that you had dozens of candidates immensely more qualified than her. One, in particular, was extremely well suited. I could pull her resume if you'd like to reconsider your decision."

"She has a Ph.D. and graduated at the top of her class."

"Yes," Gene said. "But from a state school, Sir."

Sir Bentley shrugged his shoulders.

"You can't have everything. Besides, she has other talents."

Gene nodded and looked down at the floor. Sir Bentley laughed.

"You look like your dog just died."

"I'm sorry, Sir, but I'm concerned that your latest venture could be derailed by an unqualified individual chosen for the wrong reason."

Sir Bentley harkened back to the weekend in Las Vegas where he had managed to achieve his favorite business transaction; the double consummation. First came the signing of the contract that would pay Genevieve a quarter million a year to purportedly lead a research project cataloging native plants. And the longer she remained unaware of his real motive of expanding into the burgeoning market of biopiracy, so much the better. The second act of the double consummation was an evening of drunken, explosive lovemaking that had left him both depleted and desperate for more. As anxious as he was to add biopiracy to his portfolio of global enterprises, he was even more interested in getting in her pants again.

"Are you still here, Sir?"

"Just give me a moment."

Sir Bentley sniffed the air, then shook his head and looked back at his assistant.

"Was it that good, Sir?"

"You have no idea, Gene."

"That is correct, Sir. I wouldn't. I've never even met the woman. But we still have time to replace her with someone immensely more qualified."

"Give it a rest, Gene. Okay, I think I'm ready."

Sir Bentley stood and slipped on his suit jacket.

"The press conference, yes. I believe the media are anxiously awaiting your arrival."

Sir Bentley snorted.

"They're jackals waiting to rip the flesh off my ass. What am I supposed to be talking about?"

"Just a short update on your European operations. Your talking points are already on the teleprompter. You don't need me there, do you, Sir?"

"Nah, you'd just screw it up."

Sir Bentley tugged his lapels and admired himself in the mirror.

"Let's just hope I don't have to stand there and answer a bunch of questions."

"At a press conference? What are the odds?" Gene said.

Sir Bentley nodded and harrumphed his way out of the office. Gene poured a small shot of brandy into a snifter and downed it in one gulp. He closed the door and helped himself to another.

4

Several years ago, Bentley Carruthers, a budding entrepreneur with a well-earned reputation for always being on the lookout for his next score, was knighted through a bizarre set of circumstances that included a brief, yet torrid, affair with the nubile sixteen-year-old daughter of a British Duke; forty-third in line to the throne and a direct descendant of the nineteenth century Earl of Earls.

Earl^2, as he was known to his friends, had led a small group of British forces into an obscure battle in an obscure South American country against an obscure band of indigenous gypsies.

Or traveling musicians.

Sir Bentley could never keep that part of the story straight.

The intrepid band of wandering minstrels had proven themselves a worthy foe when, as the legend goes, they lured Earl^2's force into a snake-infested lagoon and proceeded to keep them pinned down for several weeks using a variety of primitive weaponry. At this point, the real story becomes obscured.

Most historical accounts focus solely on the bravery of the British when faced with an enemy amazingly proficient with weaponry consisting of makeshift lutes and rhythm sticks. One account attributes the British demise to the minstrel's ingenious use of a complex series of mangrove catacombs and mazes carved through the lagoon. The troops diligently, yet unsuccessfully, tried to navigate their way through the dense jungle and hung tough until the intrepid Brits were ravaged by malnutrition and dehydration, snake bites and crocodile attacks. Only the troop's intrepid leader, the soon to be re-titled Earl of Mangrove, survived the ordeal. He returned home a war hero, was awarded a large country estate and lived the rest of his life in opulent seclusion.

The real story, as Sir Bentley learned in a post-coital conversation with the descendant Duke's sixteen-year-old daughter, was that the British troops, after having been helplessly lost in the jungle for a month under Earl^2 leadership, had stumbled into a remote community where a music festival, headlined by the aforementioned intrepid minstrels, was in progress.

Bentley scoffed as the young girl, between nibbles to his neck and chest, began to recount the story. Unable to convince him, the girl hopped out of bed and strolled naked to her parent's bedroom and soon returned holding an ancient leather diary. She climbed back in bed and began reading verbatim from Earl[2]'s detailed account.

Being an acquirer by nature, Bentley was already making plans for absconding with the diary even before the girl had finished reading. As she continued reading from the yellowed diary, Bentley, surprisingly found himself thoroughly engrossed in the story and paying scant attention to the girl's breasts, now serving as the perfect bookstand.

At the festival, the Brits had discovered a large vat of what appeared to be tea and proceeded to knock back several cups of the bitter, yet thirst-quenching beverage. As they would soon discover, the party punch contained not only tea but also large quantities of native hallucinogens. After several more hours of smoking powerful local cannabis through bamboo bongs, the troops developed a serious case of the munchies and headed back into the jungle in search of the nineteenth-century version of a 7-11. Their circuitous route eventually led to the discovery of a wild boar not pleased by the prospect of being dinner for a group of wildly hallucinating soldiers. The boar dashed for cover into the nearby mangrove swamp and all the troops, sans Earl[2], followed.

Soon joyful hoots and hollers became whispers of "Who goes there?" Soon the whispers were replaced by shouts of "Where the hell are we?" After several days, the cacophony of frantic, well-schooled British accents was replaced by silence.

And had Earl[2] not been discovered doing the horizontal Mambo with the tribal chief's third wife, he would have come to his demise right alongside his mangrove-challenged troops. Instead, Earl[2] was dragged naked from the hut and tied upright, four-poster style between two trees. The tribal council called an emergency meeting where, between slugs of tea and pulls on the bong, they discussed his fate. They voted 13 to 12 to let him live to serve as a warning to other imperialists about the fate that awaited those who dared invade their jungle in search of treasure or conquest.

Or their wives.

So Earl^2 was released.

But not before the chief had personally pruned the vast majority of the Earl^2's manhood off with a crude but effective version of garden shears. The tribe's medicine man applied a sticky, stinking concoction to the remaining inch and a half to stem the loss of blood and handed Earl^2 a week's supply of water and a small pouch of the killer weed. The tribe turned him loose with a rudimentary map that guided him out of the jungle and eventually back to civilization where he caught a ship back to England.

Upon hearing the actual events that had resulted in the loss of several of Britain's finest, the ruling authorities took the only course of action they deemed viable. They hired the best public relations firm of the day who punched up the story and created a national hero. After thoroughly enjoying a few weeks of good publicity punctuated by several public appearances, the ruling authority proceeded to bestow the new title and then banished the newly-christened Earl of Mangrove to his privileged life of seclusion with the stern warning to keep his mouth shut.

Sir Bentley smiled as he replayed the story in his mind and the afternoon the secret of the Earl of Mangrove's family history was revealed.

During their post-coital conversation Lady Prunella, wife of the Duke of Courvoisier and a direct descendant of the Earl of Mangrove, entered the bedroom and screamed. Several chaotic minutes involving the frantic search for the keys to the handcuffs ensued. Bentley and the girl soon found themselves face to face with Lady Prunella and the Duke in the downstairs library.

Certain his burgeoning empire and already shaky reputation would be dealt a fatal blow; Bentley prepared for the worst. However, he departed the Duke's estate thirty minutes later with the promise of knighthood secured. Through her parent's screaming litany Bentley discovered that contrary to everything she had told him during their brief courtship, she'd not only been sexually active, but downright promiscuous. To Bentley's surprise, her liaisons included half the house staff, a couple of British rock stars, three members of Parliament and, in an apparent effort to offset bad grades and increase her chances of being accepted into a top-tier university, several tenured professors from Cambridge and Oxford.

Fearing that public disclosure of another tawdry affair would be worse than their daughter's actual encounter with the predatory purveyor of perversity, they quickly acquiesced to Bentley's demand for knighthood. In return, Bentley agreed to Lady Prunella's demand to stay away from her daughter as well as the Duke's stern warning to keep his mouth shut. The Duke made the appropriate inquiries and with little fanfare, Bentley was knighted and banished from England by the ruling authority.

Sir Bentley, now firmly ensconced in New York as both magnate and quasi-royalty, loved holding court, espousing opinions on a multitude of topics ranging from the glories of global capitalism to the perfect wine served to compliment and offset the mild gaminess of roasted, wild pheasant.

Sir Bentley also had Earl^2's diary safely tucked away in his office safe.

5

"Just get your ass over there, secure the area and wait for my instructions. Can't you just do that without having to ask me a thousand questions? I'm paying you a boatload of money to do one simple thing. Something you've probably done a thousand times before. You're a soldier. Go do some soldiering."

Sir Bentley finished his tirade and stared up at the ceiling.

"I'm not a soldier." Doc's voice was calm, almost serene.

"Excuse me?" Sir Bentley looked back at the man sitting on the other side of the desk.

"I'm not a soldier. I'm a warrior."

"Is there a difference?"

"There's a huge difference, but probably not one you'd understand."

Doc began examining his fingers. He chewed off a nail fragment and spat it into the air. It landed near Sir Bentley on the desk. He glared at Doc and snapped his fingers in Gene's direction. Gene bit his bottom lip, shot Doc a dirty look, but wiped up the fragment with a napkin and dropped it in the trash can. Doc smiled at Gene who stood behind Sir Bentley and continued to glare back at him.

"Why don't you try to enlighten me?" Sir Bentley leaned back in his chair and waited.

Doc stared off into the distance. "A soldier is often asked to do things for the wrong reason. A warrior always does his best to do the right thing for the right reason."

"And the right reason in your case would be for money."

"No, that's a mercenary. Right or wrong never drives the behavior of the mercenary. In fact, it rarely even enters his mind."

Sir Bentley snorted and checked his watch. "Cocktail?"

"Vodka. Three ice cubes."

Sir Bentley snapped his fingers at Gene. Gene scowled but strode to the bar that ran along one wall of the office.

"On second thought," Doc said. "Make that four ice cubes."

Gene glared at Doc but remained silent.

"So doesn't what you do qualify you as a mercenary?" Sir Bentley said.

"Not at all. Like I just told you, I'm a warrior. I just happen to be a warrior who makes a lot of money."

"Thanks for the clarification." Sir Bentley rose and stood behind his desk. "Look, just put your team together and get your ass over to that island. Put your surveillance operation in place and then just sit tight until I get there. And for chrissakes, don't kill anybody. The last thing I need is the Indian government on my ass because you've blown away a bunch of natives."

"And my money?"

"As we agreed, I'll deposit half in your account today, and you'll get the other half when you finish."

Doc stood up and arched his back. He nodded and extended his hand. Sir Bentley shook it and put his hands in his pocket.

"I'm late for a meeting, but Gene will fill you in on the rest of the details." Sir Bentley paused at the door and turned back.

"It's rather strange that your background check turned up absolutely nothing. It's like you never existed. I find that highly irregular."

"What would you like to know?"

"Well, for starters, how is it possible for anyone to do that?"

"I always pay cash, and I never vote."

Doc smiled at Sir Bentley.

"Hmmm. You're a very strange man."

"Yeah, I get that a lot. Warriors are often misunderstood. The same way geniuses and creative souls usually are."

"I'll try to keep that in mind next time I run into Stephen Hawking or Sting. By the way, aren't you going to ask me about the reason?"

"The reason?"

"Yes, if you only do things for the right reason, don't you want to know what it is?"

"I haven't done anything yet."

"That's what I've been trying to tell you." Sir Bentley shook his head and glanced at Gene. "But aren't you the least bit curious?"

"Not really. I just assumed it was related to you making another billion or two."

"No, it's nothing like that. The money is simply a byproduct. The reason is for the betterment of mankind and the preservation of the American way of life." Sir Bentley winked at Doc and opened the door.

"Ah, an oldie but a classic. And all this time I thought you were just another pig at the trough."

"Is that a good enough reason for you, Mr. Warrior?"

"It's a bit clichéd but close enough."

"Close enough to be worth a couple of million bucks for you to find out?"

"What can I say? Warriors gotta eat too."

Gene and Doc watched Sir Bentley close the door behind him, and Gene handed Doc a small tumbler of vodka. Doc took a sip.

"Make that four ice cubes? Did you enjoy that one did you?"

"Just making sure you're staying on your toes."

Doc crossed to the door, opened it and scanned the hallway in both directions. Satisfied they were alone, he closed the door and nodded at Gene. Gene slipped behind the bar and located the wall safe hidden behind a large oil portrait of Sir Bentley. He removed a piece of paper from his vest pocket and began working on the combination.

"Officious little prick isn't he?" Gene said. "How the hell did you get us into this one?"

"Samuels. Sir Bentley fancies himself as a bit of man of espionage, and he just happened to step on some toes."

"He stepped on Samuels' toes? Stupid bastard."

"As Sir Bentley would say… indeed. Samuels asked Summerman to do a little research from the other side, and he found out that Bentley was the guy behind an Italian weapons company that's been selling some very nasty shit to some very nasty people."

Gene opened the safe, removed a small leather diary and handed it to Doc who immediately began taking pictures of each page with his phone.

"Summerman strikes again. Having a part-time ghost in the Posse comes in handy, doesn't' it?"

Doc chuckled as he continued to quickly snap photos of each page. When he finished, he nodded at Gene, who gingerly wiped the diary clean of fingerprints and returned it to the safe. They both sat down and sipped their cocktails.

"Where is Summerman? He hasn't checked in a while."

"He's on the island with Merlin."

"You got Merlin to go to a bug-infested island? This is I gotta see. What's your secret?"

"I have my methods," Doc said. "I convinced you to work for Sir Bentley, didn't I?"

"Don't remind me. But it's quite a lifestyle; I'll give him that. Hey, I'm sorry I couldn't convince him to use the scientist you wanted on the job. For some reason, Bentley is fixated on the one he hired."

"He's probably trying to get in her pants." Doc drained the last of his cocktail and rattled the ice cubes in Gene's direction.

Gene rolled his eyes but refreshed the drink and handed it back.

"I gotta tell you, Doc, posing as this guy's humble manservant is testing my boundaries."

"I'm sure it is. But it still beats the hell out of federal prison, right?"

Gene took a long sip of brandy and stared out the window.

6

Merlin limped his way across the dining room and plopped down into one of three overstuffed chairs triangulating the table. Summerman, examining the wine list, glanced up at his friend.

"Comfy?"

Merlin shrugged and casually scanned the room. He reached down below the table and stroked Murray's head.

"I've been better."

"Order some fish." Summerman laughed without looking up from the wine list. "Think of it as payback."

"You're funny for a dead guy."

Merlin stared at his big toe wrapped in a huge bandage. Summerman looked at Merlin's foot and sniffed the air.

"You been working your magic?" he said. "That smells great."

"Yeah, after I took a hit bath in hot water with a ton of isopropyl, the kid from the beach brought me some oil. It's some combination of lavender, basil, and coconut."

Merlin twisted the top off a bottle of water and took a sip.

"I finally got the image of that naked woman out of my head."

"Most men would have that burned into their brain forever. You can't wait to get rid of it."

"The whole episode was nothing more than temporary insanity."

"Need doggie...woof?" Summerman said, laughing.

"And I trust you'll take that one to your grave."

Summerman smiled at Merlin and waited.

"Shit. Never mind. Clumsy reference. Just keep your mouth shut. I have a reputation to maintain. And I shudder at what I might have done if the antidote hadn't been so successful."

"Well's it nice to have you back." Summerman refocused on the wine list.

27

"What's with the third chair? You finally teach Murray how to use a knife and fork?"

Summerman put the wine list down.

"I invited Dolphin Girl to join us."

"You're unbelievable. Let's hope the dining room isn't clothing optional like the rest of this place."

"Naked beach, good." Summerman shook his head. "Naked dining room, not so much." He leaned forward and whispered. "After I got you back to your room, I was headed towards the bar when I heard moaning coming from the hut next door. It sounded like someone was in pain. So I knocked on the door and guess who answered?"

"Dolphin Girl."

"Exactly."

"Was she in pain?"

Summerman stuffed half a dinner roll into his mouth. "No, she was fine. I was just surprised to find out that she's in the hut next to mine. I can't believe we've been here three days, and I just figured that out."

"You're slipping."

"She peeked out through a crack in the door wet and naked."

"And you believe that this is of interest to me for what reason?"

"I think she might have been having sex."

"I think that's something humans do from time to time," Merlin said. "You're the ex-rock star. Certainly, that doesn't surprise you."

Summerman washed down the roll with ice water.

"I've been watching her since we got here, and she's always alone."

"So you've been stalking her?"

"Not stalking, observing. I've seen a lot of people hit on her, but she doesn't seem interested at all."

"Maybe she has a boyfriend."

"Then why isn't he here?"

"Jesus, Summerman. If I wanted to have conversations like this, I would have stayed in high school."

"You graduated high school at eleven."

"Just to get away from conversations like this."

"You're no help."

"Maybe she prefers women."

28

"God, I hope not. For my sake."

Merlin laughed.

"Maybe she has a proclivity for inanimate objects."

"If that's it, she does one hell of a solo act."

"Good evening, gentlemen. I hope I'm not late."

Summerman stood up to greet Genevieve, who was wearing a bright green sarong and sandals. Her hair, unconstrained, trailed down the length of her back. The sarong matched the color of her eyes perfectly, and Summerman grabbed her outstretched hand and kissed it gently. Merlin made a brief attempt to struggle to his feet then fell back into his chair defeated.

"Not at all, you're right on time."

Murray woofed softly, climbed out from under the table, and nuzzled her leg.

"Well, look who's here." She knelt and stroked the dog's head. "Does he go everywhere with you?"

"Absolutely."

"The management doesn't have a problem with you bringing your dog here?"

"Murray doesn't like to be told no."

Summerman pulled the empty chair back from the table and gently slid it forward as she sat down. He sat down and beamed at Genevieve as she unfolded her napkin and smoothed it out across her lap. She stared out at the sunset then momentarily closed her eyes to enjoy the cool breeze that wafted through the thatched dining room. She opened her eyes and focused her attention on Merlin.

"And how are you feeling?"

Merlin wiggled his big toe and shrugged his shoulders.

"I'm fine," he said. "It's still numb, and I'm not sure what he put on it, but it seems to be working."

"Hmmm," she said, staring down at the large bandage. "Earlier on the beach, it had a rather off-putting smell. Now I'm picking up, what is that, jasmine?"

"Yes, among others," Merlin said, studying his menu.

"I'm glad you're feeling better."

She reached across the table and patted Merlin's hand.

Merlin's eyes narrowed as he glanced down at her hand and then glared at her across the table.

"Merlin," Summerman said. "Just relax."

"Who knows where that hand has been?" Merlin shrugged. "No offense. I just don't like people touching me."

She pulled her hand back.

"Really? I certainly didn't get that impression this afternoon."

"Momentary lapse of reason. See what I mean, Summerman? If this story gets out, my reputation is ruined." Merlin hid behind his menu. "I'm thinking about having the lobster."

"The clinical diagnosis is asexual-phobic," Summerman whispered to Genevieve.

"I heard that," Merlin said.

Summerman watched Genevieve as she looked out at the horizon. Her smile refused to disappear and grew even deeper when she caught his stare.

"Yes?" she said.

"I'm sorry," he said. "I know it's rude of me to stare, but you are breathtaking."

"That's very sweet."

"Of course, I'm sure you've heard that many, many times. I'm not saying it as a pickup line. Although if you were that way inclined I'd be most honored to share your company. I mean..."

"Take a breath, Summerman." Merlin peered over his menu briefly and then disappeared from view.

Genevieve effortlessly deflected the conversation as she studied the menu. "Let's see what we have tonight. I think I'm in the mood for fish."

Summerman, embarrassed, studied his menu and looked up as Bantu approached the table.

"Good evening, my friends," he said. "It's good to see you again." He focused his attention on Merlin. "And how are you feeling?"

"Very good, thanks to you," Merlin said. "I don't know what you used, but it seems to have done the job."

"Good, very good. Just a secret ancient remedy that's been handed down," Bantu said.

Genevieve looked up from her menu and gave Bantu her undivided attention.

"Fascinating. A secret ancient remedy. Do tell."

Bantu smiled back at her.

"Don't tell. Hence the term, secret."

Genevieve's smile disappeared. "I see."

"Don't you do anything but work, Bantu?" Summerman said. "Early this morning I saw you getting the kayaks and jet skis ready for the day. Then you hustled cocktails all afternoon. And now, you're working the dinner shift."

"This is nothing," Bantu said, spreading his arms to encompass the entire resort. "Compared to my previous job, this is a vacation."

"What do you normally do?" Genevieve said.

"I make Cloudlifters at the new GlobalCon factory," Bantu said. "Or at least I used to."

"GlobalCon?" Merlin said. "You mean to tell me those bastards have a factory here?"

"Yes, it's been in operation about six months now," Bantu said. "It was part of the post-tsunami recovery effort. A sneaker factory, plus this resort."

"You mean to tell me that GlobalCon owns this place?"

"Yes," Bantu said. "They are the only two businesses on the entire island. In fact, they are only businesses the island has ever had."

"Now I get it," Merlin said. "Doc. I should have known when he said he had a surprise for us."

"What's that?" Genevieve said. "Doc?"

Merlin glanced at Summerman, who was staring at him. Summerman slowly shook his head at Merlin, who nodded.

"It was just something my doctor mentioned," Merlin said.

"Your doctor had a surprise for you?" Genevieve said.

"Sure. He's a doctor. They always find something, right?"

"Sir Bentley Carruthers strikes again," Summerman said.

"Yes, Sir Bentley," Bantu said. "He is a very rich and powerful man."

"He's a prick," Merlin said.

"Here we go," Summerman said.

"Mr. Global," Merlin continued. "Posing as the champion of development in the impoverished, third-world."

"He has created many jobs," Bantu said.

"Sure," Merlin said. "And he pays people a buck for a twelve-hour day gluing and sewing strips of leather."

"Actually, it's two dollars a day for sixteen hours. But we do get paid overtime for anything over that."

31

"Unbelievable. See what I mean?" Merlin glanced back and forth between Summerman and Genevieve.

Genevieve stared down at her menu and avoided eye contact.

"So they're making Cloudlifters here?"

"What are Cloudlifters?" Summerman said.

"It's Sir Bentley's new line of sneakers," Bantu said. "The Cloudlifter: It's the sleeker, non-squeaker sneaker."

"Maybe I'll have the boar," Genevieve said.

"That scumbag," Merlin said. "Here he goes again marketing his crap to a bunch of kids who can't afford it," Merlin said. "And paying some already overpaid basketball player twenty million a year to endorse them."

"Yes, the inner-city children of poor nations around the world who currently go without shoes," Bantu said, reciting from memory.

"I'm sorry to tell you this, Bantu," Merlin said. "But the next child from a poor nation ever seen wearing Cloudlifters will be the first. Those shoes cost more than a lot of families see in a year."

"What do you mean?" Bantu dragged a chair to the table and sat down.

"Those shoes go for about two hundred a pair," Merlin said.

"Two hundred what?"

"Dollars. U.S. dollars."

"That's impossible," Bantu said. "I have heard stories that they were expensive, but I find that hard to believe."

"Believe it," Merlin said.

"Does anyone want wine with dinner?" Genevieve said.

"Great idea," Summerman said.

"So is that what happened to your hand, Bantu?" Merlin said.

"Yes." Bantu looked down and spoke to the floor. "I was working overtime a few weeks ago, and I momentarily lost concentration while I was stitching sneaker tongues."

"You mean to tell me that the stitching is still there?" Merlin said.

"Oh, no," Bantu said. "They got all that out but apparently the cross-stitching the factory uses fused the skin of my fingers together."

"Certainly, there's a doctor around here who could take care of that," Summerman said.

32

"There is a doctor from the Indian mainland who visits once a month, but I can't afford it," Bantu said. "Hopefully, someday I will be able to get it fixed."

"Doesn't the factory provide health care benefits?" Summerman said. "Certainly, they should take care of it since you were injured on the job."

"They told me they have no obligation in this case since it was a self-inflicted injury caused by negligence on my part." Bantu bowed his head. "I'm such a, how do you say it, klutz?"

"This is unbelievable," Merlin said. "And you can no longer work at the factory?"

"Not until I'm able to fix my hand. Making Cloudlifters is a two-hand job. But they did find me a job here at the resort. For that I'm grateful."

Merlin looked back and forth between Summerman and Genevieve. "Can you believe this?"

"Can we please just eat dinner?" Genevieve reached across the table and gently placed a hand on Merlin's arm. Merlin stared down at her hand, and Genevieve slowly pulled it away.

"Yes, let's order," Summerman said. "After all, this is supposed to be a vacation."

"Screw the vacation." Merlin staggered to his feet. "Come with me, Bantu. We need to talk."

Merlin limped off towards the beach, nodding his head for Bantu to follow him. Bantu slowly rose and followed. He paused long to chat briefly with another waiter. The waiter looked at Summerman and Genevieve and waved at the departing Bantu.

"I'm going to go with the boar," Genevieve said.

"Sounds good. How about you, Murray. One woof for the boar, two woofs for steak."

Murray woofed twice from under the table.

"Amazing," Genevieve said.

"He knows what he likes." Summerman reached under the table and stroked the dog's head.

Their new waiter approached the table. "Good evening. Are you ready to order?"

"Yes, thanks," Summerman said. "We'll both have the boar. And bring two of your biggest Porterhouse steaks, medium rare. And three baked potatoes."

"Excuse me?" the waiter said, glancing back and forth between them.

"Problem?" Summerman said.

"No, sir. It just seems to be a lot of food for two people."

"The steaks are for him." Summerman pulled the table cloth back to reveal Murray who was staring up at the waiter.

The waiter jumped back before recovering. "Wow. That is a very large dog. Does he bite?"

"Only if the service is slow," Summerman said.

The waiter nodded nervously and kept one eye on the dog.

"Two boar, two large Porterhouses. Would you like any appetizers? Maybe a nice side of spinach for your dog to go with his steaks?"

Murray growled softly from under the table.

"He doesn't like spinach," Summerman said. "Just the three baked potatoes will be fine. Thanks. And bring us a nice bottle of red."

"Yes, sir." The waiter backed away from the table and hustled towards the kitchen.

"I bet you always get great service," Genevieve said.

"You have no idea."

Genevieve watched Merlin and Bantu talking outside the dining room. "Does he always get that way?"

"Merlin has issues on top of issues," Summerman said.

"He does seem committed against what he perceives to be injustice."

"He is. We all are."

"All of you?"

"We have a small group that hangs around together. And when we see people who aren't able to defend themselves, we tend to react."

"I see."

"It's sort of a hobby," Summerman said.

Genevieve looked out towards the beach and watched Merlin's flailing hands move rapidly back and forth across the setting sun.

"What do you think he's going to do?"

"I have no idea. But it's usually a lot of fun to watch," Summerman said. "But let's talk about us." He squeezed her hand and caught her completely by surprise.

"Us?"

Genevieve frowned and sat back in her chair as the waiter arrived with their wine. He poured a small amount into Summerman's glass and waited for the performance. Summerman waved him off.

"Just go ahead and pour," Summerman said. He looked at Genevieve. "Unless you'd like to do it."

"No, I'm sure it's fine."

"At these prices, I sure hope so."

The waiter filled both glasses and departed. Genevieve remained sitting back in her chair but maintained eye contact.

"So tell me all about, Genevieve," Summerman said.

"Genevieve is all by herself and will be here for a while," she said. "What else would you like to know?"

Summerman sipped his wine.

"That will do just fine for now."

Genevieve smiled and looked out towards the sunset. The sun touched the horizon, and when she cocked her head to adjust her view, Summerman watched as the setting sun peered back at him from one of her emerald eyes. He spent the next several minutes sipping his wine and staring at the beautiful tropical postcard reflected in a vision.

7

He woke to the sound of the Gods clearing their throats. The rhythm of the rain pounding on the roof lulled him back to sleep, but another long, loud rumble from the skies caused him to sit up on his thatched mattress and pay attention. He glanced outside through the open-air hut at the wall of water cascading off his roof. He took a deep breath and smiled: How he loved the sound and smell of hard jungle-rain.

He checked the fire and was pleased that his method for ensuring that embers survived the night continued to work. The idea had come to him in a flash, much like others had arrived during his lifetime. The morning ritual of starting the tribal fire had grown tiresome. As Chief, one of his duties was ensuring that fire was always available. And over the course of many years, he had tried many times to figure out how to make the fire last through the darkness into morning without having to tend it himself or assign the task to someone else.

For countless moons, he had done just that. Adults assigned the responsibility for tending the night fire had invariably given the task to one of their children which the Chief found troublesome since children needed their sleep.

During one of their tribal festivals, Chief noticed that the in-ground pits they used to cook continued to smolder for hours. He began tinkering and came up with a way to use stones to cocoon a section of the night fire. He placed glowing embers on top of a small piece of teak, an extremely hard wood that took forever to light and even longer to burn. A hollow bamboo reed inserted into the side of the small stone structure provided enough air to the fire, and Chief happily discovered, come morning, the piece of teak continued to glow. The simple task of adding dried coconut husks reignited the flames, and the problem had been solved. From that point on, each family in the tribe tended their fire and everyone's sleep dramatically improved.

His sleep had become restless since the arrival of the gang down at water's edge. For months they had watched from a distance as the machines dropped from the sky and the intrusion began. Sights and sounds previously unknown to the tribe caused debate among the elders and had led some to believe that they were being invaded. Chief knew from his personal adventure long ago in the outside world that their arrival was simply an example of what Outsiders did; they arrived and usually stayed.

Using all his abilities and power as Chief, he had convinced the tribe that preparation for war was not the way to respond to the scene playing out on their beloved island. Although he had initially decided agreed to send scouts to observe and report back on what was taking place at water's edge, he had since changed his mind and pulled them back closer to the tribe. He knew that his son would soon return with fresh information about the outside world and possibly be bringing with him a trusted Outsider.

For years the gods had been providing signs of the outside world's incursion. Distant flying objects in the sky crossed the village each day and reports of fast machines speeding past the new structure at water's edge were common. Chief, while proud of the tribe's advancements, knew that their technologies were no match for those of the Outsiders. In his head and heart, the places he searched for answers, he knew, from the time of his own journey into the outside world to the present day, the gap had only widened.

Chief waited for the water to boil and made tea. He tied the leather wrap around his waist and stepped on the porch as the rain subsided. A group of small boys, naked and covered in mud, were chasing each other through the puddles. He chattered at them, mildly poking fun and warning them that their mothers would not be pleased with them. They laughed and chattered back at him and dashed off in search of bigger puddles. Chief smiled and shook his head at the sight. Such happiness, such carefree attitudes, and simple pleasures taken from a simple rainstorm. Chief knew that their lives were about to change. He could only hope it would be for the better.

Another round of throat-clearing arrived punctuated with the dangerous crackle of light. Chief chattered at the boys again, his voice lower, more commanding. The boys listened, glanced up at the sky and made a dash for their huts. Chief waited until they returned safely to their mothers and inspected the skies. This storm appeared larger than the last and Chief knew that the chores would have to wait. Chief, happy for the day off, nodded up at the Gods in approval and went back to bed.

8

Bantu woke to the sound of the pounding surf accented by the incessant squawking of seagulls fighting over breakfast. He sat up in bed, if a stack of palm fronds piled on a hard-packed dirt floor could accurately be described as a bed, and enjoyed the breeze. He lit the small camping stove he had found on the beach and put on water for tea. Stepping outside the small open-air shanty, he made his way to the makeshift shower he'd constructed from an oil drum, a piece of garden hose, and the sprinkler head from a watering can.

He removed the sprinkler head, put the hose in his mouth and sucked until he tasted cool water. He crimped the hose, reattached the sprinkler head and draped the hose over a tree limb. He stepped under the stream of water and scanned the empty beach. Bantu's eyes traveled north to the top of the island.

"Tomorrow."

He enjoyed a long rinse as he stood motionless under the water. Bantu was amazed that three years had passed since his departure and how fast the time had gone. Tomorrow he would return with tales of the Outsiders and their strange world. He would be welcomed back as a heroic pioneer, and the tribe would listen carefully as he recounted his experiences. Some would quake with fear while others would choose not to believe. His father would expect to hear answers to the question of what to do. And that was where Bantu needed help.

Bantu pulled the hose from the oil drum and draped it over a tree limb. He stood still and air-dried in the breeze. Glancing once again down the beach in the direction of the resort, he saw Dolphin Girl approach the water's edge. Naked, as she always seemed to be whenever she was near the water, she waded into the shallow water and then disappeared. Several moments later she resurfaced about a hundred feet from shore. Her early morning ritual continued to fascinate and intimidate him, and he was mildly annoyed when his morning ritual was interrupted by the sight of a man hobbling with way down the beach. Bantu grabbed his sarong and tied it around his waist. He walked towards the beach and waited.

"There you are. Good morning."

"Good morning, Merlin. Can I fix you a cup of tea?"

"Tea? No, thanks. I've had coffee."

"Come in," Bantu said, leading the way back into the hut. "I'm afraid it's not much of a home."

Merlin glanced around the hut but found nothing to comment on.

"Where is Summerman?" Bantu said.

"I haven't seen him this morning. He was talking with Genevieve when I went to bed last night."

"Do you think, what is the term Outsiders use, he got lucky?"

Merlin glanced in the direction of Dolphin Girl, who was back on shore toweling off.

"Luck is for suckers."

"What?"

"Nothing. Well, are you ready for your big day?"

"I must admit that I'm having some second thoughts. The factory manager does not like questions. Especially from his workers."

"Just leave the questions to me," Merlin said. "I know how to deal with these corporate hacks."

"But Summerman told me you can… "

Bantu trailed off and looked down at the floor.

Merlin's eyes narrowed.

"And just what did Summerman tell you?"

Bantu looked up at Merlin and shrugged his shoulders. "He said that you have the ability to insert yourself and alter the current reality."

"And he would be correct," Merlin said.

Bantu stared down the beach. "There's a reality I wouldn't mind altering."

"A bit smitten are we?" Merlin said.

"Smitten? I don't know that word," Bantu said.

"Smitten. Intrigued by, taken with," Merlin said. "Got the hots for?"

"Oh. Got the hots for," Bantu said. "Yes. Very much so."

"Yeah, well, get in line with the rest of the testosterone-challenged." Merlin noticed the blank stare Bantu was giving him.

"Forget it. We should get going."

"Are you sure about this, Merlin?"

"Bantu, you need to stop worrying. I'm going to take care of you. And you're just going to have to trust me."

Merlin wheeled on his good foot and headed outside. Bantu frowned and remained motionless in the center of the dirt floor. Merlin paused at the doorway and peered back in.

"What's the matter?"

"It's just that I've heard that before from others."

"What? The just trust me line?"

"Yes. I've noticed that Outsiders tend to say that more frequently than they seem capable of actually honoring."

"Well, Bantu, I'm not your normal Outsider. And you can trust me on that."

"Yes, Merlin." He shook his head. "Maybe repeating it over and over makes it mean more."

Bantu followed him outside to the path that led to the factory.

"This path is overgrown." Merlin slowly inched his way through the thick growth and brushed vines away from his face. "Ugh. I don't usually do this sort of thing."

"What sort of thing?"

"Commune with nature. Are there snakes around here?"

"Yes." Bantu casually strolled along the path. "And you can trust me on that."

9

Raining again.

Cursing everything that had become his lot in life, Gilbert glanced up from the production report he was reviewing and stared out through the glass windows of his second-floor office. He scanned the factory floor below on the lookout for recalcitrant workers. Gilbert remained vigilant against slackers attempting to extend their break beyond the allotted ten minutes or finding other ways to shirk their duties. All of these ploys, he was convinced, were designed to block his relentless pursuit of the daily production quota of 9,600 pairs of Cloudlifters. To the marketing morons in New York they might be the sleeker, non-squeaker sneaker, but to Gilbert, they were merely an assemblage of leather, rubber, and glue that, like his workforce, needed to be jammed and molded into a cohesive unit.

He polished off the last of his doughnuts, the sole benefit of being stuck on this shithole island with two hundred ungrateful workers, crocodiles, and the occasional fourteen-foot python like the one last night that had managed to work its way into Gilbert's bed. From a deep sleep where the repeating erotic dream had turned real, he felt a soothing, massage-like pressure work its way up his leg at the exact moment gentle kisses filled one ear. Fully aroused, Gilbert awoke when his dream companion, the naked woman from the beach, began applying the death crush. He opened his eyes to the sight of the python staring at him.

The python flicked its tongue and squeezed harder. Gilbert glanced down and realized that the snake was wrapped around his torso and had no intention of letting go. It was at that moment that Gilbert did what he later determined any other sane person facing a similar situation would do: He screamed and had a massive bowel movement. Moments later, after a gut-wrenching stench had filled the room, the python relaxed its grip and began to rapidly flick its tongue in and out. The tongue continued to test the air and the python slowly slithered its way off the bed. As the snake retreated, Gilbert gently raised one hip to assist the python's retreat.

Once certain that the python was out of striking distance, Gilbert grabbed a nine-millimeter pistol from his nightstand and fired seven shots from close range, two of which hit the snake. And after watching the now headless creature for the next hour to make certain it wasn't playing possum, Gilbert dragged its dead carcass outside along with his mattress and unceremoniously conducted a midnight bonfire.

The recent opening of Sir Bentley's luxurious five thousand dollars a night resort, a place he could neither afford nor was particularly welcome at, had done little to alter Gilbert's total hatred of everything the island had to offer.

Except for the doughnuts.

But even his beloved doughnuts, a daily baker's dozen of delectable treats, came with a price. And it was a hefty price that manifested itself in a 300-pound pastry chef named Hilda who loved to intersperse her lovemaking with a form of combat she had perfected during her days as a sheep shearer in the Australian outback. Gilbert visited her three nights a week where she would make him strip and proceed to vigorously wrestle him into submission. When she was satisfied that he had given her his best effort, she would straddle him from behind, a hand-rolled cigarette dangling from her lips, lock one arm around his throat and shave him head to toe with a pair of electric clippers. Their post-coital ritual included a wide variety of German pastries and heavy doses of styptic powder slathered on dozens of nicks and cuts she invariably inflicted as she maneuvered the humming shears over and around layers of belly fat.

Gilbert dreaded the humiliation and constant itching of new hair growth. He also detested Hilda's strategic use of mirrors that provided a panoramic, 360-degree view of their naked machinations. Gilbert had watched himself perform acts he wouldn't have believed possible. This former choirboy and cheerleader, this increasingly despotic factory manager, this burgeoning mass of humanity who had gained eighty pounds in a few short months, now found himself near breaking point.

Perhaps it was caused by an increasing sense of isolation from living in such a remote area.

Perhaps it was a bizarre subconscious drive for humiliation on his part

Perhaps it was the outlet he needed from the daily pressures of making his production quota.

Gilbert knew the answer to each rationalization was a simple no.

Certainly, the remoteness and daily pressure were factors, but they remained manageable realities. And humiliation was something Gilbert preferred to give rather than receive. In the end, Gilbert knew the answer behind his willingness to participate in the bizarre ritual that combined shearing and sweaty sex with a chain-smoking masochist.

Simply put, the doughnuts were that good.

Gilbert licked powdered sugar off his fingers as he studied the production report. He shook his head in disgust at the number on the final page. He pushed a button on his phone and his assistant entered the office.

"Yes, Mr. Gilbert." The assistant closed the door and stood at attention.

"Nilesh, have you seen yesterday's numbers?" Gilbert waved the report in the air and dropped it on his desk.

"Uh, yes, I have Mr. Gilbert." Nilesh cleared his throat. "I produce the report, sir."

"Well, then you should know that this is unacceptable." Gilbert stood up and stared out the window down at the factory floor. "We missed our quota. That's the third time this month. No, this simply won't do."

"We missed by six pairs, sir. We can certainly make that up before the end of the month." Nilesh stared down at the floor.

"Let me ask you a question. Does 9,594 equal 9,600? "

"No, sir."

"And isn't 9,600 our daily quota?"

"Yes, sir."

"And isn't it your job to make sure we produce 9,600 pairs of Cloudlifters a day?"

"Actually, sir." Nilesh cleared his throat. "With all due respect, I believe that is your job. My job is to help you."

"Well, since you're the only one in management who can communicate with these people, I have a somewhat different

44

interpretation of whose responsibility 9,600 pairs a day is. Are we clear on that?"

"Yes, sir."

"Two hundred people work here. That's an average of forty-eight pairs per worker each day?"

"Yes, sir."

"Sixteen hours of work. Three pairs per worker per hour. Are you following my math?"

"Yes, sir."

"Am I going too fast for you?"

"No, sir."

"Good. Now get over here and translate."

Nilesh approached the desk and picked up a microphone. Gilbert flipped a switch and a loud squeal filled the office and factory below.

"Damn," Gilbert said. "Nothing works around here."

"Would you like that translated, sir?" Nilesh said.

"No, smart ass. Just hold on a minute." Gilbert lowered the volume and stood facing the windows with his arms folded behind his back. "Okay, I'm ready."

"What would you like me to tell them, sir?"

"Tell them that I am extremely disappointed that they missed yesterday's quota."

Gilbert began rocking back and forth on his heels.

"Guan so meo for tos so."

Two hundred women and young children below paused from their work and stared up at the two men in the window. Several people nodded; other heads dropped towards the floor in embarrassment.

"Tell them that being part of a team often means individual sacrifice."

Nilesh translated the slogan into native tongue and waited for Gilbert's next instruction. Gilbert stared down at the factory floor and frowned.

"They don't seem to be responding," Gilbert said. "I'm not feeling the love. How about some respect down there. Tell them their great leader would appreciate some sign of support for his efforts."

"Yes, sir," Nilesh sighed and then spoke into the microphone. Loosely translated, he said, "Doughnut Boy feels neglected. Everybody in the room should identify the biggest prick on the island, then stand and salute him."

Small knowing smiles filled the worker's faces as they stood and saluted Gilbert. Gilbert puffed his chest out, harrumphed and returned the salute. The workers waited silently for the next round.

"Tell them, we need to continue pulling together as one cohesive unit," Gilbert said.

Nilesh nodded and spoke into the microphone.

"Fat boy wants to know, who's got the doughnuts."

Down below, several workers chuckled. Gilbert turned to Nilesh.

"Why did they find that funny?"

"Well, sir," Nilesh said. "In our culture, teamwork and good humor go hand in hand."

"I see, I see." Gilbert rubbed his chin. "Tell them; I see a bright future for this factory based on their skills and dedication to our company."

Nilesh nodded and spoke into the microphone.

"Doughnut boy's pants split when he bent down earlier this morning."

The workers laughed out loud. Nilesh beat back a smile and looked at Gilbert, who was staring down at the factory floor in amazement.

"Unbelievable," he said. "They work sixteen hours a day, yet they continue to laugh and smile. Tell them they have my admiration. And, don't forget our factory slogan. Long live the Cloudlifter."

"Doughnut Boy wants you to know that he likes to wear women's dresses with his Cloudlifters."

The factory became a chaotic mess of humanity as people fell on the floor laughing. Far above, Gilbert and Nilesh watched the outburst unfold. Eventually, the laughter subsided, and Gilbert turned to Nilesh.

"Most inspirational, sir," Nilesh said.

"Well, what can I say? It's a gift."

"Indeed it is, sir. Any other thoughts you'd like to share with them at this time?"

46

Gilbert looked down at the factory floor and shook his head.

"No, I don't think so. Just tell them to get back to work."

"The fat prick says break's over."

Down below, the chuckles and chatter stopped as people returned to their workstations. Nilesh turned off the microphone and stood at attention. Gilbert's intercom buzzed. A woman's voice.

"There are two men here to see you, sir."

"Two men? Here? Who?" Gilbert flipped through his schedule. "I don't have anything calendared."

"A young gentleman by the name of Bantu and another man. An American I believe, sir."

Gilbert looked at Nilesh. "Bantu? Does that ring a bell with you?"

"I believe he used to work here until a recent accident," Nilesh said.

"Ahhh, yes. The idiot who fell asleep at his sewing machine and stitched his fingers together?"

Nilesh bit down on his lip. "Yes, I believe that would be him, sir."

"An American? Probably some tourist who wants a tour of the factory. Or maybe a reporter. Go check them out and report back."

"That won't be necessary." Merlin limped through the door trailed by a nervous Bantu. "Why don't you just check me out yourself?"

"Why don't you tell me your name? That way security will know what to call you when they throw your ass out of my factory."

"Hi, Nilesh," Bantu said.

"Hi, Bantu. How are you doing?"

"I guess we'll see." Bantu shrugged and leaned against the wall at the back of the office and stared at Doughnut Boy.

"My understanding," Merlin said, slowly pacing back and forth in front of the desk, "is that you recently saw fit to terminate the employment of this young man."

Gilbert's eyes darted back and forth between Merlin and Bantu. He sat down at his desk, put his feet up and placed his hands behind his head. He stared up at the ceiling and then glared at Merlin.

"What business is that of yours?"

"Let's just say it interests me and leave it at that," Merlin said.

"Lawyer?"

47

"Hardly."

"Reporter?"

"Nope."

"Communist?"

"What?"

"Commie. You know, up the workers, support the common man, all praise Fidel. United we stand. Commie."

"Do I look like a communist?"

"Actually," Gilbert said, scratching his chest. "You don't look like much of anything."

Merlin's eyes narrowed, and he took a step towards the desk.

"If you're trying to intimidate me, it won't work." Gilbert continued to scratch at the new hair growth. "So why don't you and your little friend there go take a hike? In his condition, he's of no use to me at all. And when he's got his problem fixed, he can come see me and maybe I'll give him his job back."

"And how would you suggest he pay for his surgery?"

"Not my problem, man. Maybe he should have saved some of his salary," Gilbert said.

"You mean from his measly two dollars a day?" Merlin said. He placed both hands on the desk. Gilbert rose from his chair.

"Yeah," Gilbert said, leaning forward until both men's faces were inches apart. "From his measly two dollars a day. And in case you're wondering, those two dollars makes us the highest paying employer on this whole stinking island."

"There are only two places to work on the island," Merlin said. "And Bentley Carruthers owns both of them."

"Merlin," Bantu said, "let's just go. I just want to get the rest of my personal belongings and get out of here."

"Ah, Sir Bentley," Gilbert nodded his head. "Now I get it. You're one of the anti-globalists. What is with you people? We're here to help these people. We try to lift them out of poverty, and you ride in here on your white horse crying exploitation. Let me tell you, the vast majority of those people down there are grateful to us. That two dollars a day goes a long way where they come from."

"It's not two dollars a day," Bantu said.

"What are you talking about?" Gilbert said. "I sign the checks."

"It is two dollars before you take out the 36 cents for breakfast and lunch."

"What?" Merlin said.

"Hey," Gilbert said, "Nobody is forcing you to take eat at the cafeteria." Gilbert shrugged and waved an arm dismissively in Bantu's direction. "I'm not running a day care center around here."

"You son of a bitch," Merlin said.

"Okay, conversation's over," Gilbert said. He picked up the phone and barked. "Call security."

"Let's go, Merlin," Bantu said, tugging at Merlin's sleeve. "I just need to pick up my things at my workstation." He looked at Gilbert. "That's okay with you, isn't it?"

"Makes no difference to me," Gilbert said. "As long as I'm sure they belong to you and not the factory."

Two large men entered the room and closed the door behind them. They folded their arms and waited for instructions.

"Tell them to follow these men downstairs and then escort them off the premises."

Nilesh translated, and the two security men nodded but stared at Gilbert through narrowed eyes.

Bantu led the procession out of the office with Merlin, Nilesh and the security officers trailing close behind. A few moments later, after descending the short flight of stairs, Bantu opened the door to the factory floor and was soon surrounded by dozens of workers who shook hands – Bantu used his left – and slapped him on the back. The security officers smiled as they watched the reunion but gently nudged Bantu in the direction of his workspace.

"You back, Bantu?" said a young girl of around thirteen.

"No," Bantu said. "No, not back."

"But why, Bantu?" the girl said. "You work so hard."

Bantu merely nodded his head up at the second-floor window where Gilbert, arms folded behind his back, stood watching.

"Oh, him," the girl said. "He no good."

Bantu smiled at her and continued towards his workspace where he opened a drawer and removed a leather bag. He slung the bag over his shoulder and nodded at Merlin.

"Bantu," Merlin said. "I'm sorry. Trust me. I'll think of something."

They headed towards the door but stopped when they heard Gilbert's voice over the intercom.

"Stop. I'll be right down. Do not leave."

Gilbert disappeared from the window, and the sound of heavy footsteps were heard as Gilbert made his way down the stairs and huffed and puffed his way through the door.

"Where do you think you're going with that?" Gilbert looked at the workers standing around watching. "Get back to work."

Gilbert put his hand on his hips and tried to appear menacing while trying to catch his breath.

The workers glanced around the room. They stood their ground.

"I said get back to work," Gilbert said. "Please tell me you don't need that one translated."

"Cao ma son fuow yucka."

A ripple of laughter flowed through the room.

"What did she say?" Gilbert said.

"Sorry, sir," Nilesh said. "I didn't hear her."

"Liar. All right, I'm only going to say this one more time. Get back to work."

Nobody moved. Gilbert shook his head in disgust. "Fine. I'll deal with all of you later." He reached for Bantu's leather bag. "Let's just have a look at what you've got inside the bag."

Bantu recoiled and stepped out of Gilbert's reach. Several workers surrounded Bantu and, given his short stature, he disappeared from view.

"Where did he go?" Gilbert stepped towards the group that was shielding Bantu from view and started roughly tossing members of his workforce aside. A gasp went up from the crowd, and the security guards quickly moved forward.

Gilbert snapped at the security guards. "Help me find him."

The two guards ignored the command and began helping the women and children to their feet.

"Fine," Gilbert said. "I have to do everything around here." Gilbert pressed forward into the mass of workers. He continued to shove anyone within reach out of the way and onto the floor. "Come here, you little munchkin. Where the hell are you?"

Bantu eased his way through the back of the crowd and hid behind a large cabinet that contained pieces of leather and various glues. He peered around the corner just in time to see Gilbert make the decision that would prove to be his downfall.

Gilbert stormed through the crowd like a wild bull and came face to face with two young girls who stood defiantly with their

50

arms locked. Using every particle of his sugar-charged 300-pound force, he bowled over the two young girls and left them writhing on the cement floor in tears. The crowd, now on the verge of full-scale revolt, surged forward. Unfortunately for Gilbert, the two girls were the twin daughters of one of the security guards.

Commerce, being no match for family well-being, momentarily took a back seat. Both security guards made a dash for Gilbert, lifted him off the ground, and carried him by the elbows across the factory floor. Gilbert's legs bicycle-pumped in perfect synchronization with the security guard's steps until he was pinned against a large aluminum workbench. Gilbert felt the cold metal against his face as he struggled against the combined force of a large man on each arm.

Several moments passed as the workers stared at the scene in front of them. A young boy of about twelve separated from the pack and walked slowly in Gilbert's direction. He leaned in and stared at the side of Gilbert's face that was still splayed against the cold metal.

"What do you want?" Gilbert said.

The boy walked past Gilbert and opened the door of the cabinet Bantu was still hiding behind. He grabbed a long black strip of leather, a sneaker tongue complete with the Cloudlifter logo, and a large container of glue. He carried both items back to where Gilbert was and placed the sneaker tongue upside down the workbench. Gilbert squirmed as the boy poured glue on the sneaker tongue. As if he were making a peanut butter sandwich, the boy meticulously applied copious amounts of glue to the leather strip with a large wooden tongue depressor.

Gilbert, up to that point unclear about the boy's intention, had a moment of clarity and frantically tried to break free from the security guard's clutches. The security guards took this opportunity to strengthen their grip.

The boy completed administering the glue and picked up the sneaker tongue with one hand. Gilbert stared at the boy and then at the slowly approaching gooey strip of leather. Gilbert responded in much the same way he had to the python. Gilbert did manage to avoid a bowel movement, but his open-mouthed scream was exactly what the young boy was looking for. Gilbert felt the warm glue cover his tongue as the large leather strip stretched his mouth further open. A few drops trickled down the back of his throat, and he gagged and breathed through his nose.

"Gao wen fofu tak indo meow," the boy whispered into Gilbert's ear.

"Ga?" Gilbert said, his wild eyes frantically scanning the room for translation.

"He said not to close your mouth for at least five minutes, or you'll never get it open again."

Nilesh smiled at the young boy who was peering out from behind one of the security guards.

"Aghh...fu..gah." Gilbert's eyes rolled back in his head as beads of sweat dripped down his forehead. A ten-inch piece of shiny black leather, highlighted with the blue and yellow Cloudlifter logo poked its way past Gilbert's lips and teeth and rested on the cold aluminum, along with several puddles of drool.

The young boy picked up the glue container and poured small amounts on the floor near Gilbert's feet. He lifted Gilbert's right foot and dropped it down on the glue spot. He repeated the process with the other foot and then proceeded to glue Gilbert's palms to the workbench. He then stepped back to admire his work and nodded at the security guards to let go of their prisoner.

Everyone stared at the immobilized, spread-eagled factory manager. Other workers began gluing strips of leather and complete sneakers, to Gilbert's body. Gilbert soon resembled a display rack at Foot Locker. But unlike the racks containing footwear accessible from a gentle, one-finger spin; Gilbert didn't rotate.

The workers listened to Gilbert's muffled whimpers, then grew bored. Slowly, yet with a renewed sense of purpose, they headed back to their workspaces, collected their personal belongings, and left the factory. They paused at the door and removed the cheap sandals they were required to wear, and purchase for sixty-seven cents. Once outside, they felt the warm sand work its way into their toes as they shuffled away from their former place of employment and stepped back in time to the life they previously led and, for some now slightly obscured reason, left behind.

10

I'm a total idiot."

Summerman glanced up from the fruit salad he was devouring and wiped mango juice off his face. "This mango is unbelievable." He speared the last few pieces of fruit, gulped them down and stretched back in his lounge chair.

"Did you hear what I just said?"

"Uh-huh," Summerman said, turning his attention to Dolphin Girl, who was performing a series of aquatic somersaults about fifty feet offshore.

"And?"

Summerman waited until she disappeared underwater then looked at Merlin.

"Oh, you wanted a response," Summerman said. "I thought you were just feeling sorry for yourself. Let's see, someone with absolutely no authorization, went into a privately owned factory, caused a worker revolt, and watched while the manager got duct taped to his equipment."

"No, not duct taped. They used glue," Merlin said.

"And then you just left the poor guy there," Summerman said. "All in all, a very productive morning."

"The guy's a complete prick," Merlin said.

"All we had to do was hang out and wait until Doc got here. And you couldn't even do that. We've got this beautiful resort, and the sightseeing is incredible. Look at that. Man, I wonder how she does that."

"It's not like I was the one holding him down. I was just an innocent bystander."

Summerman cocked an eyebrow in Merlin's direction.

"It's total exploitation," Merlin said.

"You're a guest here."

"Some of them couldn't be more than twelve years old."

53

"And that surprises you? Jesus, Merlin. We see it all the time. But we can't do everything. Besides, it's none of our business."

"We've never let that stop us before."

"You're right. Allow me to rephrase. It's not why we're here." Summerman glanced over at Murray, who was preparing to start working on a dead fish washed up on the beach.

"Murray, you touch that fish, and you're banished from the beach for the day."

Murray turned his head and woofed at Summerman.

"You know the deal. No playing with stinky dead fish."

Murray stood at water's edge and waited.

"Come on over here and I'll order you a steak."

Murray wagged his tail and trotted towards Summerman.

"You know that's what he wanted all along, don't you?"

Merlin laughed and stroked the dog's head.

"Of course, I do. But have you ever tried to get the smell of dead fish off a dog?"

"Sure. It's very high on my list of things to do. So you're just gonna stand by and let it continue."

"No, I'm going to lie here in my lounge chair, sip another cocktail, and watch Dolphin Girl work her magic. That is if I can get a moment's peace."

"Typical."

"I'm on vacation."

"We've got work to do."

"You mean you've got more to do?" Summerman sat up his chair. "The factory's closed, the manager has mysteriously disappeared, and now Bantu has been fired from his job here at the resort. I can't wait to see what you've got left up your sleeve. What's next? Are You gonna organize a hunger strike? Maybe boycott papayas?"

"Funny," Merlin said. "I would have thought you might be at least mildly supportive."

"Merlin, when you punched the fruit vendor in Indonesia for allegedly short-changing you, who was there?"

"He did short change me," Merlin said. "Is it my fault the guy didn't understand exchange rates?"

"Who was there for you?" Summerman said.

"You were."

"And when you almost got arrested in Amsterdam for refusing to pay the taxi driver?"

"He took the long way to the airport," Merlin said.

"And then in Paris when you got in that dust-up with that French politician. Sweet Jesus, Merlin, the man invited to complete strangers to dinner, and you start telling French jokes?"

"I had too much wine," Merlin said.

"Then you start negotiating with one of the women at his table."

"I was just trying to save you some money. You're the one who pointed out that she was a hooker."

"I said she was a real looker, you idiot."

Merlin fell silent and pouted.

"All I'm saying, Merlin, is that, as your friend, I've been there for you. That is what friends do. However, friends also have the responsibility to tell each other when to back off. And as soon as Doc gets here, we're going to have more than enough to do."

Summerman stared at Merlin who refused to make eye contact.

"Merlin?"

"What?"

"Do you hear what I'm telling you?"

Merlin stared out to sea.

"Maybe."

"Hi, Merlin. Summerman."

Both men turned to see Bantu, dressed only in a pair of shorts and carrying his waiter uniform.

"Hi, Bantu," Merlin said. "Look, I need to apologize again for what happened."

Bantu shook his head vigorously.

"No. No apologies needed. I was about to quit my job here at the resort anyway."

"But what will you do?"

"I'm going home." Bantu stared up towards the rainforest that filled the center of the island, now completely shrouded in mist.

"Where is your home?" Summerman said.

"Here," Bantu said, spreading his arms.

"Here?" Merlin said. "There's nothing here except that stupid factory and the resort."

"My home is up there," Bantu said.

"What's up there?" Merlin said, squinting into the distance.

55

"My tribe," said Bantu. "The WeAreWee. That's the closest translation I've been able to come up with."

"WeAreWee?" Summerman pondered the moniker. "Oh, I get it. Because you're so small. WeAreWee, as in tiny."

"Yes," Bantu said, "In our language, the full translation is the little people who live with the snakes in the big jungle amid the clouds."

"That is a mouthful," Summerman said.

"Tribe?" Merlin thought for a moment and then nodded his head. "Now I get it."

"Son of a bitch," Summerman said, glancing at Merlin. They nodded at each other and fell silent.

"And I have a favor I need to ask."

"How can we help, Bantu?" Summerman said.

"It's a rather strange request," Bantu said. "And you are under no obligation. But it would mean a lot to me since you are the first two Outsiders I've met who I trust," Bantu said, glancing back and forth between the two men. "Well, that is not completely accurate. There were two women on the mainland who taught me many things, including English. But that's a long story."

"All the good ones are. And we've got all day." Summerman drained the last third of his cocktail and waved to the waiter. "By all means, please continue."

56

11

The extraction process Gilbert had devised to escape the clutches of the glue used to secure his palms and feet had, in his estimation, been ingenious; at least as an initial concept. Implementation had been more problematic. He'd spent the first hour waiting for someone to arrive and assist. But as time passed, Gilbert realized, unless he wanted his final legacy to be one of starvation or death by noxious fume inhalation, his escape would be up to him and him alone. With both arms and feet firmly secured he realized that the only appendage available to him was his tongue, now enhanced with several inches of leather sneaker-tongue.

He'd spotted a small jar that held a paintbrush and contained a solvent his workers used to remove glue when they'd made yet another of their countless mistakes. He extended his head forward and attempted to knock the jar over with his new tongue. His first few attempts to control the massive leather protrusion proved futile but on his fourth attempt, he managed to tip the jar over. He waited expectantly as the contents of the jar began to ooze across the workbench and towards his right hand. A rush of anticipation flared as he felt the first drops touch his pinkie and he wiggled and jiggled the tip of the digit until it popped loose. Using the pinkie to direct more of the precious solvent towards the remaining fingers, he eventually managed to free the rest of his right hand. His initial jubilation was cut short when he noticed several layers of skin forming a perfect handprint on the workbench. Trying not to obsess about the blood seeping from his fingers and palm, Gilbert began the painful process of freeing his other hand. Soon he was staring down at another handprint. He held both hands up and watched them pulse and drip blood.

The unbearable pain Gilbert felt was diminished to some degree by the effects of the glue he'd been unwillingly sniffing for the past hour. Giddy, yet nauseous and in a state of mind-numbing agony, he stared at his hands and watched the blood drip onto his shoes.

Remembering a first aid class he'd taken as part of the mandatory orientation program he'd been forced to endure before his arrival on the island, he raised both arms above his head. Much to his surprise, the technique of raising wounded appendages above the head did stop blood flow. Assuming the same pose he'd used last year in Amsterdam to surrender to the rabid junkie who was robbing him, he stared down and began to develop a plan to free his feet.

He scanned the workbench for another jar of the solvent and spied a small putty knife. He lowered one hand, felt the blood begin to seep and reached for the jar. Despite his woeful condition, he giggled as he knelt down and poured some of the liquid around his feet and waited for it to start working on the glue. He raised his arms back above his head, holding the putty knife gingerly in his right hand. The solvent wasn't working on the soles of his boots as it had on his flesh. He wiggled and jiggled and giggled in his boots with little success. He cursed and poured the remainder of the solvent and waited some more. To no avail, another round of wiggle and jiggle and giggle ensued.

And it was at that point that Gilbert had an epiphany. Others would probably have defined it differently with a cock of the head and a simple "Duh." Gilbert dropped the putty knife, looked towards the heavens and extended his Stigmata palms upward.

"Il ert, umtimes u r uch a umb uck."

Gilbert knelt down, untied the laces and stepped out of his boots.

He avoided the trail that connected the factory with the southern end of the island. Afraid to return home or the resort where an angry mob of ex-workers might be waiting in ambush, he headed into uncharted territory.

Later, he would attribute that unfortunate decision to the effects of the glue.

Two days into his fruitless search for the trail that had led him away from the factory and up into the dense jungle in the first place, Gilbert remained hopelessly lost.

12

Summerman readjusted the pillows and sank deeper into bed. He closed his eyes and listened to the surf as gently rolled landward. He'd finally convinced Genevieve to a late night cocktail in her hut but still put his chances at consummation well below fifty percent.

"I thought maybe tomorrow we'd take a hike somewhere. Do some exploring," Genevieve called from the bathroom.

"I'm afraid that's going to be a problem."

Genevieve appeared in the doorway with a puzzled expression. "Problem?"

"I was going to tell you, but then I guess I just forgot." Given the fact that Summerman hadn't been thinking about anything except how to get her into bed, he wasn't surprised.

"What's the problem?"

"Merlin and I have agreed to go with Bantu back to his village at the top of the island."

"What do you mean his village? Apart from the resort and factory, I've been told that this island is uninhabited." Out of view, she pulled on a thick bathrobe and sat on the edge of the bed.

"It's a bit strange." Summerman couldn't ignore the fact that she was adding layers of clothing the closer she got to the bed. Not a good sign he decided. "Bantu comes from some remote tribe that lives up in the rainforest and now he's going home after a three-year adventure out in the real world."

"That's odd." She casually examined her arms for sun damage. "And he's invited you and Merlin to join him. That seems even stranger."

"That's what I thought too. Apparently, Bantu's been asked to bring back a person from the outside world for the tribe to interact with. That was based on the assumption that Bantu could find someone he trusted."

"And that's you and Merlin?"

"I think it's more Merlin than me. I'm going along just to make sure Merlin doesn't get himself in trouble."

"So this tribe is dangerous?"

"Not according to Bantu. But who knows. It appears this tribe has been isolated from the outside world for centuries. As hard as it is to believe, apparently nobody knows they're there."

"Okay, Summerman," she said. "What is it that you and Merlin are up to?"

"What?"

"Who are you working for?"

"What on earth are you talking about?"

"You expect me to believe that the two of you just happened to show up on this island and are suddenly invited to visit some remote tribe nobody on the planet has ever seen?"

"Actually," Summerman said. "Yeah, I do." The lie rolled effortlessly off his tongue, and he waited.

"Hmmm," Genevieve said. "Well, it sounds fascinating. Any chance I can tag along?"

"Absolutely not," Summerman said. "Who knows what it's like up there? And if anything ever happened to you..."

"What could happen?"

"Have you seen some of the creatures that live on this island?" Summerman said, propping himself up on his elbows.

"They're just snakes and insects. And I am a trained ethnobotanist. I'm pretty used to harsh environments."

"No, I'm sorry," he said. "Bantu specifically said that it was just the two of us. At first, he didn't even want to include me until Merlin insisted."

"So you're just going to leave me here while you go off on the adventure of a lifetime. Well, thank you very much for that." She stood up and yawned. "I think I'll pass on that nightcap."

"Genevieve, please," Summerman said. "Look, there's nothing I can do. We'll probably just go up there, meet a few of the elders, and then head back. I'll be back before you know I'm gone."

"Assuming I'm still here," Genevieve said.

She crossed to the door and held it open. Summerman got the message and waved goodnight as he left. Genevieve watched the gentle surf touch sand as she sipped wine and considered her options.

13

Merlin zipped the small backpack, then folded his arms through the straps and pulled it onto his shoulders. Murray, anxious for his latest adventure to begin, wagged his tail and nudged Summerman's leg with his nose. Bantu, barefoot and shirtless, stood in the doorway holding a large bamboo stick that was sharpened to a point on both ends.

"What the hell am I doing here?" Merlin said.

"Hey, it's your fault," Summerman said. "We could be relaxing on the beach waiting for Doc, but you just had to stick your nose in, didn't you?"

"We should get started," Bantu said, squinting against the early morning sun. "Are you sure Murray will be okay going out into the jungle? We have a long day ahead."

"He'll be fine. I'm carrying extra food and water. And I never go anywhere without him." Summerman chuckled. "He's kind of like my two hundred pound American Express card."

Bantu stared blankly at Summerman.

"That was bad even by your standards," Merlin said. "Well, I'm glad he's coming along. I always feel safer when he's around."

He knelt and rubbed the dog's head.

Merlin and Summerman followed Bantu out of the hut and trailed closely as he led them up the path that led to the now abandoned factory.

"I heard some shouts coming from your room last night," Merlin said, already struggling to catch his breath. "And they weren't shouts of passion."

"Yeah," Summerman said. "Genevieve was pretty pissed she couldn't come along."

"Why on earth would she want to leave the resort to go trekking through a jungle?"

"She's interested in exploring the native fauna."

Merlin looked at his friend and shook his head.

"Every time you get a whiff, you're brain completely shuts down. I know you're dying to get into her shorts, but there's something about her I don't trust. It's like you never get the whole story when you're talking with her. Plus, she asks a million questions."

"She's a scientist. You should understand her level of curiosity."

"She's up to something," Merlin said. He scanned the island that stretched out before them and shook his head. "I hate the outdoors. What the hell am I doing here?"

"Because it's what the Posse does?"

"Don't give me any of that one for all, all for one crap. I'm only doing this to help the kid out."

"Aren't you curious about seeing this tribe?"

"Maybe a little. But I'd be just as happy if you took photos and showed them to me later."

"How are we doing back there?" Bantu called over his shoulder.

"Are we there yet?" Merlin said.

Bantu giggled and waved his arm, urging them to keep up.

"Nimble little bugger, isn't he?" Summerman said, picking up his pace.

Merlin nodded as they approached the factory. Bantu led them past the empty buildings and onto another path almost hidden from view. Soon their pace slowed due to the foliage that thickened as they began a slow ascent. A few hundred feet further the path ended. Bantu stopped and waited for his two companions to catch up. Murray discovered a large puddle of rainwater next to the side of the trail and began slurping loudly. He then decided to cool off further by rolling in the middle of it.

"You lost already?" Merlin said, staring at the impenetrable jungle that now surrounded them.

Bantu giggled again and wiped the sweat from his forehead with the back of his hand.

"I can't believe I'm finally going home."

Summerman glanced at Merlin, cleared his throat and then addressed Bantu. "Is there anything we should know about your tribe, Bantu?"

"I'm going to need a little clarification here, Summerman." Bantu chuckled.

"Well done, Bantu," Summerman said, laughing. "Well, for one thing, you said that they've had no contact with the outside world."

"That is correct," Bantu said, poking the bamboo stick into the nearby foliage.

"Are they a friendly lot?"

Bantu's eyes sparkled, and he winked at Summerman. "Are you wondering if you're going to be the guests of honor at some cannibalistic ritual dinner?"

"No, I wasn't," Summerman said. "But now that you mention it."

Bantu laughed.

"Don't worry, my friend. My tribe has an abundance of food, and we also place a high value on the human spirit. And as long as you're with me, no harm will come to you."

"And if we weren't with you?" Merlin said.

"That would not be good," Bantu said.

"Ah, shit," Merlin said as he stepped, face-first, into a massive spider web. He began extricating himself from the cotton-candy like threads.

"Watch out for that one," Bantu said.

Merlin froze and glanced back and forth. "I'm going to need some clarification here, Bantu."

Bantu pointed to the owner of the web, a large, brightly-colored spider about the size of his fist. Murray moved next to Merlin for a closer look at the web.

"Jesus Christ. Does it bite?"

Merlin took two steps backward and stood behind Murray.

"Only if you get too close."

"Deadly?"

"Only about half the time."

"What about the other half?" Merlin said.

"You just wish you were dead."

"You're a funny guy, aren't you? Are there a lot of these around?" Merlin said, maneuvering his way around the web.

"Let's hope not," Bantu said. He continued to poke his bamboo stick into the nearby thicket.

"What are you doing?" Summerman said.

"Checking for snakes."

"Lovely." Summerman scanned the ground near his feet. "And I guess there are a lot of those around as well."

"Snakes?" Bantu said. "Not as many as there are spiders. But, yes, we have many snakes here."

"Deadly?"

"Only if you get bitten by one of the poisonous ones."

"Any other deadly creatures we should know about?" Merlin said.

"You got a death wish?" Summerman laughed and adjusted his backpack.

"Sure, easy for you to say. You'd just need to wait it out for a few months."

"What?" Bantu said.

"Nothing," Summerman said, glaring at Merlin. "He's just babbling."

Bantu speared the bamboo stick violently into the underbrush and then lifted it high in the air. Murray woofed and went on point. Attached to the end of the stick was a huge snake speared through the head.

"Watch out for ones like this."

Summerman and Merlin stared at the dead, yet still quivering reptile.

"Cobra," Merlin said.

"Yes," Bantu said. "It's the only snake we try to kill whenever we see one."

"Are there any more around here?" Merlin said, snuggling close to Summerman.

Bantu giggled and pushed forward.

"You may as well ask why the sky is blue. Come."

Merlin and Summerman closed ranks and inched forward directly behind Bantu. They continued to hack their way through the dense groundcover for a few hundred yards until the foliage cleared and they found themselves standing on a section of rock, coral and sand. They sat down to catch their breath and gulped water. Murray discovered another large puddle and took another roll.

"Look up there," Bantu said, pointing at a waterfall in the distance.

Water cascaded off the face of a cliff and plunged several hundred feet, then disappeared past the foliage.

"Freshwater," Bantu said. "It's what sustains my tribe."

"Where does it end up?" Merlin said.

"You'll see."

Bantu hopped to his feet and looked up at the mid-morning sun. Summerman and Merlin followed as Bantu led them across the rock and coral. Soon, they were again confronted by thick foliage, this section even denser than before.

"I was hoping we'd be able to stay on the rock," Merlin said.

"If you follow that path, eventually it leads back down to the beach by the resort."

"Bantu, I don't want to be critical," Merlin said. "But if that path leads to the resort, why didn't we just take that on our way up?"

"Because it winds back and forth for several miles. It would take us forever. Plus, it's very dangerous."

"Let me guess," Merlin said. "Snakes, right?"

"Yes, but this time of year I worry more about the wild boars."

"Wild boars." Merlin shook his head. "Of course. Silly me."

Bantu giggled. "The boars roam all over the island," Bantu said. "But during mating season they tend to stay close to that path."

"And there's a lot of these wild boar around, I assume," Merlin said.

"Oh, my yes."

"Deadly?"

"Debatable," Bantu said, wiping sweat from his forehead. "But the males can be very territorial. Getting gored by a three-hundred-pound boar is not something I'd recommend."

"Noted," Summerman said.

Merlin looked at Summerman and shook his head.

"What the hell are we doing here? I could be sitting in the air-conditioned bar, and you could be ogling Dolphin Girl's hooters."

14

Dolphin Girl was, at that very moment, ogling her hooters. More accurately, she was staring at the bizarre insect that had dropped from a branch and wiggled its way inside her shirt. By the time she knew it was there, it was securely attached to her left nipple. The insect, a bright red-green creature that looked like a cross between a centipede and a leech, seemed quite content with its new found home. Genevieve flicked the bug with her finger which only annoyed the bug, and she felt dozen of little legs dig deeper into her aureole.

"Merde."

She grabbed a pack of Gitanes and lighter from her pocket as she unbuttoned her shirt. She felt the sting expand, and she pondered the long-term consequences of insect toxins versus the short term effects of third-degree burns to her left nipple. She took a drag on the Gitanes, flicked the cigarette clear of ash and slowly maneuvered it under the nipple. Grimacing, she waited as the insect initially tightened its grip but was then overcome by the glowing cigarette. The invader fell to the ground, and Genevieve stomped on it. She turned her attention to her already blistering nipple. She cut a small piece from a nearby aloe plant, gently rubbed it around the nipple, and slipped her shirt back on. She sat down on her backpack and slowly worked her way through the rest of the cigarette and tried to get her bearings.

She heard the rustling of palm leaves and then caught a glimpse of him out of the corner of her eye. Genevieve ducked behind a large palm frond and peered out at the strange man. He was short and fat, wild-haired and wild-eyed, and clad only in a primitive loincloth that appeared to have some form of writing on it. Caked in mud and blood, with a black tongue that protruded several inches and flapped against his chin as he walked, Genevieve believed she was about to become one of the first people on earth to have direct contact with a member of Bantu's tribe. Despite his bizarre appearance and bug-eyed stare, Genevieve felt excitement and anticipation rather than fear. As he drew nearer, she stepped out from behind the palm and made eye contact. She waited for a reaction, but he only continued to lurch forward and stare at her wildly.

Genevieve, confused, was consumed by one question.

Why on earth was this guy surrendering to her?

"Ot n e onuts?"

"I'm sorry," Genevieve said, extending her hand. "I don't speak whatever language that is?"

"Uh?"

"No, I don't. Do you speak English?"

"E…ya."

"Of course, you don't speak English. How silly of me." She pondered for a moment. "Parlez vous Francais? Merde. This is going to be a problem. My name is Genevieve." She pointed to herself. "I'm Genevieve."

"E…ya. I…O…U."

"I'm sorry, I'm not following. And you don't have to keep your hands up in the air. I'm perfectly harmless."

"Ops ta bud."

"Ops ta bud? Ops ta bud." She shook her head. "Sorry. I've got no idea what you're talking about."

"I ands," Gilbert said, nodding his head at his extended hands. "Ops ta bud."

Genevieve stared at the stranger's palms, wrapped with what appeared to be a mixture of mud and grass. She then looked back at the bug-eyed man. He opened his mouth and wiggled his massive tongue in her direction which she interpreted as a form of tribal come on.

"Not on your life," she said, shaking her head. "You surrender, I get naked? Sorry, that ain't gonna happen." But Genevieve was forced to admit to herself that the tongue was intriguing.

"Ah…ter."

Genevieve did her best to comprehend what the man was trying to say, but her concentration was broken by the wildly flapping tongue. He nodded in the general direction of the canteen draped around her neck and continued to wiggle the tongue.

"You'd like a drink of water? Is that it?"

The stranger nodded his head vigorously and lurched forward. Genevieve took a step back but removed the canteen from her neck. The man dropped to his knees, tilted his head back, and opened his mouth. His arms remained outstretched and reminded her of a short, fat version of Tim Robbins in Shawshank Redemption. Genevieve poured from a distance and watched as water bounced off the man's tongue and face. She leaned closer and poured directly over the tongue and into the man's mouth. She continued until the backwash threatened to choke him. He coughed, stood up, and blinked at her.

"U ay ve I ife," he said, smacking his lips the best he could.

"You're welcome." Genevieve frowned. "I think."

"Ot n e onuts?"

"You said that before," she said. "Ot n e onuts? What is that?"

"Onuts. Onuts."

Genevieve shook her head and pulled the pack of cigarettes out of her pocket. She extended the pack in his direction. "Gitanes?"

"I ont oke," he said, shaking his head. "I ant ohnut."

"You and that damn ohnut," she said, exhaling smoke. "Do you and your tribe live around here?" Genevieve extended her arms hoping to help translate the question.

The stranger shrugged his shoulders and waved his arms helplessly. They remained above his head.

"Are you lost? Did you get separated from your tribe?"

The question was close enough for Gilbert. He nodded his head vigorously.

"I see," she said. "Say, how about I help you find them?"

Gilbert smiled, and his tongue flapped rapidly back and forth.

"Damn," Genevieve said, mesmerized by the tongue. "The women in your tribe must be a happy lot."

"Ot?"

"Never mind. So, Mr. Jungle Dweller, which way should we go?"

"Ow te uck sud I O?"

"Ow te uck...mais putain," she said, crushing out her Gitanes on the ground. "I say we head up. How's that work for you?"

Gilbert shrugged his shoulders and waited.

"Okay, follow me," she said, starting to make her way through the thick foliage.

Gilbert watched her cargo pants stretch tight as she bent down to step under a spider web stretched between two palm fronds. Despite the relentless pain that surged through his arms, he smiled and followed close behind.

"Ice ass."

15

Doc felt the Gulfstream's landing gear drop and opened his eyes. Esmeralda, sitting directly across from him, glared at him and then hid behind her magazine. Doc shook his head and glanced behind him where Freak and Bob Garbo were discussing the most effective use of concussion grenades. Actually, Freak was doing all the talking. Bob Garbo just sat staring out the window possibly contemplating the effectiveness a concussion grenade would have on his chattering travel companion.

"We're about five minutes out," Doc said.

"Great. I can't wait," Freak said.

Bob Garbo turned in Doc's direction and nodded.

"Go screw yourself, Doc," said the voice from behind the magazine.

"Jesus, Esmeralda. Why don't you just tell me what I did to piss you off so I can apologize and we can put this behind us?"

"You don't know? And now you expect me to tell you?"

"I'm sure it could be any number of things. You've got quite a list."

"You got that right."

"So let's get it on the table."

"You'd like that, wouldn't you?"

"It has to be better than talking to a copy of Mercenary Monthly. What do you say?"

She licked her finger and turned the page.

"In your dreams."

The plane taxied to a stop, and Esmeralda stormed past the waiting jeep and walked towards the resort. Doc supervised the transfer of luggage and equipment from the plane to the waiting jeep and hopped in the front passenger seat. Bob and Freak climbed in the back, and the jeep sped towards the resort. Moments later the jeep slowed, and Doc cooed the offer of a ride. Esmeralda, without breaking stride, took a long pull of tequila and continued to stomp her way up the hill. Doc shrugged his shoulders at the driver, and they sped off.

"Look like you ain't getting any tonight, Doc," Freak said, leaning forward towards the front seat.

"What was your first clue? She'll be fine," Doc said.

"When?" Freak said.

"Sometime."

Doc pulled down his baseball cap and checked the rearview mirror.

"Women. Who knows why they do the things they do, right?" Freak nodded at his profundity and slapped both men on the back. Doc and Bob continued to ignore him for the rest of the short trip to Nirvana.

16

Freak spent no time thinking about or debating the definition of who he was or why he did it. He was a mercenary, pure and simple. He just wasn't very good at it.

If someone was paying him enough, he would go anywhere, do anything, and kill anybody. Born thirty-three years ago as the only son of Gerald and Meredith Hana in Scranton, Benjamin Hana came into the world with the label 'destined for greatness' bestowed upon him by his chronically underachieving parents. Young Benjamin's accomplishments hovered between mediocre and incompetent. Cursed with a limited intellect, an appearance described by his prom date as ghoulish, and a temper unsuited for someone destined to have the living shit kicked out of him on the playground, young Benjamin found school and life challenging.

Hated by people, avoided by dogs, and with no sense of direction, Benjamin spent his childhood alone and lost, figuratively, and often literally, left without a clue about his actual whereabouts in life. His father, one evening after spending several hours searching for his son who'd gotten lost walking home from school, remarked that Benjamin could get lost in a closet. And the very next day at school, Benjamin managed to prove him right.

But despite the tribulations young Benjamin faced during the first nine years of his life, things took a disastrous turn when a famous franchise opened a new restaurant near his house. The opening of the restaurant coincided with the start of the school year and Benjamin's new fourth-grade teacher, on the first day of class, had called young Benjamin, Benny. The smartest girl in class, someone young Benjamin had already pegged having the potential to end up a real bitch, put two and two together and cried out to the class, "Hey, Benny Hana. Bring me an order of egg rolls."

Not surprisingly, the new nickname stuck and young Benjamin became the constant target of barbed gems from children and adults alike. Even his teacher, a young woman driven by the need to be adored by her students, joined in the fun. And one night in tears,

Benny Hana related one of the teacher's comments that had brought the class to their knees.

"You know, Benny," she had said during a World War II history lesson, "You don't look Japanese."

His father, feeling an enormous amount of guilt for laughing at the story, along with the marital impact of the 'No Action Until Further Notice' sign Mrs. Hana had posted near their bed after her husband's ill-advised comment, tried to make amends with a surprise trip to the restaurant on Benny's birthday. Finding the food pedestrian, yet mesmerized by the chef's knife work on display a few feet in front of him, Benny identified his career path. He was going to be a soldier. A weapon's expert and extremely proficient with knives. Benny slipped a ten-inch knife under his sweater when the chef and his parents weren't paying attention, and a lifelong pursuit began. After slicing off the tips of two fingers, he doubled his effort. Benny began practicing every day after school in the nearby woods, but his poor sense of direction slowed his training until Benny discovered that he could indeed throw a knife at a tree and make it stick as long as he didn't particularly care which tree he hit.

By the age of sixteen, he had added pistols, slingshots, and nunchucks to his slowly burgeoning skill set. As questions and complaints began to build in the neighborhood about broken windows, missing pets, and other close calls that left local families hunkered down in their homes at night, Benny decided he was ready to take his act on the road. Benny made the decision to join the army and, after fully convalescing from his fourth nunchuck concussion acquired during an energetic, yet directionless, practice session, he bid his parents goodbye.

Desperate to hit their aggressive recruiting target, the Army accepted Benny's falsified birth certificate and looked the other way when it came to his grades and IQ score. They also acquiesced to his request for a formal name change. After careful consideration and a thirty dollar filing fee, Benjamin Hana became Freak. Hair-triggered and directionally-challenged, Freak somehow made it through basic training and achieved marksman status. His drill sergeant, who lost two hundred bucks on the bet, was stunned when he saw Freak's final test score. The sergeant was convinced, but could not prove, that Freak and his cross-eyed fellow trainee had somehow managed

74

to hit each other's targets in a bizarre, yet impressive, display of target range crossfire.

The score, while barely passing, secured Freak's spot, and he was shipped to Bosnia and assigned to a security post where he managed on his first day to wound three local women riding their bicycles home from work. Freak had been target shooting at the empty six-pack he'd drunk while on duty, but several ricochets had found their way into the ankle, elbow and right buttock of the three women. The army investigated the incident, denied any involvement, but did agree to pay the each woman thirty grand as a gesture of international goodwill.

By the time the payments were made, Freak was already on his fourth assignment. None of his commanders could stand looking at him, nor could any of them ever get comfortable knowing that Freak was armed and somewhere in their vicinity. After being held accountable for four incidents of friendly fire, and being suspected of six others, Freak was visited one morning by a colonel carrying honorable discharge papers and a one-way ticket back home. Unwilling to return to ongoing local ridicule, combined with the prospect of the bitter Scranton winter, Freak joined the Navy and assigned to a frigate patrolling off the coast of Antarctica.

His Navy career proved to be even more short-lived. One clear, blue day amid the bright white of the icebergs, Freak, bored out of his mind and freezing his ass off, began firing his rifle from his post near the bow of his boat. After indiscriminately firing a few hundred rounds at the massive blocks of ice, Freak paused to admire his work when he noticed streaks of red staining the pure white ice. Despite his defense that he hadn't been aiming at the napping polar bears because he'd been clueless they were even there, Freak received yet another honorable discharge as part of the deal cut between the Navy and several nations with environmental and financial interests in the ice flow known as Antarctica.

With his face and name now plastered on every animal rights website, Freak found his notoriety oddly pleasing. Despite the increased level of hostility he now endured, Freak remained defiant and adopted the persona of a hostile, D-list celebrity; a calculated look made complete by the full-length white fur coat he wore and accented with a shoulder strap of empty shell cartridges. Freak spent a whirlwind two months in California auditioning unsuccessfully for several adventure reality shows. All the various producers had concluded that whatever ratings bump Freak might generate, they couldn't ignore the litigation risks.

Freak, resplendent in his white fur, began stalking the streets of West Hollywood talking to himself. While blending in perfectly, he quickly became a nuisance and well known to local law enforcement. After a heated conversation with several members of the LAPD, he found himself missing the structure and protection of the armed forces.

Knowing that his total lack of a sense of direction would probably not bode well for a career in the Air Force, he wandered into a Marine recruiting center one afternoon and offered his services. The sergeant in charge of recruiting took one look at Freak, reviewed his file, and laughed, and laughed, and laughed.

Freak left the recruiting center completely pissed off as the sergeant wiped away tears of laughter. Down the street, he found his last option; the Coast Guard. Desperate for additional personnel and misinterpreting Freak's experience with weaponry as a positive addition to their ranks, the Coast Guard assigned Freak as a gunner on one of their newest cutters equipped with the latest in Homeland Security firepower, a prototype computer-controlled 76-millimeter cannon that fired 100 rounds per minute. Freak, overjoyed at the prospect of having this amount of firepower at his fingertips, could barely constrain himself from banging in a fresh set of coordinates and letting it do its thing.

Unbeknownst to Freak and everyone else, with the exception of a few senators on the appropriation committee, the weapon was manufactured by an Italian firm whose major stockholder was none other than Sir Bentley Carruthers. Also unknown was the fact that the only thing preventing the prototype from being installed on hundreds of naval vessels around the globe at a tune of ten million a pop was a successful live test.

Freak's cutter had been assigned the plum assignment of patrolling the waters off the coast of Hawaii where, on most days, the crew spent their time fishing off the back of the boat and keeping a close eye out for that major threat to national security, topless sunbathers. Bored out of his mind one day, Freak wandered unsupervised into the control tower and began fiddling with the controls.

Before he could even utter the words, "Uh-oh", the massive cannon began firing. Freak ran from the control tower but stopped on the lower deck to marvel at the show. It took two minutes for technicians to stop the balky prototype and it was later revealed that close to three hundred shells were fired. And if it hadn't been for the fact that one private yacht had drifted into the path of two of the shells, the incident would probably have been forgiven, if not forgotten.

One of the shells took out the stern of the yacht with a glancing blow. The other had entered and then exited the bow without exploding. However, the magnificent private yacht, The Pleasure Y, soon began to sink. Freak, along with the rest of the crew and several other witnesses on various craft and whale watching cruises, was stunned to see the sight of a naked man and woman appear on deck and raise their arms in surrender.

Sir Bentley Carruthers, Freak decided, wasn't in bad shape for a guy his age but what drew most of the attention was the naked redhead standing next to Sir Bentley. She was Bentley's soon-to-be-ex personal assistant, and the sight of her frantically waving her arms and bouncing up and down on the sinking yacht brought cheers and hoots from the Coast Guard personnel and polite, yet enthusiastic, golf claps from the elderly whale watchers.

Assuming that he was under attack from a reported renegade band of pirates who'd been terrorizing private yachts off the coast of Niihau, Bentley had given no thought to clothing on his way out of the stateroom and onto the deck. With his Viagra-fueled erection holding firm even in the face of personal tragedy and a stiff breeze out of the north, Bentley failed to notice the number of onlookers armed with digital cameras. Before he had time to lower his arms, the photos of him and his assistant went viral. Accompanying the photos were sketchy details about Sir Bentley's clandestine affair, the massive holes in the yacht, and testimonies regarding the impressive debut of the 76-millimeter cannon. Subsequent postings included photos of the assistant's former career as a pole dancer, along with hints and whispers about the potential involvement of Sir Bentley's wife in the attack.

His wife, while playing no role in the initial attack, did finish the job three days later when The Pleasure Y mysteriously exploded while undergoing repairs in dry dock. Due to his wife's personal holdings in Sir Bentley's companies and Wall Street jitters about what the dumping of that many shares would do to the stock price, Sir Bentley agreed to a permanent separation from his emotionally scarred wife. The agreement was straightforward. The couple would lead separate lives, Mrs. Bentley would keep her stock but have no direct say in the day to day operations, and neither one, under court order, could ever speak publicly about the events of that day.

Sir Bentley quickly recovered the 200 million the separation cost him when the prototype was approved for full deployment. The Coast Guard breathed a huge sigh of relief knowing they'd dodged a public relations disaster and, after the media frenzy had died down, they focused their attention back on the real cause of the entire affair. The Coast Guard brass acknowledged, despite Freak's total incompetence and inability to follow the simplest order, he had managed to shorten the cannon's approval process by at least a year. So the brass decided to reward Freak by not throwing his ass in jail. Three weeks after blowing Sir Bentley's yacht out of the water, Freak left the Coast Guard newly promoted to Ensign and armed with his third and final honorable discharge.

17

Bob Garbo, classically trained pianist and fluent in seven languages, was the quietest person on the face of the earth. Or at least that was Doc's opinion. During their quasi-job interview three years earlier conducted during Bob's second set at the piano bar of the airport Marriott outside of D.C., Doc made several futile attempts to flush out Bob's impressive but sketchy background he'd learned through the military intelligence grapevine.

As a devotee of the philosophy, if it ain't written down; it never happened, Bob didn't do resumes. As such, Doc had probed, circled back, reframed and eventually quit asking. Doc had initially considered shyness as the explanation for Bob's recalcitrance. But after watching him use his left hand to hold the melody line together while using his right to immobilize a drunken software salesman who was talking over Bob's jazz interpretation of Strangers in the Night, Doc scratched shyness off the list. Over time, Doc had come to understand that Bob Garbo was simply a man who didn't need words to make his point and that he preferred total seclusion to the company of others.

His reticence led to widespread reports that Bob was a distant relative of his Garbo namesake, Greta. One day on the firing range, when Doc inquired about any potential truth to that rumor, Bob shook his head no. When Doc had asked if he was certain that his family lineage had not crossed paths at some point with the reclusive actress, Bob nodded yes. When Doc asked how he could be so sure, Bob's nostrils flared in anger in the face of what he considered incessant questioning. But unable to identify a suitable non-verbal response to the question that wouldn't injure his new employer, Bob, through narrowed eyes, replied, "Cuz." Doc had nodded and left him alone, in part out of respect for Bob's privacy, but to a large extent because Bob was holding a high-powered rifle and could shoot the ass out of a fly at fifteen hundred yards. Over three years working together on a part-time basis, Doc had developed a reliable approach to use with the Silent One. Doc would gently ask Bob to do something and then get out of his way.

Freak had enough experience working with Bob to know better, but his lack of self-control and self-awareness had made him oblivious to the number of times Bob had come close to slitting Freak's throat in the dead of night or putting a bullet between his eyes. The only thing preventing Freak from becoming a casualty of not-so-friendly fire was the fact that the idiot was Doc's ex-brother in law.

Nine hours into their trek from the resort into the jungle had left both men tired and cranky. A light rain began to fall, and the steamy fog that wafted through the foliage slowed their already sluggish progress. Apart from the several miles he had hiked that day, the major contributor to Freak's anger and discomfort were the two backpacks, ammo belts and the case of Kingfisher he kept alternating between arms. Freak had long given up trying to stop the flow of stinging sweat pouring into his eyes. Bob, carrying a backpack and rifle, led the way through the thick jungle. He peered through the large palm leaf, then held up a hand and stopped.

Freak groaned as he placed the beer gently on the ground and removed the ammo belts. He slipped on the wet grass as he removed the backpacks. Both packs, holding various explosives, crashed to the ground. Freak dove for cover behind a large rock. Bob laughed, then shook his head in disgust and cracked open a beer.

"What?" Freak said. "You got a problem, Mute Boy? You try carrying these things."

Bob held a finger to his lips demanding quiet. He turned away and peered through the palms. He slowly scanned the horizon, sat down on the damp grass and began working on his beer.

"Warm," he said, wiping his mouth with the back of his hand.

"No shit, Sherlock." Freak grabbed a beer. "Gee, eighty degrees all day in this jungle humidity. Who would even think that beer would get warm?"

Bob burped, crumpled the empty can and reached for another.

"I'm going to die of a heart attack lugging this crap around."

Bob smiled.

"Fuck you, Mute Boy. How about you start carrying your share of this shit?"

Bob yawned and looked up at the rain that was beginning to fall harder.

"How did I end up in the middle of this jungle?"

Freak put his hands on his hips and glanced around at the thick foliage.

"Money," Bob said. He drained his second beer.

"Do you have any idea what we're even supposed to be on the lookout for?"

Bob shrugged and reached for another Kingfisher.

"Unbelievable. I'm stuck out here with the snakes and spiders, looking for who knows what, while that prick Doc is drinking martinis and banging the crap out of Esmeralda. I get to schlep around a couple of hundred pounds of firepower with a silent-era Tarzan."

"You Jane," Bob said.

He burped loudly and massaged his neck.

"Funny," Freak said, grabbing another beer. "Yeah, you Jane. That makes perfect sense. I've been wondering about you for a while now. Just don't try anything while we're out here. I should warn you. I sleep with a knife."

Bob gave Freak a dead-eyed stare as he removed a massive hunting knife from its sheaf and began to clean his fingernails.

"Man, I'm dehydrated. Feel my head. I think I'm running a fever." Freak took a step in Bob's direction.

Bob laughed and pulled the brim of his Yankees cap down. He returned the knife to its sheath and removed a piece of equipment from the small bag. The high-tech device, a combination video camera, and GPS system, was the last of the forty they'd spent the day installing based on the coordinates Doc had provided. Bob placed the device on a rock surrounded by damp ferns and checked to make sure the lens was unobstructed. He wiped his hands on his pants and pointed to a nearby clearing.

"There." Bob easily hoisted his backpack and strolled towards the clearing.

"There what?" Freak said.

"Camp."

"Camp? Out here? Are you out of your mind? We've got plenty of time to get back to the resort if we hustle."

"No," said Bob, not bothering to glance back at the protesting Freak.

"Look, Mute Boy. All we had to do was lay in the cameras and the GPS. And you just finished the last one. So we're done. That was all the instructions I got. Did Doc tell you to do something different?"

Bob stared at Freak.

"Oh, pardon me. My mistake. Nobody tells Mute Boy what to do. For chrissakes, what did he ask you to do?"

"Stay."

"And?"

"Watch."

Freak shook his head in disbelief. "Stay. Watch. What the hell are you, a Golden Retriever?"

"Woof."

"Funny. What else did he say?"

"Wait."

"Wait for what? A sign from above?"

Bob shrugged and began assembling a small tent.

"Were you dropped on your head as a child? You know they do make words that have more than one syllable."

"Indubitably," Bob said.

"Huh?" Freak said, taking another look around at his surroundings. "Well, screw him. I'm going back."

"Good." Bob began collecting leaves and small pieces of wood into a pile near the tent.

Freak shook his head, then stood up and grabbed one of the backpacks. He adjusted the strap, knelt down and grabbed six more beers. He took two steps but then paused.

"Do you think there are animals out here that feed this time of day?"

"Yup."

"What kind?"

"Hungry ones," Bob said, striking a match to the kindling.

"I'm serious. You think there are things like… tigers?"

Bob considered the question and shrugged.

"Well, I know there are snakes."

Bob blew on the flickering flame until it flared and took hold.

"If it's a choice between sleeping next to you in a tent and worrying all night if you're going to slit my throat or try to slip me the high hard one, I'll take my chances. I'm outta here."

Freak slung a second bag, this one long and narrow, over his shoulder and headed back through the thick group of palms they had just cut their way through. Bob leaned back against a rock, stretched his legs out and opened a fresh beer. He took a quick inventory.

Fire. Decent food. Half a case of beer.

And no sign of Freak.

Life was good.

**

Freak grumbled the first quarter mile and then took a wrong turn that led him further up into the island and away from the resort. About a mile later it dawned on him that he was hopelessly lost. One would think that a person with honorable discharges from three branches of the U.S. military would know the difference between north and south and be able to remember that the sun did indeed set in the west. However, this proved not to be the case as Freak wandered aimlessly for the next two hours through the dense jungle increasingly shrouded in mist.

Pissed off and out of beer, Freak stopped to take a leak against a thicket of ferns. Halfway through emptying his bladder and down to 96 bottles of beer on the wall, Freak felt what he assumed was an insect biting the back of his neck. Freak slapped at the spot in question. His fingers brushed against what felt like feathers, but he didn't have enough time to comprehend either that likelihood or potential implications. Seconds later, Freak dropped to his knees and murmured something about 95 bottles as he fell forward, face-first into the foggy, urine-drenched ferns.

18

Bantu stopped and pressed a finger to his lips. Merlin and Summerman fell silent and waited for further instructions from Bantu. They'd been walking for hours, and all three were tired, hungry, and increasingly cranky. Murray was slowing down as well, except for the tail. That continued to keep perfect time.

Bantu took a deep breath and expelled a loud bird-like sound that caused every flying creature within a mile to take wing. Silence soon returned to the jungle and Bantu stood still apparently waiting for some form of response to his call. He didn't have to wait long.

A *pfffft* sound raced through the air that was followed by a soft grunt. Merlin dropped to his knees on the soft undergrowth. Summerman watched as Merlin began to spasm.

"What are you doing down there?"

"I don't know," Merlin said as he pitched forward face-down into a small patch of ferns.

"Oh, no," Bantu said.

He dropped to his knees, rolled the unconscious Merlin over and removed the small feathered dart imbedded in the side of his neck. Bantu frantically removed the leather pouch draped over his shoulders and rummaged through it. He extracted a small handful of a sticky substance and forced it down Merlin's throat. He worked his hands up and down Merlin's throat, then sat down to wait.

Pfffft.

Summerman recoiled as another dart whizzed past his head and hammered into a nearby stalk of bamboo.

"Tuber," Bantu said, shaking his head in disgust.

"Not tuber. Dart." Summerman and Murray dove for cover behind a rock. "And I'm assuming they're poisonous."

"No, the guard on duty must be Tuber. He's probably forgotten to be on the lookout for me. He never pays attention in meetings. He's what you Westerners call, what's the term I'm looking for?"

"The village idiot?"

84

"Exactly," Bantu said, scrambling to his feet. "That's Tuber."

"Probably not the best person to give poison darts to."

Bantu nodded and repeated the bird call.

Merlin moaned and blinked rapidly until his eyes managed to stay open. "Where am I?"

"Good question." Summerman peered over the rock he and Murray were hiding behind.

"What's going on?"

"The village idiot is firing poison darts at us," Summerman said, scanning the horizon.

"That's nice," Merlin said as he curled into a ball and began dozing.

"Wake him up," Bantu said. "He needs to stay awake."

Pffffft.

The dart veered high and left, and Summerman caught a glimpse of it as it flashed by and disappeared into the jungle. He gently slapped Merlin's face repeatedly. Merlin moaned and cursed at him, but did manage to stay awake.

"He's not used to visitors," Bantu said.

"No shit," Summerman said, shaking Merlin's shoulders.

"Cut it out," Merlin said. "Stop hitting me, you fuck."

Bantu began yelling in native tongue. Summerman couldn't understand a word but was certain the message contained several expletives. Bantu stopped ranting and waited. Summerman pulled Merlin to a sitting position.

"Think he got the message?" Summerman said.

"With Tuber, one never knows," Bantu said, scanning the trees for signs of the sentry.

Eventually, they heard the return call. It went on for several seconds and Bantu listened closely. He shook his head. "Yeah, it's Tuber."

"What'd he say?"

"He recited the recipe for roasted wild boar," Bantu said. "It's his favorite."

"This is the guy you assign to protect your tribe?" Summerman said, climbing to his feet.

"It's the safest place to put him. Nobody in the tribe likes having him around. He makes everyone nervous. This is probably the first time he's ever had to defend his post. But I need to warn you not to underestimate him. He's not bright, but he's very fierce. So while you're here, do your absolute best not to make him angry."

"Anger can be a cleansing emotion," Merlin said.

"Is he going to be okay?" Summerman said, kneeling over Merlin and looking into his vacant stare.

"He'll be fine. But without the antidote I gave him, he'd be, as you say, toast."

Bantu giggled at his joke and waved towards the trees.

"Nasty little thing," Summerman said, examining the sharp feathered object. He rolled it in his fingers and gingerly tested the tip with his index finger. "So he just got lucky on that first shot?"

"Please don't play with that," Bantu said, taking the dart and dropping it into his leather pouch. "No, the first shot was what you should expect. The other two were warning shots."

"Don't warning shots usually come first?"

"Like I say. It's Tuber," Bantu said.

He raced in the direction of a small man who was holding a blowgun in one hand and waving frantically with the other. Summerman watched Bantu and the man hug, slap each other's back and chatter loudly. When the initial joy of their reunion subsided, Bantu pointed back at Summerman and Merlin. Tuber's demeanor immediately changed. He stared menacingly and slowly pulled the blowgun to his lips. Bantu tapped the blow gun away from his mouth, but the intense stare continued.

Tuber then noticed Murray staring at him and took two steps backward. He chattered at Merlin and glanced back at the massive dog.

"What's wrong with him?" Summerman said.

"He's wondering what kind of tiger Murray is and which one of you has the ability to tame him."

"Just tell him that Murray is a dog and that he won't hurt him."

Bantu thought in silence.

"Maybe we should just let Tuber believe you're the one who tames the tigers. It might come in handy."

"Handy? I'm going to need some clarification here, Bantu."

"Well, for one, he will revere you. No one has ever been able to tame the mighty tiger. And you won't have to worry about him shooting any more darts in your direction."

"Works for me." Summerman bowed at Tuber. "The Great Tiger Tamer at your service."

Tuber flashed a smile at Summerman and returned the bow.

"How about that? It's working," Summerman said.

"Unbelievable," Merlin said. "What about me?"

Tuber glared at Merlin and snarled.

"I don't think he likes you," Summerman said.

"There's a surprise. Get in line, pal." Merlin turned to Bantu. "Tell him I'm Summerman's assistant."

Bantu chattered at Tuber, who listened and then blew a raspberry in Merlin's direction.

"I don't think he's buying it," Summerman said.

"Just stay close to me and you'll be fine," Bantu said.

"What the hell are we doing out here?" Merlin said.

Summerman glanced around and rubbed Murray's head.

"I have no idea."

19

"What the hell are you doing out here?"

"I av o I e a."

Genevieve sat down on a patch of sand to catch her breath. She studied her traveling companion sitting across from her and tried to comprehend the notion that he seemed perfectly content to wander around in circles staring at her tits. Over the past three hours, he continued to stumble through the jungle, often falling and causing additional damage to his face and arms. His leather-like tongue, baked in the hot sun, twitched back and forth. He panted at her like a Saint Bernard in heat.

"I must be going crazy in this sun, but I'm sure I can smell acetate." Genevieve lighted yet another Gitanes. Stress? Being lost in the jungle? Natives with twelve-inch tongues? Whatever the reason driving her increased nicotine intake, she made a silent vow to cut back.

"It da goo," Gilbert said, pointing at his tongue.

"I hate to say this since I consider myself an extremely culturally sensitive individual, but that's an ugly language."

"It ot my ag ugg."

"Kind of proves my point, doesn't it?"

"Uck U," Frustrated, he tugged violently at the strip of leather protruding from his mouth.

"I wonder what they call you."

"Uh?"

"Your name. I was just wondering if you have a name."

"Il ert."

"Il ert, huh? Is there any tribal significance associated with that? What am I asking you for? Do you even know the way back to your village?"

Gilbert grunted and shook his head. "Ot illage?"

"Putain," Genevieve said, taking a long drag from her Gitanes. "This is hopeless. Is everyone from your tribe like this?"

"Ibe?"

Genevieve shook her head and picked up a small stick and traced patterns in the sand. She stopped when Gilbert started squealing excitedly. He slid towards her, and she scrambled backward, dropping the stick in the process. Gilbert slid a leg forward and grabbed the stick with his toes. Genevieve watched as Gilbert worked the stick between his big toe and then squeezed his foot tight. Tentatively, he began writing in the sand.

"This ought to be good." Genevieve extinguished her cigarette and buried it in the sand. She tried to read upside down but then sat down next to Gilbert and followed along as he slowly worked his way through the process.

"My...name...is...Gil...bert."

Gilbert grunted loudly, glanced up and offered a prayer of thanks to heavens, then clapped his hands in jubilation. That proved to be a major error in judgment as both palms immediately began seeping blood. Too excited by his communication breakthrough to be deterred, Gilbert raised both hands above his head and continued his footwork.

"Your name is Gilbert?" Genevieve stared at him. "You're not from the tribe?"

Gilbert shook his head.

"Then who the hell are you and what on earth are you doing out here in the jungle?"

Gilbert scrawled his response.

"Lost," Genevieve said, reading from the sand.

"Es," Gilbert said, "I ost."

Gilbert wiped away his previous responses with his other foot and then began writing again.

"I...am...fact...ury...man...ager. You're the factory manager. The Cloudlifter factory?"

"Es, es, es," Gilbert said, unable to contain his excitement.

"Not that it matters," Genevieve said, staring down at his hen scratching. "But that's not how you spell factory."

"O uck urelf," Gilbert said.

"Excuse me? Did you just tell me to go fuck myself?"

Gilbert flushed with embarrassment and scribbled the word sorry in the sand.

"I should hope so," Genevieve said. "There's no need to get snarky."

Genevieve watched as Gilbert scribbled in the sand.

"They glued your hands? Who? Oh, your workers. You must be quite the manager." Genevieve chuckled and reached for a fresh cigarette.

Gilbert nodded and scribbled, trying to ignore the cramps working their way up his leg.

"And your tongue too?"

Gilbert nodded again and leaned his head forward so she could take a closer look.

"Merde," Genevieve said, gently grabbing the strip of leather protruding from his mouth. "That's stuck, isn't it?"

"Uckin a."

"Can I help?" Genevieve said, reading aloud. "Well, there's some plants around here that I could mix with some water that might keep your hands from bleeding and maybe take away some of the pain, but I don't think there's anything I can do about that tongue."

Gilbert scribbled some more.

"Cut it?" Genevieve said. "Oh, I get it. You want me to cut the leather."

"Es," Gilbert said.

"Okay," Genevieve said, beginning to root through her bag. She pulled out a hunting knife and held it up in front of Gilbert.

"E air ul."

"What? Oh, sure, I'll be careful," Genevieve said.

Gilbert leaned forward, opened his mouth as wide as he could, and closed his eyes. Genevieve, trying desperately to avoid the odors that had accumulated during his ordeal, slowly began slicing away hunks of leather. Minutes later, she put the knife down and leaned in for a closer examination.

"Well, I think that's about as close as I can get. There's still about a quarter inch left along your tongue, but I'm not comfortable going any further."

"Thatth okay," Gilbert said. "Oh, thatth's tho much better. Thank you."

"It's nice to be able to understand you," Genevieve said. "Nice to meet you, Gilbert. I'm Genevieve."

"You'll have to excuse me for not thaking hands. Oh my, I theem to have a bit of a lispth."

Genevieve giggled.

"Tho glad you're finding it tho funny."

"I'm sorry, Gilbert," she said, biting her lip to suppress the laughter.

"I hate thith island. It's thuch a thithole."

"I think it's fascinating," Genevieve said.

"You're more than welcome to it." Gilbert stood up and glanced around. "You wouldn't know the way back to the rethort by any chance would you?"

"Sure," Genevieve said, standing up. "All you need to do is follow the sun and work your way down towards the beach."

"The thun?"

"As long as you keep the highest point on the island on your left as you head back down, the sun will be setting right in front of the resort. You can't help but eventually run into it."

"The thetting thun. Of course. Now I remember."

"Now let's see what we can do for those hands of yours before you go."

20

Doc glanced back and forth between the six different monitors that had been installed in the living room of their suite now named Command Central. He glanced up as Esmeralda approached carrying a cup of coffee. As he sipped, he studied her eyes for signs of possible reconciliation, but his hopes were dashed when she gave him the finger and sat down in a chair with her back to him. She began studying a map of the island and sipped her coffee in silence. Doc shook his head and refocused on the monitors. Moments later, he flipped a switch and spoke into his headset.

"This is Command Central. Hey, Bob Garbo. Wakey, wakey."

"Yeah," boomed the reply through the speakers.

Esmeralda wheeled in her chair and glared at Doc. He looked at her sheepishly and lowered the volume.

"How is it out there?"

"Hot."

"Thanks for the update," Doc said. "What do you do, Bob? Allocate yourself a certain number of words per day?"

"Funny."

"You could learn something from him," Esmeralda said, not looking up from the map. "Hi, Bob."

"Morning."

"The reception's great, Bob. This new gear seems to be working just fine, so I think you should move to phase two and see if you can get at least a couple of cameras closer to the village before the end of the day."

"Okay."

"Get in as close as you can without being seen. I want to have a couple of days to observe them without them knowing they're being watched. Bentley says they're dangerous, but I think he's lying."

"Undoubtedly."

"Hey, put Freak on for a minute. I want to make sure he stays under control and doesn't start shooting the place up."

92

"Gone."

"What do you mean he's gone? Where the hell did he go?"

"Somewhere."

"That son of a bitch," Doc said. "Had he been drinking?"

"Yup."

"Please tell me he didn't take a rocket launcher with him."

"No."

Doc paused to consider Bob's response. He looked at Esmeralda to see if she comprehended the message. She shook her head no.

"No, you won't tell me no because that would be a lie, or no he didn't take it with him."

"First."

"So he's wandering around out there with a rocket launcher?"

"Yup."

"Shit."

"Yup."

"What else has he got with him?"

"Beer."

"Goddamn it," Doc said. "No way you could find him is there?"

"Pardon?" Bob said, his voice rising slightly.

"Sorry," Doc said. "Of course, you could find him. What I meant to say is would you?"

"Depends."

"Right, of course," Doc said. "Phase two, or find Freak." Doc looked at Esmeralda, who was now paying close attention. "Tell you what. We'll keep our fingers crossed that he doesn't blow up the tribe before we can get in there. Just proceed with phase two."

"Good."

"Fuck him, right?"

"Yup."

"Command Central out."

"Later."

21

As they approached a seemingly impenetrable part of the jungle, Bantu stopped and turned to face Merlin and Summerman. He was beaming and hopping up and down with excitement.

"Are you ready?" he said.

"If you're referring to a shower, absolutely."

Merlin picked bugs out of his hair and off his shirt.

"Ready for what, Bantu?" Summerman said.

"To meet my family and the rest of the tribe."

Merlin and Summerman glanced at each other, and Summerman nodded.

"Bantu," Merlin said, placing an arm on his shoulder. "We need to talk."

"Of course," Bantu said, sitting down on the grass and nodding at Tuber to do the same.

Tuber followed suit and stared at Murray. Murray stared back and wagged his tail. Tuber smiled at Summerman and then glared at Merlin. He removed the long bamboo cylinder he used to fire his darts with and began polishing it with a piece of cloth. Between wipes, he glanced back at Merlin through narrowed eyes.

"What would you like to talk about?" said Bantu.

Merlin paralyzed with fear, felt his stomach roll.

"Well," said Merlin, pointing at Tuber. "That. Is that the reception we can expect from the rest of your tribe?"

"No, not at all. I'm sure that most of the tribe will be more than welcoming. That is, once they get past their initial shock at meeting Outsiders."

"I'm going to need some clarification here, Bantu."

Summerman placed his hand on Merlin's shoulder in an attempt to calm him down. "If you could, Bantu, define what their initial shock might include."

Bantu thought for a moment and then scratched an itch on the top of his head.

"Let's see," he said. "Everyone will be most intrigued by your arrival. And Murray will, of course, attract much attention. Most will just follow my father's directions. Some will probably run and hide until they discover that it's safe to come out."

"I can live with that," Merlin said. He glanced at Summerman, who nodded his agreement.

"A handful will be suspicious and potentially dangerous. But don't worry. I will take care of that."

"How exactly is that going to work?" Merlin said.

"The stigma of shooting me by mistake with a dart would cause great shame to the offender, and make my father quite angry," Bantu said. "So just make sure you stay very close to me the first couple of hours."

"That's not going to be a problem," Merlin said. "Like white on rice."

"So the two of us are going to be the first Outsiders to come in direct contact with your tribe?" Summerman said.

"Well, a long time ago, a ship did land on the island, and a small band of men came ashore to explore."

"And how did that end?" Merlin said.

"According to legend, not well," said Bantu.

"So you're saying that your tribe has used violence in the past," Merlin said.

"Can you name one anywhere that hasn't at one time or another?"

"Good point," Summerman said.

"But that was a long time ago. And since I'm the one bringing you, you'll be fine," Bantu said, clamoring to his feet. "But please remember to stay close."

Tuber began running his fingers lovingly through the feathers of a dart. He stood up, inserted the dart into the end of the tube, then placed it to his lips and fired at a bamboo stalk about fifty feet away. The dart found its target and Tuber slowly turned his head and smiled menacingly at Merlin.

"What did I ever do to him?" Merlin said Summerman.

Summerman shrugged and closely followed Bantu as he led them further into the thick foliage.

22

"You're making it difficult for me to walk."

"You're the one who said to stay close," Merlin said, snuggled tight against their guide.

"Cobra," Bantu said, veering away from the snake that was rapidly slithering off in another direction through the grass.

In tandem, the three men shuffled their way past the snake. Murray woofed at the snake but kept his distance.

"Good boy," Summerman said.

"Smart dog," Bantu said.

"You have no idea."

Summerman chuckled and rubbed the dog's head.

Tuber hung back but soon caught up, the dead snake draped over his shoulders.

Merlin looked towards the heavens. "Just kill me now."

Tuber grunted as if somehow comprehending Merlin's plea. He smiled menacingly, obviously pleased by the prospect.

"Let's not give him any ideas, okay?" Summerman said.

Bantu led them through another dense area overgrown with bamboo; then a pathway opened up. They walked a short distance and then Bantu paused at what appeared to be the edge of a cliff. He stared out and began to weep.

"I'm home."

Summerman and Merlin, wild-eyed, stared down at the scene below.

"I didn't expect this," Summerman said.

"It's so...," Merlin said.

"Beautiful," Summerman said.

"Yes," Merlin agreed, nodding his head. "But there's more to it than that."

"Serene."

"Yes. That's it," Merlin said. "Serene."

Below them, a valley opened up in front of them that stretched across the entire top of the island. The jungle canopy, while still dense, seemed to part in the middle allowing the midday sun to shine brightly down upon the village. Dozens of nearly identical huts made of wood with thatched roofs circled one immense structure. Several fenced gardens sprouted a variety of plants and flowers. Other fenced areas contained what appeared to be pigs. Behind the village on one side, a majestic waterfall cascaded water off its rocky cliffs into a small lake that lay below. Children of all ages splashed and swam in the lake, and their chattering and laughter drifted upwards.

"Bantu," Summerman said, taken aback by the scene below. "I'm sorry, but I just assumed your tribe would have been hunters and collectors. You know, tribal."

Bantu laughed as he continued to look down at the village.

"We've been here a very long time," he said. "Several generations ago it was determined that it was much easier to farm than hunt."

"How the hell did they figure that out all by themselves?" Merlin said.

Bantu, mildly offended, turned towards Merlin.

"Are you saying my people aren't smart enough to figure out how to plant and grow food?"

"No, that's not what I meant, Bantu." Merlin's face flushed with embarrassment.

"What I think he meant, Bantu," Summerman said. "Is that your tribe seems very developed."

"Of course, it's developed," Bantu said. "We've been here for thousands of years. Even if it happened by accident, eventually we were bound to figure some stuff out."

"Sorry," Merlin said.

"Holy shit," Summerman exclaimed, pointing to the distance past the village.

"What?" Merlin followed Summerman's stare.

"It can't be," Summerman said. "How the hell did they get here?"

"No one knows," Bantu grinned from ear to ear. "I've missed them."

"All I see is a couple of giant gray rocks." Merlin continued to squint into the distance. "Wait. No way."

"Yes," Bantu said. "Elephants."

"This is unbelievable," Summerman said.

"We can only guess that they swam here from a nearby island or were on some ship that sunk nearby," Bantu said. "It continues to be a mystery."

"How long have they been here?" Summerman said.

"For many, many generations. Every few years a new baby elephant arrives. That's the only time we need to be careful when they're around. Most of the time they're quite tame. Like pets. Sometimes they wander into our gardens and have to be chased away."

Tuber began chattering and pointing down at the village. Bantu listened and then turned to Summerman and Merlin.

"Tuber's hungry," Bantu said.

"I could eat," Merlin said.

Tuber stepped down onto the narrow pathway that led down to the village and extended an arm out off the edge and strained on tiptoes until he secured the end of a large vine secured to the branch of a towering pine tree. He held the end of the vine and offered it to Merlin.

"What? I'm sorry, I don't speak gibberish." Merlin looked at Bantu for clarification.

Bantu chattered with Tuber and then frowned as he stared down off the edge of the path that led down to the village. Bantu shook his head at Tuber, who chattered back at Bantu. He waved the end of the vine in front of Bantu as he continued his diatribe, now louder and more direct. Bantu continued to shake his head no. Tuber offered the end of the vine to Merlin and Summerman, who stared back oblivious.

"He says he's invented a faster way to get down to the village," Bantu said.

"What?" Merlin said, pointing at the vine. "On that thing?"

"Yes," Bantu said. "But if I were you, I'd take the path."

"He wants me to swing down several hundred feet on that vine?" Merlin said.

Bantu nodded, and Merlin turned to Tuber, who continued to wave the end of the vine in his direction. "Sorry, Tuber, ain't gonna happen."

Tuber listened and then looked at Bantu for translation. Bantu shook his head again and Tuber, apparently not being used to having his offerings refused, stomped his feet on the hard-packed earth and glared. Merlin leaned in close to Tuber and stared into his eyes as he spoke.

"No way, Tarzan."

Tuber, not thrilled with Merlin's tone, growled and bared his teeth. Merlin took a step back but continued to maintain eye contact. And then Tuber apparently bored with the conversation, shrugged his shoulders, wrapped his feet around the end of the vine, and then jumped off into space.

"Sweet Jesus," Summerman said, staring down at the rapidly descending Tuber. "Look at him go."

Murray barked at Tuber's rapid departure.

"You've seen him do this before?" Merlin said.

"No," Bantu said. "But he's always building tunnels and other things to help get around the island faster. He just finished making this one as a surprise for me. And he was hoping one of us would go first."

"I bet he was," Merlin said, staring down.

They watched as Tuber dropped free-fall for about fifty feet and then altered course to a forty-five degree angled descent as the vine tightened. Somewhere around a hundred feet off the ground, Tuber appeared to pick up speed, and he caught the attention of several tribesmen.

"This is not good," Bantu said.

"The vine's too long," Summerman said.

"Yes," Bantu said, leaning his head over the edge of the path for a clearer view.

"He's gonna kill himself," Merlin said.

"He'll be okay," Bantu said. "He's stupid but very tough."

Tuber's return to the village came up a bit short; about five hundred feet short to be exact when he ran out of available altitude with still about fifty feet of vine remaining. He landed with a loud thwack that reverberated across the valley. Whatever screams or moans he may have uttered in those final few seconds were muffled as he plunged face-first into what initially appeared to be a small sand hill but later proved to be the home of several million fire ants. Tuber was pulled back into consciousness as ants began gnawing on his body. Dazed and limping badly, he made his way through the village smacking and slapping at the ants with both hands past the laughter of his fellow tribesman until he reached the nearby lake. He jumped in and stayed submerged until the ants had either drowned or departed for dry land. Eventually, he crawled out and collapsed on the bank, wracked with pain and embarrassment.

Bantu, Merlin, and Summerman, with Murray in close tow, inched their way down the narrow pathway leading to the village.

23

Chief knelt down to inspect the water level of the rice paddy then chattered with one of the workers. He watched while the worker increased the flow of water through the bamboo irrigation system, then nodded and walked towards a smoldering pit. He sniffed the aroma and peered over the edge noting that the two enormous boars, slaughtered that morning, were close to being ready.

Glancing around for something else to do, he focused on a group of children sweeping the wooden pathways around the village. The children were spending as much time laughing and hitting each other with the bamboo brooms as they were sweeping dirt, but the Chief noted that progress was being made so decided to make his way towards the group of elders sitting under a large Gurjan tree. He chattered with them for a few minutes and then looked around the village.

Many years ago he had led the effort that had allowed the tribe to stop their constant movement in search of food. As soon as they had developed the ability to grow and harvest rice and penning animals for later slaughter, the tribe's life had dramatically improved. With their basic needs for food and shelter solved, Chief had led the tribe into a phase of village life he called Katatna; the quest to make life easier. Three simple objectives dominated Chief's approach to ruling his tribe: No one ever goes hungry. Everyone must be safe. Good and bad follow every choice.

No one was more aware than he of the potential for bad that could come from Chief's request of Bantu to bring an Outsider into the village. Many elders, both privately and in public, had spoken critically of this decision. But Chief knew from what he had seen from the Outsiders at water's edge that they were coming.

And coming closer all the time.

Chief also knew that the tribe's survival would depend on the reactions when the initial encounters took place. From his experience in the outside world many years ago, he knew that the Outsiders came from a different environment and that their tolerance for dissent was often limited. Violence, Chief knew, was an option they would use and was one that his tribe could not survive, no matter how bravely they fought in the face of danger. But his opinions had often fallen on deaf ears during recent elder meetings as the date of Bantu's return approached. If Bantu did indeed return with an Outsider, Chief would need to be watchful for tribesmen wanting to take matters into their own hands. One poison dart at the wrong time would be unfortunate; the return fire of the Outsiders would be fatal to the tribe.

Chief shook away the burdens of leadership with a cool drink of water and a glance at a group of children learning how to weave bamboo leaves into baskets and roofing. He smiled and looked at the sun slowing appearing through the clouds. The rains had departed and tonight's dinner would take place under a clear sky and full moon.

Chief heard the call before he saw them. Four men, along with what appeared to be a small tiger, were standing at the top of the ledge that provided safe passage into the village. One of them was waving, and Chief returned the welcome. Bantu, standing between two Outsiders, was jumping up and down with excitement. The two Outsiders were staring off into the distance. Chief focused on the fourth man and held his breath. Being the only brother of his dearly departed wife had brought Tuber into Chief's family, and Chief had, for years, secretly tried to identify ways to give him back.

Chief knew that Tuber had taken Katatna to heart. Unfortunately for the young man and the rest of the tribe, the ability to make life simpler took more than heart. Tuber's lack of mental agility, combined with his fierce stubbornness, had earned him the nickname, Yowza; one who is a great danger to himself and others. However, given Tuber's mean streak and proficiency with a blowgun, it was not a nickname anyone used when he was within earshot.

Chief stared in disbelief as Tuber grabbed a large vine and launched himself off the rock ledge. He began a rapid descent towards the village. Chief listened closely but couldn't decide if Tuber's screams were some form of war cry he had come up with whether he was merely terror-stricken. Chief watched as Tuber approached and then shook his head at the length of the vine.

"Yowza," Chief whispered as Tuber smacked loudly into the nest of fire ants.

The villagers waited silently and then broke into shrieks of laughter as Tuber slowly emerged from the sand covered in ants. The children followed his meandering path towards the lake and taunted him from a distance.

Chief made a mental note to have one of the tribesmen remove the vine before one of the children decided to take a ride, then walked to the bottom of the path and waited for his son and his two guests to arrive.

24

Doc studied the monitors and marveled at the quality of the color. Vibrant greens accented with reds, yellows and blue were pleasing to the eye but Doc, if he was going to be able to complete his mission and get off the island, needed more than something he might see on the Discovery Channel. The process repeated itself endlessly; his eyes would focus on a monitor for signs of human life, then he would move to the next screen. He sipped his coffee and slumped further down into the thick leather chair. Mind numbingly boring, he decided. But better than schlepping his way through another snake-infested jungle. Or another barren desert with only the sight and smell of a camel to keep him company.

He glanced at Esmeralda but discovered her chair was empty. For the past few days, she had been distant and distinctly pissed off. Doc tried to remember the specifics of their current battle, but nothing definitive came to mind. Esmeralda had been doing her best to work her way through the resort's ample supply of fine tequilas since they'd arrived. Normally, that was positive for Doc since, after three shots of liquid gold, Esmeralda's pattern was to stop yelling at him and take out her anger on him physically. Well versed in the science of pain management, Doc would smile and take everything she could offer.

Since they touched down two days ago, Esmeralda had broken her pattern. While the level of anger she expressed towards Doc had, if anything, even deepened, she had stopped using him to defuse it. Doc had caught her flirting with one of the guests at the resort but rather than feel any anger of jealousy of his own, he had felt nothing. Esmeralda had disappeared for long stretches, and Doc could only assume that she was somewhere around the resort the beach breaking in a new thoroughbred.

A knock on the door interrupted Doc's thoughts, and he opened it to find a young Indian man holding a silver tray. Doc devoured his

104

omelet, washed it down with two more cups of coffee, and pondered the idea of room service while on surveillance.

He refocused on the monitors and noticed that several of the views had changed over the past hour.

"You've been busy, Bob Garbo."

He noted the GPS coordinates displayed on each monitor and checked his map of the island. There was no sign of the village, but Doc knew that Bob would have at least one camera covering the tribe in place before the end of the day. Once Doc had the chance to observe the tribe's actions and movements for a few days, he would decide on an appropriate course of action. After that, who knew? He frowned and felt another pang of restlessness that had recently returned after months of conscious sublimation. Buddha, buried beneath layers of self-doubt and daily life, was struggling to get out and back to the center of his consciousness. With his Bodhisattva-quest a distant memory, Doc often wondered why Buddha simply didn't give up and move on to a more worthy subject.

Perhaps, by refusing to give up on the unworthy, Buddha was merely trying to prove his point about the struggles inherent in the search for enlightenment.

Perhaps the unfailing faithful were the easy part of his job and, to stretch and test his abilities, Buddha devoted the majority of his efforts on the hopeless.

Perhaps Buddha had more than enough capacity and energy to deal with everyone regardless of their spiritual state.

Perhaps Buddha just hung out and didn't give a rats ass about who followed him or didn't.

Perhaps Buddha just had a soft spot for Doc.

Whatever the reason, Buddha was rumbling in Doc's head and heart of late and was showing no signs of going away.

And that fact alone gave Doc hope.

He continued working his way across the monitors enjoying the views of jungle foliage. He watched a cobra slither its way in and out of view. He turned up the volume and listened to a variety of sounds drifting in and out of range. He moved to the monitor furthest on the left and his heart jumped. Doc scrambled to the console that controlled the cameras and zoomed in.

"What the hell?"

Doc rolled his chair forward and reached out his hand, gently stroking the figure displayed on the monitor. His thoughts headed back to memories from eight years ago in Marseilles. Three months of intensity he had never experienced before or since, completely severed by the mere fact of life getting in the way of two people who would have loved nothing more than to spend the rest of their lives doing exactly what they'd been doing since they'd randomly met in a café.

He remembered the day perfectly. A warm June afternoon filled with the sounds and smells of the nearby wharf where fishermen were unloading their daily catch. Doc had been in search of coffee, and when presented with the choice of two competing cafes, he had chosen the one on the left, thus altering his life forever. One split second decision had brought her into his life. Three months later, several weeks after deciding that his life was now forever linked with hers, they had been pulled apart. Eight years later she was unknowingly looking at him through a video monitor. What on earth she was doing in the middle of the jungle, he had no idea. But she was back.

"What are you doing?"

Doc turned away from the monitors and saw Esmeralda staring at him.

"Just working."

"That's all you ever do."

She grabbed a bottle of tequila and headed back towards the door.

"You're glowing," Doc said.

"Am I? I hadn't noticed."

Doc smiled at her and shook his head. She stared back blankly.

"What?"

"Nothing. It's okay, Esmeralda." Doc began stuffing items into a backpack. "I know what's going on. And it's okay."

"I have no idea what you're talking about," she said, taking a long pull from the bottle of tequila.

"I'm heading out."

"Where? Out there?"

"Yeah." Doc zipped the backpack.

"Why on earth would you do that?"

"Why would I do that? Uh… I'm starting to get worried about Freak."

Doc glanced upwards and hoped that Buddha would forgive the lie.

"Since when? That little prick has given you nothing but trouble since he started working for you."

"He's still one of my guys, and you never abandon one of your own."

"I see." She eyed him suspiciously. "Okay, don't worry about me. I'll be fine."

"I'm sure you will."

"What's that supposed to mean?" she said, taking another long pull of tequila.

"Nothing," Doc said, searching the room for his binoculars. "But intermission is almost over. Shouldn't you be heading back?"

"Yeah, probably," Esmeralda said. "I mean, I guess I can find something to do."

"Just try to keep an eye on the monitors from time to time. Actually, just bring him here with you. That way you can kill two birds with one stone if you know what I mean."

"Now you're not making any sense at all," she said, raising the bottle to her lips.

"It's okay, Esmeralda. It had to happen sooner or later. But I'm curious. What was it that put you over the edge?"

Esmeralda stared at him with a glazed expression.

"I don't know. It's just something in me. It's probably my fault."

"Of course, it's your fault," Doc said, laughing.

"Fuck you, Doc."

Esmeralda wheeled and stormed out of the room, slamming the door behind her.

"Get ready, whatever your name is," Doc said. "You're in for a wild ride."

Doc pulled the backpack onto his shoulders and tightened the straps. He glanced at the monitor and stared at the figure who was now sitting quietly on a rock smoking a cigarette.

"Genevieve," he whispered.

He glanced up at the ceiling.

"Thank ya, Buddha."

107

25

Merlin looked around the large, open-air hut. Massive tree trunks stripped of their bark and stained provided support to the perimeter of the circular structure that reached, at its apex, a height of thirty feet. Light rain was falling but the roof, comprised of thatched bamboo leaves, beat back the moisture. Bantu, still holding his father's hand, stared up in awe, then knelt down and ran his hands along the smooth, polished wooden floor. He began chattering excitedly with his father.

"This is new," Bantu said, providing much-needed translation for Merlin and Summerman. "Our tribe's new community room."

"It's incredible," Merlin said. "But how on earth did your tribe-?"

He stopped when he saw Bantu's eyes narrow.

"Yes?" Bantu placed his hands on his hips and glared at Merlin. "By all means, please continue."

"No, I didn't mean to-"

"What I think he means, Bantu," Summerman said. "Is what tools were used to do the work?"

Bantu chattered with his father who nodded his head and then scowled at Merlin.

"Yes, that's what I meant. No disrespect intended, Bantu."

Merlin glanced back and forth between Bantu and his father and decided that narrowed-eye stares must run in the family.

"It's an amazing structure, and it looks like something you'd see at the resort down on the beach."

While Bantu's father didn't speak English, apparently he had picked up at least one word; resort. He began shouting, waving his arms, and stamping his feet to punctuate whatever point he was making. For the third time that day, Merlin took a step backward.

Bantu calmly spoke to his father, who stopped shouting but fixed a cold stare on both men.

"It's not our resort for chrissakes," Merlin said.

"Drop it," Summerman said, digging his fingernails into Merlin's forearm.

"We may not have many of the newer tools, but we do very well with what we have," Bantu said. He chattered at his father who nodded in agreement.

"And everyone works very hard," Bantu said.

"It's not like I made the decision to build the thing," Merlin said.

Summerman shrugged his shoulders. Bantu nodded and then continued.

"The roof is woven from fresh palm leaves and allowed to dry. We apply a mixture of plant extracts and a bit of rubber paste for waterproofing."

"That's pretty smart," Merlin said.

"Yes," Bantu said, rolling his eyes at his father. "We have our moments." Bantu chattered briefly with his father who listened, then laughed.

"And as you've noticed, we have an abundance of different trees. We chop them down and use them as the foundation for our huts."

"You have axes?" Summerman said.

"Yes," Bantu said. "They're built with stone and wood and held together by the dried skin of the pig. Very basic but, with practice and diligence, they work quite well.

"But the floor, and the tables and chairs," Summerman said, admiringly running his hand over one of the chairs. It's so smooth."

"Sandpaper," Bantu said. He rubbed both hands together to help translate for his father. "My father came up with the idea several years ago."

"Really?" Summerman said.

"It's quite amazing," Bantu said, beaming at his father. "You take a dried bamboo leaf, apply a layer of glue and then pour sand on top. You end up with a piece of sandpaper that lasts a couple of hours."

"Impressive," Summerman said.

"Yes, my father has invented many things to make our lives easier," Bantu said. He chattered to his father who listened, then smiled.

"Booga-wooga-nooga," he said, nodding his head up and down vigorously.

"Excuse me?" Merlin said.

Bantu laughed and playfully punched his father's arm.

"Booga-wooga-nooga is one of our tribe's favorite expressions. The English translation is, you bet your sweet ass."

"Booga-wooga-nooga," Merlin said, laughing along.

"Booga-wooga-nooga." Chief nodded his head and smiled.

Chief chattered at Bantu and pointed at Murray. Bantu nodded and smiled.

"My father says that Murray is a magnificent animal."

"Tell him, thank you very much. Would he like to pet him?"

Bantu translated, and Chief nodded. He knelt down and tapped the floor. Murray trotted over and accepted Chief's rubs and scratches. Chief chattered at Bantu.

"My father is very impressed by your ability to tame such an amazing creature."

"Actually, it's not that hard. Murray does most of the work."

26

Follow the thun, follow the thun, follow the thun."

Gilbert continued to repeat his new mantra and stumble his way through the jungle back to what passed for civilization in this God forsaken place. His progress was slowed by the piece of equipment he had discovered not long after he had reluctantly left the buxom French woman. She was certainly out of his league but long periods of isolation made people do strange things, a fact he had learned from own experience on the island. Who'd have ever thought that he, a charter member of the Little Rock chapter of Metrosexual Mensas would have ever agreed to have kinky sex with a bizarre pastry chef simply because of the quality of her doughnuts? Had Gilbert and the French woman ended up paired together for several days in isolation he fantasized about what might have happened under cover of darkness surrounded only by the cries of wild animals and a cozy campfire. But Gilbert's survival instinct and desire to get the off the island had won out over primal lust, given his longshot odds of actually ever nailing the black-haired beauty in the first place.

He had spotted the Army-green metal case from a distance and approached it cautiously. With absolutely no idea of how it got there, Gilbert opened the case to find a gleaming piece of high-tech weaponry. Despite the fact that he had no idea how to operate the device, Gilbert slung the strap over his shoulder and immediately felt somewhat safer as he continued his descent through the jungle.

**

Sir Bentley lowered the landing gear on the Gulfstream and dropped from four thousand to five hundred feet in a matter of seconds.

"Man, this baby really handles," Sir Bentley said, glancing back over his shoulder.

If Gene was impressed by the aerodynamic features of the jet, it went unnoticed. His head was buried in an air sickness bag.

"Gene, you puke on my carpet, you'll be sorry."

Sir Bentley eyed the approaching runway.

"Get me out of this thing," Gene said.

"Don't worry. It won't be long. We'll get some color back in you."

"Green is a color," Gene said, retching again. "You sure you got a license to fly this thing?"

"Almost." Sir Bentley's head jerked as the wheels touched the ground and the jet bounced down the runway until he managed to bring it to a stop. "Perfect landing."

"Define perfect."

Buddy Quizling, Sir Bentley's personal lawyer, fought back the return of breakfast, unbuckled his seatbelt and took a deep breath.

"Perfect, as in you're still alive." Sir Bentley lowered the stairs, and the heat and humidity greeted them.

"Sweet Jesus," Buddy said. "This better be worth it."

"I'm gonna die." Gene clamored down the steps and dropped to his knees as he vomited the final vestiges of last night's lamb vindaloo onto one of the plane's wheels.

Sir Bentley glared at his assistant but said nothing. Gene climbed to his feet and belched.

"C'mon," Sir Bentley said, climbing into a nearby jeep. "The natives are getting restless."

"Yeah, I'm sure," Buddy said, falling into the backseat. "A bunch of Neanderthals still eating tree roots and struggling to walk upright. This whole operation ought to take about five minutes."

The fireball exploded directly in front of them. The force of the blast and the subsequent wall of flames that rose several hundred feet into the air initially had Sir Bentley's undivided attention. Moments later, when he realized exactly what he was witnessing, the fireball lost some of its magnificence.

"My factory," Sir Bentley said, unable to take his eyes off the giant fireball. "Those jungle bunnies blew up my factory."

"Man," Gene said, peering up from the backseat. "That's some serious firepower."

"This changes everything," Sir Bentley said. "No more negotiations with these people."

"What the hell are you talking about?" Buddy said. "At least give me the opportunity to do my job. We haven't even started negotiating."

"Yeah, well," Sir Bentley said, scowling at the red-blue ball of flame. "Then we won't be starting."

Sir Bentley, Buddy, and Gene ducked for cover as objects began to rain down on them.

"What the hell is this?" Gene said, holding up a smoking piece of orange leather.

"That's a Cloudlifter. Or at least it was," Sir Bentley said.

"It's a shoe?"

"It's the sleeker, non-squeaker sneaker."

Gene flipped the hot object back and forth between his hands. "Yeah, I can see that."

**

Gilbert gently placed the rocket launcher down and stared in disbelief at what he'd just done. He had absolutely no idea how such poor aim could have enabled such a perfect direct hit, but he wasn't about to complain. As Sir Bentley's plane had descended into view, unmistakable from the massive dollar sign painted on the tail, Gilbert had snapped. Every frustration he had felt over the past several months, exacerbated dramatically by his recent foray into the jungle, had instantly crystallized into one clear, concise thought: Blow the prick out of the sky.

He had worked his way into a clearing, opened the case, and extracted the rocket launcher. Guessing as to the proper way to load a rocket into the weapon, he had chosen well. But he had no indication of the force the rocket launcher produced when fired. The initial burst from the launcher caused him to lose his balance, and he'd executed a perfect ninety-degree turn to the right. The rocket grazed the tops of some nearby palm leaves and disappeared.

Moments later, Gilbert heard the thunderous explosion, and he knew exactly what he had done. After peering around the palms and then staring up at the huge ball of fire racing towards the heavens, Gilbert waited for pangs of remorse. When nothing of the sort occurred, Gilbert sat down and watched as the fireball grew, rolled into itself, and exploded again. He calmly weighed his options as

114

thousands of Cloudlifters, mostly in pieces, dropped from the sky and were swallowed by the jungle.

"The thleeker, non-thqueaker, theaker indeed."

Gilbert laughed menacingly, and his eyes grew and stayed wild. He placed the still warm launcher back in its case, ran a hand lovingly over the remaining rocket, and snapped the case tight. He stood up, draped the strap over his shoulder and continued his journey back down the hill towards the resort. With one rocket left and with Sir Bentley now on the island, Gilbert knew there was still work left to do.

But first, he needed a doughnut.

27

Merlin and Summerman continued to be amazed as they followed Bantu and his father on the guided tour through the village. Over the past hour, they had visited one of the family huts where they'd been stared at by several small children and their mother who'd been cooking what appeared to be soup over an open fire. With Bantu's encouragement, the children had managed to overcome their initial fear and were eventually coaxed out from behind their mother's legs to accept the chocolate Summerman offered. Several minutes later, they were all best buddies with Murray, who stayed behind as they continued the tour.

Bantu and his father led them towards a fenced area that stretched over an acre and contained hundreds of different plants. The fence was built with bamboo stalks that had been bound tightly with the vine that Tuber had unsuccessfully used to swing back into the village. Several adults were tending the garden and doing their best to keep a variety of bird species at bay.

"This is a very sacred place," Bantu said. "This is where we grow our plants."

"For food?" Summerman peered over the fence at the unfamiliar plants.

"No. These are for making our medicines."

Bantu followed his father through the bamboo gate. He motioned Merlin and Summerman through the gate and closed it behind them. The workers immediately stopped what they were doing and rushed to welcome Bantu home. After the hugs and kisses, Bantu introduced Merlin and Summerman. The workers, although wary, smiled and waved, then returned to their work.

Merlin stared at the long, perfectly maintained rows of plants and spotted a large wooden structure at one end of the garden.

"It collects rainwater," Bantu said, anticipating the question. "We have several of them."

"Carved out of wood?" Summerman said, stepping closer to inspect the structure.

"Yes," Bantu said, and then laughed. "It's one of the worst jobs you can be assigned. It's usually given as a punishment when people break one of the tribe's rules."

"Someone has to carve these out from a solid block of wood?" Summerman said.

"Yes," Bantu said. "As you can imagine, it's most tedious."

"But why put it way out here in the garden instead of near the village?" Merlin said. "That seems a bit…"

"Yes?" Bantu's eyes narrowed. "Seems a bit what?"

Merlin lowered his head briefly and then looked up at Bantu. "What I was going to say is that it seems a little strange that you would do that."

"Fair enough, my friend," Bantu said.

He began chattering with his father and the workers.

"I wish you'd stop doing that," Summerman whispered to Merlin.

"I've got a serious case of foot in mouth going on here, don't I?"

"Watch this," Bantu said.

Merlin and Summerman watched as one of the workers removed a block of wood from the bottom of the structure. Moments later they heard a soft hissing sound near their feet. They looked down and saw small patches of moisture begin to appear near the plants.

"An irrigation system?" Summerman said. "Are you kidding me?"

Bantu beamed and draped an arm around his father's shoulder.

"Another of my father's inventions."

"Booga-wooga-nooga," the Chief said.

It was booga-wooga-nooga's all around for several seconds as Chief's sentiments were echoed by the tribesmen.

"As you can see," Bantu said, pointing at a piece of bamboo about three inches in diameter protruding from the bottom of the structure, "we've inserted this into the rainwater barrel and then we use smaller pieces to create a set of pipes. If you dig into the dirt about an inch down, you'll see small pieces of bamboo with tiny holes. The system lets us easily control the amount of water. I'm sure you get the picture."

"It's a drip system," Merlin said.

"I'm not familiar with that term," Bantu said. "But yes, it does come out in drips. And during those times when the rains don't fall, we use this to make sure our plants stay healthy."

"Amazing," Summerman said.

"Looking for ways to make life a bit easier isn't something only Outsiders do, Summerman."

Bantu chattered with his father who nodded and then patted his son on the shoulder. They walked a short distance away from the village until they reached the entrance to what appeared to be a cave.

"Stay close and watch your step," Bantu said, following his father through the entrance.

Merlin and Summerman entered and found themselves standing in a cave about twenty feet wide and twice as long.

"Bats?" Merlin said.

"Not during the day," Bantu said.

His father began chattering loudly and, from the back of the room, a figure emerged. He was carrying a small torch which he dipped into a bowl of liquid. The torch flared, and he proceeded to light several other torches sitting on the floor. Light filled the room, and the man then recognized Bantu. They hugged for several seconds and then Bantu pulled the man towards Merlin and Summerman.

"This is my younger brother, Ganesh."

"Nice to meet you," Summerman said, extending his hand.

"Hi, Ganesh," Merlin said.

Ganesh beamed and hugged Bantu again. Bantu's father watched the scene with joy then turned all business as he approached one of the wooden shelves that held dozens of small wicker baskets.

"This is the most sacred place of all," Bantu said, staring around the cave. "This is where we keep all of our medicines."

"Medicines? What kind of medicines could you people possibly...." Merlin smiled at Bantu. "I'm not surprised, Bantu. Please, continue."

Summerman chuckled and sat down on a nearby rock.

"We have medicines for everything. That is one of the main reasons for our longevity," Bantu said.

"Longevity?" Merlin said. "What are you worried about? You can't be any older than twenty, Bantu. And your father doesn't look a day over thirty-five."

"I am afraid, my friend, that you are quite mistaken."

Bantu chattered with his father and brother who both laughed loudly.

"They say you need to learn how to count," Bantu said.

"Okay, I give up," Merlin said. "How old are you guys?"

"Well, we don't use your calendar as you might imagine. We keep track by the number of full moons during one's lifetime."

"Is that why you have all those different stacks of rocks along one side of the village?" Summerman said.

"Very good, Summerman," Bantu said. "Every full moon a rock is added to everyone's stack. My father is about to celebrate his one thousandth moon."

A bewildered Merlin glanced at Summerman, and then stared at Bantu's father who grinned back at him.

"And that would make him 83?"

"Give or take, yes," Bantu said.

"No way," Merlin said.

"Unbelievable," Summerman whispered. "He looks like he could run a marathon."

"Booga-wooga-nooga," Merlin said.

"Ah, yes, the marathon. I saw one of those during my trip. I suppose he could, but undoubtedly he would ask the question why anyone would ever want to."

"Well, yeah, there is that," Summerman said. "So, Bantu, if your father is 83, how old are you?."

"Six hundred and fifteen moons. That's 51 by your calendar."

"We thought you were a young man," Merlin said.

"In my tribe, I am."

Bantu approached holding three small wooden drinking cups. He handed one each to Merlin and Summerman and kept the third for himself.

"What's this?" Summerman said.

"Think of it as what you call a multi-vitamin. It's for warding off diseases. And my father is quite insistent that, since we've been

119

in contact with the outside world, that we drink this every day for the next several days."

Merlin sniffed the cup and found the smell neutral. He looked at Summerman and held his cup up in a toast.

"When in Rome, huh?"

"Bottoms up," Summerman said, chugging it down.

Merlin followed suit and they handed the cups back to Bantu just before they collapsed unconscious on the floor.

28

Doc felt it before he heard it. Through years of experience in battle, he had developed a sixth sense about impending explosions, and he knew that the air seemed to grow still just before all hell broke loose. In the distance, he had heard the unmistakable, gentle swoosh of a rocket launcher being fired. He stopped in his tracks, listened closely, and then heard the massive explosion. When he saw the fireball appearing above the jungle, he shook his head in disgust.

"Goddamn you, Freak."

Doc heard a nearby rustling noise and immediately went on full alert. He knelt behind a palm frond, peered through, and then slowly worked his way through the foliage in the direction of the sound.

And then he smelled it; upwind, also unmistakable. A rush of memories flooded back and overwhelmed him. He edged his way through a maze of overgrown fronds and leaned against a large rock. Another waft of the distinctive smell drifted by and he smiled. He peered around the edge of the rock knowing that the creator of the odor in question, a freshly lit Gitanes, was nearby.

When he first saw her, he waited until his heart had stopped trying to beat its way out of his chest before working his way closer. She was even more beautiful than the last time he had seen and her jet-black hair, tied back, continued to trail the length of her back. She was staring at the huge ball of flame with a confused look on her face but other than that, she seemed at ease and completely comfortable in the dense jungle that surrounded her. She took a sip of water, then another drag from her cigarette as she continued to stare at the fire in the sky.

Doc slid to his stomach and began inching his way along the ground to her left. He worked his way closer until he was lying on the ground about three from her right foot. He stared up at her magnificent legs and waited until she was about to take another puff.

"Don't you know those things will kill you?"

Genevieve's scream and jump backward were impressive, and Doc roared with laughter as he jumped to his feet and beamed at her. Genevieve blinked and shook her head in disbelief.

"Doc?"

"How are you, Genevieve?"

"What? You? Here?"

"Just thought I'd drop by and say hi."

Doc closed in for a hug.

"Eight years?"

Genevieve wrapped her arms around him and didn't let go.

"Yeah. Marseilles."

"I heard you were dead." She planted a fierce kiss.

Coming up for air, Doc said, "Just wishful thinking for some folks."

"God, I've missed you," she said, squeezing him even tighter.

"Feel like saying hello the way we used to?"

"You bet I do."

Doc worked them carefully to the ground. He spotted a sandy portion among the ferns and rolled them on to it. Genevieve, without breaking the kiss, reached for her bag and pulled out a small blanket. Doc managed to unfold it and eventually they managed, more or less, to get on top of it.

"You still single?" Doc said.

"We wouldn't be doing this if I weren't."

Genevieve peeled her shirt off. Doc gasped for breath.

"Tres Magnifique."

"I see your French is still abysmal," Genevieve said, using her legs to work her pants down to her ankles. "How about you? Are you unattached?"

"I will be very soon."

"Shouldn't you at least buy me dinner first?" she said, digging her nails deep into his back.

"I'll buy you anything you want," Doc said. "But first things first."

"You ever leave me again, I'll kill you."

"I'm staying right here."

Genevieve rolled over on top of him, and Doc closed his eyes as their bodies got reacquainted. She murmured into his neck. Doc opened his eyes, prepared to respond but stopped short when he caught a glimpse of what was staring at them.

"Uh-oh," he said.

Without slowing down, Genevieve said, "What's wrong?"

"Someone's watching us?"

"Merde. Cobra?"

"I wish. Much worse."

Genevieve climbed off and sat on her knees peering at the object in question.

"A camera?"

"Yeah." Doc managed a nervous smile and small wave to the fisheye lens.

"Who the hell would put a camera out here?"

"Me."

"Merde. You're working out here, aren't you?"

"Why else would I be here?"

Genevieve laughed.

"You're something else. So who have we been putting on a show for?"

"Never mind."

He grabbed a sock and covered the lens. Doc pulled her back down onto the blanket.

"Now, where were we?"

29

Where the hell is he?"

Sir Bentley's tone left no doubt that he expected an answer but Esmeralda, semi-conscious on the bed and increasingly smitten with Gene, either didn't hear or chose to ignore the question.

"I fly halfway around the world, and this is what I get? Third rate jungle video and some skank hammered on tequila?"

"Why don't you come over here and take a little nap with me, Gene." Esmeralda gently patted the sheets and then Sir Bentley's insult registered.

"Hey, who are you calling a skank?"

Sir Bentley ignored her and sat down in front of the wall of video monitors. He began fiddling with the controls and searched the screens for signs of life.

Esmeralda patted the sheets again and winked at Gene, who was sitting in a chair next to the bed. She arched her back, sighed and beckoned again for him to join her. Gene started to get up out of his chair but caught Sir Bentley's glare and decided to stay put.

"You're no fun," Esmeralda said, yawning deeply. "Don't know what you're missing."

"Maybe later," Gene said.

She closed her eyes and immediately began snoring.

Sir Bentley crossed to the bed and shook Esmeralda's shoulders. Getting no response, he gently slapped the side of her face. She murmured and kissed the air.

"I think she likes it," Gene said.

Sir Bentley shook his head in disgust and returned to the monitors. "Where the hell is he?"

"Nobody has seen him since this morning."

Sir Bentley snorted and looked around. "Where is my stupid excuse for a lawyer?"

"He's in the bar." Gene scanned the monitors. "Man. That is one dense jungle. Glad I'm down here."

"Yeah, me too," said Sir Bentley. "I hate snakes."

"Look at the size of that one," Gene said, zooming in on one of the screens. "What is that?"

"Do I look like a snake charmer?"

"So what do we do?"

"I guess we wait," Sir Bentley said.

"Doc is out looking for one of his men."

Sir Bentley and Gene glanced at Esmeralda, who was sitting upright with her bare legs dangling over the edge of the bed.

"I thought you'd be out for hours," Gene said.

"Well, you thought wrong," she said. "I've got a killer headache." She hopped up out of bed not bothering to button her shirt and staggered towards the bathroom. Moments later she returned carrying a handful of aspirin that she popped and washed down with a long swig of tequila. "I've gotta stop drinking in the afternoon. It fucks up my whole day."

They watched Esmeralda remove her shirt, poke a finger into her bare breasts to test for sunburn and pull on a tee shirt.

He and Gene raised eyebrows in approval and watched as she lit a cigarette, grabbed the bottle of tequila, and sat down in front of the monitors.

"So one of his men is missing?"

"Yeah, his stupid brother in law, Freak. If we're lucky, maybe he'll get eaten by a crocodile."

It took a moment for the name to register with Sir Bentley.

"Freak?"

"Yeah. And the name fits him perfectly."

"Ugly? Dumber than dirt?"

"That would be him," Esmeralda said.

"Did you say his brother in law?"

"Yeah." Esmeralda brushed her hair back from her face with the hand she was using to hold the cigarette. "Shit," she said, frantically swatting at her head.

Gene cringed at the smell of burnt hair and gently removed the cigarette from her hand. After making sure she hadn't set herself on fire, he returned the cigarette.

"Thanks," Esmeralda said, sliding her fingers up his leg.

"Yeoww," Gene said, jumping out of his chair as the cigarette came to rest on his inner thigh. "Damn, that hurts. Look, lady, you

125

want to set yourself on fire that's one thing, but try not to take me with you, okay?"

"Ooh, a feisty one," Esmeralda said, taking a long drag on her cigarette. "I like that."

"Can we please get back to business?" Sir Bentley said.

"Oh, let's," Esmeralda said, staring blankly into the monitors.

"Doc brought Freak with him?" Sir Bentley said.

"Yeah. He said he was going to give him one last shot," Esmeralda said. "He says he has some sort of responsibility to take care of the idiot. Personally, I think it's some form of penance." Esmeralda belched loudly. "Doc felt obligated after the divorce. I don't get it myself but what are you gonna do? Family, you know?"

"Unbelievable," Sir Bentley said. "I thought I'd seen the last of that cretin."

"What? You know Freak?"

"Yeah." Sir Bentley flashed back to the day when Freak had managed to blow his yacht out of the water. "We've met."

"Lucky you." Esmeralda crushed out her cigarette and took a long pull of tequila. "More oxygen has-" Esmeralda stopped short when she heard Sir Bentley howl.

"Gene, zoom in on camera five. Now."

Gene did as instructed and all three stared at the monitor in question.

"Man, look at them go at it."

All three were unable to take their eyes off the couple performing on camera with their backs to them.

"Wow." Sir Bentley whistled softly. "Most impressive."

"Jungle love," Esmeralda said, lighting another cigarette without taking her eyes off the screen. Her expression changed as a face appeared in the monitor. "Doc? You two-timing son of a bitch."

Sir Bentley laughed and studied the screen.

"So he's out on surveillance is he? Funny name for it."

"He certainly is getting in for a close look," Gene said.

"That two-timing son of a bitch." Esmeralda hurled the empty tequila bottle out the open window, over the balcony and into the swimming pool directly below the suite.

Sir Bentley continued chuckling until another face came into view. "Genevieve? How could you?"

"Is this the one you've been telling me about? Your plant specialist?"

"Yes," Sir Bentley said.

"Man, she's hot," Gene said. "Damn, what happened to the picture?"

The screen went blank but all three continued to stare until it became clear that the image wouldn't be returning.

"He was taking her against her will." Sir Bentley started pacing. "That must be it."

"That's a laugh. Doc has never had to take it in his life," Esmeralda said.

"Yeah, Bentley," Gene said. "I think women taken by force usually try to get their legs closed, not the other way around."

"Didn't you see the way she was clawing at his back?"

"Yeah. The lucky bastard. She was really into it."

"Bullshit," Sir Bentley said. "He overpowered her. And camera angles always lie. Or maybe he was holding a knife on her and she had to go along."

"I don't know, Sir," Gene said, stealing a glance at Esmeralda who continued to stew.

"I'm telling you he forced himself on her," Sir Bentley said. "Get packed."

"Get what?" Gene said.

"Packed. We're going."

"Into the jungle?"

"No, to fucking Disneyland," Sir Bentley said, heading towards the door.

"If you don't mind, I'm gonna wait here," Esmeralda said, stretching out on the bed. "I'll deal with him when he gets back."

"Bent, c'mon," Gene said, holding up his hands in protest. "What the hell do you think the two of us are going to be able to do out there?"

"Well, we can start by finding her," Bentley said. "We're leaving in ten minutes so get ready."

He stormed out and left the door open.

"I thought he'd never leave." Esmeralda yawned and closed her eyes. "Doc, I'm gonna cut your balls off."

Gene glanced at the snoring woman, took a final look at the monitors and closed the door behind him.

127

30

Merlin woke up to the sight of one of the ugliest people on the planet staring at him from a foot away. He reached out and stroked Murray's head who was standing guard over Summerman. Merlin nudged his comatose friend and poked his head and shoulders until he reluctantly sat up. He blinked at Merlin, then at the ugly man.

"How long have we been out?" Summerman said.

"Probably about for one slice of moon."

"Ah, my little tribal timekeeper. You going native on me already?" Summerman rubbed the sleep out of his eyes.

"Like that one, did you?" Merlin said. "What the hell was that we drank?"

"You speak English," said Ugly Man.

Merlin and Summerman glanced at each other and then back at Ugly Man.

"All current evidence notwithstanding, yes. I'm Merlin. This is Summerman."

"You can call me Freak. Summerman, huh? Is that your dog?"

"Yeah. He's all mine."

"I don't think he likes me. Does he bite?"

"Only strangers who ask dumb questions."

"What?"

"Just keep your movements at snail pace and you should be fine."

"I need your help."

Summerman stared at Freak's face. "I'm sorry. But I'm not a plastic surgeon."

"What?"

"Nothing," Summerman said. "How did you get here?"

"I got darted and dragged here by a couple of those jungle bunnies."

He caught the glare Merlin, and Summerman were giving him and began backtracking. "Hey, I'm sorry. I didn't mean anything by that. I love black people."

128

"Jungle bunnies?" Merlin said.

"Look, I said I didn't mean it," Freak said, his anger rising. "What is your problem?"

Merlin stood up and took a step towards Freak, who was still sitting on the floor with his hands behind his back. Freak tried to hop to his feet but collapsed.

"How come you two aren't tied up?" Freak attempted to chew through the leather ties. "Bastards have probably got my rocket launcher too."

"Rocket launcher?" Summerman said.

"Yeah, I'm part of a covert mission to take this place by any means possible. But don't say anything, it's a secret."

"Freak, that's your name, right?"

"Yeah."

"Covert mission? You wouldn't be traveling with Doc White by any chance would you?"

"Yeah, he's my ex-brother in law."

Summerman glanced at Merlin, who shook his head. "We finally get a chance to meet the famous brother in law."

"Well, I don't know about famous. I do have a rather impressive military record, but I don't know if I'd call myself famous."

"Well, Freak, why don't you tell us a little bit more about what you're doing here?"

Pffft.

Freak reached for the side of his neck, but his hand dropped away. He fell forward unconscious.

"What are you doing?" Summerman said.

"Wow." Merlin stared at the blowgun. "I hit him."

"Well, it's a little hard to miss from three feet. Why did you go and dart him?"

"I don't like the prick."

"Don't you think it would have been better to keep him conscious so we could try to figure what he's up to and maybe find Doc?"

Merlin stared off into the distance.

"Maybe."

31

Gilbert slowly worked his way between two identical plants with thorns longer and sharper than the needles used to stitch Cloudlifters. He sucked in his rumbling stomach. Although currently empty, it was still twice the size it was during his pre-doughnut island days. He meticulously pushed one of the branches away from his path and stepped forward. He released the branch, and it snapped back into place, grazing the side of his leg.

"Thit," he said, examining the blood already seeping through the scratches on his left leg.

He surveyed his progress; a foot and a half and now surrounded by hundreds of the thorns. He glanced over his shoulder and realized moving backward was not an option. Still sucking in his massive gut, he looked down and discovered that only an inch of space existed between his navel and another plant branch that threatened him from the front. Struggling from lack of oxygen, his face reddened as another wave of panic raced through his system. Frantically searching for an escape route, Gilbert's knees threatened to buckle, and his lower back spasmed. Faced with the choice between falling face first and deal with a full-body piercing or the consequences of a more localized attack, Gilbert closed his eyes and sucked oxygen. He screamed as thorns pierced his soft white underbelly. Wildlife within a five-mile radius scattered.

He opened his eyes and stared down at the blood streaming down his stomach. The pain hammered him, and he dropped to his knees.

The thorns released as his knees touched the ground and the branch snapped forward and quivered inches from Gilbert's face.

He waited until they came to rest and grunted as he worked his legs out from under him. Sitting on the ground between the two massive plants, he slowly removed the case holding the rocket launcher from his shoulder and slid it forward towards his feet. He leaned back on his elbows and gently worked his way down until he was lying on his back. Using the back of his heels for leverage and pushing with his hands, Gilbert inched his way forward and under the remaining thorn-covered branches. Eventually, he staggered to his feet and examined his wounds, noting, with some degree of satisfaction, that the bleeding had stopped.

Gilbert slung the case back over his shoulder, checked the high point on the island and the sun to make sure he was still heading in the right direction and sniffed the air. The unmistakable scent of Hilda's doughnuts beckoned, and his stomach rumbled. No longer needing the landmarks to help him find his way back to the resort, Gilbert trudged forward using his nose to lead the way.

Ten minutes later he came over a small crest of land, and several thatched roofs came into view. He made his way to the dirt path and fell twice in excitement as the resort drew closer. Gilbert veered right as the scent of deep-fried pastries grew stronger. He soon entered the back door of the kitchen. Hilda, stuffing custard into a large batch of chocolate éclairs, jumped back in fear at the first sight of the disheveled, bloodstained creature standing in the doorway. She picked up a large knife and held it in front of her as she backed up.

"Hilda. Itths me."

"Gilbert?"

"Yeth."

"Jesus, mate. You scared the bloody crap out of me. I thought you might have gotten blown up at the factory. What on earth happened to you?"

Gilbert stared lovingly at the éclairs.

"It's a long thory."

"What's that thing in your mouth?"

"Later," Gilbert said, drooling. "I'm famithed. Can I pleathe have a doughnut?"

Hilda smiled and put the knife down. She placed a tray of the éclairs on the table, and Gilbert scrambled into a chair and began wolfing them down. Upwind, Hilda watched as he inhaled the first half-dozen. Gilbert took a break to catch his breath, wiped chocolate from his mouth with the back of his hand, and then began to sob uncontrollably.

"There, there, baby," Hilda said, patting his shoulder. "It's okay. You're home now. Tell you what, why don't we get you in the shower and then I'll fix us a nice quiet dinner."

Gilbert nodded his head and rubbed his eyes.

"What on earth were you doing out there in that jungle?"

"Trying to thurvive."

"Well, it's nice to see you haven't lost your sense of humor, even in the face of your factory blowing up. Such a shame."

"Yeth," Gilbert said, reaching for another éclair. "Itth a real pity."

No, you idiots. It's this way."

Gene and Buddy did a 180-degree turn and looked at Sir Bentley, who was pointing towards a spot on the horizon. He was dressed in a bright yellow safari suit and wearing a pith helmet. A new pair of yellow Cloudlifters and knee socks completed the ensemble.

"Are you sure, Bent? You sure we haven't been walking around in circles?" Gene said.

"Yeah, I agree," Buddy said. "This place looks awfully familiar."

"It all looks familiar. It's a jungle."

"Sweet Jesus. Try to relax," Gene said, sitting down on his backpack. "I just think we're lost, that's all."

"We're on an island," Sir Bentley said, scanning the surroundings. "How the hell could we get lost?"

"I don't know," Gene said, opening a beer. "But I've been lost before, and this looks a lot like it."

"It has to be this way," Sir Bentley said, staring through a pair of binoculars. "Let's go."

"Whatever you say," Gene said, climbing to his feet.

"I have to find her," Sir Bentley said, tightening the straps of his backpack. "And when I rescue her and prove that no man can match my abilities, not to mention charm, she'll come around. You just wait. You'll see."

"You're sure he was taking her against her will?" Buddy said.

"Absolutely."

"The bastard," Buddy said.

Gene decided against further debate concerning Sir Bentley's delusions that Doc had forced himself on Genevieve. Even though he had never had the opportunity to experience the phenomenon personally, Gene knew that a woman who was able to massage her partner's shoulder blades with the bottom of her feet during coitus was offering encouragement, not protest.

"What did you have the place insured for?" Gene said as they resumed their trek.

"What?"

"The factory. How much coverage did you carry on it?"

"A hundred million," Sir Bentley said, working his way around an enormous deciduous tree. He tapped the trunk and looked up. "What is this, teak?"

"Wouldn't have a clue," Buddy said, briefly interrupting his snake patrol to glance up at the tree.

"This has gotta be worth a fortune," Sir Bentley said.

"Sure," Buddy said. "As long as it was chopped down and cut into pieces."

"Well, sure. That's the only way it's worth anything."

Gene shook his head and resumed scanning the brush as he trudged forward. "A hundred million?"

"Yeah," Sir Bentley said. "What about it?"

"I just thought that it couldn't have cost you more than twenty or thirty million to build it."

"Twenty-five. I saved a bundle by using local labor." Sir Bentley puffed with pride. "But as far as the insurance company knows, it cost me eighty. Plus, you have to factor in the appreciation of the land value since it was built, plus the proximity to the resort, lost production time, you know the drill."

"So by doing absolutely nothing except watch the thing blow up, you made seventy-five million today."

Sir Bentley smiled for the first time all day.

"Yeah. Somewhere around there."

"Nice work if you can get it," Gene said.

"Hey, if you can't figure out a way to turn a nice profit during a time of disaster, you don't deserve to be rich in the first place."

"Turning Disaster Into Opportunity. There's the title for your next book," Buddy said, tossing his empty beer can into the foliage.

"Hmmm." Sir Bentley considered the possibilities. "Yeah, that might work. But I'd have to downplay the human suffering angle. Wouldn't want to come across as a heartless prick."

"Perish the thought," Gene said. "So after we find her, then what?"

"I'm not sure," Sir Bentley said, hacking at a series of overhanging vines with a machete.

Buddy sat down on a rock and opened a fresh beer.

"Why don't we just sneak into the village, grab a bunch of the plants, and hop in the Gulfstream. We put the chemists to work while I start drawing up some patents."

"Just like that?" Sir Bentley said, shaking his head in amazement.

"Sure, why not?"

"For a corporate lawyer you don't know much about globalization, do you?"

"What's to know? A little local knowledge, cheap workforce, no regulations. Make it cheap and ship it out. Sell a bunch, make a bunch more. It's a freshman b-school 101 course. It's a 101, baby. A 101 all the way."

"You should stick to being a lackey, Buddy. You know, play to your strengths," Sir Bentley said. "Subtlety is what's needed here. This thing is worth billions. Besides, without understanding how the plants are used, we could spend years trying to figure it out in a laboratory. With local knowledge, we can cut our time to market by at least ninety percent. We need to co-opt the medicine man, the guy who has the history either in his head or written down somewhere."

"Co-opt?"

"Yeah, you know, build up some trust," Sir Bentley said.

"You mean before you screw the shit out of them," Gene said.

"Exactly."

33

Freak heard the sound of wooden flute and opened his eyes. He blinked several times to make sure he wasn't dreaming. A young woman, naked from the waist up with perfect skin the color of mahogany, was sitting on the floor a few feet away creating a lilting melody through a carved piece of bamboo. Freak stared at her until he caught her eye and then his heart melted when he saw the smile.

She chattered at him briefly, arched her back to better display her breasts, and resumed her song. Freak propped himself up on his elbows and watched and listened. The music was like nothing he had ever heard before, which wasn't surprising since Freak had been a devotee of classic metal since the age of twelve. Although the music the young woman was playing didn't induce the desire to dive headfirst from a stage into a mosh pit, Freak did find it soothing.

He stared at the bare-breasted woman gently exhaling into the flute. Freak was most definitely relaxed. And aroused. In fact, he was hard as the piece of bamboo she was blowing.

Freak's current state of arousal had not gone unnoticed and the young woman, without breaking melody, nodded her head at the bulge threatening to burst out of his cargos.

"Must be the music," Freak said, red-faced and laughing.

The young woman paused long enough to slide closer towards his bed, chattered briefly and resumed playing.

"You're really good with that thing," he said. "By the way, I'm Freak. I'm sorry, but I don't speak Jungle-ese."

She slid a few feet closer, chattered and started to play again.

"You're very beautiful," Freak said. "And I know beautiful when I see it. I've been all over the place. Plus, I've got three honorable discharges and was almost on TV."

The young woman giggled and slid closer until she was within touching distance, a possibility that Freak was giving serious consideration.

A loud, angry chatter filled the hut. Tuber, apparently angrier with the young woman, scowled at both of them. The woman, now also angry, chattered back at Tuber as she approached him. Standing face to face, they jawed at each other for about a minute until the young woman smacked Tuber over the head with the bamboo flute and stormed out. Freak leaned forward in the hope of catching a final glimpse of her before she disappeared, then cowered in fear as the strange man approached.

"Hey, man," Freak said. "I didn't do nothing. She was coming on to me."

Tuber chattered at Freak in a loud, high-pitched screech.

"I'm sorry, man. Like if she's your girlfriend or something. Look at me; I'm tied up. What could I do?"

Freak held up the leg in question, and Tuber lost some of his anger.

"Yeah, that's right. I'm a prisoner. Nothing I can do. Mind you, not that I wouldn't jump all over that if I had half a chance."

Tuber listened closely and cocked his head.

"You're not getting any of this, are you?'

Tuber chattered a brief response.

"What I mean is that she's hot. Premium quality. Double P. P squared. Get what I mean? Nah, you're not getting any of this."

Tuber squinted at Freak with a confused look on his face.

"Pussy? Liquid gold? Y-town?"

Freak slid into a singsong rap and got rolling.

"Magic in a pot, she's hot, when she's lookin' for that spot, in da pot." Freak paused and waited for a response.

"Nothing, huh? How about her ass? That little grass skirt she's wearing ain't never gonna hide that thing from public view. C'mon man, you must have got that one. You know? Booty, wonderbooty, bootylicious, the naked glute suit? A round mound of sound if slapped hard when bound. You like that one? That's from a rap I've been working on. I call it Get Off With The Freak On Ya."

Tuber's eyes narrowed and he grunted at the rambling man spraying spittle. He took a cautious step backward.

"Nothing, huh? Let's see," Freak said. "What about her titties? C'mon you gotta understand that one. Christ, she's got em out there in the open saluting the world. Titties? You know titties?"

Tuber listened closely and then tried the word.

"Ti...tee."

"Yeah, that's it, man. Titties. You got it. The twins. Ear warmers. Sweater puppies. The Magic Muffins. Yeah, it's all that."

"Ti...tee," Tuber said, shaking his head.

"Yeah, you know what I'm talking." Freak laughed. "Titter magic."

Tuber stared at Freak with a blank expression.

Freak cupped his hands under his breasts and mimicked the young woman blowing on the bamboo flute. He made a squeezing motion with his hands and licked his lips.

Tuber snarled in comprehension.

Pffffft.

"Oh, shit. Not again."

Freak hit the floor with a dull thud.

34

The celebration began just before sunset with a display of drums and chants that would have been right at home at Mardi Gras; as would the copious amounts of a milky, banana-scented liquid the adults were knocking back by the cupful. Everyone in the tribe banged incessantly on instruments of various sizes that had dried pigskin stretched tight over wooden frames as they chanted in an off-pitch sing-song manner.

"Well, it's nice to see they're not good at everything," Merlin said, recoiling from the sound that reverberated across the village.

"Yeah," Summerman said, taking his seat next to Merlin at the table of honor. "But they are loud. I'll give them that."

Bantu, led by his father, entered the hut, and the pace and volume of the chants and drums increased to the point where the wooden floor began to vibrate. Chief led Bantu to his seat next to Summerman and then raised his arms to silence the crowd. The drumming and chanting drifted away and soon the only sound was the loud voice of Tuber who continued to harangue his girlfriend in a corner of the hut. Chief waited until he caught Tuber's eye and glared at him. Tuber flushed with embarrassment and sat down in a huff next to the red-faced flute master.

Silence filled the room.

Summerman leaned closer to Bantu. "What's the matter with him?"

"He believes he has lost face with the tribe. Shilila played the song of love on her flute to someone else. To an Outsider no less," Bantu whispered.

"Jealous, huh?"

"Extremely," Bantu said, nodding his head. "So much so that he's planning on challenging him to a duel."

"A duel?" Merlin said, eavesdropping. "How cool is that."

"It's not what I had hoped to see on my first day home," Bantu said. "But Tuber has every right to defend his honor."

139

"Doesn't the woman get a vote in this?" Summerman looked at the young woman who continued to glare at Tuber.

"Oh, most certainly," Bantu said. "But choosing an Outsider, no offense, would be most difficult for the tribe to accept."

Merlin glared at Freak.

"Especially when the Outsider in question is such a wonderful human being."

"He is a rather strange fellow," Bantu said. "And tomorrow we will deal with him. But tonight, it's time to, how you say, party down."

Merlin and Summerman laughed and joined in the toast Chief was proposing to his returned son. They took a long swig of the banana liquid and smacked their lips.

"This tastes sweeter than the other one," Merlin said.

"Yeah, but it's pretty good," Summerman said. "What is this, Bantu?"

"It's a fermented combination of banana, papaya, and rice."

"Fermented? You mean alcoholic?"

"It depends on which barrel you're drinking from." Bantu pointed at three large containers along one side of the wall. "The one on the left is for the children. That's just a punch. The one in the middle is fermented and will cause you to slur and stagger if you drink enough of it."

"What about the barrel on the right?" Merlin said.

"You don't want to drink from that barrel," Bantu said, sipping from his cup.

"Too late for that," Summerman said, draining the last of his drink.

"Yeah, we've been drinking out of that barrel since we started. What's the matter with it?" Merlin said.

"Oh, my," Bantu said, "You've been drinking from the elder barrel?"

"The elder barrel?" Merlin said. "Pardon my ignorance, Bantu, but what in the elder barrel?"

"Just some special plants and herbs," Bantu said. He turned and chattered quietly with Chief, who was sitting on his left.

The Chief stared at Summerman and Merlin and chattered back at Bantu under his breath.

"What?" Merlin said. "What are you two talking about?"

"It's nothing," Bantu said, closely studying their faces. "How many have you had?"

"This is number three," Summerman said. "Hey, Bantu, have you always had that thing growing out of the side of your neck?"

Before Bantu could respond, Chief stood up to address the tribe. He chattered, paused to allow a brief round of applause and drumming to rise and subside, then continued with his speech. He nodded at Bantu, who stood up and waved to the tribe.

"Who are you, lizard boy?" Merlin said to the figure sitting next to him. "And what have you done with Summerman?"

Summerman stared at the creature sitting next to him and said,

"Wow, you should get that thing checked out by a doctor."

"What thing?" Merlin said, touching his face with hands of rubber.

"That big hole in the center of your face," Summerman said, extending his finger and inserting it into one of Merlin's nostrils.

Merlin swatted the finger away and stared out at the tribe sitting on the floor.

"Sweet Jesus," Merlin said. "They're melting."

"They're not melting," Summerman said, staring out at the crowd. "But I sure would like to know how they do that two head trick."

Chief chattered to the tribe and then pointed at Summerman and Merlin. Bantu gently poked Summerman in the ribs.

"Stand up and wave," Bantu said. "You're being introduced to the tribe."

Summerman and Merlin grinned at each other and then stood up and nodded to the tribe as they banged on their drums. Chief chattered some more and then shook his head as he noticed Merlin wander off from the table towards the elder barrel. Bantu hopped to his feet and gently pulled Merlin back to his seat as the tribe roared with laughter.

"We're a hit," Merlin said, slumping back into his chair.

"Doesn't that thing hurt?" Summerman said, fixated on Merlin's face.

"I can't feel a thing."

35

Want some more?" Doc said, holding up a piece of roasted boar.

"No, thanks. I'm full," Genevieve said, lighting a Gitanes. "And sore."

Doc smiled and chewed. "Eight years. We've got a lot of catching up to do."

"Yes, but we're not going to be able to do it in one day." Genevieve stood and arched her back. "But it's nice to see you haven't slowed down."

"You bring it out in me," Doc said.

"Okay," she said, edging closer to the fire. "Now that we've got that out of the way, I think it's time we had a little chat."

"You mean the 'what's a nice guy like you doing in a place like this' chat? That one?"

"Exactly."

"I was wondering the same thing about you," Doc said.

"I'm working for Sir Bentley Carruthers," Genevieve said.

"Really? That's funny, so am I."

"Doing what?"

"According to him, making the world safe for democracy." Doc stuck his knife into the side of the roasted pig suspended above the fire and wiped his hands.

"Ever the noble warrior, eh Bodhisattva?"

"It's been a long time since anybody's called me that." Doc stood up to stretch his legs.

"Still going the Buddhist route?"

"I'm trying, and failing miserably."

Genevieve laughed and took a drag on her cigarette.

"Well, the path towards enlightenment can be a slippery pursuit," she said.

"Don't I know that," Doc said.

He stretched out on the ground and stared up at the stars.

"You're always so hard on yourself, Doc," Genevieve said, gently stroking his hair. "So, what on earth are you doing out here?"

"Ostensibly to get a handle on the tribe that lives here. Bentley says they're sabotaging his operations."

Doc chuckled and grabbed a cigarette from her pack.

"You sound skeptical."

"I don't believe a word coming out of his mouth. As far as he's concerned, I'm here with a security team to keep him safe. But I'm here to see what he's up to in a couple of areas. He pissed off some very dangerous people with some weapons technology he's trying to sell to about fifteen different countries. Stopping that is my primary objective but, while I'm here, I decided to find out about his plans to move into biopiracy. What are you doing for him?"

"He's paying me a boatload of money to catalog native plants."

"Interesting."

"He says he's building a native plant museum."

Doc laughed.

"I couldn't say no to the money." Genevieve crushed out her cigarette. "He was looking for a way to get me on his payroll."

Doc thought for a moment and then smiled at her.

"Please don't tell me you've been sleeping with Sir Bentley."

"I'm not. Well, I did once, twice if you count the brief slip in the shower."

"I see," Doc said.

"But I was excited about the job offer. We were in San Francisco at one of his mansions. I drank a ton of champagne, and I hadn't had sex in months."

Doc laughed again. "Take a breath. And I wasn't asking for details."

"I know, but it's become a real problem. I sleep with him, and it's like he owns me."

"People like him don't like to be told no. And I can certainly understand why he wants a return visit after having it once, twice if you count the slip in the shower."

"Ha-ha. Very funny."

Doc rolled onto to his side and stared into her eyes.

"So what's the old coot like?"

"I thought you didn't want details."

"Well, maybe just a couple."

143

It was Genevieve's turn to laugh.

"Actually, he looks pretty good for a guy his age. And he knows his way around a woman's body."

"He's certainly had enough practice."

"The Viagra helped. But it was strange. About five minutes in, he starts telling me how much he loves me, how he wants to take care of me, and that all I need to do is commit to him, and he'll make sure I never want for anything."

"I guess you could do worse," Doc said.

"Sure. But when I looked into my future all I could see was him, eighty and naked, inching his way across the bedroom with major wood and a walker."

Doc roared with laughter.

"When he laid it out, it was like he was trying to close a business deal and I was just one more acquisition."

"But you took the job."

"Yeah. And for the past several months I've been on the road."

"Ducking him?"

"I've been doing some research work, but yes, I'm ducking him. But he calls me every day to check up on me. What am I doing? Who am I with? When am I coming back to the States? And after he's played twenty questions, he wants phone sex."

"Can't blame him for that. And this supposed museum?"

"The story is that he wants to create a museum with me as its head that houses artifacts from remote civilizations. He plans to specialize in the cataloging of ancient tribal remedies derived from native plants."

"And then sell them out of a new pharmaceutical company," Doc said.

"That makes sense. The majority of Western drugs all started with some form of native plant. I'm not sure, but he has been extremely anxious for me to get here and begin exploring the plant life. What's so special about this place? If you've seen one jungle, you've seen them all, right?"

"He's looking for the tribe that uses them."

"And they're here on this island?"

"They most certainly are," Doc said.

144

"I've always heard tales, mostly folklore I'm sure, about remote islands in this area where many of the native plants contain magical cures for just about anything that ails you. When I was doing my dissertation, I remember hearing rumors about some British explorer who'd kept a private journal about his trip down in this area. Apparently, the journal contains descriptions about a remote tribe that had incorporated hundreds of indigenous plants into their daily life. But I've never seen any proof of it."

Doc removed his phone and located the photos he'd taken of the journal. He handed it to her and waited as she flipped through the photos.

"This is amazing. I was convinced that it was just folklore being kept alive by the plant scientists. The ongoing quest for the fountain of youth. There's nothing like a good fantasy to help drive research grants and endowments. The story always stayed with me because of the explorer's name who later got knighted. The Earl of Mangrove."

"That's the guy. And the name of the family that was behind Sir Bentley's knighthood and subsequent drumming out of England."

"Bentley was forced to leave England?"

"He certainly was. It's not well known, but Bentley got caught banging the sixteen-year-old daughter of the Duke of Mangrove," Doc said.

"Sixteen?"

"Yeah. And to avoid public embarrassment they cut a deal with Bentley to take his knighthood, keep his mouth shut, and get out of town. That's when he moved to New York."

"He got knighted for screwing a teenager?"

"If I remember, the award was for extraordinary services rendered to the Empire."

"He wasn't that good." Genevieve stretched out.

"But the Viagra helped, right?" Doc said, laughing.

"If you're into that sort of thing."

She pulled Doc down on top of her.

36

Bob Garbo placed the final camera on the outskirts of the village and looked down into the valley that stretched out before him. Torches hung from bamboo reeds like streetlamps and various fire pits added to the light and shadows that flickered in the distance. The drumming and chanting had grown sporadic as the night sky fell into complete darkness. Bob flipped the switch on his communication system and whispered into the darkness.

"Base."

He waited for a response and then tried again. Hearing only silence from the other end, Bob climbed to his feet and considered his options; head down into the village, camp here for the night, or return to the resort. He checked his backpack and discovered he still had a half bottle of scotch. He headed back into the jungle about a hundred yards and found a clearing that provided adequate cover. He assembled his tent, rolled out his sleeping bag, and took a sip of scotch. The tribe was partying, and they weren't going anywhere. Plus, he needed to speak with Doc. Or at least that crazy bitch Esmeralda.

**

"Esmeralda, you are tres magnifique. Que belle. Mon dieu, be still my beating heart."

"Speak English, Frenchie," Esmeralda said, violently thrusting her hips down onto the ribcage of her companion.

"You are, as you Americans put it, great in ze sack."

"Tell me something I don't know." Esmeralda rolled over onto her back, dragging her partner along for the ride. "Hand me that bottle of tequila." Esmeralda took a long pull, resealed the top and tossed it onto the floor.

"C'mon, Frenchie. You Paris guys are supposed to be such great lovers," she said, slapping his ass. "Show me what you've got."

"Shouldn't you answer that?"

"It can wait."

**

"Hey, Bob Garbo. You there?"

Bob rolled over and sat up inside his sleeping bag.

"Doc?"

"Yeah, it's me. Hey, I haven't heard from you all day. Is everything okay?"

"Fine."

"Good. So we're all set."

"Yeah."

"Have you been updating Esmeralda?"

"Tried."

"Tried? She's not answering?"

"No."

"What the hell is she doing?"

Bob stayed silent.

"Right," Doc said. "Why am I asking you? Let's try her again. Keep the line open and we'll try for a three-way hookup."

"Okay."

**

"Calling Command Central. Come in. Are you there, base?"

"Allo?"

"Who is this?"

"This ez Piqûre."

"Who?"

"I am Piqûre. Ze lead singer and bass player for Les Gendarmes."

"Les what?"

"Les Gendarmes...ze Police. We ez a tribute band."

"I can barely hear you. Turn up the volume. "

"Turn up ze what?"

147

"The volume. What the hell are you doing on this line?"

"You called. I answered. Who ez this I am speaking with?"

"That's none of your goddamned business. I can't hear a word you're saying. Turn it up. Do you see the red button on the bottom of the receiver?"

"Ze red button?"

"Sweet Jesus. Yes, the volume control is at the bottom. Press the red button that says max."

"Oh, allo, Max."

"You idiot. I'm not Max. Look, just put Esmeralda on."

"She ez in ze bathroom."

"Well, tell her to get her ass out of there and get on the radio."

"Hey, Esmeralda," Piqûre yelled. "Get your ass out of there and get on ze radio."

"Is that Doc?"

"No, it ez someone called Max."

"Just put her on the goddamn phone," Doc said.

"Hang on, Max. I'll be with you in a moment."

"Who the fuck is Max?" Esmeralda said.

"How should I know? He ez your friend."

"It's not Max. Jesus Christ. Will you just put Esmeralda on the line?"

"What does he want?" Esmeralda said.

"He wants to speak with you."

"Ask him if Doc is there."

"Ez Doc there?"

"This is Doc."

"Oh, allo, Doc. Say goodbye to Max for me."

"Tell him to go fuck himself."

"She says to go fuck yourself, Doc."

"Put her on the goddamn phone. Now."

"You don't have to be rude, Doc. Esmeralda ez taking shower."

"Ask him if he's still banging the one with black hair," Esmeralda shouted.

"Are you still banging-"

"I heard her. Tell her, it's none of her business."

"Doc says it ez none of your business, Esmeralda."

"Is that right?" Esmeralda said. "Well, then tell him it's none of his business that you and I have been banging each other for the past two days."

"Is this Doc your boyfriend?" Piqûre whispered.

"Former," Esmeralda said.

"Is he a large man? Perhaps dangerous?"

"He's a trained killer."

"Then perhaps we should not tell him."

"Goddamn it. You big baby." Esmeralda stalked into the bedroom trailing water. "Give me the goddamn phone. I'll tell him myself." She snatched the phone out of his hand. "Doc, you two-timing prick. I'm gonna cut your balls off and throw them in a shredder. You no good sonofabitch."

"Doc?" Piqûre said. "What ez it you have done?"

"Shut up, Frenchie. And go shower. As soon as I get off the phone, you and I are going another round."

"Yes, of course," Piqûre said. "Whatever you say." He leaned close to the phone. "Goodbye, Doc. Good luck."

"Who the hell is that?" Doc said.

"None of your business," Esmeralda said reaching for the tequila bottle.

"Bob, you there?" Doc said.

"Yup."

"Great. The Silent One on line two. Did you tell him about your appearance on camera today, Doc?"

"Yeah, well, what can I say?"

"You can say goodbye, asshole."

Esmeralda cut the connection and took a long swig of tequila.

"Man, what a piece of work," Doc said.

"Indeed," Bob said.

"Have you finished setting up all the cameras?"

"Almost."

"So you'll be done in the morning?"

"Yeah."

"Well, it looks like Esmeralda's not going to play."

"Pissed."

"Yeah, she certainly is. Look, I'm a little busy here at the moment," Doc said, trying to continue the conversation while Genevieve was nibbling at his neck. "One of us should probably

149

head back to the resort just to make sure everything's all right down there. Do you mind taking a look?"

"Nope."

"Thanks, Bob. I owe you one. And just to be on the safe side, keep your distance from her when you get there."

"Absolutely."

"Okay, I'll touch base with you sometime tomorrow and we'll-"

Doc moaned.

"I'm out."

"Enjoy," said Bob Garbo.

37

The only things that Summerman remembered about the previous evening were colors, two-headed monsters, and the wild boar. The morning jungle, filled with vivid greens and yellow, had lost the red and purple hues that dominated last night's sky. He scanned the horizon and listened for the sounds of the village yet saw or heard nothing except the rattle of bamboo gently swaying in the wind and the cacophony of birdlife chattering about what to have for breakfast.

He remembered deciding to go for a walk to clear his head. This had proven costly since, rather than negate the hallucinogens, Summerman's visions increased as he ventured out of the village. He remembered feeling a sense of invincibility rather than panic as he and Murray, who miraculously had become an actual tiger, trekked on through the night.

Past the two-headed cobra, around the thousand-foot waterfall and into the purple banana plants. He remembered the misty rain that burned his skin, yet left no scar. He remembered the wild boar that had crept up behind and spoken to him.

"Nice dog," the boar said.

"Thanks. He's my best friend."

"Good choice on your part. You lost?" the boar said.

"I'm not sure," Summerman said. "Where am I?"

"You're the ghost. Don't you know?"

"I'm not a ghost at the moment."

"That's okay. I'm not a boar. I'm in disguise."

"Who are you?"

"I'm Chief."

"Chief? From the tribe?"

"Yes."

"You could have fooled me," Summerman said, staring at the tusks protruding from the side of its face. "You sure look like a boar."

151

"Thanks."

"You're performing shape shifting?"

"Yes."

"And now you're speaking English?"

"Maybe you're just hearing me in my native tongue."

"I see. So where are we?"

The boar looked around, then back at Summerman.

"The jungle, I think."

"Yes," Summerman said, running his fingers through his hair. "The jungle. Now I remember."

"But we could be anywhere. The zoo. A theme park. Perhaps, even Wonderland."

"Or maybe the Land of Oz?"

"Sure," the boar said. "Whatever works for you."

"But definitely not Kansas."

"No," laughed the boar. "Definitely not Kansas."

"So what are you doing up at this hour?" Summerman said.

"I'm talking with you."

"Yes, of course. I've never seen a pig with zebra stripes before."

"I'm in transition. And don't call me a pig."

"Sorry. Transition, huh? I guess everybody wants to be something else."

"Not everyone," said the boar, nodding his head in the direction of the village. "Some folks just want to be left alone."

"Yes. So tell me, what's it like being a boar?"

"As hunter, great. As the hunted, less so."

"Makes sense. Where are you going?"

"Home," said the boar.

"To see the wife and kids?"

"Yes. To see the wife and kids."

"You're a lucky man, er, boar."

"Indeed. Goodnight, my friend. And be careful out here. Bad things are about to happen."

"Bad?"

"Yes."

"To whom?"

"How the hell should I know? I'm only a boar."

Summerman watched him waddle off. Moments later, the boar stopped and turned.

"Oh, and if I were you," said the boar. "I'd lay off the elder barrel. You might end up doing some strange things."

"Like talking to a pig?"

"There's no need for name calling," said the boar, resuming his journey.

An early morning shower brought him back to the present. Summerman rested on a rock surrounded by tall bamboo. Murray was exploring the nearby plant life and finding much to keep him occupied. Summerman listened as the rain tapped against the palm leaves and then built into a constant rhythm. And then above the rain, he heard the sound of a woman's screams and moans.

**

Genevieve rolled over in the sleeping bag and reached for a Gitanes. Doc climbed out of the sleeping bag and pulled on his pants and shirt. He poked his head outside the small tent and watched the rain for a moment and then stretched out next to her.

"I've got to get some work done today," Doc said, nuzzling Genevieve's neck. "But it can wait."

"Please, Doc." She laughed. "Don't start. We're going to kill each other if we keep this up."

"Maybe it will rain all day, and we'll be forced to stay here."

"It'll stop soon." Genevieve watched cigarette smoke drift upwards. "Are you going to the village today to make contact?"

"I'm not sure," Doc said, extracting a hand-held device from his shirt pocket. "Let's see what Bob Garbo has been up to."

Doc stared at the screen and flipped through the different camera shots that now surrounded the village from a distance.

"Let me see," Genevieve said, sitting up. "Merde, this is incredible. Where on earth did you get this technology?"

"You don't want to know."

Genevieve switched from one camera angle to another and continued to shake her head in amazement.

"Are those sidewalks?"

"Yeah, looks like it. Probably made of wood."

"Water towers, fences, and look at those huts. They're incredible."

"Pretty advanced."

"They seem very peaceful. I mean they're all smiling and laughing. Not a care in the world."

"Wait until I get there," Doc said.

"Doc you are not going to hurt these people. Do you understand?"

Doc poked his head outside the tent as the rain subsided.

"Doc? Did you hear me?"

"Yeah, I heard you. But I'm working here."

"And hurting people is what you do, right?"

"Sometimes, yeah."

"And this time?"

"I won't know until I get a chance to see them up close."

"Doc, I'm warning you."

"Shhh," Doc said, holding up a hand. "Someone's out there."

"What?" Genevieve scrambled out of the sleeping bag and pulled her clothes on.

Doc patted her arm and gestured for her to be still. He checked the magazine of his nine-millimeter pistol, grabbed two additional clips of ammunition, and a large hunting knife. He pulled on his boots and turned to face her.

"Listen," he said. "I need to go see what that is. So just stay here." He handed her what looked like a pistol. "This is a flare gun. If anyone shows up here, just fire it into the air. I'll be right back."

"Doc," Genevieve said. "Who on earth could be showing up out here in the middle of the jungle?"

"My point exactly." Doc inched his way out of the tent. "I'll be right back."

**

Sir Bentley, Buddy, and Gene ate well that morning courtesy of the chef who had packed a large bag of goodies before they'd left Nirvana. Various cheeses and canned smoked oysters perfectly complimented the fresh lox and bagels that had survived the moist jungle air just long enough to remain edible. They washed it all

154

down with a chilled bottle of Dom, then headed deeper into the jungle with full bellies and an early morning champagne buzz.

"Man," Buddy said, staring around blindly at the impenetrable thicket that surrounded them. "I am so lost."

"It's gotta be here somewhere," Sir Bentley said, glancing up at the sky, desperate for any form of assistance. "It's an island for chrissakes. How is it possible to get lost on an island?"

"Australia's an island. Greenland's an island."

"And your point is?" Sir Bentley said, glaring at Gene.

"Forget it." Gene stopped in his tracks. "Well, what do you know?"

"Hah," Sir Bentley said. "I told you we weren't lost."

"That's a tent. And it looks just like our tent."

"So that's where he's holding her." Sir Bentley crept towards the small tent partially obscured by palm leaves.

"I don't know, Bent," Gene said, shaking his head. "From what I saw-"

"I'm telling you," Sir Bentley said, his voice a rage-filled whisper. "He's taking her against her will."

"Yeah," Buddy said. "Strong will. Weak won't."

"Shhh."

**

In the early morning light, Doc slowly stalked his prey from behind. Holding a twelve-inch knife, Doc bent one of the man's arms back and grasped his wrist tight. The man yelped in pain and tried to glance backward, panicked by his unseen assailant. Doc pressed the knife deeper into the man's throat until the skin threatened to split.

"What are you doing out here?"

"Nothing," the man croaked.

"Summerman? I thought you were waiting back at the resort. What the hell are doing out here?"

"Hopefully," Summerman said. "It's just an elder barrel flashback."

Murray tore through the foliage snarling and snapping his jaws. He stopped suddenly, wagged his tail, then draped both paws over Doc's shoulders.

155

"Murray, how's my boy?"

Doc sheathed his knife and scratched Murray's ears.

"Some watchdog. You're a little late, Murray," Summerman said. "What's the matter? The heat getting to you?"

Murray woofed but otherwise ignored the comment.

**

"This'll smoke them out." Sir Bentley pointed at the tent. "Fire."

Doing his best TV-cop imitation, Buddy pointed the flare gun he'd found lying on the ground, slipped on the wet grass as he went into his crouch, and inadvertently pulled the trigger. Bentley felt the sear of hot flare piercing his left calf. The flare glanced off his leg, ignited the tent, and then disappeared into the jungle torching several palm leaves as it roared away at low altitude.

"You dumb shit. Goddamn, that hurts." Sir Bentley examined the six-inch burn on his lower leg.

"Nobody here," Buddy said, glancing around the remains of the rapidly disappearing nylon.

"You're a genius, aren't you?" Sir Bentley said, blowing on his leg. "Your powers of observation are breathtaking."

"Hey, screw you, Chicken Little. You're the one who came up with the idea of attacking an empty tent."

"What on earth are you doing here?"

All three men turned to see Genevieve making her way through the jungle and heading in their direction.

"Thank God you're safe," Sir Bentley said.

"Safe?" Genevieve said. "Why wouldn't I be safe?"

"She doesn't look like a hostage," Buddy said. "In fact, I'd say she was glowing."

"Shut up, Quizling." Sir Bentley refocused his attention on Genevieve, who was doing her best to work a brush through her tangled hair. "I saw you yesterday being taking against your will. By that animal, Doc."

Genevieve stopped brushing her hair and glared at Bentley.

"You were watching? How dare you spy on me."

"Well, it was a little hard not to given the camera angle," Gene said.

"I wasn't spying," Sir Bentley said. "I just happened to be in the command post reviewing the monitors when the two of you appeared. Did he hurt you?"

"I'll survive."

Genevieve resumed her attempt to brush dead bugs out of her hair.

"I knew it," Sir Bentley said. "You poor girl. Well, you're safe now."

"Bentley. I'm fine. Now if you don't mind, I have some things I need to take care of."

"They can wait," Bentley said. "But for now, we're heading back to Nirvana."

"I'm not going anywhere," Genevieve said.

Sir Bentley glared at her and slipped into his best CEO voice. "Excuse me? Do I need to remind you who you work for?"

"Bentley, please. Don't even start-"

"Ah," Bentley said, cutting her off with a wave of his hand. "Normally, when one of my employees demonstrates such poor performance, not to mention the fact that you consistently fail to report in, you could have been dead for all I knew." Bentley paused to take a breath. "Normally, the employee in question would be fired on the spot."

"Bentley, I have three notebooks filled with notes and sample species from my travels up to this point."

"But nothing from this island, right?"

"No, but what do you think I'm trying to do out here in the middle of this jungle?"

"Ah." Bentley cut her off with another wave of his hand. "You've had plenty of time. What have you been doing since you got here?" Bentley extracted a hotel bill from the jacket of his safari suit and read along during his harangue. "Let's see. Six days total. Seven pay per view movies, jet ski and hang glider rentals, hundreds of dollars in room service charges, three thousand dollars of wine."

"Don't blame me," Genevieve said. "You're the one who put the wine list together. For chrissakes, Bentley, you're charging two hundred bucks for a bottle of Egyptian red that sells on the street in Cairo for fifty cents."

"Do not take that tone with me," Bentley said, his eyes narrowing. "Let me remind you of some basic facts. I'm Sir Bentley

Carruthers. I own business operations on four continents and forty-seven countries. I own this island. And, until I say otherwise, I own you. Are you ready to deal with that?"

Genevieve lit a Gitanes and casually blew smoke skyward.

"Yeah. And I'm the great piece of ass that got away. Deal with that."

Sir Bentley's face turned bright red and flirted momentarily with purple. "I risk my life trekking through this jungle to save your life, and this is what I get? But putting my sense of gallantry and courage aside for the moment, I just have one question for you."

"Yeah?"

"Is this your best work?"

"Go screw yourself."

"Ah, the standard response of the intellectually overmatched." Sir Bentley snorted with contempt.

"Go screw myself, indeed. And having experienced firsthand the great piece of ass in question, that's undoubtedly my preferred option."

"Whoa, Bentley," Buddy said. "That's a cheap shot even by my standards. And I'm a lawyer."

"Quizling, shut your mouth. When I want your opinion, I'll give it to you."

Genevieve focused on her breathing and smiled at Bentley.

"Okay, Bentley. We'll do it your way. You want to go back to the resort. Let's go."

"Finally, some common sense prevails," Bentley said. "And as far as my head of security goes, I'll deal with him later."

"You'll need an army."

"That can be arranged," Sir Bentley said, as he followed Genevieve and her magnificent, gently swaying backside through the dense foliage.

38

Merlin listened to Chief's chattering, punctuated with laughter and gyrations, then looked at Bantu for translation.

"My father says that he is glad you're here and hopes that you can give good counsel."

"That's it?" Merlin said. "He talked for two minutes, and that's all he said?"

"Well," Bantu said, a smile forming on his face. "He did have a few observations about your experiences with the elder barrel last night."

Merlin cringed and smiled wanly at Chief.

"It was the dancing wasn't it?"

"Yes," said Bantu laughing. "My father says that your dancing makes Tuber appear God-like."

"I have no rhythm," Merlin said. "By the way, what do you put in that punch?"

"Like all of our tribal remedies and medicines, that is kept secret."

"Unbelievable. Any sign of Summerman yet?"

"No," Bantu said. "He was last seen walking out of the village talking to his hand."

"I'm getting a bit worried," Merlin said. "Perhaps we should send out a search party."

"If he doesn't return by afternoon, that is something we will consider," Bantu said. He then chattered with his father who nodded in agreement.

Shouts of excitement and cheers erupted throughout the village, and the three men looked out through the hut.

"It's time," Bantu said, helping his father to his feet.

"You're not going to let them duel are you?" Merlin watched the villagers stream towards the community hut.

"It is an accepted part of our culture," Bantu said. He chattered with his father who nodded.

"Booga-wooga-nooga," Chief said, rising to his feet.

"Come," Bantu said, leading the way out of the hut. "You are the first Outsider to witness this."

"What about Freak?"

"Yes, of course. He too will bear witness, but I guess his impressions will be different from yours." Bantu said. "I don't like his chances."

The three men followed the rest of the tribe into the community hut and took their seats of honor on the inside edge of the circle of people ringing the floor. A rhythmic beat comprised of two handclaps followed by one loud smack of the palms on the wooden floor began. It started softly and built into a sustained, thunderous sound that reverberated throughout the valley. Merlin listened as the roar build and then he began to sing off key.

"We will, we will, rock you."

Chief stared at Merlin.

"What are you doing?" Bantu whispered, glaring at Merlin.

"It's something we do at our sporting events."

"Well, don't," Bantu said. "It's annoying my father."

"Well, excuse me." Merlin glared at Chief, folded his hands and pouted.

Loud booing and hissing broke out as Freak was led into the hut. He glared at the crowd and gave them the finger which didn't register with the tribe. However, when he picked his nose and flicked the booger into the front row, things threatened to turn ugly.

Chief rose majestically to his feet and commanded silence. The brief lull ended when Tuber, clad in paint, leather, and feathers strode confidently into the hut. The crowd gave him a standing ovation, and he bowed. He glared at Freak, who hacked up a loogie and fired it in Tuber's direction.

Tuber approached Flute Girl whose aloofness was disappearing from the excitement. She glanced back and forth between the combatants and covered her eyes with both hands. Tuber and Freak were led to the center of the room where they stood glaring at each other.

Bantu hopped to his feet and approached both men. Bantu chattered loudly to the crowd who nodded and roared their approval. He chattered briefly with Tuber, who had already extracted his dart gun and was gently stroking the feathers of one of the darts that

160

hung from a belt on his waist. Bantu waved to a tribesman who approached Freak carrying a dart gun and a belt of feathered darts. Bantu secured the belt around Freak's waist.

"Okay, dickhead," Freak said. "What's the deal here?"

"This is called Gwanganna."

"Gw…an..ga…," Freak said.

"Never mind," Bantu said, shaking his head. "I guess that's not important. It's very simple. You and Tuber will stand back to back and, on Chief's signal, you will each take ten steps and then turn and fire. The first person to go down, and stay down, loses."

"Piece of cake," Freak said, blowing into the dart gun.

"But I must stress that you do not try to cheat by taking less than the required ten steps," Bantu said.

"What happens if I do?"

"Community participation," Bantu said, pointing around the circle of tribesmen brandishing dart guns and smiling at Freak.

"Got it," Freak said. "Thanks for the safety tip."

Tuber growled at Freak.

"What is your problem?" Freak took a step towards his opponent and did his best Tyson.

"Okay," Bantu said, nodding at his father.

Chief raised an arm skyward. Bantu put both combatants back to back and returned to his seat. The Chief lowered his hand and shouted. Tuber and Freak placed the loaded dart guns to their lips and slowly marched off the ten paces to the accompaniment of the crowd counting their progress.

Merlin leaned forward in his seat and stared into Freak eyes. Flute Girl peeked through her fingers. Chief and Bantu carefully studied both men's movement as the thunderous count approached the magic number. On guna, which Merlin assumed was the tribe's word for ten, Freak, drawing upon his basic training with the Army, dropped to the floor and rolled. Tuber wheeled and fired a dart. It whistled across the hut, past the spot where Freak's head was supposed to be, and hit Merlin in the middle of the forehead. Immediately, Merlin's eyes glazed over, and he slumped backward in his chair. Freak, coming to rest on his elbows in a prone position, fired a dart of his own. His abysmal sense of direction again raised its ugly head as the dart headed ninety-degrees off target and imbedded with a loud thud into the side of Chief's neck. Soon, Chief joined the unconscious Merlin on the polished wooden floor.

Dozens of concerned tribesmen clamored to their feet and rushed towards Chief, who was splayed on the floor in a non-leader-like fetal position.

Shouts of anger and finger pointing ensued with the confused Freak, still prone with dart gun pressed firmly to his lips, being the sole focus of the angered mob's attention. Tuber, initially unsure of which dart had hit the Chief, remained tentative but grew more confident as he assessed the crowd's reaction.

Freak seized on the momentary confusion, leaped to his feet, and dove out one side of the hut falling eight feet and landing on a particularly prickly jungle fern. Yelping and limping with pain, but quickly gathering his composure, Freak surveyed the situation and decided to make his escape by heading towards the northeastern side of the island. Tuber dashed outside and caught a glimpse of the hobbling Freak working his way past the vegetable gardens, around the boar pen, and through the rice paddies. Tuber fired two darts from his long-range dart gun and chattered angrily as they fell woefully short.

And then Tuber had a brainstorm.

He raced to the metal container he'd taken from the intruder during his capture. For the past day, Tuber had been drawn to the polished metal object and was told by Bantu that the object was one of the Outsider's weapons. Bantu had also told him, in the strongest terms possible, not to play with it since it could do much damage. Given the circumstances, Tuber believed that he was now perfectly within his rights to ignore Bantu's warning.

Tuber extracted a large cylinder from the metal case and inserted it into the end of the tubular structure that resembled, to some degree, his beloved dart gun. Tuber rested the loaded rocket launcher on his shoulder, dropped to one knee, and attempted to fix the weapon on the hobbling Freak about to disappear into the jungle on the far side of the village. Tuber scrunched his shoulder and held the rocket launcher tight against the side of his face. He adjusted his aim one final time, attempting to allow for the wind which always dramatically affected the flight of his feathered darts, closed his eyes, and fired the weapon.

Had the rocket launcher's instruction manual been written in tribal tongue, perhaps the course of events might have been altered. Upon firing the weapon, Tuber was violently propelled forward facedown into the mud. He dropped the weapon, struggled to his feet and wiped enough mud away from his eyes to follow the path of the rocket. Despite searching the afternoon sky for any sign of the rocket, the only thing Tuber witnessed was Freak disappearing into the jungle.

The rocket in question, although unseen by the mud-faced Tuber, was indeed airborne at that very moment.

Tuber, with absolutely no training in the operation of the SkyWriter, had almost managed to successfully pull it off. But he had failed on one vital detail; which end of the launcher the rocket was fired from. The rocket, fired at a forty-five-degree angle, sped off towards the southwest.

Tuber took one last forlorn look at the distant jungle that now protected the escaped Outsider and then headed back inside to check on the condition of Chief. His stomach rumbled with hunger, and he caught a glimpse of Flute Girl sitting by herself in a corner of the hut. Deciding that she would be easier to deal with on a full stomach, Tuber headed for the food table and grabbed a small bunch of bananas.

Out of sight and out of mind, the rocket was now someone else's problem.

39

Bob Garbo watched the events unfold from his perch atop a massive tree near the edge of the village. Through binoculars, he watched and laughed as Freak hobbled his way past the vegetable gardens, rice paddy, and pigpen, chased by one of the tribesmen. A bad ankle was slowing his escape but Bob, between laughs, nodded in mild admiration as Freak made his way through the village and disappeared into the jungle. He focused the binoculars on the pursuer who was chattering wildly and watched as he opened the case to the rocket launcher.

"Don't."

Bob watched as the tribesman somehow managed to load and fire the weapon from his shoulder backward. Bob looked up and caught a glimpse of the rocket as it disappeared over the jungle rooftop. Bob checked the GPS coordinates on his handheld device. He waited a few seconds and checked them a second time. He repositioned himself in the tree and activated the communication system.

"Esmeralda."

Bob waited.

Nothing but dead air.

"Esmeralda?"

Bob looked at his watch.

"Esmeralda."

"Allo? Ez that you Max?"

"Max?"

"Allo? Doc, ez that you? Allo? Who ez this?"

"Bob."

"Bob? Bob who?"

"Garbo."

"Like ze famous actress?"

"No."

"Okay. Allo, Bob. Nice to meet you. How may I help you?"

"Esmeralda."

"Esmeralda ez sleeping. Can I take ze message?"

"Okay."

"Will I need a pen?"

"No."

"Okay, Bob. What ez ze message?"

"Incoming."

"Incoming? That ez ze whole message?"

"Yeah."

"Okay, Bob. But can I ask you, what ez incoming?"

"Rocket."

"Okay, Bob. Got it. Ze incoming rocket."

"Hide."

"Hide? Is that another part of ze message?"

Bob shook his head and exhaled loudly.

"Allo? Bob?"

"Yeah."

"Who is it?" Esmeralda asked.

"Ahh, good you are awake. It ez Bob."

Bob waited through the rustling of sheets and whispers.

"Garbo? Is that you?"

"Yeah."

"Sorry, I was just taking inventory." Esmeralda yawned. "What's up?"

"Incoming."

"What?"

"Yeah."

"What?"

"Rocket."

"Now?"

"Yup."

"How long have we got?"

"Minute."

"A minute? As in one?"

"Yup."

"One of the SkyWriters?"

"Yup."

"Fuck."

"Yup."

From the other end of the line, Bob heard the explosion and the sound of breaking glass along with a string of French expletives.

"Out."

**

Sir Bentley huffed and puffed up the hill, worked his way through a set of palms and stared down at the magnificent stretch of beach that housed Nirvana. On the tarmac, private jets sat glistening in the sun, while, offshore, three luxurious yachts gently rocked in the calm bay waters. A couple of dozen guests, a number representing approximately half of the ultra-exclusive resort's capacity, lounged on the beach and around the pool. Sir tipped his pith helmet back, put his hands on his hips, slid one foot forward, held the pose, and proudly surveyed the scene playing out below.

"Get your camera out, Gene," Genevieve said, staring at Sir Bentley. "He's about to claim this land for England."

"My dear," Sir Bentley said, not glancing back at her, "This resort is the culmination of twenty years of hard work. It's just a pity you've decided to turn into such a bitch of late. Who knows, a piece of this might have been yours."

"I'll stick to plants," Genevieve said.

"Can you two just stop bickering long enough for us to get down this last hill? I need a cocktail and a shower," Gene said.

"What's that sound?" Genevieve said.

"Airplane, maybe?" Buddy said.

All four caught sight of the rocket at the same time.

"What the-" Gene said.

"What on earth is that?" Genevieve said.

"It's a SkyWriter," Sir Bentley said.

"A what?" Buddy said, staring up at the rapidly descending rocket.

"It's a shoulder-fired rocket."

"How the hell do you know that?" Buddy said.

"Because I make them," Bentley said.

"I thought you made sneakers," Buddy said. "I didn't know you make weapons."

166

"Hardly anybody does," Bentley said, his eyes darting back and forth between the rocket and the resort. "No, not my resort. Hit one of the yachts. Please."

"What do you know?" Buddy said. "How about that? Sir Bentley's an arms dealer. So that thing is called the SkyWriter?"

"Yes," Sir Bentley said, staring at the descending rocket. "It's the lighter, quieter, all-nighter fighter."

"I guess we'll see how quiet it is in a few seconds," Genevieve said, focused on the rocket bearing down on the resort.

A swoosh, bang, and a boom later, all four stared down at the fireball that consumed a large section of the resort. A series of smaller explosions popped and crackled, then disappeared.

Sir Bentley wept as he stared down at the disaster.

Gene shook his head and draped an arm over Bentley's shoulders.

"Man, you are gonna get your ass sued over this one."

Sir Bentley blubbered but then sighed and adjusted his pith helmet. "Okay, let's go check it out."

"I'm right behind you, Sir," Gene said.

"Wait," Sir Bentley said, his eyes frantically scanning the surrounding jungle. "Where the hell did she go?"

**

"What's the matter?"

"Be quiet," Doc said, cocking his head to one side. Goose bumps, provoked by the familiar sound, appeared on both his arms. "Shit. Come here, Murray." He pulled Summerman behind a large rock and crouched next to him as he continued to scan the sky.

"Freak, you friggin moron."

The name registered with Summerman.

"Freak? Your idiot of a brother in law? Ugly, rotten attitude, carrying a rocket launcher?"

"Yeah," Doc said. "How'd you know that?"

"He's at the village. He got captured by one of the tribe's lookouts and was dragged in yesterday."

"That figures. He's such a putz." Doc continued to stare up at the sky and then pointed. "Look."

"Is that what it looks like?"

"If it looks like a shoulder-fired missile, then yes."

Summerman watched the missile roar directly overhead.

"Where's Merlin?"

"He's with the tribe. At least I guess he's still there. I'm a little fuzzy about some of the details."

"I thought I told you to wait at the resort until I got here."

"Well, Merlin decided to do a favor for Bantu. He's the Chief's son."

Doc glared at Summerman but then cooled off.

"Okay. No harm, no foul."

**

"Hold still you big baby."

Gilbert struggled but was pinned in place by two enormous legs wrapped around his waist and an arm strong enough to bend steel lodged against his throat. He looked down at his bare chest that had turned crimson.

"I'm bleeding. Jesus, Hilda. Be careful with those things."

Hilda, a lit Marlboro fluttering in the corner of her mouth, paused. "What'd you say? Couldn't hear you over the razor."

"I said I'm bleeding. You're taking out chunks of skin."

"Occupational hazard."

Hilda applied liberal doses of Mercurochrome to Gilbert's chest wounds. Her haphazard administrations left long red tributaries flowing down his chest.

Gilbert screamed, as he frantically tried to escape her clutches. "Let me up. Now."

"You're no fun." Hilda released her grip. "You're just not the same since you got back from the jungle."

"What have we got to eat around here?" Gilbert said.

"There's a ton of stuff in the walk-in coolers. The one on the left is full of desserts, and there are a couple of trays of fresh pastries. Help yourself." She lighted another Marlboro.

"Then get your ass back here. We need to shave your back."

Gilbert harrumphed his way to the walk-in cooler and pulled open the massive steel door. He closed the door and studied the shelves containing cakes, pies and an assortment of plastic containing holding a variety of icings. And then he spied what he was looking for. A huge tray of freshly-baked pastries beckoned.

Halfway through his first chocolate cruller, the blast knocked him to the floor. Briefly unconscious, he awoke drenched in custard and chocolate sauce. But the steel door to the walk-in cooler had done its job. Gilbert staggered to his feet, wiped his face and sampled the custard dripping from his fingers. Nodding his approval, he picked his way through the debris and pushed the release knob on the door. Gilbert stepped through and found himself standing outdoors. More than a little perplexed, Gilbert scanned the area that used to be the kitchen and located the only item that appeared undamaged; the electric razor.

Hilda was gone.

This Gilbert knew instinctively when he exited the walk-in. The breeze shifted in his direction, and a whiff of chocolate drifted past him. At this point, Gilbert choked up and began sobbing. Someone had killed his friend, his only true comrade on this God-forsaken island. The only person he could share his true thoughts with. Someone had eliminated his lover. It had been a bizarre affair, yet intimate on many levels. Gilbert wiped his eyes with the back of his hand, custard mixing with his blood and tears. Someone had taken her away. The 300-pound chain-smoking combination of womanhood and rugby player. Her angelic face. Her relentless passion. Her bluntness, refreshing and unique in these days of political correctness. Another wave of sadness washed over him. Gilbert sniffed loudly and wiped his eyes with the sleeve of his shirt. Gradually, he composed himself and his breathing returned to normal as the tears stopped.

And then another thought popped into Gilbert's head. Initially, he was merely saddened as he pondered the implications. Then anger ignited and flared until it matched the fire raging through the resort.

If Gilbert had been thinking clearly, he would have realized his anger was premature. By simply checking the other walk-in cooler she had wandered into in search of protein, he would have discovered the mildly-concussed Hilda gnawing on a turkey leg.

Gilbert pounded his fists together.

He stomped his feet like a three-year-old sent to bed without dessert.

He cursed the heavens and vowed revenge.

He turned murderous as he considered the possible perpetrators of this hideous crime.

The former sneaker factory manager with a bad attitude and inherent dislike and mistrust of workers, morphed into mercenary.

Gilbert turned his face to the sky and roared with fury.

Someone had killed the Doughnut Maker.

40

As the fire began to subside, seven jets on the tarmac played a dangerous combination of Chicken and Bumper Cars as their pilots frantically attempted to get airborne. Topless sunbathers hurriedly retied their tops and headed below deck as the private yachts hoisted anchor and bolted for the high seas.

The entire group of resort staff and factory workers, led by Hilda, commandeered a flatboat used to ferry supplies to the resort. Hilda, confident that the eight dozen pastries she'd packed would be sufficient if she didn't pig out, calculated that the trip back to the Indian mainland would take four days as currently mapped. However, she knew it would take less than a day if the captain ignored all the scheduled stops and kept the throttle down. Anxious to hit dry land and begin a well-deserved European vacation, she worked her way into the captain's quarters with a tray of chocolate crullers and proceeded to close the deal.

Two hours after the missile strike, the island was devoid of everyone associated with the business of making sneakers or serving umbrella drinks to the uber-rich.

Sir Bentley fumed as he surveyed the damage. Although the guest villas were undamaged, the kitchen and dining room would require extensive rebuilding. Bentley, trailed by Gene and Buddy, headed towards Command Central to prepare for the next phase of what he had codenamed Operation FUBAR.

"Why don't we just get the hell out of here?" Gene said.

"And just surrender to a bunch of Neanderthals?" Sir Bentley said.

"They seem pretty well armed for Neanderthals," Buddy said.

"Well, somebody is arming them, and I plan on finding out whom. And my money is on Doc."

"Doc? No way, Bentley," Gene said.

"The burnout turned misogynist. You saw with your own eyes what he did to Genevieve."

171

"Yeah, I saw it," Gene said. "Maybe he can give me some pointers."

"What?"

"Nothing."

"Well, at a minimum, maybe we should call in reinforcements," Buddy said.

"The last thing I'm going to do right now is let anybody on the outside know what's going on here. If this gets out, I'll have both the U.S. and Indian governments all over my ass. Plus, I'd be a laughingstock."

Gene and Buddy stared at Bentley's canary-yellow safari suit, knee socks, and sweat stained pith helmet. They glanced at each other and shook their heads.

"Yeah, we wouldn't want that to happen," Buddy said.

Sir Bentley didn't even slow down as he reached the door to Command Central. He burst into the room with Gene and Buddy trailing close behind. Sir Bentley glanced around the room.

"Esmeralda," Sir Bentley said. "Are you in here?"

"Allo?"

"Who's that?"

"It ez I. Ez that you, Max?"

"Max? No, it's not Max. And where the hell are you?" Sir Bentley continued to scan the room for signs of life.

"I am here. Ez that you, Bob?"

"No, it's not Bob. This is Sir Bentley Carruthers and I'm ordering you to show your face."

A small nervous man crawled out from under the bed.

"Sir Bentley Carruthers? Ze famous sneaker maggot?"

"That's magnate, you moron. Now who are you and where is Esmeralda?"

"I am Piqûre. And Esmeralda is gone."

"Gone?" Gene, shocked, stared down at his feet. "Oh, no."

"What happened?" Sir Bentley said.

"The rocket came. Then she left."

"Damn," Gene said. "What a way to go."

"But she should be back soon."

"Back?" Buddy said.

"Yes," Piqûre said. "She went to ze bar. But she'll be back. You like to wait?"

172

"Out of my way, Frenchie."

Sir Bentley brushed past him and sat down in front of the blank monitors. He fiddled with the controls, then smacked the top of the table with his palm.

"Shit, they're all dead."

"Yes, ze pictures went off when ze rocket go boom-boom."

The door opened, and Esmeralda entered carrying a box.

"What a war zone. But I salvaged what I could. Only six bottles of tequila made it, but there's a case of vodka."

She noticed they had visitors.

"Bentley, you're back. Hey, Gene."

"How ya doing, babe?" Gene said, pointing both index fingers playfully at her.

"Right back at ya."

Esmeralda winked at him and nodded her head in Buddy's direction. "Who's this?"

"I'm Buddy Quizling. Sir Bentley's personal lawyer."

"Good luck with that," Esmeralda said, cracking the seal on a bottle of tequila.

"I missed ya, Gene."

"Right back at ya."

They both laughed, and Gene accepted the bottle she handed him.

"What is going on around here?" Bentley said, throwing his arms into the air. "We're under attack and you two are acting like you're in goddamn high school."

"Ooze attacking?" Piqûre sat down on the edge of the bed. His eyes darted back and forth nervously.

"That goddamn band of jungle dwellers. Who do you think?" Sir Bentley said.

Piqûre cowered and pulled the blanket up around his chest.

"I don't know," Piqûre said. "I thought maybe it was Max."

"Who the fuck is Max?"

"You do not know?" Piqûre said.

"No, I don't," Sir Bentley said. "If I knew who he was, why would I be asking?"

"That ez a good question."

Sir Bentley stared at the Frenchman and then focused on Esmeralda.

173

"So what do you have to say for yourself?"

"What?" she said. She took a long pull of tequila.

"Maybe you should give that a rest," Buddy said.

"Hey, what can I say?" Esmeralda said, taking a long swig. "Medicinal purposes, baby. We've just gone through major trauma here." She looked at Bentley who continued to glare at her. "What is your problem, Bentley?"

"You are here to protect and defend my interests."

"I am? I thought we were here to rip off a bunch of defenseless natives." She lighted a cigarette and waved it back and forth as she talked. Gene shuffled two steps to his right. "Although we may need to revise the defenseless part."

"Whatever," Sir Bentley said. "Regardless, so far you're doing a shitty job."

"Hey, Bent, nice outfit by the way. I think Mr. Rogers had the same one in magenta. Look, Doc gave me specific instructions to monitor the surveillance system and until that SkyWriter took out your resort, that's what I was doing."

"Well, you can forget Doc," Sir Bentley said. "From this point forward, I'm driving the bus."

"Fine by me." Esmeralda sat down in a chair and waited for instructions. "Well, Commander, now what?"

"Yes, yes, we need a plan don't we?" Sir Bentley began pacing. "I'm thinking counterattack." Bentley's concentration was interrupted by a loud knock. "Who is it?"

"It ez probably Max."

"Will you shut up?" Sir Bentley said, crossing to the door. "Who is it?"

"Sorry, but that's classified information unless I know who I'm speaking with."

Sir Bentley jerked the door open and stared in disbelief when he recognized the man standing in front of him.

"Uh-oh," said the disheveled man.

"You."

"Hello, Sir Bentley."

"Well, just when you think your day can't get any worse."

"Yeah, well, I'm still really sorry about your yacht, Sir Bentley. May I come in?"

174

"If you must. Just stay clear of the knives and flammables." Sir Bentley pulled the door open. "C'mon."

Freak hobbled his way through the doorway. He glanced around the room and nodded in everyone's general direction.

"Ez that you, Max?"

41

Merlin stared at the blood covering Bantu's hand and then studied his face. Bantu's expression remained unchanged as Chief meticulously worked his way between his son's stitched fingers. He placed the razor-sharp stone on the table, dabbed at Bantu's hand with a damp cloth and examined his work. The bleeding stopped, and Chief picked up the stone and finished slicing away the final inch of skin between Bantu's first two fingers. He reapplied the cloth to stop fresh bleeding, gently pulled the two fingers apart and chattered at his son. Bantu responded, made a scissor move with his fingers and put his hand back down on the table.

"What did he just say?" Merlin said.

"He said I was a total idiot for doing this to myself," Bantu said.

"Doesn't it hurt?"

"No, my father gave me some medicine for the pain." Bantu pointed at a small bamboo container.

Merlin sniffed the sticky paste and recoiled from the smell. "Yuk. What the hell is this stuff?"

Bantu chattered with his father who looked at Merlin and shook his head.

"It's just a mixture of some traditional plants," Bantu said.

"What did you just say to your father?"

"I asked him if I could tell you how it's made."

"And he said no?"

"He said you haven't proven yourself worthy yet," Bantu said. "And he is still blaming you for bringing the man named Freak into the village."

"Not worthy? I've told him five times already," Merlin said. "I've never seen the guy before in my life."

Merlin glared at Chief, who stared back while casually running his thumb across the edge of the cutting stone. Chief chattered without taking his eyes off Merlin.

"What did he say?" Merlin said.

"Never mind," Bantu said.

"No, I want to know." Merlin continued to play stare-down with Chief.

"He wonders if you and the man called Freak are the best the Outsiders have to offer."

"Well, you can tell your father to go fuck himself," Merlin said.

"That would not be a good idea."

"Yeah, maybe you're right." Merlin finally broke eye contact. "Hey, what about Summerman?"

"Oh, he likes Summerman," Bantu said. "He says he has a well-developed soul. And is good with animals."

Bantu translated his last comment for his father.

"Booga-wooga-nooga," Chief said, nodding his head. He returned to his work slicing the skin between Bantu's second and third fingers.

"I can't believe that doesn't hurt," Merlin said. "I'd be rolling on the floor in agony."

"Not if you were given the right medicine," Bantu said, watching his father's movements.

"How on earth did you people learn all this?" Merlin said.

Bantu glared at Merlin and chattered at his father. Chief stopped and waved the stone in Merlin's direction.

"You people?" Bantu said. "Now you have offended us once again."

"I didn't mean anything by it," Merlin said. "It's just that, well, you live way out…"

"We may live remotely but why should that mean we are ignorant about the ways of the earth?"

"Yes, I know all that," Merlin said. "But you're completely cut off. Since I've been here, I've seen how you grow food, irrigate your crops, even how you make booze. And it looks like you've got medicines and ointments and who knows what else to cure a bunch of different ailments. All I'm asking is how the hell did you do it?"

"With practice," Bantu said, making the scissor movement with his second and third fingers. He nodded at his father who smiled, applied the cloth and then started working on the final two fingers.

"But you're so civilized," Merlin said, staring at Bantu's hand.

Bantu laughed and chattered with his father who laughed along with his son. Chief waved both arms in the air and made a Boogie Man face at Merlin. Bantu roared with laughter.

"My father wonders if you are afraid of the dark and evil spirits."

"Is that what he really said?"

Bantu winked at his father. "Close enough." Bantu repositioned his hand on the table. "Merlin, my friend, just try to remember that we've been here for centuries."

"Yeah, but still, you've developed a remarkable society."

Bantu smiled and chattered with his father who smiled at Merlin and bowed his head in appreciation.

"He liked that one?" Merlin said.

"Yes." Bantu wiggled his fingers in the air and smiled at his father. "My father liked that one very much."

42

"Team FUBAR. Fall in."

"Fall in?" Esmeralda, fighting a massive hangover, shuffled forward into line. "I'll be lucky if I don't fall down."

Sir Bentley, nattily attired in a freshly-pressed, canary-yellow safari suit with matching Cloudlifters, tilted his pith helmet back and paced as he surveyed the troops.

"Today is a day that will live in infamy," Sir Bentley said.

"Now that's original," Esmeralda whispered to Gene as she swayed back and forth with a glazed expression on her face.

"Shhh," Freak said, "I'm trying to listen to our leader."

"You're such a suck-up." Esmeralda burped loudly. "Man, I feel like shit."

"No talking in formation," Sir Bentley said.

He continued pacing until he came to a stop in front of the camouflaged-clad Freak. His face, along with the rest of his exposed skin, was covered in black.

"What's your deal?"

"Camouflage, sir," Freak said, a crisp salute punctuating his response.

"And the black face?" Sir Bentley said.

"For night surveillance purposes, sir," Freak said, offering another salute.

"It's seven o'clock in the morning," Buddy said.

"Yeah," Freak said, turning his head ninety degrees to address the lawyer. "But it's not going to stay there is it?"

"He az a good point," Piqûre said.

"Quiet," Sir Bentley said, continuing to stare at Freak's face. "Is that shoe polish?"

"Yes, sir," Freak said. "Captain Freak could not locate his face paint, sir."

"Captain?" Gene said.

"Yes, Captain Freak."

179

Gene laughed.

"Just until the sun comes up. In this heat, by noon you'll be Captain Alice Cooper."

"You just worry about yourself, Private Gene. I'm now in charge of the airborne division."

"Airborne?" Esmeralda said, then coughed loudly and spit on the ground. "Man I gotta cut back." She shook her head and tried to regroup. "You're in charge of airborne. Airborne what?"

"Yes, airborne," Freak said. "Control of the skies is key to winning a ground assault."

"Color me inattentive but I don't think I saw any F-15's sitting on the tarmac," Esmeralda said.

"Adaptability is a central component of today's army."

"Wouldn't airborne refer to ze Air Force?"

"Whatever, Frenchie," Freak said, glaring at Esmeralda. "While you were off doing body shots with Private Gene last night, I was conducting reconnaissance work."

"Esmeralda," Piqûre said. "You and Gene?"

"I thought something seemed different last night," Esmeralda said, puzzled.

"You were great, baby," Gene whispered.

"How could you?" Piqûre said. "You said I was ze only one."

"Relax, Piqûre. It was just the Herradura talking." She dismissed the Frenchman with a wave of her hand. She leaned closer to Gene and whispered, "Was I really good?"

"You were fantastic, baby," Gene said, gently brushing her hair back from her face.

Esmeralda nodded and began swaying. She grabbed Gene's shoulder for support, and he took the opportunity to run his hand down her back and gently squeeze her left bun.

She held up both arms in protest and shook her head.

"Don't do that. I'm not in the mood."

She coughed and spat a vile yellow sputum near one of Sir Bentley's new Cloudlifters.

"Putain." Piqûre glared at Esmeralda and kicked the dirt. "Salope. Je m'en fou."

"English, Frenchie," Freak said. "When you're in America, you'll speak English."

"But we are not in ze America," Piqûre said.

"As soon as I plant a flag we will be," Freak said.

"People!" Sir Bentley said, clapping his hands rapidly. "Let's focus here."

"You're just pissed because she prefers me, Frenchie," Gene said, ignoring Sir Bentley.

"What a laugh," Piqûre said. "Ha, ha, ha, ha, ha. A woman preferring ze crass American over ze Frenchman."

"That Tweety Bird suit is making me sick," Esmeralda said, unable to maintain eye contact with Sir Bentley.

"It ez definitely yellow," Piqûre said.

"The one color a Frenchman has no trouble identifying," Freak said. Gene and Buddy joined Freak in laughter.

"Team FUBAR. Come to order." Sir Bentley stomped a Cloudlifter on the ground.

"What's the matter, Frenchie?" Gene said. "Can't stomach the fact that a woman with Esmeralda's class and style would prefer someone like me? Isn't that right, Esmeralda?"

"I'm gonna puke," Esmeralda said.

"Exactly," Piqûre said, nodding his head. "That ez my reaction as well to that preposterous notion."

"No, I mean it," Esmeralda said, lurching forward. "I'm gonna puke."

And she did.

All over Sir Bentley's new Cloudlifters.

Team FUBAR, with the exception of the retching Esmeralda, quietly shuffled three paces left.

"Tequila, broiled salmon, and pistachio ice cream is not a good combination." Esmeralda groaned as she stared from her knees at the spattered sneakers.

"The fishy-squishy, post-puker sneaker," Gene said.

"You're going on report, Private Gene."

Sir Bentley scuffed the sand in an attempt to get vomit off his Cloudlifters. "Shit. They're ruined. Get on your feet, Lieutenant."

Gene helped Esmeralda to her feet. She wobbled momentarily like a tenpin, then came to rest.

"Now if we can continue without further interruptions," Sir Bentley said, regaining his composure. "We are dealing with an enemy here that has shown no reservations about using deadly force to achieve its objectives."

"Sir, if I may?" Freak took out a small pad and pen to take notes. "What are the enemy's objectives?"

"To drive us from the island, of course, Captain Freak. They have, without provocation, blown up my Cloudlifter factory that, by the way, provided over two hundred well-paying jobs to people devastated by the recent tsunami. And just when their lives were returning to some form of normalcy, these savages, yes, I said it, savages, have somehow managed to procure, no, managed to steal one of our most advanced weapons and use it to destroy Nirvana."

"The heartless bastards," Freak said.

"Indeed, Captain Freak," Sir Bentley said. "I'm glad someone in this operation understands what we're dealing with here."

"Uh, Commander Bentley," Gene said, raising his hand. "How could a bunch of primitive jungle-dwellers, as you so lovingly call them, figure out how to load and fire this advanced weapon, much less hit their target?"

"Okay, okay." Sir Bentley scratched his chin and began to pace again. "Fair question. Let's brainstorm it."

"Maybe they just got lucky," Freak said.

"Perhaps," Sir Bentley said. "But we can't take that chance."

"Maybe the tribe is an outpost full of spies for the CIA," Buddy said.

"To do what?" Freak said. "Spy on snakes? What an idiot."

"Well, it's better than your maybe they just got lucky idea," Gene said.

"Watch yourself, Private Gene. You're talking to a Captain."

"Really? You got promoted? What a joke. By the way, Captain, your mascara is running."

"Quiet in the ranks," Sir Bentley said. "I will not tolerate discord among the troops."

"You're a little late, Bentley," Esmeralda said. "My theory is that the tribe has cable and spends a lot of time watching the History Channel."

"Shut up, you drunken slut," Sir Bentley said. He took a menacing step towards her.

"Watch it, Bentley." Gene stepped forward to block Sir Bentley's path. "She may be a drunken slut, but she's our drunken slut."

"Get back in ranks, Private."

"You want a piece of me?" Esmeralda said.

"I eat women like you for breakfast," Sir Bentley said.

"You should be so lucky, Bent," Esmeralda said. She coughed, then hacked and fired a yellow-green loogie onto one of Bentley's sneakers.

Sir Bentley stared down in disbelief.

"Maybe ze just had help," Piqûre said, casually shrugging his shoulders.

Sir Bentley looked up and turned to the Frenchman. "What was that?"

"I said maybe ze just had help."

Sir Bentley considered the idea and started to slowly nod his head. Moments later, the nod turned bobble-head. "Yes. Of course. They had help."

"According to you, no one has ever even made contact with them," Gene said. "Who the hell could possibly be helping them?"

"I'll tell you who," Sir Bentley said, pointing a finger at Esmeralda. "Her boyfriend Doc, that's who."

"Ex-boyfriend," Esmeralda said. "Jesus Christ, Bent. If Doc was planning on blowing up your factory and resort, he wouldn't need any help. Especially from some primitive tribe that lives in the middle of the jungle."

"But don't you see? Now it all makes sense. They're the perfect cover story. No one would ever suspect him," Sir Bentley said, wearing out the small patch of sand on either side of him. "So, not only does this despicable human being take women by force, he also conspires with the enemy."

"He's a traitor," Freak said, scribbling frantically in his notepad.

Esmeralda leaned closer to Gene.

"Doc would never take anybody by force. He might be a total prick, but he's a gentleman prick."

"The way they were going at it, if she was protesting, I'd like to see her when she's really in the mood," Gene said.

"That two-timing son of a bitch. I'm gonna cut his balls off."

"Silence," Sir Bentley said. "This requires a slight modification to our plans. From this point forward, members of Team FUBAR have permission to shoot Doc White on sight."

"Bentley, you're going to get all of us killed," Esmeralda said. "For chrissakes, the man is dangerous. Especially when he gets pissed off. Don't piss him off, Bentley."

"I don't know this guy, Bentley, but maybe you should listen to her."

"A lawyer says something smart." Gene nodded at Freak. "Right that one down, Alice."

"He's a traitor," Freak said.

"You idiot," Esmeralda said. "Without him, you would have been foreclosed from the cardboard box you were living in. You're a moron. He's your brother in law."

"Ex-brother in law," Freak said. "And he's crossed the line. I, for one, am not afraid of him."

"Thanks for proving my point." Esmeralda shook her head to clear cobwebs. "Bentley, just do the right thing and call this off. Or better yet, let's just hop on your Gulfstream and go home. I'll make us a pitcher of margaritas for the ride."

"Listen to her, Bentley," Buddy said.

"Typical," Sir Bentley said. "Let's just give up without a fight. He's just one man."

"Bentley, if you piss him off, he will cut us into small pieces and feed us to the crocodiles," Esmeralda said.

"Really?" Piqûre said.

"There's a rumor that one time he killed seventeen union guys just for trying to organize the commercial fishermen in Marseilles."

"The Holy Mackerel Massacre? That was him?"

"Yes, it was," Esmeralda said.

"I remember that. The price of John Dory went through ze roof."

"I can't believe the cowardice I'm witnessing. He's only one man," Sir Bentley said.

"Well, actually, sir," Freak said. "He does have one other person at his disposal."

"Shit, that's right," Esmeralda said.

"Yes, of course," Piqûre said. "Max."

"Who the fuck is Max?" Sir Bentley said.

"He ez a very dangerous man."

"How many times do I have to tell you? There is no Max," Esmeralda said. "Jesus, I forgot all about him."

"Who?" Sir Bentley said.

"Garbo."

"Who?"

"Bob Garbo," Freak said.

"Oh yes, of course, "Piqûre said. "How could I forget Bob?"

"Who is Bob Garbo?" Sir Bentley said.

"Ex-Special Forces," Esmeralda said. "Grew up on the plains in Canada and learned cross-country skiing at an early age. Expert sharpshooter. Rumored to have been a Canadian spy who infiltrated Russia in the late seventies and worked his way onto their Olympic Biathlon team where he won silver at Sarajevo. Got recruited by Langley, underwent extensive cosmetic surgery and spent several years playing piano at the Marriott airport lounge near Dulles. He was spying on politicians who were divulging military secrets to weapons manufacturers."

Sir Bentley coughed softly. "Big guy, real quiet?"

"Yeah, why?" Esmeralda said.

"Never mind," Sir Bentley said, staring down at the sand. "Continue."

"After he ratted out a couple of Senators and one still unidentified arms merchant, he went underground. Details are pretty sketchy after that. He surfaced about a few years ago when he started working with Doc part-time."

"I see," Sir Bentley said. "Good with a rifle, huh?"

"If they're inside a mile, Bob will smile. That should tell you all you need to know."

Sir Bentley turned to Freak. "How confident are you in your ability to provide adequate air protection?"

"Not a problem, sir," Freak said, snapping off another salute. "But with double the capacity, it would be even stronger."

"Double the capacity?" Buddy said.

"Yeah," Freak said. "I could use another guy. Or even her."

"Not a chance, Freak Boy," Esmeralda said.

"Well, I can't do it," Sir Bentley said. "I need to run things on the ground. Private Gene?"

"Hey, boss," Gene said. "You've already witnessed firsthand my air sickness problem."

"Yeah," Sir Bentley said, fixing his stare on the Frenchmen. "How about you?"

"Me?" Piqûre said, pointing a finger at himself. "I am only here so I can keep an eye on Esmeralda and ze weasel here. Ow can I do zat if I'm in ze air?"

Sir Bentley nodded and then turned to Freak. "Looks like you're on your own, Captain Freak."

"I'll do it."

All eyes turned towards the voice. But it was the massive bare belly with puncture wounds and dozens of scabs along with the occasional tuft of hair that caught and held their attention. The man wore a loincloth and a pair of orange Cloudlifters that had seen better days. A headband made of woven palm fronds held back his remaining wisps of hair. He was carrying a cricket bat in one hand and an almost empty tray of pastries in the other.

"Gilbert?"

"Yeth, Thir Bentley," the wild-eyed man said, his intense stare focused solely on the magnate. "It'th tho nice to thee you."

43

Doc cocked his head to one side, touched his traveling companion on the shoulder and held a finger to his lips. Summerman nodded and stood quietly waiting for further instructions. Murray followed suit and crept silently next to both men. Doc slowly worked his way through a section of dense foliage, used both hands to spread two massive palm fronds and peered through. Summerman peered over the shoulder of the kneeling Doc.

"What is it?"

"Shhh."

"Another snake? Man, I hate those things."

"Will you be quiet," Doc said.

"I'm sorry, but I hate snakes."

Doc slowly turned his head and glared at Summerman. Summerman turned silent. Doc inched his way forward with Summerman pressed against him. Doc pointed his finger at Summerman and then pointed to the ground.

"Oh, no," Summerman said. "You're not leaving me here alone."

Doc repeated the gesture and stared at him with dead eyes.

"Okay," Summerman said. "You convinced me."

Doc stepped through the two large palm fronds and disappeared from sight. Summerman sat down on the ground and scratched Murray's ears as he glanced around and peered through the palms in search of Doc.

Doc, already thirty feet ahead, focused his attention on the figure that was sitting on a rock facing a small stream. He stalked from behind until he was within arms-length and leaned in even closer.

"I thought I told you those things will kill you."

Genevieve screamed, coughed up a lungful of smoke, and fell off the rock onto the adjacent moss.

"Goddamn you, Doc."

187

She jumped to her feet and punched his arm.

"Merde. You son of a bitch. Don't do that."

Doc laughed and then turned to see Summerman appear through the foliage.

"Over here, Summerman," Doc said, reaching out to hug Genevieve.

"Get away from me," she said, then relented and returned the hug.

"I couldn't resist," Doc said. "Summerman, I'd like you to meet Genevieve."

"We've met," Genevieve said. "Hi, Summerman. C'mon here, Murray."

She began petting the dog.

"Genevieve, I thought I told you to stay put at the resort," Summerman said.

"You told her?" Doc said. "That was your first mistake. Never tell Genevieve to do anything."

Genevieve laughed and gave Doc a deep kiss.

"You know me so well," she said, coming up for air.

"Am I missing something here?" Summerman said.

"We go way back."

Doc ran a hand down her back and left it resting on her hip.

"Cross this one off the list," Summerman said.

"What's that?" Doc said.

"Nothing."

A bolt of lightning flashed, and thunder rumbled and reverberated across the jungle.

"That came up fast," Genevieve said, staring up at the blackening sky.

"I've got a tarp in my pack," Doc said, scanning the immediate area. "Let's get it up over there." He pointed to a large flat rock sheltered by thick foliage. "This could flood down here."

"Flood?" Summerman said, glancing out over the small stream directly in front of them. "What are you talking about?"

"You're welcome to stay down here if you like," Doc said. "I'm sure the two of us could find some way to amuse ourselves."

Another bolt of lightning accompanied by thunder arrived. Doc dashed off in search of his pack and Genevieve and Summerman followed Murray towards the large rock.

"Boyfriend?"

"Oh, he's much more than that," Genevieve said.

"I missed my chance didn't I?"

"I'm afraid so, Summerman. Sorry."

"Just my luck."

**

Team FUBAR, under an increasingly anal set of instructions from Sir Bentley, began assembling the bright yellow tent just as the first raindrops fell.

"No, that's not right," Sir Bentley said, staring down at the misshapen collection of canvas and aluminum.

"What are you doing?"

"Don't yell at me, Tweety," Esmeralda said, swigging from a bottle of tequila. "What do the instructions say?"

"These instructions are useless," Gene said, turning the piece of paper over repeatedly. "Seven languages and not one of them English."

"Goddamn them," Sir Bentley said.

"Who?" Gene said, still examining the instructions for clues.

"My manufacturer in China. I specifically listed English as one of the languages. Who the hell would make something for the U.S. market without assembly instructions in English?"

"You make this thing?" Esmeralda said, "Jesus, Bentley, is there anything left you don't make?"

"I call it the Cloudsleeper. It's the Safer, Self-Inflating, Sweet Dream Maker. This is just a prototype." Sir Bentley grabbed the instructions from Gene. "It won't come on the market until next year. I'm targeting the military and the outdoor markets."

"Can't wait to see what it looks like," Buddy said, laughing.

"People," Piqûre said, hands on hips. "It ez starting to rain. Come on. There are only four pieces of metal. How hard can it be?"

"Try that one in that one," Esmeralda said, pointing at the sections of metal poles Gene was holding.

"Hey, look at that," Gene said, holding up the assembled tent piece. "It works."

"Well, if anybody would know what goes in what hole, it would be her," Sir Bentley said.

"Watch yourself, Commander," Esmeralda said. "I've been known to snap."

"Hurry, please," Piqûre said.

"What's the matter, Frenchie? Afraid of a little water?" Gene said.

"It ez not a little water I am afraid of. It ez a lot of water that worries me."

"Just hang on," Gene said, assembling the second tent pole. "Okay, that should do it."

"Finally," Sir Bentley said, approaching the tent. "Now watch this." He reached down, flipped a lever, and the floor of the tent began to fill with air. Moments later, the bottom of the tent had become a thick air mattress. "Pretty cool, huh?"

"Not bad, Commander," Buddy said as all five climbed inside the four-person tent.

They elbowed each other for space, now cocooned from the raindrops spattering against the outside of the tent.

"It ez cozy in here," Piqûre said.

"Snug as a bug in a rug," Buddy said.

"Nice," Sir Bentley said.

"Thanks. Now get your hand off my ass, Bentley," Esmeralda said, inching her way closer to Gene.

**

Doc leaned back on his elbows and watched as the rain intensified. He stroked Genevieve's jet black hair and counted his blessings.

Summerman looked at them and said, "Sorry to be the third wheel here. If it weren't raining, I'd take Murray for a walk and leave you two alone."

"Don't worry about it, Summerman," Genevieve said, lighting a fresh Gitanes.

"Have you decided what we're going to do with the tribe yet?" Summerman asked.

"I have no idea. I haven't even seen them yet."

"They're amazing. So remote but very advanced."

"Doc isn't going to do anything to them. Are you?"

Genevieve looked at Doc and waited for a response.

190

"I'm working here," Doc said. "You know what that means."

"I certainly do. Bad things are about to happen to a lot of people."

"And you're lily-white in all this? Is that what you're trying to tell me?" Doc said.

"I'm just here to catalog plants."

"Yeah," Doc said, "And there really is an Easter bunny."

"Bentley never said anything about hurting these people. In fact, the way he made it sound was that they were ready to talk with us."

"Ready to talk? That's where I'm supposed to come in," Doc said. "Helping them get ready to talk."

"How could I forget? That's one of your specialties, isn't it?" Genevieve crushed her cigarette on the rock.

"Why are you getting pissed at me?" Doc said, tightening the rope that was holding one side of the tarp up. "You knew what you were getting into as soon as you signed on to work for him."

"I had no idea it might involve anything like this," she said, staring out at the rapidly swelling stream.

"C'mon, Genevieve," Doc said, laughing. "That little girl act might work on someone like Summerman. But you're talking to me now. No offense, Summerman."

"Oh, none taken."

"You're such a bastard sometimes," Genevieve said, hugging her knees with both arms.

"Yeah, I know," Doc said. "But do you think people like Bentley make billions of dollars by being nice to other people? Or by playing it straight?"

"I'm just here to catalog plants."

"Repeating the same lie over and over again doesn't make it true," Doc said.

"How much money are we talking about here?" Summerman said.

"Well, if the rumors are true about the range of remedies they've developed, we're talking billions," Doc said.

Summerman rubbed his forehead and said, "They're true. I've seen them."

Doc stared at Summerman until he continued.

"There's a huge cave just outside the village they showed us that has hundreds of different plants and containers. At first, I didn't think too much about it, but when I saw the guards outside I did wonder."

"Hundreds you say, huh?"

"Yeah. And I've seen what a few of the remedies can do."

"The fish bite on the beach," Genevieve said, nodding her head. "That was incredible. It was like that poultice simply pulled the toxins out of your friend's system."

"Yeah," Summerman said. "Billions?"

"Sure," Doc said. "Think about it. Everybody is looking for the magic pill these days. Longevity, anti-aging, super-vitamins, extra lead in the pencil."

Summerman laughed. "So why doesn't he just go in and take them? Why the hesitation?"

"Because he needs more than just the plants," Doc said.

"He needs the local knowledge about how they're combined and used," Genevieve said.

"Exactly. And that's where you come in, my dear. At least on one part."

"I catalog, classify them, Document how they're grown and interact, look for potential spinoffs."

"But Bentley needs local knowledge," Summerman said.

"Absolutely. Local knowledge could shorten his research and development efforts to almost nothing. He wouldn't have to do trial and error in the lab if he was just told how these remedies were developed."

"What a prick," Summerman said. "There should be a name for scumbags like him."

"There is," Doc said. "Bio-pirate."

"You learn something every day," Summerman said.

"Bio-piracy. It goes on, but you don't hear a lot about it. The drug companies send out emissaries to find indigenous people with traditional medicines that could sell. They isolate some plant compound or whatever they can find and whack a patent on it. And then it hits the market with a cute label and catchy slogan."

"What about his sneakers? He's making a fortune on those," Summerman said.

"He won't stop making those," Doc said. "But next on his wish list is a global drug company. Big pharma means big money. Really big money. But before he can go much further, he needs local knowledge."

"He needs Chief."

"Chief?"

"He's the head of the tribe. Bantu's father."

"Bantu?" Doc said.

"He's the guy we've been trying to help. He's the one who invited us back to meet his tribe."

"The one from the beach," Genevieve said.

"Yeah. By the way, how old do you think he is?"

"He's probably early to mid-twenties," Genevieve said.

"He's fifty," Summerman said.

"No way."

Summerman nodded his head and recoiled as thunder and lightning popped directly overhead.

"And this Bantu speaks English?" Doc said.

"Yes, he's been out in the real world for the past few years."

"Does Bentley know about him?"

"I doubt it," Summerman said. "But his factory manager knows him since he worked there."

"Gilbert," Genevieve said.

"You know him?" Summerman said.

"Yeah, I met him in the jungle a couple of days ago."

"What?" Doc said. "Out here?"

"He was wandering around lost. He said he was heading back to the resort. What's left of it."

"What happened to the resort?" Summerman said.

"A rocket hit it."

"So that's what happened to my communication system," Doc said. "I can't get in touch with anybody."

"Well, Bentley, as you can imagine, is pretty pissed about the rocket."

"He should be. It was one of his," Doc said. "If I know Bentley, he's planning retaliation. We just need to find the tribe before he does."

"I'm not going anywhere in this rain," Genevieve said, lighting another Gitanes.

"You were smart to move us up the hill," Summerman said. "That stream is turning into a raging river."

193

Tip the ocean ninety degrees and pour: That's how hard it was raining.

Team FUBAR huddled in their tent that had started cozy but soon became oppressive. The sides of the tent flickered with a strobe light intensity from the lightning, and a light cloud of mist rose from the air mattress floor.

"It never rains like this in France," Piqûre said.

"This isn't rain," Gene said. "It's a steam bath."

"Stop whining, Private Gene," Sir Bentley said. "It will be over soon."

"God, I feel like shit," Esmeralda said.

"Stop chugging tequila," Sir Bentley said. "Your liver is probably speaking Spanish by now."

"It helps me forget where I am," Esmeralda said.

"You don't have a clue where you are?"

"I'm stuck in a tent in the middle of the jungle with you. Damn, it's not working." Esmeralda laughed and took another long pull from the bottle.

"Some vacation," Piqûre said, picking at his new Cloudlifters.

"You're on my payroll now," Sir Bentley said. "So you can quit whining."

"You are not at all like the recent article I read about you in ze airline magazine."

"That was a good article," Buddy said.

"I certainly would hope so," Sir Bentley said. "It cost me a fortune."

Esmeralda placed a hand on Gene's shoulder, leaned forward, and ripped an enormous fart that echoed off the air mattress and reverberated through the tent.

"Ooh. Mon dieu. Esmeralda, how could you?"

"Whew. Much better," Esmeralda said. "That salmon didn't agree with me."

"Exactly what part of the fish did you eat?" Sir Bentley said, waving his pith helmet in the air.

"Wow." Gene gasped for breath. "Hey, Frenchie. Open the zipper and let some air in."

"But it ez raining."

"Would you prefer this?" Gene said.

"It ez a good point." Piqûre pulled the zipper down halfway and stuck his head outside. Moments later, he pulled his head back in and stared at the other members of Team FUBAR with a blank expression.

"What?" Sir Bentley said.

"Ez's very strange," Piqûre said.

"This whole trip has been very strange," Buddy said. "I think we can handle it."

"We're moving," Piqûre said.

"Not until this rain lets up were not," Sir Bentley said.

"No," Piqûre said. "Now. We are moving now."

"What are you talking about?" Bentley scrambled over the Frenchman to look outside. Moments later, he pulled his head back in and stared at the others with the same blank expression.

"We're moving."

Gene stuck his head outside and left it there as the rain pounded down. "We're floating down the middle of a river."

"Indeed. It ez true."

"Let me see." Esmeralda scrambled across the air mattress to join Gene. "Flash flood?"

"Yup."

"Where do you think we'll end up?" Esmeralda said.

"Perhaps downstream?" Piqûre said.

"You're a big help," Esmeralda said, coming back inside the tent. "Open the other flap so we can at least see where we're going."

Piqûre complied and peered out through the meshed vent. "This ez not good."

"Man, we're flying," Esmeralda said, staring at the foliage that now formed the banks of the river.

"Smooth ride, though," Sir Bentley said. "Gene, remind me to add that to our marketing brochure."

Gene nodded and joined the others as they peered out the mesh window.

"The tent is working as a sail," Esmeralda said. "We need to cut it. Who's got a knife?"

Team FUBAR patted the pockets of their shirts and pants in vain.

195

"Some wilderness team," Esmeralda said, tearing at the tent fabric with her teeth. "Man, this stuff is tough." She gave up and stared back out through the vent.

"Gene, make sure we add durable," Sir Bentley said.

The tent swerved left, and all four tumbled and bounced and rolled on the air mattress.

"Bentley. Move the hand," Esmeralda said.

"Sorry."

"We are picking up speed," Piqûre said. "How ez that possible?"

"We're gonna die," Buddy said, staring at a huge rock directly in front of them.

"Merde."

"Get out of my way, Frenchman" Sir Bentley peered out the porthole. "Damn. That's a big rock."

"What do we do, Sir Bentley?" Piqûre said.

"How the hell should I know?"

"Well, after all, you are ze famous maggot."

"Magnate, you moron." Sir Bentley tugged his pith helmet further down onto his head. "Team FUBAR, permission granted to make suggestions."

"Well, for starters," Buddy said, "We need to miss that rock."

Sir Bentley nodded in agreement. "Okay, all together now," Sir Bentley said, beginning to chant. "Miss the rock. Miss the rock."

"Oh, yeah, like that's gonna work," Esmeralda said.

"That ez your plan, Sir Bentley?"

"You got anything better?" Sir Bentley said, staring wild-eyed through the window.

"He az a good point," Piqûre said, glancing at Esmeralda.

Team FUBAR followed their leader as the tent sped on.

"Miss the rock! Miss the rock! Miss the rock!"

**

Summerman opened his eyes and yawned. Doc and Genevieve were already awake and staring out at the torrent of water that raced past about twenty feet in front of them.

"Good nap?" Doc said.

196

"I've never figured out what is it about rainstorms that make me sleepy."

"It still hasn't let up," Genevieve said.

"I think it's raining harder," Doc said.

"Look at that current," Summerman said. "You wouldn't survive five minutes in that."

Murray barked loudly. The others followed his stare. They heard it coming moments before they saw it. And then a tent raced past and disappeared downstream.

"Did you see that?" Summerman said, his eyes blinking in disbelief.

"I'm not sure," Doc said. "What did you see?"

"A floating yellow tent with screams coming out of it."

"Yeah," Doc said. "That's what I saw."

"You thinking what I'm thinking?" Summerman said, glancing at Doc.

"Yeah. I think Sir Bentley Carruthers has just arrived."

**

"Safer, Self-Inflater, my ass." Esmeralda bounced the empty bottle off the mattress and folded her arms. "We're fucked."

"We missed the rock didn't we?" Sir Bentley said.

"And how many more are we headed right into?" Genevieve said, returning Bentley's glare.

"Yeah, Bentley," Buddy said. "This is not good. We're sitting ducks here."

"You two are a couple of total defeatists," Sir Bentley said. "What about you, Frenchman. You got anything left?"

"Quack, quack," Piqûre said. "I am sorry, Sir Bentley. I think I am too paralyzed with ze fear to be much help."

"We could jump," Gene said.

"We could drown, too," Esmeralda said.

"There is that," Gene said. "We could throw a rope and try to lasso something on the river bank."

"Got any rope?" Esmeralda said.

"Nah."

"What ez that sound?"

The rest of Team FUBAR cocked their heads and listened.

"It sounds familiar." Esmeralda peered out through the vent.

"Yeah, it does. But I can't quite place it," Gene said.

"I recognize that sound. A couple of weeks ago I was in Niagara Falls," Sir Bentley said.

"Dirty weekend, Bentley?" Buddy chuckled.

"No, I was trying to buy the Canadian side. That's the sound of a waterfall."

Team FUBAR fell silent and pondered.

"Uh-oh," Sir Bentley said.

"Yes, it does look like ze river disappears up ahead," Piqûre said. "That does it. Next year, I'm vacationing on ze Riviera."

"And we're coming up on some trees," Gene said. "They look like big bamboos."

"Okay, team, let's get ready." Sir Bentley knelt and folded his hands in prayer. He looked skyward. Team FUBAR immediately understood their leader's directions and sprang into action.

"Hit the trees! Hit the trees! Hit the trees!"

And they did.

The force of the impact drove all five of them forward into a clump of bamboo. Only the cushion provided by the air mattress kept them from being crushed between the trees and the force of the current. Piqûre, sitting at the front of the tent, caught the worst of it. His nose broken, bled profusely for thirty minutes. Esmeralda chipped a tooth on a tequila bottle but otherwise escaped undamaged. Gene and Buddy suffered minor cuts and bruises. Sir Bentley was unscathed, although he did need to change into a new safari suit after they safely made ground. Bentley swore it was simply rainwater that had drenched his suit but the whiff of urine the others picked up whenever downwind of the yellow-clad magnate told otherwise.

44

Bob Garbo, perched high in a tree and cocooned in a waterproof poncho, watched the floating yellow tent race past his line of sight and then rubbed his eyes. He'd been living in jungle isolation only for a few days, an insufficient amount of time for the onset of hallucinations. But a speeding tent in the middle of a tropical storm on a remote island stretched the boundaries of reality.

As the rain subsided, he returned his binoculars to the case hanging around his neck and carefully worked his way down the tree back onto solid ground. Approaching the riverbank, he tested his communication device and discovered that it still wasn't working. Left with no other alternative, he fell back on a well-tested method for contacting colleagues during field operations. He whistled and waved at Doc on the other side of the river.

"Garbo," Doc called. "Where the hell have you been hiding?"

Bob pointed up at the tree.

Doc looked up and nodded, then waved him over. Bob waved back and studied the raging water.

"Who the hell is that?" Summerman said, staring across the river.

"Bob Garbo."

"Who's he?"

"One of my part-timers." Doc caught Summerman's confused look. "No, not like you. Not that kind of part-timer. But he's excellent and has a hard-on for Sir Bentley."

"He's going to have to wait until the level drops," Summerman said. "That current's too strong to swim. Plus his pack looks heavy."

"Don't bet on it."

They watched Bob walk upstream about a hundred yards.

"Watch this," Doc said.

Bob stopped and stripped down to his shorts. He removed a plastic bag from his pack, placed his belongings inside, then covered it with the bag and tied it tight.

"What is he doing?" Summerman asked.

"He's going to join us." Doc pointed to a nearby patch of sand. "Right there."

"There? Right now? No way."

"Want to make it interesting?"

"How much?" Summerman said.

"A hundred bucks?"

"Make it a thousand."

"Lucky you can afford it, huh?"

Bob glanced across the river and studied the current. He walked another twenty yards upriver and approached the water's edge holding the pack in front of him. He placed the pack in the water, tested its buoyancy and pushed off. He kicked his legs as the current grabbed him and began crossing the river at a thirty-degree angle. As he approached the other side, he tucked his legs and pulled up on the pack. His feet hit the sand, and he popped upright, the pack still clutched in both hands. He tossed it on the sand and smiled.

"Where the hell did you learn how to do that?" Summerman said.

"Raging Waters," Garbo said, extending his hand.

Summerman returned the handshake and said, "I'm Summerman."

"Bob Garbo."

"And this is Genevieve," Doc said.

Bob glanced at her and looked back at Doc.

"Marseilles?"

"The very one," Doc said, beaming.

"Nice to meet you, Bob," Genevieve said. "I'm sorry, but I don't think Doc has ever mentioned you before."

"Good."

"The communication system is out since the rocket took out a piece of the resort," Doc said.

Bob raised an eyebrow.

"I'm not sure who did it, but my money is on Freak," Doc said.

"Tribesman," Bob said, shaking his head.

"Really? But Freak had to be involved."

"Absolutely."

**

Freak took a step back and admired his creation. Gilbert, who'd waited out the storm sitting in the equipment shed working his way through the last tray of pastries, grunted and staggered to his feet.

"Whatcha think?" Freak said, lovingly running his hand across the aluminum frame of one of two identical contraptions.

"What are these things for?"

"What the hell do you think? They're for flying." Freak tightened the banana bicycle seat he'd removed from a Lady Schwinn.

"I'm taking the one with the riding lawn mower seat, so this one is yours."

"Mine?"

"Yes, Assistant to the Admiral of the Air Force. It's yours."

"Admiral of the Air Force? I thought Admiral was a naval title." Gilbert tightened his headband and loosened his belt.

"Yeah, but I thought it was a nice touch since, by the time this mission is over, it may involve a sea component."

"Sea component? You mean like when these things crash into the ocean?"

Freak ignored the comment and began pacing back and forth.

"Let's commence with your training."

"There is no fucking way I'm getting strapped into that thing," Gilbert said.

"Need I remind you, Assistant to the Admiral of the Air Force, you volunteered for this mission. And you are under the direct command of me as the Admiral in question."

"I don't care if you're Queen of the Navy."

"Who told you about my nickname?" Freak said, coming to a sudden stop.

"What?"

"Nothing. Well, that is indeed most unfortunate." Freak resumed pacing. "Then I guess my only other option is to restrict you to barracks and place you on limited rations."

"So my choice is to strap myself into that thing or stay here at the resort while you head back into the jungle? Gee, Admiral, not the briar patch."

"Okay," Freak said. "Then I guess you'll just miss out when our new supplies arrive."

"Supplies?"

"Yes, I just re-ordered. They should be here tomorrow. And they include twelve dozen assorted cakes and pastries."

"Bullshit."

"Okay," Freak said. "Have it your way."

Freak turned away from Gilbert and began tinkering with one of the makeshift aircraft.

"You ordered pastries?"

"Uh-huh," Freak said, not looking up from his work. "And that's not counting the six Boston Cream pies."

Gilbert stared at his feet for several seconds and looked up at Freak.

"I love Boston Cream Pie."

"Who doesn't?"

"Okay, I'm in."

"All right," Freak said. "That's more like it. Fall in."

Gilbert looked around the tool shed and spread his arms with a confused look on his face.

"Close enough."

Freak grabbed a six-iron from a set of clubs sitting in a corner. Using the iron as a pointer, he described the features of his creation.

"You're looking at the prototype of what I call the Freakster." Freak paused for a moment to let the name register and continued with a flourish.

"It's the latest in air support weapons systems that creatively combines standard and high-tech components into a highly-versatile, low-altitude aircraft that is an essential addition to any counter-insurgency arsenal."

"Are you training me or trying to sell me a car?"

"I'm still working out the marketing pitch so excuse me if I ramble a bit."

"How about the Thrashing, Splashing, Come See the White-Trash Crashing?"

"Obviously, you're not a marketer," Freak said. "First, I need to point out the wingspan of sixteen feet. Not a problem when above tree level but an important safety consideration when flying low between bamboos."

Gilbert nodded and yawned as his blood sugar began to drop.

"And notice the lightweight aluminum frame construction along with the latest in ultra-light, yet ultra-sturdy, airlift components."

"Airlift components? It's a hang glider with bicycle wheels."

Freak held up a hand. "At first glance, it may appear."

Freak removed a small piece of tarp from behind the banana seat.

"What's that?"

"The engine," Freak said. "It's a John Deere taken from that riding mower. Given your extra girth, I decided some additional lift capability was required."

"It'll never get off the ground," Gilbert said.

"I wouldn't be too sure of that, Assistant to the Admiral."

"What's under those?" Gilbert said, pointing to the piece of tarp on each side of both hang gliders.

Freak snatched the tarps away as if Gilbert had asked what was behind door number three. He held the pose and beamed at Gilbert.

Gilbert recognized the object immediately and felt his sphincter tighten. "You're going to fire missiles from a hang glider?"

"What good is a fighter plane without a weapon system? And the SkyWriter is the latest in portable, high-tech weaponry."

"You said six Boston Cream pies, right?"

Freak nodded his head, his eyes glazed with excitement.

"Okay, Admiral. Let's go get some natives."

"That's what I like to hear," Freak said.

"Just one question." Gilbert eased his way onto the banana seat. The seat disappeared, and the aircraft squeaked and moaned from the weight. "What is this thing?"

"Walkie-talkie," Freak said.

"Does it work?"

"Of course, it works," Freak said, pressing a button on the bright red plastic device.

"The farmer in the dell, the farmer in the dell." The snippet ended and was replaced by Freak's voice. "Testing. Testing, one, two, three."

Gilbert stared at the plastic toy duct taped to the hang glider and shook his head in disbelief.

"Testing, testing," Freak said. "I'm not happy about the music selections, but there was nothing I could do about it."

"Fisher-Price?"

"Hey, as Rumsfeld says, you go into battle with what you have, not with what you wish you had."

Gilbert read from the side of the walkie-talkie. "For ages 3 to 8." He looked at Freak, who was pulling on a pair of shiny metal goggles. "Sounds about right."

45

Merlin inhaled deeply to savor the smell as he scooped the fried rice concoction into a coconut shell. He chewed slowly as he listened to Bantu chatter with his father. He tasted pork, garlic and onion as well as other spices he couldn't identify. He paused, mid-swallow when Chief's voice rose, and he saw the finger pointed in his direction.

"Now what?"

"My father is concerned, that is all." Bantu dropped his head and resumed eating.

Chief continued his rant and waved both arms in the air. He glared at Merlin and shoved his bowl of food away.

"He's pissed off about something." Merlin flashed a smile in Chief's direction. "Why I have no idea. I've barely said a word to him in two days."

"I'm afraid that is the problem," Bantu said, refilling his bowl. "He believes that your silence speaks for itself."

"Tell your father that every time I open my mouth around here, I seem to get hit with a poison dart. So is it any wonder I'm a bit hesitant to offer suggestions?"

"He does not believe you are qualified to speak on behalf of the Outsiders."

"Not qualified?"

"He says he would be more comfortable receiving counsel from Summerman. But he has disappeared. But my father's anger is mainly with me. He believes I have failed."

"How have you failed?"

"By not bringing someone back to the village with the ability to speak on behalf of the Outsiders."

"There's only about seven billion people on the planet, Bantu. Who could speak for all of them?"

"From my travels, it was evident there are many who do just that," Bantu said.

"Perhaps you should tell your father that the wisest men are those who do not push their beliefs on others."

"It is not your beliefs that are the source of his anger. It is your lack of ideas."

"Lack of ideas? Who the does he think he's talking to? I've got a great track record."

"Perhaps. But how does that help our tribe? How does that help us identify ways to deal with the arrival of the Outsiders?"

"Well, I'm certain I'll come up with something very soon."

Bantu chattered with Chief, who listened and then snorted.

"Bullshit," Chief said.

"Bullshit. I'll tell you what's bull-," Merlin cocked his head. "Hey, that was in English."

"Remember that my father ventured out of the village many years ago himself on a similar trip as mine. He still has a few favorite words and phrases."

"Yeah." Chief pointed his finger at Merlin. "Bullshit."

"Well, then let's see if you understand this one, Chief. You're a total pain in the ass."

Chief lowered his finger but maintained eye contact.

"Fuck you," Chief said.

"Perhaps bringing you here was not a good idea." Bantu placed a hand on Merlin's shoulder. "Perhaps it is up to us to decide how to best move forward."

"Fuck me?" Merlin pushed Bantu's hand away.

"Oh, no," Bantu said. "Now you've done it."

Chief, his face purple with rage, rose to his feet and began chattering loudly.

"Now what did I do?"

"You pushed my hand from your shoulder."

"That? So what? That was nothing. I was just reacting."

"In our tribe, the resting of one's hand on another's shoulder is the most sincere gesture of friendship one can make. And to refuse it is serious."

Chief stormed around the hut, his voice loud enough to cause tribesmen outside to pause from their assigned chores. Merlin stood and watched the Chief stomp his way back and forth across the hardwood floor.

"Chief, relax," Merlin said. "It didn't mean anything. I'm sorry."

Chief glared at Merlin and chattered nonstop.

"He doesn't get like this often." Bantu approached his father. Chief waved him away and continued to circle the perimeter of the hut.

"Bullshit," Chief said. "Bullshit, fuck you. Bullshit."

"These usually don't last long," Bantu said. "He'll calm down in a minute."

Merlin stared at the wild-eyed Chief.

"I just wanted to spend a few quiet days on the beach. I guess that was just too much to ask for."

"You were selected as one of the chosen ones, Merlin," Bantu said, his voice calm and quiet. "Perhaps it is time for you to start living up to my choice."

"And do what? Tell you how to stop development? Slow down the advance of Western civilization? Millions have died trying to do just that. I'm not some miracle worker."

"So you're saying that we have no choice, no way to deal with it?"

Merlin extended both arms in desperation.

"I don't know what I'm saying, Bantu? In the end, maybe your tribe could count your blessings that you've somehow managed to avoid it for this long."

"We like our life," Bantu said.

"I completely understand," Merlin said. "It's fantastic in many ways."

"Then help us."

Merlin exhaled loudly and nodded his head.

"Okay, I have no idea what I can do without the rest of my posse, but I'll try."

"That is all we can ask," Bantu said.

He chattered with Chief, who listened carefully, then nodded.

"My father says thank you."

"I didn't hear him say anything," Merlin said.

"Now who's being the pain in the ass," Bantu said.

"Booga-wooga-nooga," Chief said.

"Look, Chief," Merlin said, extending his hand. "I'm very sorry, and I will do my best to help."

207

Chief stared at Merlin's handshake offer as he listened to Bantu's translation. He grunted but did not return the handshake.

"He could at least shake my hand," Merlin said.

"That gesture has little meaning in our world," Bantu said.

"Oh, right," Merlin said, extending his arm towards Chief's shoulder.

"No," Bantu said, jumping forward. "Now is not the time for you to-"

Bantu's warning came too late as Merlin rested his hand on Chief's shoulder. Chief stared at the hand and chomped down on it like it was a slice of pizza.

Merlin's howls reverberated across the jungle as Chief held on for dear life.

46

You hear that?" Doc said.

Bob Garbo stopped in his tracks, cocked his head to one side and pointed towards the northwest.

"How far away do you think it is?"

"Mile."

Doc nodded and smiled.

"It's kind of like the good old days out here, isn't it? No high-tech surveillance or communication systems. Just following our instincts and training."

Bob nodded in agreement and looked over his shoulder for Genevieve and Summerman. Doc also paused to look back at the section of thick jungle they had cut their way through.

"Where the hell are they?" Doc said.

Bob shrugged his shoulders.

"Genevieve?"

"Doc, we need a little help back here," Genevieve said.

Doc and Bob took a few steps, and Bob grabbed Doc's elbow and pointed at the ground about a hundred feet away.

"Holy shit," Doc said.

"Yeah," Summerman said. "Murray, stay. Get back here."

"How many are there?" Doc said.

"I see two," Genevieve said. "But I've heard that paralysis by fear can cause double vision.

"That's odd," Doc said. "Usually, they're solitary creatures."

"Well, it looks like this group went condo," Summerman said. "And I don't think they're very receptive to visitors. Murray, stay."

Summerman grabbed Murray's collar and held on for dear life.

Bob Garbo reached into his pack and pulled out a pistol.

"Silencer," Doc said.

Bob nodded and screwed the device onto the barrel of the pistol. He crept forward in search of a clear line of sight.

"Don't move," Doc said.

"That won't be a problem," Summerman said.

"Have you got a good hold on Murray?"

"As good as I'm going to get."

"Both of you need to stay exactly where you are. Do not move."

Genevieve and Summerman, face to face with two hissing cobras preparing to strike, looked at each other and nodded. Seconds later, the heads of both snakes exploded in front of their eyes as two soft pops punctuated the air.

Murray woofed in surprise.

"Who is this guy?" Summerman said.

"Clear."

Bob returned the pistol to its holster.

Genevieve and Summerman stared at Bob as they approached. Bob had already moved on and was intensely studying a hand drawn map. Murray nudged his leg in thanks and Bob knelt down and scratched Murray's ears.

"You can't fall behind," Doc said.

"I had to pee," Genevieve said.

Doc nodded and looked over Bob's shoulder at the map.

"I heard screaming," Summerman said.

Doc and Bob both nodded without looking up. Summerman glanced at Genevieve.

"Nice to see people so focused on their work."

Genevieve laughed and lighted a Gitanes.

"Okay, Doc," she said. "We must be close. Now, what?"

"Well, according to Summerman, when he and Merlin went in earlier they weren't attacked."

"Yes, but we were being escorted by the son of the chief."

"Still," Doc said. "From what you've told us, it doesn't sound like they're headhunters."

"What about the dart guns?" Genevieve said.

"Probably just used for hunting and defensive purposes," Doc said.

"Defensive purposes as in attacking uninvited visitors?" Genevieve said, taking a long drag on her cigarette.

"You just watched Bob shoot the eyes out of a couple of snakes from a hundred feet away. You don't have anything to worry about."

"That's exactly what I'm worried about," Genevieve said. "I'm telling you for the last time; you are not going to hurt these people."

Doc scratched his head and wiped sweat from his brow with his shirtsleeve.

"Genevieve, I told you that nothing is going to happen unless they provoke us."

"Well, I'm sorry, Doc," she said. "But I know how short your fuse is."

"My fuse is fine. Look, would you rather have Bentley get there first?"

"No," Genevieve said.

"Thank you." Doc turned his attention back to the map. "Yeah, from what we just heard, it has to be in that direction."

"Yup," said Bob.

"So how do you plan on going in once we find it?"

Genevieve crushed her cigarette with her boot.

"Slowly and quietly," Doc said.

Bob Garbo nodded in agreement and put the map back in his pocket.

47

Freak pulled the starter cord, and the twelve-horsepower John Deere engine roared to life. He stared down the incline of the service road that stretched across the back of the resort and looked at Gilbert's butt cheeks that completely engulfed the banana seat. He was holding onto the aluminum frame of the hang glider as if his life depended on upon it.

Which it probably did.

"Piece of cake," Freak said, glancing back and forth between the service road and the Freakster II. "All you have to do is let the engine do its thing until you hit about twenty miles an hour, then lean back as far as you can to help the wind get under the mainsail."

"Then what?"

"Keep climbing to about a thousand feet and the breeze should take you right to the center of the island."

"Should?"

"Probably."

"Most inspirational, Admiral." Gilbert scratched his chest as he stared at his aircraft. "How will I know when I'm at the right altitude?"

"If you get to the point where you can't see shit, you'll know you're too high."

"Oh, that's helpful. And then what?" Gilbert said, squeezing the life out of the aluminum frame.

"Pray the wind doesn't drop."

Freak performed a final inspection of the aircraft and slapped Gilbert on the back.

"Don't worry, from up there you'll see the village without any problem. Just keep circling and wait for my command."

"I don't like this," Gilbert said.

"Just keep saying to yourself, pastries and Boston cream pie, oh my. Think of it as your mantra."

Freak repositioned the hang glider until it was headed straight down the access road and engaged the makeshift gearstick. The glider lurched forward, and Gilbert gripped the frame tighter. The craft began to pick up speed and Gilbert felt the breeze against his cheek.

"Pastries and Boston cream pie, oh my. Pastries and Boston Cream Pie, ooooooh...."

The sound of the John Deere and the rustling wind drowned out Gilbert's cries as the Freakster II raced down the incline and slowly lifted off. By the time Gilbert opened his eyes, he had already sailed past the resort, and the only thing he could see below him was the deep blue of the ocean. He tugged hard on the right side of the frame, and the aircraft reluctantly turned back towards the island.

"Whew," Gilbert said. "What do you know? I'm flying."

The farmer in the dell, the farmer in the dell..."This is Freakster I calling Freakster II. Come in, Freakster II."

Gilbert pressed the Send button on the Fischer Price intercom. Hi-ho, the Derry-o, the farmer in the dell.

He waited for the music to end. "This is Freakster II."

The farmer takes a wife, the farmer takes a wife.

"How goes it up there, Assistant to the Admiral?"

Hi-ho, the Derry-o, the farmer takes a wife.

"So far so good. It's a little sluggish, but it's getting better the higher up I go."

The cat takes a rat, the cat takes a rat.

"I'm right behind you for now, but I'm going to pass you and take the lead as we head inland. Try to maintain eye contact. Oh, and one more thing."

Hi-ho, the Derry-o, the cat takes a rat.

"What's that?"

The rat takes the cheese, the rat takes the cheese.

"Your butt cheeks are showing. See if there's something you can do to remedy that situation. Freakster I out."

Gilbert glanced over his shoulder, then looked back down at the rapidly disappearing ground and decided that showing a little butt crack was the least of his worries.

Hi-ho, the Derry-o, the rat takes the cheese.

"Freakster II out."

Above the constant drone of the engine, Freak heard his stomach rumble.

"Hmmm. Cheese. That's sounds good."

48

Doc held up his arm, and the others stopped in their tracks and waited for instructions. They had made their way into a clearing, but still surrounded on all sides by thick jungle. Doc cocked his head back and forth and listened intensely. Taking his cue, Bob Garbo reached into his pack, grabbed the pistol, but kept his hand inside hidden from view.

A high-pitched sound came from their right which was quickly repeated from their left, then from behind. Palm leaves rustled, and a figure stepped through the foliage and stared at them. He was holding a blow gun in one hand and making hand gestures with the other. A metal case hung from his shoulder, and he stared at Summerman. Moments later, three other figures appeared left, right and behind at ninety-degree angles forming a diamond-shaped pattern.

"Tuber," Summerman said.

"You know this man?" Doc said, not taking his eyes off the tribesman.

"Yeah, we've met." Summerman attempted a small wave.

Tuber snarled and raised the blowgun to his lips. Bob started to pull his pistol, but Doc placed his hand on Garbo's forearm and shook his head.

"He's from the village," Summerman said. "And he's a few bananas short of a fruit salad."

"He's from a remote tribe in the middle of the jungle," Genevieve said. "What'd you expect? A Harvard man?"

"No, that's not it," Summerman said. "His tribe calls him the village idiot."

"The village idiot carrying a rocket launcher," Doc said. "How the hell did he get his hands on that?"

"From that other idiot, Freak," Summerman whispered. "It's not loaded is it?"

"Jesus, I hope not," Doc said. "And why are you whispering? He hasn't learned to speak English has he?"

"Jesus, I hope not," Summerman said. "I just called him the village idiot."

Doc continued to watch Tuber, who finally recognized Summerman. He maintained his glare but lowered the blowgun from his mouth.

"What are you going to do, Doc?" Genevieve said.

Doc pondered the question and looked at Bob, who remained on point, his hand clutching the pistol.

"I don't know about you, Garbo, but I'm thinking if they were going to try to kill us, they would have done so already," Doc said.

"Yup."

"And rather than us wear ourselves out trying to find this damn village, maybe we should just let them take us there."

"Yup."

Murray trotted towards Tuber and sat down in front of him. His tail wagged back and forth. Tuber stared down at the massive dog and tentatively touched his head. Murray licked his hand, and Tuber smiled.

"Now there's something you don't see every day," Bob said.

The other three stared at the suddenly verbose mercenary.

"What?" Bob said.

"Good boy," Summerman said, beaming with pride.

"Unbelievable," Doc said. "Besides, it's such a beautiful day. I don't feel like killing anybody at the moment, do you?"

"No," Bob said.

Doc and Bob slowly raised their arms in surrender. Summerman and Genevieve followed suit. Murray glanced back at them, then hopped to his feet and placed both paws on Tuber's shoulders.

49

Sir Bentley paced back and forth along the edge of the rapidly receding riverbank. He grunted, reviewed his notes and sat down on a rock. Esmeralda took a long pull of tequila and offered it to Gene who declined. Piqûre also refused as he sat down in the sand to stretch his legs.

"This place sucks," Piqûre said, glancing around the dense foliage. "Does anyone have any idea where we are?"

"Yeah," Esmeralda said. "We're lost."

"Team FUBAR is not lost," Sir Bentley said. "Not lost, I tell you. We're in a planning phase."

Buddy shrugged at Esmeralda, who scowled and pumped a fist up and down in Bentley's direction. She took another swallow, checked the level in the bottle, and returned it to her pack.

"I wonder how many different creatures there are out here that can kill you?" Buddy said, burning a leech off his arm.

"Including Bentley?" Esmeralda said.

Gene, Buddy, and Piqûre laughed. Sir Bentley was not amused.

" I've read that people should be particularly careful in the jungle after torrential rainstorms. Apparently, flash floods can create havoc among indigenous animals," Sir Bentley said.

"Havoc like being swept away in a tent?" Esmeralda said.

"I was thinking more along the lines of crocodiles and snakes," Sir Bentley said.

"Ooh, I don't not like ze snakes."

"Then keep your eyes open, Private," Sir Bentley said. "Because I am sure that we weren't the only creatures dumped here. And research shows that it's the initial hours after a storm when most snake attacks occur."

Piqûre stared at Bentley with a puzzled expression.

"What's the matter?" Sir Bentley said.

"What is…ze Cur?"

"What?"

"Ze Cur. What is it?"

"What the fuck are you talking about?" Sir Bentley said.

"You said this is ze time when ze snake attacks ze Cur. So I ask you, what is ze Cur?"

"A cur is a mongrel dog," Gene said.

"What is ze mongrel dog doing way out here in ze jungle?"

"Beats me," Gene said.

"You moron," Sir Bentley said, dumping sand out of his soaked Cloudlifters. "When snake attacks occur. O-cur. When they happen. Got it?"

"Excuse me," Piqûre said. "I am so sorry if English ez not my first language. Plus, it ez such an ugly language."

"Watch it, Frenchie," Buddy said. "Don't start bad mouthing the U.S.A."

"I was talking about ze language, not ze Americans. Tout le monde de merde."

"Speak English," Buddy said.

"Go fuck yourself," Piqûre said. "Ez that English enough for you? You...you corporate hack. You...you scumbag. What do you throw when you ze a lawyer drowning? A very big party. You sycophantic bottom-feeder."

"Man he's got you pegged, Quizling." Sir Bentley laughed and gave the Frenchman a doff of his pith helmet.

Buddy stared at Piqûre, then laughed and slapped him on the back.

"Not bad, Frenchie. Almost like being at a board meeting."

"It ez a gift," Piqûre said, puffing with pride.

"Bentley," Esmeralda said. "Do you have a plan or not?"

"Hold your drawers. I'm working on it," Sir Bentley said.

"Maybe ze cavalry will arrive," Piqûre said. "Just like in ze movies."

"Or our Air Force," Gene said.

"Jesus, I forgot all about him. Can you believe that guy? I should have had him shot after he blew up my yacht. Air Force? What on earth could he possibly expect to fly around here?"

"How about a hang glider equipped with a lawn mower engine, and armed with a couple of SkyWriters?" Gene said.

Sir Bentley chuckled.

"Good one, Private Gene. Now that is something I'd like to see."

Gene pointed up at the two objects flying at very different altitudes, approaching from the east.

"Well, here's your chance." "Well, here's your chance."

**

Freak stared back as the village disappeared from view and then focused his attention on the jungle rooftop that was looming about a half-mile in front of him. He glanced around for signs of Gilbert's craft. Unable to make a visual sighting, Freak fiddled with his intercom and activated the signal.

The wheels on the bus go round and round.

"Freakster I calling Freakster II. Come in, Freakster II."

Round and round, round and round.

"Freakster II. You found a new song, Admiral? Over."

The wheels on the bus go round and round.

"Yeah, I found a bunch of them. It's the big yellow button underneath the speaker. We've got Twinkle Twinkle Little Star, Itsy Bitsy Spider, and When You Wish Upon a Star. Got any preference? Over."

Round and round, round and round.

"Completely your call, Admiral. But I do need to mention that I think I'm losing altitude."

I know, it's only rock and roll, but I like it.

"What the hell? Over."

I know, it's only rock and roll, but I like it.

"Good choice, sir. Not something I'd expect from a children's toy, but definitely a classic."

Well, I like it, like it, yes, I do.

"Damn, somebody has been screwing with our communication system. Either that or we're getting crosstalk from somewhere. You're losing altitude because the wind is dropping. Prepare to jettison your engine. Over."

"Jettison, sir?"

The radio screeched, then the music stopped.

"There, that should do it. Yes, Assistant to the Admiral, jettison your engine now. Over."

219

"And how do you propose I do that, sir?"

"Cut the duct tape, moron. Over."

"And I'll gain altitude?"

"Let's hope so for your sake. Or it's over. Over."

"I need to pee."

"Then pee. Who's going to see you? You're in the middle of the jungle. Just remember to pee with the wind. Over."

"Freakster II. Over. And probably out."

Gilbert leaned back. The banana seat groaned under the weight, but held. He used his pocketknife to slice away the thick layers of duct tape that was holding the engine in place. Gilbert watched as the lawn mower engine fell away and disappeared towards ground. He felt the rapid movement upwards as the breeze caught his now lighter craft. Gilbert managed to unzip his trousers and lift his legs as he relieved himself amid the sounds of the gentle flapping of canvas and a cool ocean breeze in his face. Gilbert closed his eyes as his bladder emptied and he repositioned his weight on the banana seat.

"Aaahh."

He didn't even see the other members of Team FUBAR below staring up at him as he passed over the jungle rooftop. He also didn't see the hundred and fifty foot Gurjan tree a directly in his path.

**

"What on earth is he doing?" Sir Bentley shaded his eyes with a hand as he stared up at hang glider.

"Believe it or not," Esmeralda said, looking through binoculars. "I think he's flashing us. Yuk." She handed the binoculars to Gene. "If I were him, I wouldn't be advertising."

Gene looked through the binoculars and took several steps to his left as he saw the stream of liquid begin to fall from the sky.

"Hey, Bentley, you might-"

"Be quiet, Private," Sir Bentley said, eyes skyward.

"Okay," Gene said.

"That's strange," Sir Bentley said "Is it raining again?"

"No, I don't think so."

Gene focused the binoculars on Bentley's confused expression.

"Just a little friendly fire."

220

50

Doc sat quietly with his hands folded in front of him and waited for the two men to stop chattering amongst themselves. He looked at the fourth man sitting at the table with a large poultice covering his left hand.

"What happened to you?" Doc said.

"The fucker bit me," Merlin said, pointing at Chief.

Doc frowned but said nothing as he continued to wait for the chattering to stop.

"Okay," Bantu said. "My father is ready to speak with you."

Doc nodded and looked at Chief. Their eyes locked, and Doc recognized the look; prideful, questioning, with a touch of defiance. Chief chattered at him briefly without breaking eye contact.

"My father would like to know why you are here."

"I was sent," Doc said, looking directly at Chief.

Bantu nodded, translated and listened to Chief's response.

"Are you a dangerous man?"

"Dangerous?" Merlin said. "Talk about the pot calling the kettle black."

Doc slowly turned towards Merlin and waited until he had his undivided attention. "I would appreciate it if you would just sit there quietly," Doc said, his voice barely above a whisper. "Do I make myself clear?"

Merlin nodded and picked at his poultice.

Doc resumed eye contact with Chief. "Yes, I can be a dangerous man."

Bantu began translating, but Chief stopped him with an upraised palm. He nodded at Doc and chattered briefly.

"Why were you sent?" Bantu said.

"Because you have something that someone else wants."

Chief listened to the translation, nodded and pondered his next question. Bantu listened to his father and then spoke to Doc.

221

"My father has no idea what our tribe could have that would be of interest to the Outsiders, but he would like to know if you will simply take it from us if we choose not to give it you."

Doc thought for a moment and felt the breeze brush his cheeks. He glanced outside and watched Genevieve, freshly bathed with her hair still wet. She strolled through one of the gardens followed by Summerman and several members of the tribe who were fascinated by the statuesque goddess with jet black hair. Doc smiled, certain that the fact that she was only wearing a sarong tied around her waist was contributing to the level of interest she was receiving. Virtually all of the women in the tribe were topless but, judging from the expressions on the tribesmen's faces along with the winks and nudges they shared, daily exposure to female breasts had done little to dampen their appreciation for the truly magnificent.

Doc looked at Chief, who was staring at Genevieve. Chief slowly shook his head in admiration. He chattered with Bantu, who chuckled and nodded his head.

"My father is very impressed with her."

Doc took another look at Genevieve and looked at Chief.

"She is magnificent, isn't she?" Doc said.

Without waiting for the translation, Chief said, "Booga-wooga-nooga."

"I was surprised when your father agreed to let her visit your garden," Doc said.

Bantu translated, and Chief laughed and responded.

"My father says that any man who could say no to her should probably not call himself a man in the first place."

Chief smiled and chattered.

"My father says that she is the sort who makes one believe in the power of the gods," Bantu said.

"Your father is a very wise man," Doc said.

Chief leaned forward conspiratorially, thrust an index finger in and out of a knot hole in the table and pointed at Doc and then at Genevieve.

"Do the two of us?" Doc grinned. "Tell your father, yes, as often as I can."

Bantu translated, and Chief roared with laughter. He then chattered at Bantu and sat back grinning in his chair with his arms folded.

222

"My father says he may be very wise," Bantu said. "But you are very lucky."

"Booga-wooga-nooga," Chief said, staring outside at the garden. He then grunted at Doc.

"Yes, I owe you an answer to your question. Tell your father that I don't know what I will do if that occurs, but I will do my best not to harm anyone in your tribe."

Bantu translated, and Chief stared at Doc as he listened and seemed satisfied for the moment with the answer. Chief stroked his chin and spoke to Bantu.

"My father would like to know what we have that the Outsiders want."

"Your plants and medicines," Doc said.

Chief listened and then scowled. He chattered loudly and waved his arms in the air.

"My father says that those are sacred items. They give life and keep the evil spirits at bay."

"I understand," Doc said. "But in the outside world, they would also do one more thing."

"Make money," Bantu said.

"Yes, they would make money. A lot of money."

Bantu chattered with Chief, who nodded and shook his fist angrily at Merlin.

"There he goes again," Merlin said. "What the hell did I do?" Merlin then raised his voice as if volume would assist comprehension. "He's the one who wants your plants," he said, pointing at Doc. "Why are you mad at me?"

Doc let Merlin's outburst slide, then stood up and walked to the entrance of the hut. He stared up at the sky along with Bob Garbo, who was sitting on the front step.

"Is that who I think it is?" Doc said.

"Yeah."

Chief approached and peered over Doc's shoulder. Chief growled when he recognized one of the pilots. He poked Doc in the ribs and pointed up at Freak, who was circling overhead.

"Yes," Doc said. "He's one of mine. Tell your father I'm sorry, but he's my brother-in-law."

Bantu translated, and Chief nodded as he continued to stare up at the two strange contraptions weaving their way back and forth across the village.

Tuber recognized his nemesis and raced back and forth under Freak's flight pattern firing darts straight up into the air. He continued to reload and fire until one of the darts returned to earth and pierced the back of his neck rendering him unconscious.

Chief shook his head sadly and chattered commands to a small group of tribesmen who reluctantly left the garden to tend to the loudly snoring Tuber. Chief chattered at Doc and pointed at Tuber lying on the ground.

"My father says he understands," Bantu said. "Tuber is my father's brother-in-law."

"Family, huh?" Doc said to Chief.

"Booga-wooga-nooga," Chief shrugged and then chattered at Bantu.

"My father says that it appears we are being invaded and would like to know if there are more of you on the way."

"There are always more of us."

51

Doc laughed as he casually waved the back of his hand to shoo away the pairs of eyes peering over the top of the wall of the hut. He rolled over and spooned the sleeping Genevieve. She stirred and edged back against him, and he shook his head in amazement at his newly rediscovered recovery powers.

"Don't even think about it."

She rolled over to face him.

"It's not me," Doc said. "It's your fault."

"Guilty as charged."

She sat up noticing the remaining pair of eyes. "We've got company."

"The kids are amazed by you."

"They're sweet. The adults too."

"No natural enemies for centuries will do that for you."

"That's about to change," Genevieve said.

Doc got up and pulled on his shorts. He sat back down on the edge of the mattress and stared outside.

"I can't believe the vegetation. And some of these trees are amazing. What's the name of that one?" Doc said, pointing at a tree that towered over a hundred feet.

"That is Dipterocarpus Turbinatus. The Gurjan tree. They can grow up to two hundred feet. Gurjan oil is used to treat respiratory problems, and it also relieves skin irritations like eczema and rashes."

"So Bentley is right about this place being a potential goldmine?"

"From what little I've seen, I'd have to say yes."

Doc rubbed his hand over the shiny hardwood floor.

"Is this teak?"

"No, the floors are made from Padouk."

"I love the red color."

Genevieve looked around the hut and marveled at the simple, yet elegant, design. She stared up at the woven thatched roof and admired the teak table and chairs. A set of bowls made from coconut shells rested on the table next to a woven vase that contained freshly cut orchids.

"How did they do all of this?" she said.

"What? Build their civilization?"

"Yes. It's primitive but, at the same time, very advanced."

"Combine a natural sense of curiosity with work ethic and unlimited time and I guess you're bound to figure some stuff out."

Doc waved to the pairs of eyes that had reappeared over the half-wall, then faked a playful charge in their direction. The eyes disappeared, and they heard laughs and giggles.

"I've been in over sixty countries, and I've never seen anything like this place. They farm, they build, and they invent. Did you see the sandpaper they've come up with?"

"No," Genevieve said, running a brush through her hair.

"I asked Bantu how they managed to get the finishing touches on these floors and those sidewalks, and he showed me how they make sandpaper."

"With sand?" Genevieve said, examining the ends of her hair.

"Funny," Doc said. "They take the dried palms they use to make their baskets and these roofs, apply an adhesive they've developed and then dip them in sand. It doesn't last long, but it obviously does the trick."

"It must take them months to finish one of these huts."

"Yeah, you and I wouldn't want to do it, but they just keep at it. I asked the Chief about his philosophy of work and he said, 'Go slow, but never stop.'"

"I'm surprised they've been as welcoming as they've been. I was expecting a different reaction."

"We might still get it," Doc said. "Chief knows he has a problem with the long-term survival of his tribe. Their numbers are going down, and that factory and resort scared the shit out of him. So if Bentley does something stupid, Chief's mood is gonna change in a hurry."

"Something stupid like flying hang gliders over the village?"

"That moron. That was something only Freak could come up with. I should have let Bentley shoot him when he wanted to."

226

"So what do we do? Put a search party together and try to find him?"

"No, we just sit tight and wait for him to show up. Until then, we just keep watching and learning as much as we can."

"I could spend years cataloging the plants on this island." Genevieve stretched out on the mattress. "And I can't wait to see this cave Bantu keeps talking about."

"He's interesting," Doc said. "Three years out in the real world and he seems to have survived it pretty well."

"He's definitely his father's son."

"Yeah. I haven't heard what happened to his mother."

"Snakebite."

"Tough way to go."

"Yeah. She was off somewhere by herself, and they didn't find her until it was too late."

"You be careful out there," Doc said.

"Bantu has already given me some of the antidote to carry around."

Doc nodded and stared into her eyes.

"Come back to bed," Genevieve said, arching her back.

"Good idea," Doc said, stretching out on the mattress "I could use forty winks."

Genevieve rolled over on top of him and tied her hair back as she straddled him.

"You'll get ten and like it."

52

"This is delicious."

Summerman slurped down the last of his fish soup and refilled his coconut bowl.

"Yeah," Bob said, studying Merlin over the top of his bowl.

"You don't talk much do you?" Merlin said.

"No."

"Well, maybe you should try. It would be good to know a little bit more about what the hell you're doing here."

Bob stared at Merlin as he continued sipping his soup.

"Unbelievable," Merlin said. "That's just rude."

"Merlin, please give it a rest," Summerman said.

"Well, it is rude," Merlin said. "I'm sick and tired of his cloak and dagger routine. I've been stuck in this place for days now. I want to go home, or at least back to the resort."

"Go," Bob said.

"Just like that, huh? It's as simple as just leaving. Even when my job isn't finished here yet," Merlin said.

"Job?"

"Yes, my job. Our job," Merlin said.

Bob Garbo shrugged and refilled his bowl.

"Look, I know you work with Doc, so that carries a lot of weight, but you don't intimidate me in the least and-"

Bob placed his hand firmly on Merlin's forearm and stared at him with dead eyes.

"Stop."

Merlin nodded, pushed his bowl away and sat back in his chair with his arms folded.

"I want out of here," Merlin said.

"It won't be long," Summerman said. He looked towards the door. "Here comes trouble."

Tuber, showing no side effects from the encounter with the dart, entered the hut and helped himself to a bowl of soup. He glanced around the table and fixed his gaze on Merlin. He snarled and held his blow gun up to his lips.

"What the hell did I ever do to this guy?"

"He just doesn't like you," Summerman said.

"Tell him to get in line," Merlin said.

Bob Garbo laughed, then stood up from the table and left the hut.

"He makes me nervous," Merlin said. "I sure hope Doc knows what he's doing bringing this guy along."

"Me too," Summerman said. "I've seen him shoot."

53

Buddy watched from a distance as Sir Bentley sat on a rock and made notes. Bentley's pith helmet was pushed back, and sweat dripped off his forehead and spattered his notepad. Buddy wondered, in a combination of awe and amusement, what possessed the billionaire to keep moving forward buying, developing, acquiring, and, in all likelihood in this situation, stealing what he wanted to further his empire. Sir Bentley noticed Buddy's stare and waved him over.

"You seem troubled, Private Quizling."

"I have a lot on my mind, Commander. Plus, this is the first time I've ever been lost in the jungle."

"Team FUBAR is not lost, Private." Sir Bentley slipped the notepad back into his shirt pocket. "We are merely weighing our options."

"I can only identify two, Sir Bentley. Get to the village or go home."

"That's a somewhat limited vision, but then you are only a private."

"But I'm on the verge of becoming a very rich private," Gene said.

"Yes, you should do quite well on this deal."

"That's what I would like to discuss. My end of the deal."

Sir Bentley turned towards Buddy, raised an eyebrow and waited.

"Mind you, the original deal we struck where I'd get five percent of the profits of whatever products ended up being developed. But it was based on my administrative work only."

"And?"

"And now I'm out here doing, what would you call this, field research? I'm participating in the procurement process, so to speak."

"And because of this procurement participation, you believe you are now entitled to a higher percentage?"

"Yes, Commander. I do."

"I see." Sir Bentley removed his pith helmet and scratched his head. "Private Quizling, do you know what five percent of a billion dollars is?"

"C'mon, Bentley, I've worked for you for ten years now. Let's drop the whole Commander shit shall we?"

"I believe adherence to military tradition and protocol builds cohesion."

"Have it your way. But in answer to your question, yes, I do know what five percent of a billion is."

"And based on the business plan for this venture, what is the estimated profit over the first ten years?"

"Somewhere between three and five billion," Buddy said.

"So you can expect to make somewhere in the neighborhood of two hundred million dollars."

"Yes, Commander. Based on the structure of our current arrangement."

"But you now consider that insufficient?"

"Yes, Commander. I believe I am entitled to a larger percentage. Somewhere in the neighborhood of fifteen."

Sir Bentley laughed and stared at his lawyer.

"Fifteen percent? For what?"

"For keeping my mouth shut."

"Excuse me?"

"Sorry. For keeping my mouth shut, Commander."

"About what?"

"Oh, just a little story about the rape and destruction of an ancient civilization on a remote island you recently purchased. I'm sure every media outlet on the planet, not to mention the U.S. and Indian governments, would be fascinated to hear the details."

"You really are a bottom feeder aren't you, Private Quizling?"

"I'm one of the biggest, Commander. Isn't that why you hired me?"

"Yeah, it was. But there is another option."

"I'm all ears, Commander."

"I could just shoot you and leave your body out here for the wild boar to find."

"No, you won't do that," Buddy said, smiling.

"Really? What makes you so sure?"

"Because I've already written this sordid little tale down and sent it to my office. Along with a copy of your business plan. My staff is under specific instructions to open the sealed envelope in the event they don't hear from me."

"I see. Nice touch," Sir Bentley said.

"And although I have no idea how many people you're planning on getting rid of before you get off this island, I'm damn sure I won't be one of them."

"I'll give you ten percent."

"You got a deal, Commander. Plus, I want a promotion."

"Promotion?"

"Yeah, I've had enough of this Private shit. I want to be a Captain. Yeah, that's it. Captain Quizling."

"Okay," Sir Bentley said. "All right, Captain Quizling. It's time to start earning your ten percent. Let's go find ourselves some natives."

54

Gilbert opened his eyes when his bladder had drained and enjoyed the view. Unencumbered by the weight of the engine, the glider stabilized at an altitude of approximately one hundred and fifty feet. Unfortunately, the set of Gurjan trees looming directly ahead topped out closer to two hundred.

"Freakster II calling Freakster I. Come in Freakster I. I said this is Freakster II calling Freakster I. Where the hell are you, Freak?"

"This is Freakster I. Freakster II, state your position."

"Sitting in a fucking hang glider with my dick out and a bicycle seat up my ass, Sir."

"I've lost visual contact."

"Well, just look for the tallest trees you can find and I'll be in one of them."

"Suggest you jettison some more weight to gain altitude. Come in, Freakster II. Freakster II do you read me?"

Gilbert wasn't reading the Admiral of the Air Force at the moment because the walkie-talkie, along with everything else Gilbert could get his hands on, had been ripped free and dropped. Except for the SkyWriters bolted to the frame.

The hang glider slowly climbed as Gilbert leaned back and pulled on the steering mechanism as the Gurjans approached. Gilbert screamed and then recited his mantra.

"Pastries and Boston cream pie, oh my. Pastries and Boston cream pie, oh my."

Freakster II cleared the tops of the Gurjans by inches. Gilbert wasn't as fortunate. As the hang glider flew over the trees and continued its journey, Gilbert caught a limb in the ribs and was ripped from the banana seat. He bounced through the branches and came to rest upside down a hundred and fifty feet above the jungle floor. Gilbert opened his eyes and found himself staring at the cutest baby monkey he had ever seen. The monkey gurgled and held up a paw in his direction as an invitation to play.

Unable to move, Gilbert waved meekly at Baby Monkey hopping up and down on the branch.

"Stop jumping around. You're gonna make me fall," Gilbert said.

It wasn't Baby Monkey that made him fall. It was Momma Monkey who, due to lack of sleep or a severe case of post-partum depression, wasn't ready to accept visitors. Letting loose a howling scream that reverberated across the jungle, Momma Monkey used one arm to snatch her baby and the other to grab Gilbert. She snarled as she held Gilbert suspended in mid-air. After recovering from the initial jolt of intense pain, the first thought that popped into Gilbert's head was the question of whether or not his left thumb could support three hundred pounds.

Eleven seconds later, Gilbert learned that it could not.

Gilbert plummeted towards earth staring up at Momma Monkey's confused expression as she clutched Gilbert's thumb.

Gilbert didn't scream.

Gilbert didn't cry.

Gilbert simply let his mind do its thing as he dropped between the massive branches of the Gurjan.

He flashed back on his first Krispy Kreme he'd devoured perusing Playboy while working the graveyard shift at 7-11, forever establishing an irrevocable link between sweets and sex.

He flashed back on Hilda and their nights of pastries and passion.

He flashed back on the insanity of the past several months where he'd been responsible for managing two-dollar-a-day workers cranking out two-hundred-a-pair Cloudlifters for Sir Bentley Carruthers.

"The sleeker, non-squeaker, sneaker indeed."

Gilbert hit the ground hard, shattering his skull and virtually every bone in his body. One of his final thoughts was of a giant slice of Boston cream pie nestled between Hilda's breasts. Along with a big glass of cold milk to wash it down.

At death's door, Gilbert had no idea which direction he was heading, but he hoped they knew their pastries. And then a comforting thought emerged through his torment.

Angel's Food or Devil's Food?

He could face eternity with either cake.

Gilbert belched softly and closed his eyes.

Drawn by the smell of fresh blood, the wild boars arrived and began their recycling efforts. As the sun rose the next morning, Momma Monkey stared down from her perch high atop the Gurjan and saw no sign of the intruder.

Gilbert was gone.

Momma Monkey grunted and resumed nursing her baby.

55

"Team FUBAR, fall in."

Sir Bentley paced back and forth on the sand as he waited for his troops to line up. Esmeralda burped and shuffled into place. She leaned her head on Piqûre's shoulder, who was also groggy from lack of sleep. Only Buddy had the bounce in his step Sir Bentley wanted. Sir Bentley assumed it was due to the new terms he had negotiated. Only Buddy knew the real reason.

"What time is it?" Esmeralda said. "The sun isn't even up yet."

"I need sleep," Piqûre said. "Why don't we do this later, Bentley?"

"That's Commander. And no, we're going to do it now."

"But I have no sleep last night," Piqûre said, yawning.

"Couldn't get comfortable?" Buddy said. He wore a new pair of bright green Cloudlifters and bounced up and down on his feet.

"No, eet was not that," Piqûre said. "Eet was just that Esmeralda was particularly horny last night."

"Hey, like I told you," Esmeralda said. "Get it right the first time and we won't have this problem."

"All night with the up, down, up, down. Mon dieu. Eet ez more than I can take."

"Poor baby," Gene said. "You're outside doing the horizontal mambo with someone who doesn't know the meaning of the word inhibition, while I'm stuck in a tent with Captain Farts and Rhino-Boy. Jesus, Bentley, you'd think that with all your billions, you could find a doctor who could fix that snoring."

"I don't snore," Bentley said.

"Unbelievable," Gene said, staring at Sir Bentley then turning to face the sleepy couple. "You two must have heard him."

"No, my ears were covered most of ze night."

"I couldn't hear anything over his whining." Esmeralda laughed. "Oh, mon dieu, my pee-pee ez so sore."

"I am not a machine," Piqûre said.

236

"No shit," Esmeralda said. "Note to self. Next time, pack extra batteries."

"People, let's settle down," Sir Bentley said, clapping his hands together rapidly. "We're on a mission here."

"What's the plan, Commander? What's the plan?"

"Good question, Private, er, Captain Quizling. Our plan is to head northeast."

"And?" Gene said.

"And then we'll hit the village. Eventually."

"That's your plan?" Esmeralda said. "Just walk in?"

"Absolutely. If we survive the first few minutes, which I've calculated out to be a seventy percent probability, as soon as they learn who I am, they will at least listen to what I'm offering."

"Exactly what are you offering, Commander Bentley?" Esmeralda said, folding her arms in front of her.

"Access to and participation in a free and democratic capitalistic society," Sir Bentley said, frowning at having to explain the obvious. "The ability for them to keep living as a tribe in their village. With some minor adjustments to their lifestyle of course."

"I'm not doing this," Esmeralda said. "At first, it sounded like a pretty cool idea interacting with some ancient tribe, but now, no way. I'm not going to be a party to whatever it is you're planning."

"You don't know anything about what I'm planning," Sir Bentley said.

"I don't need to. Whatever it is, I'm sure it involves screwing these people out of something. And since you've got so much practice doing that, Bentley, you don't need my help."

"Get back in ranks." Sir Bentley took a step towards her.

"Excuse me?" Esmeralda said, wheeling around to stand nose to nose with the magnate.

"I said get back in ranks," Bentley said. "You will leave only when I say you can leave."

Esmeralda grabbed Sir Bentley's crotch and squeezed. Bentley's eyes began to water and his knees buckled. The only thing keeping him upright was the fulcrum provided by her hand.

"Effective immediately, consider yourself on leave."

Esmeralda smiled and let go. Sir Bentley dropped to his knees in the warm sand, then rolled over onto his back and groaned.

"C'mon you," Esmeralda said, pointing a finger at Piqûre. "I think I remember where I hid a case of tequila."

"Now we go back into ze jungle?"

"We never left the jungle," Esmeralda said, glancing around the foliage to get her bearings. "It's all jungle."

"This ez true."

"We're heading back to the resort. So get your ass in gear. I need a shower. If you're lucky, maybe I'll let you wash my back." She looked at Gene. "How about you Sugar Pops? Feel like coming along?"

Gene considered the idea. He looked at Sir Bentley who stared back with his hands on hips. Gene glanced back at Esmeralda. He nodded.

"I'm in."

"You desert my army, and you'll be hung, Private," Sir Bentley said. "And then fired."

"Really, Esmeralda," Piqûre said. "Ze American?"

"Maybe my friends have come back," Gene said. "And I really could use a shower."

Piqûre brightened at the prospect of a hot shower. "Very well. Au revoir, Buddee. Adieu, Commander Bentley."

"See you back at the resort," Buddy said, winking at Esmeralda.

Esmeralda, Gene, and Piqûre headed back down the path they'd created and disappeared from view. Buddy watched them leave and turned his attention to Bentley, still grimacing in pain.

"You okay there, Commander?"

"That bitch," Bentley said. "Well, there's no way for her to get off the island. I'll deal with them later."

"Don't worry about it. They're no help."

"No, they weren't. I just wish I knew where Doc was and what he's up to."

"Shit, no problem. He's still on your payroll. Plus, he's got what he wants."

"Genevieve," Sir Bentley said.

"Hey, it's her loss, right, Commander?"

"Yeah," Sir Bentley said. "Her loss. Okay, let's do this."

"How far do you think it is?"

"How far can it be? The whole island is only about eight miles wide. And we're at least two miles inland. If we assume that Freak and the Fat Man flew over the village, if we follow their path backward, we just gotta hit it."

"I completely forgot all about those two. I wonder what our Air Force is up to."

"I'm sure they'll make an appearance at some point." Sir Bentley pulled up his socks, hitched up his safari suit pants and adjusted his pith helmet.

"Unless they crash into the ocean."

He nodded at Buddy.

"Team FUBAR, move out."

56

Genevieve followed Bantu into the cave on the outskirts of the village and chattered at the tribesman standing guard. The guard did his best to uphold his end of the conversation, but he couldn't stop staring at Genevieve, wearing a yellow sarong wrapped around her waist. She smiled but didn't miss the spittle on the corner of guard's mouth. She released her ponytail and pulled her jet-black trails forward to cover her breasts. Bantu sensed her discomfort and excused the guard who reluctantly departed and made his way back to the village.

"This is it, huh?"

Genevieve peered around the circular cave through semi-darkness.

"Yes. Stay there for a moment."

Bantu lit and placed several more torches around the cave.

The cave, now bathed in light, revealed dozens of woven baskets and a wide variety of plants suspended from by what appeared to be spaghetti-thin strips of leather.

Bantu watched Genevieve's eyes dart back and forth as she studied the massive room and waited for her first question.

"It's chilly in here."

"Yes, I noticed."

Genevieve laughed and relaxed.

"Okay, what have we got here?"

"The plants you see hanging upside down are being dried. Later, they will be crushed and mixed in different combinations."

"Some of them look familiar, but there are dozens I can't identify," Genevieve said. "And I do this for a living."

"During my travels, I would always try to find these plants. I didn't find many, but then I did spend a lot of times in cities. Not much grows in concrete and metal."

Genevieve nodded and moved towards a row of baskets.

"May I?"

"Yes," Bantu said. "I don't know what is in them until I see."

"There aren't any labels." Genevieve glanced up and down the rows of baskets.

"My tribe has no written language."

Bantu pointed to his head.

"Everything is kept here. And only a few people know how the remedies are made and how they're used."

"You and your father?"

"Yes. And a few of other elders," Bantu said. "Soon we will have to decide which of the youngest will become the next knowledge keeper."

"It's passed on once a generation?"

"Yes."

"Interesting."

Genevieve removed the lid on a nearby basket. She peered inside and jumped backward as a cobra casually poked its head over the top of the basket.

"Merde."

"I'm so sorry."

Bantu flicked at the cobra's head with a stick until it retreated inside the basket. He replaced the lid and carried it to the entrance of the cave.

"Tuber continues to break the rules. He's fascinated with snakes and always tries to make one a pet. As many times as he's been bitten, one would think he would have learned by now."

"One would think," Genevieve said, lifting the lid to another basket. She cautiously peered inside.

"This is GunGunGa," Bantu said, running his hand through the herbal mixture. "For stomach problems. What's the Outsider word for sores inside the stomach?"

"Ulcers?"

"Yes, that's it. Ulcers. GunGunGa cures them."

"You mean, takes the pain away?" Genevieve smelled the mixture.

"No, it cures them."

Genevieve frowned at Bantu, skeptical.

"How is that possible, Bantu?"

"My father says it is a gift from the Gods. He always says that everything we need has been put here for us but, sometimes, it's just

241

not obvious, and we have to work hard to figure things out. Trial and error is, I believe, the term you Outsiders use."

"And you've figured everything out?"

"Oh, my no." Bantu laughed. "What would be the point of life if we ever figured everything out? But over many, many years, we have, what's the word? We have unraveled many of life's mysteries."

Genevieve put the lid back on the second basket and moved to the next.

"WooNoo," Bantu said. "It is for men who want to have…"

"For men who want to have what?" Genevieve said, examining the white powder.

Bantu stammered, then shrugged his shoulders and tapped on the side of the stone wall. He pointed towards his groin, then tapped the wall again.

Genevieve nodded in comprehension. "I see." She laughed and extended her index finger at a ninety-degree angle.

"The gift that keeps on giving?"

"Yes," Bantu said, still flushed with embarrassment. "My father developed it many years ago. He says it was the one creation that cemented his role as leader of the tribe."

"He would have gotten my vote," Genevieve said. "Does it work?"

"Booga-wooga-nooga."

Genevieve laughed.

"Please, go ahead and take some." Bantu offered her a small container.

"Really? Are you sure?"

"Yes, please do. I'm quite sure both you and Doc will be most satisfied."

Genevieve considered the idea then put a small amount in the container. She thought some more and filled it.

"Not that anyone would ever need it with you around," Bantu whispered.

"What's that?"

"Oh, nothing."

57

By the way, how do those feel?"

"What? Oh, the Cloudlifters. They're fine. But at two hundred a pair, they should give me a goddamn pedicure."

"It's paying for those damn endorsement contracts that drives the price up," Sir Bentley said, peering through yet another thicket of palms. "Amazing thing the free market. Create enough demand and people will pay anything to get their hands on it."

"How much demand do you think we'll generate on this plant stuff?"

"Are you kidding? If we find only one thing that even remotely impacts health, we're gonna make a killing. I plan on marketing it by playing up the longevity angle."

"Longevity, yeah," Buddy said. "That's something everybody needs."

"I've already worked up a couple of slogans. Want to hear them?"

"Do I have a choice?"

"Live longer and stronger before reaching the Wild Blue Yonder."

Buddy blanched.

"That sucks, Bentley. Even by your standards."

"Yeah, it sounds a bit forced. I was afraid of that."

Sir Bentley wiped his brow with his sleeve.

"How about this one? Longevity: Finally, Something to Live For."

"That's not bad. Who are you planning on signing up to endorse it? I'd probably go with an old-timer the boomers are comfortable with. You know, someone who's been under the knife but doesn't look like a shrink wrapped fossil."

"No, I'm done with celebrity product endorsers," Sir Bentley said. "All they do is screw up my margins. I'm going a completely different route on this one."

"Stock actors working for scale?"

"No, I'm gonna use one of the jungle bunnies from this tribe. Photograph him in his natural setting doing a bunch of native crap, do an infomercial that tells everyone he's a hundred and twelve years old and that the secret to his longevity is good ole Whatever I Call It, and watch them climb over each other trying to buy the shit at WalMart and Target."

Buddy laughed.

"Commander Bentley, you are one for the ages."

"Nobody just gives you a billion dollars, Captain Quizling. One has to earn it."

"Oh, I'll earn it, Commander," Buddy said. "You don't have to worry about that."

"Shhh," Sir Bentley said, holding up a hand. "There's that flute music again."

"It's nice."

Sir Bentley gasped in an excited whisper.

"There, over there. Shhh. Wow. A man and a woman. Holy shit. There really is a tribe out here."

"They're naked," Sir Bentley said. "What is that? What's he doing?"

"What?" Buddy locked his binoculars on the man. "He's eating something. It's a white powder of some sort." Buddy looked at Sir Bentley. "Jungle coke?"

"Doubtful. Coca won't grow in this climate." Sir Bentley swatted a multi-colored bug inching its way up his arm and grabbed his binoculars. "Wow. Jungle-dwelling certainly agrees with her.

"She looks pretty good." Buddy refocused on the man. "Sweet Jesus."

"What?"

"Him," Buddy said, adjusting focus. "Talk about instant wood."

"Impressive," Sir Bentley said, nodding his head. "Let's just hope it's the white powder and not the flute music that popped that puppy."

"Jesus. What a breakthrough. Instant-acting, natural Viagra. Corked bat straight from the jungle. What would that be worth?"

"Incalculable." Sir Bentley said. "Especially if I combine it with the longevity remedy. Can you imagine the power of that marketing campaign?"

"Live long and strong with a massive schl-."

"I got it," Sir Bentley said as he considered the idea.

"Catchy. But a bit graphic for the networks."

"Screw the networks," Buddy said. "We can go straight to the internet once we whack a patent on it. Word of mouth alone will sell this one. Jesus, we could promote it like a one-a-day multivitamin."

"What's a day without wood?" Sir Bentley pointed a finger at Buddy to punctuate his point.

"This is gonna be huge."

"Talk about huge," Sir Bentley said, peering back through his binoculars. "Look at the size of that thing."

"Yeah, I know, but she seems more interested in her flute than his." Buddy whistled softly.

"No, wait. I take that back."

"Wow," Sir Bentley said. "I didn't see that coming. Look at her go."

"So what do we do?"

"We follow them back to their village."

"Makes sense." Buddy sat down on the grass without breaking eye contact with his subjects.

"What are you doing?" Sir Bentley said.

"Getting comfortable. It looks like we might be here awhile."

"I gotta get some of that."

"What? Her or the boner medicine?"

"Why both, of course."

Buddy laughed and shook his head.

"Silly me. For a moment, I forgot who I was talking to."

58

Freak was now well and truly pissed off. He scanned the skies and surveyed the jungle floor. Having lost contact with Gilbert two hours earlier, Freak had traversed the area at different altitudes for signs of both his assistant as well as the members of Team FUBAR. The wind had dropped the past hour, and he was losing altitude. The tops of the massive trees that delineated the jungle canopy were drawing nearer with each loop and Freak was faced with the choice of landing or jettisoning his SkyWriters.

Another set of trees approached, and Freak panicked and lifted his legs as the wheels of his glider barely cleared the treetops. He looked down and came eye to eye with a massive monkey growling and baring its teeth at him at he drifted past. Freak spat at the monkey and laughed and then spotted something in the distance.

Gilbert's hang glider had come to rest on the top of a massive cliff that towered above the northeast corner of the island. Freak commenced his descent with a series of increasingly smaller circles until he felt the wheels of his aircraft touch ground, bounce, and return to solid ground. Freak grunted with satisfaction at his landing skills until he noticed that he was quickly running out of landing strip. He applied the brakes; which, given the low-tech nature of his operation, meant dragging both feet and, eventually, his knees along the rocky ground. The glider came to a reluctant stop near the edge of the cliff and Freak peered over the edge. Several hundred feet below, he watched the violent surf pound rocks and sand.

"Damn. That was close." Freak fought vertigo and carefully maneuvered himself backward off the lawnmower seat. He sat down and examined his bleeding knees and feet. Satisfied that he hadn't sustained severe injury, he rolled the glider back from the precipice. He crawled back to the edge of the cliff and surveyed the panoramic view through his binoculars. Freak marveled at the beauty of the ocean and the jagged cliffs that dominated this side of the island. Off to his right, he caught a glimpse of the distant resort and the airstrip where Bentley's Gulfstream sat ready for action.

"I'd love to get behind the wheel of that, baby," Freak said, admiring the sleek aircraft. "I could do some major damage with that one. Show these morons what's what."

Freak looked down through the binoculars and the magnified beach and surf rushed up to greet him. Another wave of vertigo hit and Freak rolled over on his back and struggled to catch his breath. He waited several moments and let the breeze roll over him until his stomach stopped roiling. He then stood and approached Gilbert's aircraft. The glider was undamaged apart from the banana seat that was completely bent and twisted from Gilbert's massive girth. Strands of duct tape remained from where the engine and communication system had previously been secured, but the SkyWriters still glistened in the afternoon sun.

Freak whistled and waited for a response. Hearing nothing in return except for a few quizzical squawks from some nearby parrots, Freak conducted a brief search of the immediate area. He returned to the aircraft, scanned the area one final time and placed both hands on his hips and shook his head in disgust.

"Hey. Assistant to the Admiral. I hope you realize deserters get shot for treason."

Freak removed the two SkyWriters from Gilbert's glider and, again, marveled at their light weight. He studied the flanged wings protruding from the back of each missile and then stared at the two SkyWriters already duct taped to his glider. Unable to come up with an alternative, Freak attached the new pair facing backward. He rolled his glider, now equipped with double the firepower, away from the edge of the cliff. He pushed the glider over the edge and screamed as the craft plummeted. He caught his breath as the glider eventually caught the wind and soared upwards. He maneuvered his way back onto the lawnmower seat, tightened his goggles, and turned away from the ocean back towards the village.

59

Man, I thought they'd never finish," Buddy said, following Bentley through the foliage.

"I think they stopped because they wore themselves out," Sir Bentley said, carefully stepping his way around a plant with razor-sharp needles.

"They certainly aren't setting much of a pace heading home," Buddy said, nodding at the slow moving couple about a hundred yards ahead. "Man, can you believe that guy's staying power? I think we've hit the motherlode with that powder."

"And that's just one. Who knows what else they got in their bag of tricks."

"We just have to find out where they keep it all," Buddy said.

"That's your job."

"My job? Why the hell is that my job?"

"Because while you're finding out where they keep everything and who their Medicine Man is, I'm going to be buying us time by having a little chat with their leader. Maybe he'll just roll over, and we can just help ourselves to what we want."

"What about this guy, Doc?"

"I'm not worried about Doc. But if he decides to do something stupid, there's always this."

Sir Bentley pulled a nine-millimeter from the jacket of his safari suit.

"Uh, Commander, I hate to say this, but I think this jungle heat is starting to affect you," Buddy said, following Sir Bentley's tentative steps across a small stream. "If this guy Doc has half the background you've talked about, he's gotta be dangerous."

"The guy's a total burnout," Sir Bentley said, coming to a stop. "All you have to do is look at the quality of people he's surrounded himself with. His crazy brother in law who, by the way, is now working for us. His drunken slut of a girlfriend who left my mission to go off with that goofy Frenchman. Please, Captain Quizling, don't insult my intelligence. Doc is no threat to the outcome of this mission."

"I'm just saying that you should probably be careful around him."

"Nobody messes with my possessions." Sir Bentley stared at Buddy, his eyes wide with anger. "Nobody. Got it?"

"Loud and clear, Commander."

"Well, I'll be," Sir Bentley said, standing upright and tilting his pith helmet back on his head. "The village has been here the whole time."

"Wow, look at that," Buddy said staring at the scene playing out before his eyes. "We must have walked around the outside half a dozen times."

"As of right now, that's ancient history." Sir Bentley stared down at the huts. "This place is in serious need of a makeover." Sir Bentley laughed and punched Buddy on the shoulder. "This is going to be a piece of cake."

**

"Well, will you look at who finally showed up," Doc said to Bob from their position in a Gurjan tree about sixty feet above the ground. "If they had circled the village one more time, I was gonna go out and drag them in myself."

Bob Garbo nodded silently without removing his eye from the rifle scope.

"I guess you've got Sir Bentley right between the eyes," Doc said, peering through his binoculars.

Bob nodded again and pulled the rifle stock tighter to his chest.

"I should just let you shoot both of them right now."

"Yup."

"Nah, we better let him in. Set up a chat with Chief and see if he tips his hand."

Bob Garbo shrugged his shoulders then quickly disassembled the rifle and returned it to its case. He then followed Doc down the tree.

**

"Look," Sir Bentley said, pointing at the sarong-clad woman strolling away from the main village carrying a notebook. "It's Genevieve. You better follow her and see what she's up to."

"So I'm the one who has to follow her around?" Buddy laughed as he stared at the trail of jet black hair trailing down her back. "Oh, no, Commander. Not the briar patch."

"Just get going and try not to let anybody see you," Sir Bentley said.

"What do I do if I get in trouble or need to get in touch with you?"

Sir Bentley frowned and stroked the wispy stubble on his chin.

"Good point. We probably should have some form of signal. The floor is open for suggestions, Captain Quizling."

"We've got a flare gun here somewhere don't we?"

Buddy rummaged through his pack.

"As a matter of fact, we do. How many flares do we have?"

"Four," Buddy said.

"Okay." Sir Bentley tipped his pith helmet back and began pacing. "Let's see. One flare means that you've found either the Medicine Man or where they store all the medicines."

"One flare, one discovery. Got it."

"A second flare means that you've discovered both."

"Two flares. Medicine Man plus the stash. Got it."

"A third flare means you're ready to commence with the rendezvous phase of Operation FUBAR."

"Rendezvous phase?"

"Yeah, we hightail it out of this shithole and meet back at the Gulfstream."

"Third flare. Exit shithole. Got it."

Buddy started off in the general direction of Esmeralda and then stopped. "What do I do with her?"

"Who? Genevieve?"

"Yeah."

"If she gets in the way, you have my permission to shoot her."

"That's a bit harsh don't you think?"

"She's had her chance. Not only has she proven herself unworthy, but she's also been unfaithful."

"Maybe I can talk some sense into her," Buddy said, his mind fixated on the combination of Genevieve and the white powder. He

250

shuddered with anticipation and repacked the flare gun. "Just leave everything to me, Commander."

Sir Bentley watched Buddy as he began to work his way through the plant life towards the back of the village. Now completely alone in the jungle for the first time, Sir Bentley looked around in the hope of finding solace and comfort amid the hostile environment. He found it in the form of an expertly crafted piece of metal, complete with a fifteen round clip, safely tucked inside the jacket of his canary yellow safari suit.

60

"Well, if it isn't Sir Bentley Carruthers."

"Yaaaah!"

Bentley jumped and hit his head on a low-hanging branch of the Gurjan tree he was hiding behind on the edge of the village.

"Ow. Damn it."

Bentley removed his dented pith helmet and rubbed his head. He punched the hat back into shape, pulled it back on and glared at the intruder.

"You scared the shit out of me."

Doc grinned and extended his hand.

"We've been waiting for you. What the hell took you so long?"

"I've been busy," Sir Bentley said. "What the hell are the two of you up to?"

"Who? Genevieve? I'm sure she's around somewhere."

"Don't bullshit me, Doc. I saw the two of you on camera."

Doc nodded and shrugged his shoulders.

"That was just a one-time thing. You know how it is, Bentley. Two people, alone in the jungle."

"Hmmm, I'm sure," Sir Bentley said. "Do you have any progress to report or have you gone completely native?"

"Well, I haven't been able to do too much. Still trying to build rapport, you know how that works. But I have set up a meeting with Chief."

"Chief, huh? Interesting," Sir Bentley said. "Well done there, Doc."

"My pleasure, sir. It's the least I can do," Doc said.

"Hmmm. Well then, let's do the meeting."

"I'm surprised to see you traveling by yourself, sir. I mean, what with the jungle being the dangerous place that it is."

"This place?" Sir Bentley snorted. "This is nothing."

"Of course," Doc said. "Look out there, sir. Snake."

Sir Bentley screamed and jumped backward. Doc laughed and winked at him.

"Prick." Sir Bentley picked himself up and straightened his safari jacket. "You're funny for a total burn-out."

"We should be going, sir. We don't want to keep Chief waiting."

"What's this guy like?" Sir Bentley said as he followed Doc toward the Chief's hut.

"He's a warrior."

"Really? Takes one to know one, huh? Well, why don't you let me be the judge of that?"

"Absolutely." Doc paused at the doorway of the hut and extended his arm. "After you."

Sir Bentley stepped inside the hut and glanced around at his surroundings. Surprised by the elegant simplicity of the furnishings, he sat down at the head of the table and removed his pith helmet. He turned his head towards the doorway upon hearing the angry chatter and watched as two men approached. The older of the two glared at him.

"You're in his seat," Doc said.

"Oh, so we're going to play that game, huh?"

Sir Bentley glanced at both tribesmen and slumped into the other chair.

"You really should be standing," Doc said.

"Oh, of course," Sir Bentley said, effortlessly transitioning into smarmy. "After all, one needs to be culturally sensitive." He stood up and extended his hand towards Chief. "I'm Sir Bentley Carruthers. It is my deepest honor to meet you, sir."

Chief's eyes narrowed as he continued to glare at Sir Bentley and wait for the translation. Eventually, Sir Bentley withdrew his hand.

Sir Bentley turned towards Doc and whispered, "How on earth am I supposed to communicate with this guy?"

Doc waved him off and smiled and bowed. Chief returned the greeting and sat down at the head of the table.

"I will be translating," Bantu said, sitting down to the right of his father and directly across the table from Sir Bentley.

"And who are you?" Sir Bentley wiped his brow with the sleeve of his safari suit. "Your weather is interminable."

"I'm Bantu. And this is my father."

"I see," Sir Bentley said. "You're English is impeccable. I guess you didn't learn that here."

"No."

Sir Bentley waited for a moment for Bantu to expound, then shrugged his shoulders and continued.

"Two years ago," Sir Bentley said, then paused and looked at Bantu unsure of how fast he should speak.

Bantu chattered at his father who nodded impatiently and gestured for Sir Bentley to get on with it.

"Okay, I get it. No need to get snippy. Two years ago, after the tsunami devastated many of the islands in this region, I was asked by the Indian government to assist in the recovery efforts."

Bantu chattered in his father's direction without taking his eyes off Sir Bentley.

"Play it straight, Bentley," Doc said. "He's got an incredible bullshit detector."

"They did ask me," Sir Bentley said.

"They asked you to make a contribution to the recovery effort," Doc said. "You came up with the idea to buy and develop the islands."

"A minor detail, and certainly not particularly relevant to this discussion," Sir Bentley whispered.

"Okay," Doc said, stretching back in his chair. "You've been warned."

Sir Bentley frowned at Doc and then turned the charm back on as he spoke to Chief.

"When I purchased this island," Sir Bentley said. "I had no idea that anyone lived here. I thought I was merely buying a few deserted islands that might be a good place for me to locate a few of my businesses in an attempt to bring some much needed economic development to this impoverished area."

Chief grunted as he listened to Bantu and repeated the get-on-with-it gesture.

"In my world, I am an important man," Sir Bentley said.

Chief nodded and waited.

"I have a variety of different businesses. Here on this island, I have a sneaker factory," Sir Bentley paused and spoke directly to Bantu. "Does your tribe even have a word for sneaker?"

254

"I'll figure something out," Bantu said.

"Athletic footwear." Sir Bentley lifted his foot in the air and pointed at his Cloudlifter. "It's the-"

"The sleeker, non-squeaker sneaker. Yes, we've got that," Bantu said.

"I'm impressed. You've heard the marketing campaign," Sir Bentley said.

Bantu held up the scarred hands from his sewing accident. Chief looked at the hand and growled at Sir Bentley.

"What the hell is that all about?" Sir Bentley said, turning towards Doc.

"Bantu is one of your former employees," Doc said. "At least he had an accident and was cut loose with no medical care."

Sir Bentley's face turned red as he stared at Bantu's hand.

"Well, finding adequate medical care in such a remote part of the world can be problematic. I'm sure you can understand that."

Bantu calmly translated for his father who glared at Sir Bentley and slapped the table.

"Bullshit!"

"He speaks English?"

"Just enough."

"Certainly, that was just some administrative error. My factory manager is around here somewhere, and I will be speaking with him about this matter. I will get to the bottom of this."

Chief didn't bother waiting for the translation. He sniffed the air, made a face, and laughed loudly. Doc and Bantu joined in.

"Moving on," Sir Bentley said. "In addition to my factory, you may have also noticed that I have built a magnificent beachfront resort."

Chief emitted a guttural growl.

"Please, don't use that word," Bantu said.

"What word? Resort?"

Chief growled louder and bared his teeth at Sir Bentley.

"It upsets my father very much."

"So I see. Okay, how about hotel?"

Bantu nodded and chattered briefly with his father. Bantu grinned but remained silent.

"What did he say?" Sir Bentley said.

"It is nothing," Bantu said, winking at Doc.

255

"If we're going to do business together, we need to be honest and open with each other. Tell me what he said."

"My father said, in that yellow suit, you look like a cross between a parrot and a monkey."

"Do I now?" Sir Bentley glared at Chief. "Then tell your father that means a lot coming from a fucking jungle- Ow." Sir Bentley winced from the pressure Doc had applied around his wrist. Doc glared at him and shook his head.

Chief waved his hand and stomped a foot on the floor.

"Jesus. Is this guy all business or what?" Sir Bentley said, rubbing his wrist. "You can imagine my surprise when I learned that your tribe lived on one of my islands."

Sir Bentley waited for the translation and then continued.

"I thought to myself, Sir Bentley, this is wonderful. What better way to promote cultural awareness and positive relations among different groups of people than by the mutual exchange of cultural ideas and viable economic opportunities."

"Jesus, Bentley," Doc said. "Take it easy."

Sir Bentley held up a hand to silence Doc and beamed at Chief while waiting for Bantu to finish translating. Chief listened intently without taking his eyes off Sir Bentley and gestured for him to continue.

"I said to myself, Bentley, you can provide hundreds of employment opportunities to these people. In fact, over the past couple of days, due to a series of unfortunate events I'm sure you played a major role in, I've had several positions open up at both my factory and hotel."

"You're unbelievable," Doc whispered.

"Pay attention," Sir Bentley whispered in return. "You might just learn something about how the global economy works."

"That's what we're afraid of," Bantu said. "But I'm afraid we've already learned more than enough."

Bantu chattered with his father who nodded his head vigorously.

"Booga-wooga-nooga."

"What does that mean?" Sir Bentley leaned forward in his chair.

"Loosely translated, it means you bet your sweet ass," Bantu said.

"Booga-wooga-nooga. That's a good one. Mind if I use that one?"

Sir Bentley chuckled and placed his hand on Chief's shoulder. Chief immediately tried to take off one of Bentley's fingers with one bite. Sir Bentley snatched his hand back and stared at Chief who now had a permanent snarl etched on his face.

"This guy is in serious need of some western civilization."

Bantu translated the last comment before Sir Bentley could stop him. Chief listened and then, to the surprise of the others around the table, a huge smile appeared on his face. He softly chattered with Bantu, who giggled and looked at Sir Bentley.

"My father says it would be strange taking advice about civilization from a man who walks around with his manhood on display. Especially one with so little to show for himself."

Sir Bentley glanced down at his lap. Since the flash flood, he'd being trekking through the jungle commando, and he noticed that not only was his fly open, his little turtle was attempting to poke its head through the opening. He quickly zipped up and sat back in his chair embarrassed.

"Oooh," Chief said. "Him big man." He then laughed.

"Maybe you'd like to compare bank accounts." Sir Bentley said, over the laughter. "If we could please get on with our meeting." Sir Bentley picked at what remained of his manicure and waited impatiently for the final snorts of laughter to subside.

Chief looked at Sir Bentley and chattered. Bantu listened and translated.

"My father would like to know what it is that you want from us in exchange for the privilege of being your slaves."

"Hey, my wages are competitive within the industry," Sir Bentley said. "Need I remind you that I'm the highest paying employer on this island? And with the high-end clientele, I'm sure the staff rakes in a ton on tips."

Bantu translated for his father who listened but, without any point of reference for servers, wages or tips, merely shrugged his shoulders.

Sir Bentley turned to Doc.

"Can you please do something here? What am I paying you for?"

"Well, Bentley, originally you said you wanted me to quell a factory uprising. Then it transitioned into a surveillance job. At this particular point, I'm not exactly sure what you expect me to do. Apart from stop sleeping with Genevieve."

"You said you had already stopped." Sir Bentley jabbed a finger in Doc's direction. "You lied to me." He pointed at Chief while continuing to glare at Doc. "I expect you to convince this guy that voluntarily doing business with me is in his tribe's best interest."

"And I would do that because?" Doc said, getting up from his chair.

"Because I told you too. How's that for a start?"

"Not good enough," Doc said.

Chief grunted and stood up. He chattered at Bantu and headed towards the doorway of the hut.

"My father says the meeting is over for now. He's going fishing."

"Just like that?" Sir Bentley said. "It must be nice to be able to just drop everything and go fishing."

Chief paused and waited for the translation. He chattered briefly with Bantu.

"My father says, yes, it is."

Chief wheeled on one foot and walked briskly towards the doorway. He looked back over his shoulder.

"Asshole."

61

Buddy peered over the top of the large rock he was hiding behind near the entrance to the cave. He watched Genevieve as she meticulously examined the contents of dozens of containers that sat on wooden shelves extending the length of one wall. He slid down behind the rock as he heard footsteps. One of the natives walked past him and entered the cave. Buddy peered over the rock and watched in disbelief as Genevieve and the native began conversing in English.

"I can't believe you work for that man," Bantu said.

"I take it the meeting didn't go well," Genevieve said, extinguishing her cigarette.

"It's quite amazing that one person could possess every quality I dislike about the outside world."

"That's our Bentley," Genevieve said. "Your father was not impressed?"

"My father was not," Bantu said. "He left the meeting to go fishing."

Genevieve laughed. Buddy watched her breasts softly bounce as her laughter echoed through the cave.

"Doc say not to worry, but I'm not sure," Bantu said. "Sir Bentley is a very powerful man who could bring many forces into play."

"You just need to trust, Doc," Genevieve said. "He's very good at what he does."

"And what exactly is it that he does?" Bantu said.

"Doc makes things happen," Genevieve said.

"My father says he is a warrior."

"Yes. He has been a warrior for many years."

"My father says he can trust Doc because he sees truth in his eyes."

"Doc might not agree since he's constantly searching for the truth himself."

259

Bantu nodded.

"But my father is correct? Doc can be trusted."

"Yes. I'm not sure what is going to happen, but Doc is a man of his word."

"That's all I needed to hear." Bantu led Genevieve towards the wall of containers. "Earlier I was showing you the different remedies we've developed to fight off the aging process. Should we continue with those?"

"Yes, let's do that," she said, opening her notebook.

"Jackpot," Buddy said.

**

"Smell me."

Summerman stared at Merlin, who was sitting next to him on the edge of the lake that stretched behind the village. Both of them were holding bamboo fishing poles and running out of patience.

"Are you out of your mind?" Summerman said. "You're the world's biggest germophobe. I can't believe you wouldn't even ask me that question. We've been in the jungle for days."

"I've been conducting an experiment." Merlin offered an armpit to Summerman. "No, I'm serious. Smell me."

"Get away from me."

"C'mon. Don't be such a baby." Merlin handed his fishing pole to Bob Garbo, who was sitting on the other side of him. "Smell me."

Summerman shook his head in disgust but leaned over and took a quick whiff of his friend.

"I don't smell anything," Summerman said, refocusing on the coconut attached to his fishing line that was serving as a bobber about twenty feet offshore.

"Exactly," Merlin said, taking a deep sniff. "What are the odds of that? I've been out here in this heat and humidity, climbing around and over who knows what, and here I sit, fresh as a daisy."

"That is odd," Summerman said, operating the makeshift reel to check if the bait was still inside the bamboo trap attached to the end of the line. "These traps are incredible."

"I'll believe that as soon as I catch something," Merlin said. "But isn't that amazing? I don't smell."

"And to what do you attribute this breakthrough of personal hygiene?" Summerman tossed the trap back into the water and sat back down next to Merlin on the bank.

"Bantu," Merlin said. "Who else? He showed me a bunch of herbs they use for cleaning things around the village, and I just started experimenting. It's amazing. And probably worth a fortune."

"Jesus, not you too. Isn't one invading carpetbagger enough?"

Bob Garbo stood up and silently reeled in his line. Another large fish, his sixth since they sat down two hours ago, flopped inside the bamboo trap.

"Another one? How are you doing that?"

Merlin stared in disbelief at the large fish flopping on the bank near his feet.

"Skill."

Bob Garbo reloaded the trap with fresh bait; a mixture of wild boar entrails and rotten fruit.

Chief approached the bank carrying his fishing pole and a coconut shell filled with bait. He glanced at the collection of fish next to Bob and grunted in approval as he loaded the trap with bait, gently tossed it into the water and sat down next to Summerman.

"How was your meeting with Sir Bentley?" Summerman said.

"He doesn't speak English," Merlin said. "How many times do I have to remind you?"

"Just watch." Summerman put together a strange combination of gestures and hand signals. "How was your meeting?"

Chief watched and listened and nodded his head. He sneered as he looked out over the lake.

"Asshole."

Summerman smiled coyly at Merlin and Bob Garbo.

"Don't try to tell me I don't speak Whatsittooya."

"Great. I don't smell. And you're speaking in native tongue. I think it's about time we decided to hit the road."

"Yup," Bob Garbo said.

"What's the matter, Great Silent One? You don't think we belong here?" Merlin said.

"Nope."

"And I suppose you do?"

"Nope."

"Who then? Not Sir Bentley."

Bob Garbo scoffed and refocused on his coconut bobber.

"Then who, if anybody, should be here to help these people?" Summerman said.

"Doc. Genevieve." Bob expertly reeled in another fish.

Chief grunted at the size of Bob's fish. He soon landed his own, removed it from the trap and tossed it onto the bank.

"Nice fish, Chief," Summerman said.

"Booga-wooga-nooga."

62

Waking up from his nap, Doc heard the approaching footsteps and opened his eyes. Standing in the doorway, his pith helmet angled off the side of his head, Sir Bentley glanced around the interior of the hut and nodded approvingly.

"I have to give these people credit. This is very functional."

Sir Bentley stepped inside and sat down on a chair near the bed, then continued to scan his surroundings.

"Of course, electricity and a sewer system would be a major improvement."

"They seem to be doing just fine with what they have."

Doc propped himself up in bed and folded his hands behind his head.

"Ah, yes," Sir Bentley said, examining a small wooden carving sitting on a nearby table. "The curse of the contented. That all too familiar disease. It's the biggest threat to Western civilization."

Doc gave Sir Bentley a small smile.

"Contentment. Yes, that's what it is. I've been trying to put my finger on it."

"I guess you've been too busy putting your fingers in other places," Sir Bentley said, scratching his bug-bitten arms.

"What do you want from these people, Bentley?"

"I just want what's mine."

"Bentley, a simple transfer of land ownership doesn't automatically mean you own this place."

"I beg to differ, my friend." Sir Bentley aimlessly wandered the perimeter of the hut. "You've spent your entire career trying to prove my point. Well, at least reinforce my point." Sir Bentley chuckled as he examined one of the wooden chairs. "You of all people should understand what's in play here."

"I understand what's in play. I'm just not sure I agree with it."

"As a member of my payroll, it doesn't matter. I don't give a shit what you think."

263

Doc nodded his head and glanced outside the approaching storm clouds. "How much money and power does one person need?"

"How long is a piece of string?" Sir Bentley said.

Doc chuckled and rubbed his three-day growth.

"I'm sitting on a potential goldmine here, Doc. And I'm happy to share a piece of that with you. It would be worth millions."

"I already have millions."

"No doubt ill-gotten contraband from some of your previous assignments. Perhaps you would feel differently about money if you actually worked for it."

"I spent twenty years doing the government's bidding, Bentley. Trust me, I earned every penny. Maybe you find comfort in money, but the only thing it's done for me is give me more time to think about what's bugging me."

"Ah yes, the Western Buddhist's dilemma. Constantly striving to find meaning and purpose in the incomprehensible amid the tragic suffering of the unenlightened. Thoughts to ponder while sipping your mocha-chino latte from the comfort of your Mercedes while stuck in gridlock."

"So how do you deal with all of it, Bentley?"

"What? Life? I don't give it the time of day. Self-awareness is highly overrated."

"You're a real piece of work, Bentley."

"There's not much to understand. I work. I eat. I fuck. I make money. And then I move on to the next deal."

"And that's it?"

"That's it. The same as everyone else. I just do them better than everyone else."

"So it's just a question of how zeros, right?"

Sir Bentley considered the question and then nodded in agreement. "Yeah, that's pretty much it when you boil it all down. How many trailing zeros you have."

"And this is the next deal," Doc said.

"Yes. And it looks like it could be the deal."

"You think the Indian government is going to let you get away with plundering this place."

Sir Bentley snorted.

"They don't even know this island is inhabited. There is no record of this tribe. Can you believe that? Centuries have come and gone, and these people have completely slipped under the radar. How is that even possible?"

"And if the Indian government finds out?"

"I've already taken care of that. Fortunately, the greed and corruption of politicians transcend culture." Sir Bentley shrugged his shoulders. "Let's just say that I have a few things up my sleeve should I ever be forced to use them."

"So, you're moving into the drug industry," Doc said.

"Yes, sneakers are so pedestrian, even at two hundred a pair. Mind you, the margins are nothing to sneeze at."

"Plus you've got about eighty million people in the U.S. alone that are getting old."

"Exactly. And by some strange generational quirk, most of them either think they're either destined to live forever or desperately want to. I have no idea, yet, what this tribe eats or drinks but as soon as I heard Chief was in his eighties, I knew I'd hit the motherlode."

"He's an amazing guy."

"For a savage, yeah. I'll give you that."

A whooshing sound filled the air and then disappeared.

"That sounded like a flare," Doc said.

"A flare you say? I'm afraid I'm not familiar with that sound."

A second whoosh rose up and over the hut.

"What the hell is going on?"

"Probably just the wind." Sir Bentley sat down. "So what's it going to be, Doc? Are you in or out?"

"I'm afraid I'm out, Bentley. And I'm also afraid that I might have to intervene on their behalf."

Doc got off the bed and walked to the doorway. He peered up at the sky and checked the top of the trees that were gently swaying in the breeze. "I know those were flares."

Doc grimaced as the dart pierced the middle of his back. He turned towards Bentley, his knees buckling.

"You shouldn't have done…"

"I'm sorry you feel that way, Doc. I had such plans for you."

Sir Bentley removed the blowgun from his lips and stared at it lovingly. "The sharper, smarter, jungle-darter," he said, laughing.

He knelt to check the unconscious Doc for concealed weapons and then heard the sound of the third flare. Sir Bentley Carruthers checked his watch and smiled.

"Exit shithole. Well done, Buddy. Right on schedule."

Sir Bentley walked through the doorway and stealthily maneuvered unseen through the village and headed off in search of the newly trampled trail that led back to the resort.

63

Buddy listened in amazement near the entrance as Bantu provided detailed explanations of how dozens of plants were used, either by themselves or in combination with others, to prevent or cure ailments that impacted virtually every body part. Buddy also ogled Genevieve as she took copious notes and asked an endless stream of questions. He only understood a fraction of the science being discussed, but one thing he fully comprehended was that the tribe was sitting on a pharmaceutical goldmine.

Buddy grabbed the flare gun and then crept outside the cave and fired. Bantu and Genevieve both heard the sound and looked at each other.

"What was that?"

Genevieve walked to the cave entrance and peered out. Bantu followed and looked up at the sky.

"I don't know. Maybe the wind?"

"Could be," Genevieve said. "But just to be careful, maybe it's time we headed back to the village."

"Maybe not."

Buddy stepped into view holding the flare gun in one hand and a nine-millimeter pistol in the other.

"You," Genevieve said. "Where's Bentley?"

"He's over at the village taking care of Chief and your consort, Doc."

"My father? Is he okay?"

Bantu began to trot towards the huts. Buddy pointed the pistol at Bantu and motioned him to stay put. He kept the gun on them as he fired a second flare into the sky.

"I'm afraid you won't be heading back to the village." Buddy stared at Genevieve and smiled.

She draped her hair forward in front of her chest and gently touched Bantu on the arm.

"I'm sure both your father and Doc are fine. Just don't do anything silly. Who knows what this moron is capable of."

"Moron?" Buddy said. "Who's the one holding the gun? Okay, back in the cave."

He waved the pistol menacingly and followed them into the coolness of the torch-lit cavern.

Genevieve turned her back, loosened her sarong, and pulled it up over her breasts, and retied it. She pulled her hair into a ponytail and stared defiantly at Buddy.

"Now what?"

"We're going to go on a little trip," Buddy said.

"I'm not going anywhere," Bantu said. "At least not until I'm sure my father is okay."

"As long as your father doesn't do anything stupid, he'll be fine. The same goes for the two of you."

He tossed a box of plastic bags at Bantu and dropped his backpack on the floor.

"What I need you to do is to start filling these bags with samples of everything in here and put them in that backpack."

"And then what?" Bantu said.

"Then we start our little trip."

"And if I refuse?" Bantu said.

"Hmmm," Buddy said, a grin spreading across his face. "Well, since you seem to be the one with all the knowledge, I can't shoot you, can I?"

"That would appear to be the case, yes," Bantu said.

"Then I guess I'll have to shoot her. And I would hate to do that."

"You're missing the big picture, Buddy."

Genevieve sidled over to the lawyer and gently stroked his bicep.

"How's that?" Buddy said, his arm quivering from her touch.

"We don't need him. He's spent the last couple of days giving me more information than we can use in a decade."

"Genevieve, what are you saying?" Bantu said.

"What I'm saying is mission accomplished. I've got everything I came for."

"What?" Bantu said. "But I trusted you. And Doc as well."

"Let's leave him Doc out of it, okay? I need someone who gets what it takes to get ahead in this world. No, not survive, prosper."

"You mean Sir Bentley?" Bantu continued to stare at her in disbelief.

"No, maybe Bentley twenty years ago, but he's old. I need someone who's successful and can also get my motor running."

She gave Buddy's arm one final squeeze and headed towards the shelves to begin collecting specimens.

"What do you say, Buddy? Think you're the one who can make me purr?"

"I knew it," Buddy said. "I knew you were on the take. You're my kind of girl."

Genevieve slowly approached the lawyer.

"Then you're smart enough to know that this is your chance to prove you've got what it takes. I'm going to give you a shot, so don't screw it up."

She leaned in close and gently kissed his neck.

"I expect a lot but, for everything I get, I give back double."

"You're bullshitting me," Buddy said.

"Am I?" Genevieve dug her fingernails into his upper thigh. "Aren't you man enough to at least try, Buddy? Do you think I'd spend all this time in this g place and leave empty-handed? I spent nine years studying this stuff, and I know what it's worth. And I want a piece of it. A big piece."

"What about Sir Bentley?" Buddy said.

"With these plants and our combined expertise, we don't need Sir Bentley."

Bantu continued to stare at Genevieve in disbelief.

"What's the matter with you?" Genevieve said, glancing at the crestfallen tribesman.

"I can't believe you would do this," Bantu said.

"You were the ones who wanted to join the Outsiders. Well, welcome to our world."

Genevieve nuzzled Buddy's shoulder.

"Start filling up those boxes." Buddy waved the pistol at Bantu. "And pack a couple of extra bags of that white powder."

Genevieve laughed and raked her fingers along Buddy's inner thigh. Buddy groaned and involuntarily squeezed both triggers. Fortunately, the nine millimeter's safety was on, but the flare gun

269

fired and all three stared as the flare roared across the cave, out the entrance, and into a palm tree a few hundred feet away.

"Let's hope you're not always that quick on the draw," Genevieve said, as she swayed away and resumed filling the plastic bags.

Buddy stared at her and tried to determine if he was being taken for everything he had or had just won the lottery. He studied her from behind and decided it couldn't hurt to keep his options open.

64

Sir Bentley saw the first one just after he left the perimeter of the village. Two more loomed directly ahead, one on each side of the trail. He looked up and saw four more standing on top of a cliff that seemed to emerge from the jungle canopy. During his brief stay in the village, they'd made it clear he wasn't welcome. Now it appeared they were going do everything in their power to keep him from leaving.

The first dart struck a tree about ten feet to his left. Bentley respected the warning shot and began slowly walking backward, his eyes scanning the thick foliage for alternative routes. Since he and Buddy had entered the village from a different direction, Bentley was already disoriented and unwilling to test the tribesmen's hunting abilities. Out of options, Sir Bentley hightailed it back to the village.

**

Freak had spent the afternoon at sea. Above the sea was more accurate. Several hours had passed as Freak's aircraft, caught in a swirling updraft and struggling under the weight of the four SkyWriters, had looped endlessly over the same patch of ocean. Dizzy from the constant right turn, he caught a break when the wind dropped, and he managed to break free from the clutches of the breeze. With the back of his neck blistered by the sun and out of water, the Admiral of the Air Force headed inland in the direction of the village in severe pain, dehydrated, and inordinately pissed off.

**

Buddy watched Bantu lift the pack onto his shoulders and struggle with the straps until it was fastened securely in place.

"C'mon. Let's go," Buddy said. "I still don't know why you insisted we bring him along. It would be much easier if I just dusted the Smurf right here."

"Do you want to lug that pack all the way back to the Gulfstream?" Genevieve retied her sarong around her waist. Buddy stared at her and then forced himself to refocus.

"Good point," Buddy said.

"Well, there's no way I'm carrying it," Genevieve said. She pulled a shirt out of her bag and buttoned it. She caught the look of disappointment on Buddy's face. "If you think I'm trekking through the jungle topless, you're crazy. They'll be plenty for you to ogle later, sweetie." She nodded at Bantu. "We'll have plenty of time to dispose of him along the way. C'mon, we'll take the shortcut that runs along this side of the village. It'll save us hours."

"I showed you that trail in confidence," Bantu said, struggling under the weight of the pack. "Now you're going to use it against our tribe. And to think I believed you had a heart."

"My lack of heart is the least of your problems," Genevieve said. "Just try to keep up."

"Remind me never to piss you off." Buddy chuckled as he followed both of them into the thick foliage. "And don't forget," Buddy said, gently shoving Bantu forward, "I've got this pistol aimed right at your back."

**

Sir Bentley left the trail and dashed towards one of the vegetable gardens about a hundred yards from the huts. Holding his pith helmet on his head with one hand as he ran, he glanced back and noticed that the blowgun wielding tribesmen had disappeared. Pushing his knock-kneed legs to their limit, he entered the garden and ducked down behind an enormous pineapple bush to plan his next move.

Thirty minutes had passed since he'd heard the third flare yet there was still no sight of Buddy or Genevieve. Cursing himself for his hasty, ill-planned departure and subsequent return to the village, he struggled to come up with Plan B. Preoccupied with the thought of taking a poison dart in the neck, his usual powers of concentration betrayed him. Left to ponder, he wondered if Buddy had decided to

272

screw him on the deal. He quickly discarded that idea since Buddy needed him to fly the plane away from this wretched place.

Sir Bentley then considered the possibility that Buddy had somehow managed to lure the dazzling beauty into some jungle love. He discarded that idea as well since it was too painful to consider. Or maybe she'd done something stupid, and Buddy had just gone ahead and shot her.

Oblivious to whatever actions Buddy had taken, Sir Bentley knew exactly what he needed to do. Get his ass out of this jungle and back to his beloved resort.

The next time he returned, he'd come with an army. And not the lazy-ass band of burnouts Doc had assembled.

"That's all I need." Sir Bentley nodded his head. "Some real firepower."

He peered up from behind a row of pineapple plants and saw the shadows of natives continuing their approach.

65

Bob Garbo and Chief silently compared their respective catches as they walked back towards the village. A small boy ran up to them and chattered excitedly with Chief, who handed over his fish as he listened. The boy added Bob's fish to his load and headed off. Chief nodded at Bob, and they walked towards Doc's hut.

They found him still unconscious and face down on the floor with a feathered dart protruding from the middle of his back. Chief immediately left, and Bob removed the dart and rolled Doc over onto his back.

"Doc." Bob Garbo said gently slapping his face.

Doc groaned, and his eyelids fluttered and closed again.

Bob sat down next to Doc and waited until the Chief returned carrying a cup of liquid. They maneuvered Doc to a sitting position and helped him drink. Doc gagged and blinked rapidly until his eyesight returned.

"Man, I'm slipping," Doc said, managing a brief laugh. "I let myself get darted by that little prick."

"Providence."

"I hope it was only luck." Doc stood. "What did I miss?"

Bob Garbo glanced at Chief, who stared back at them with an inquisitive look.

With a shrug of his shoulders, Bob, to the amazement of Doc, started to talk.

"I'm not sure, but no one has seen Bantu or Genevieve since they went to the cave a couple of hours ago. Bentley tried to leave the village but got spooked by some of the natives who were out hunting and is now hiding in the pineapples. And Chief and I just finished catching a shitload of fish."

Doc stared in disbelief at Bob Garbo.

"Un gwan inga gowa," Bob said, patting Chief on the shoulder.

"Booga-wooga-nooga," Chief said, holding his hands a couple of feet apart.

"He's talking about the one that didn't get away," Bob said.

"You finally start speaking, and you're multi-lingual? How the hell did you learn to speak Whatsittoya?"

"If people spent just half as much time listening as they do talking, they'd be amazed by what they could learn."

Chief chattered at Bob, who listened carefully and nodded his head.

"Chief is worried about Bantu's and Genevieve's safety."

"Tell him everything will be okay. Things are playing out pretty much the way we expected."

Bob translated. Chief nodded and chattered back.

"He wants to take Bentley prisoner," Bob said. "Maybe it's not a bad idea."

Doc glanced outside the hut and easily spotted the yellow safari suit amid the rows of pineapples.

"Maybe. But if that idiot lawyer has taken Bantu and Genevieve, he's obviously on his way back to Bentley's Gulfstream."

"And unless the lawyer is a licensed pilot, which is doubtful, they aren't going anywhere without Bentley," Bob said.

"That's right. And no one in the village saw Bantu or Genevieve come back this way from the cave?"

"No."

"They're probably taking that shortcut trail on the other side of the village Bantu was telling us about."

"So do we follow the lawyer, Sir Bentley, or both?"

Doc drank the last of the liquid, grimaced, and then handed the cup to Chief.

"Let's start by having a little chat with our friend, Sir Bentley."

**

Freak circled the perimeter of the village as he struggled valiantly to maintain altitude. Coming out of a controlled right turn, he spotted his knobby-kneed Commander crouched behind a row of pineapple bushes on the edge of the garden that fronted the village. He saw several tribesmen carrying spears and long blowguns stealthily working their way towards the garden. Freak immediately commenced a rapid descent. Cursing his lack of a communication system now that the Fisher Price had been rendered inoperable, Freak resorted to basics.

"Hey! Commander Bentley!"

Upon hearing the voice, Sir Bentley took a break from his emergent panic attack and glanced around the pineapples in search of the owner.

"Just relax, Bentley. Research shows that jungle isolation is a leading cause of imaginary voices."

Sir Bentley shifted his weight as he crouched further down behind the pineapples.

"Commander Bentley. It's me."

"I should've just stuck with sneakers."

Sir Bentley shook his head vigorously in an attempt to free whatever gremlins had taken up residence inside his head.

"Up here. Commander, I'm up here."

Sir Bentley stared up in amazement at the approaching hang glider being maneuvered by the idiot known as Freak. He caught sight of the four SkyWriters strapped to the sides of the glider. Bentley flashed back to a warm sunny day off the coast of Hawaii when the moron hovering overhead had sunk his beloved yacht. One single thought formed as Bentley watched the heavily-armed hang glider continue its descent towards the pineapples.

"Don't fucking shoot!"

Freak nodded and gave him a thumbs-up. He began another hard right turn. Out of the corner of his eye, Freak spotted several tribesmen standing on the edge of the jungle that bordered the village. They were pointing up at him and chattering excitedly.

"That'll teach you to mess with us." Freak tugged at his goggles and focused on the horizon. "Hang on, Commander. I'm coming."

"That's what I'm afraid of," Bentley said.

He watched several tribesmen begin to jog toward him. Sir Bentley looked up at the hang glider that was now only about a hundred feet off the ground and rapidly descending. He looked back and saw Doc watching him from the doorway of his hut. Chief stood beside him with a bemused expression.

Bentley heard the cackle of parrots and monkey snorts that sounded like mocking laughter. He heard the tribesmen's derisive chattering; a guttural collection of grunts and groans masquerading as a language. He watched the approaching tribesmen, drawing ever closer with spears raised and blowguns touching lips. With the jungle world closing in around him on all sides, Sir Bentley Carruthers, for the second time in two days, did something he hadn't done since he was a small child.

He peed his pants.

And then he started running as fast his little knobby-kneed legs would carry him. He jumped up from behind the pineapples and made a beeline away from the village and, he hoped, in the general direction of Nirvana.

**

"Should we go get him?" Bob Garbo said.

He smiled as he watched Sir Bentley bob and weave his way through the grassland holding onto his pith helmet with one hand.

"No," Doc said as he watched the events unfold. "I gotta see this."

Chief chattered at Bob, who nodded.

"What?" Doc said.

"Chief says he run like a three-legged crocodile."

Doc smiled as he continued to stare at the yellow safari suit that intermittently popped in and out of view amongst the tall green grass swaying in the breeze.

**

Freak dropped to fifty feet and focused on the tribesmen wielding spears and blowguns. The first dart missed, but did hit the canvas of the hang glider. Freak grabbed the dart and tossed it away. He pumped a fist defiantly at his attackers and completed another loop that brought him even closer to the ground. He drifted away from the village in the direction of the rapidly tiring Sir Bentley.

Sir Bentley peered back over his shoulder at the approaching hang glider. He slowed to a trot as Freak approached and leaned out over the edge of the glider.

"I'm here to save you, Commander."

"And how do you propose to do that?" Sir Bentley, not breaking stride, glanced up at the glider that was now directly overhead.

Freak's response went unheard as the hang glider soared past Sir Bentley and began another loop.

Sir Bentley continued to jog as he watched the glider draw closer. Freak, now a mere twenty feet off the ground, was dividing his attention between his concern for his Commander and concern for his own ass as he followed the movement of the armed tribesmen.

Freak weighed his options as he approached Sir Bentley from behind. He dangled his legs and Freak stared down at their proximity to the ground. He gulped and swallowed his fear.

"Grab my legs," he shouted.

"What?" Sir Bentley came to a stop and gasped for breath. "Grab your what?"

"My legs. I'll carry you out."

"Are you out of your fucking mind?"

"We can debate that at a later time, Commander." Freak stared intensely at his target. "But right now, I suggest you prepare to grab my legs and hold on."

"This is so beneath a man of my stature."

Sir Bentley raised both arms to the sky and grabbed Freak's ankles. Sir Bentley, airborne but being dragged through the grassland only about a foot off the ground, glanced back at the village that was beginning to disappear from view as the jungle grasses thrashed against his bare legs.

"Get this thing airborne," Sir Bentley bellowed, his legs, bent at the knee, dangling precariously off the ground.

"I'm trying, Commander," Freak said, grimacing as he pulled back on the control bar in an attempt to get more air under the sail. "I think we have a weight problem."

"Speak for yourself, soldier," Sir Bentley said. "I'm in perfect shape for a man my age."

"No, sir," Freak said, taking notice of the approaching trees. "I was referring to the total weight of the aircraft."

"Who gives a shit what you were referring to? Just get me back to my Gulfstream in one piece. And that is an order."

"Don't worry, Commander. I have an idea."

"Why doesn't that make me feel any better?"

"Just leave everything to me, Commander."

"Like I have a choice."

Sir Bentley clung desperately to Freak's ankles.

Freak continued to pull back on the control bar until the hang glider was tilting upwards at a thirty-degree angle. The aircraft rose to fifty feet off the ground. Freak began tinkering with the two SkyWriters facing backward off the hang glider.

"What are you doing?"

"I've seen the recoil these missiles have," Freak said. "Pretty bad design on the part of whoever makes them, but it might work in our favor."

"I make them."

"Really?" Freak said. "Ah, yes. Well then, very well done indeed, Commander. A most elegant design."

"It's the lighter, quieter, all-nighter fighter."

"Uh, okay," Freak said. "Hang on tight. This could hurt."

"Just get it over with." Sir Bentley tightened his grip and clamped his eyes shut.

Freak leaned back in his seat, hooked both feet behind the control bar, and reached out with both arms and fired the two SkyWriters that faced backward off the hang glider. Both rockets ignited, roared to life and disappeared off the back of the hang glider in search of something to hit.

Lost in the roar were Freak and Sir Bentley's screams as they began their rapid ascent. Sir Bentley opened his eyes and watched the treetops disappear from view. He clamored up Freak's legs until he was securely draped against the metal frame of the hang glider. He stared wild-eyed at Freak as the glider continued to climb. The only sound was the rustling of canvas piercing its way through a twenty mile an hour headwind.

"Man," Freak said. "What a rush."

Sir Bentley's mouth moved in response, but the only thing that came out were the remains of his breakfast.

**

From the confines of the verandah that wrapped around his hut, Doc stared, slack-jawed, as the hang glider soared like a crisply struck four-iron over the trees and several hundred feet into the air until it became a distant speck in the sky. The SkyWriters exploded a safe distance from the village. The tribesmen watched the explosion and ensuing grassfire and made a hasty retreat to the village. They headed straight for the Elder barrel and spent the rest of the day pursuing alternate visions. Chief scratched his head and continued to stare into the distant sky as he chattered with Bob Garbo.

"Goingo, gacka, malacka," Bob said.

Chief nodded and waved at Tuber, who was approaching with an arm draped over Flute Girl's shoulder. Reluctantly, Tuber left the young woman and joined Doc, Bob, and Chief on the verandah.

"He's going to be our guide," Bob said, nodding at Tuber.

"He doesn't look happy about it."

"I wonder why," Bob said, laughing. "Trek through the jungle or spend all night hooked up with her."

"Ah, the pesky burden of leadership," Doc said.

Chief began chattering rapidly with Bob and Tuber. Tuber nodded his head and looked at Bob. Doc waited patiently for the translation.

"Okay," Bob said. "We're all set."

"Good," Doc said. "We should probably get going."

"Chief is being a bit coy, but he says that we have a nice surprise waiting for us."

"I can't wait."

Doc smiled at Chief.

"No, he says we'll like it. Our old buddy, Tuber, is going to show us."

"All right." Doc headed back inside the hut. He paused at the doorway and looked at Bob. "Does this remind you of anything?"

"What, this situation?"

"Yeah."

"Rampant capitalism running roughshod over an indigenous population? I'm going to need some clarification here."

"New Guinea."

"Yeah. Sure, I see some similarities. That didn't end well."

"And why was that?" Doc said, leaning against the doorway.

"We never cut the head off the snake," Bob said.

"Exactly."

66

"C'mon, quit stalling. It's just a snake. Step around it."

"Why don't you try and shoot it like the last one?" Genevieve said, staring at the cobra that was prepared to strike the first person that got within ten feet of it.

Buddy removed the nine-millimeter from the pocket of his shorts and counted the remaining ammunition. He had spent nine rounds an hour ago in an unsuccessful attempt to shoot the cousin of the snake he was now watching. Unwilling to waste any more of the precious rounds, he checked the safety and returned the pistol to his pocket.

Bantu poked at the snake with a long stick, and it reluctantly crawled away.

"Some shortcut," Buddy said, motioning them forward down the trail.

"It is short," Bantu said, struggling with the weight of the pack. "It's just not safe."

"Just keep moving." Buddy warily glanced around. "I don't want to be out after dark."

Genevieve slapped at a large insect that had taken up residence on her left breast. "Merde." She examined the bite mark. "That bastard took a chunk out of me."

"He wanted to nibble your breasts. Can't blame him for that." Buddy laughed and gently shoved her forward. "Get moving."

"Oh, no," Bantu said, stopping in his tracks on the edge of the mangroves surrounding the trail.

"Now what?" Buddy said. "I've about had it. If you try to stall one more time I'm gonna- Is that what I think it is?"

"Yes." Bantu took a step backward and pulled Genevieve with him. "Crocodile."

"Of course it is. If it isn't the wild boars, the pythons and cobras, or the dung-throwing monkeys-"

281

"Save it for later, Buddy." Genevieve kept both eyes fixed on the massive reptile that was slowly maneuvering its way out of the mangroves. "What do we do, Bantu?"

"Now you want my opinion."

"Stop whining," Genevieve said, checking the ground on either side of her for a potential escape route. "Options. Quick."

"We could run," Bantu said.

"Can humans outrun a crocodile?" Buddy said.

"I don't have to worry about outrunning it."

Bantu removed the pack and slowly inched backwards

"You don't?" Buddy said.

"No. I only have to worry about outrunning you."

"Funny little prick, aren't you?"

"We could shoot it," Bantu said.

"Yeah, that's a good one," Genevieve said, lighting a Gitanes. "Good ole Wyatt Earp here couldn't hit air parachuting."

"I hit the snake. Eventually."

"Yeah, from six inches away after Bantu clubbed it to death with a stick."

Genevieve blew smoke in Buddy's direction.

"Well, I know I can hit that thing," Buddy said, pulling out the pistol. "Look at the size of him."

"Hang on."

Bantu removed the pack from his shoulders and began rummaging inside. He pulled out one of the plastic bags and applied a sticky paste to the end of a stick. He slowly approached the crocodile holding the stick in front of him.

"Jesus, Bantu," Genevieve said. "Be careful."

"Like you care what happens to me," he said, standing about six feet from the crocodile that was increasingly interested in the stick now inches from its face.

The crocodile snapped its powerful jaws, and half the stick disappeared inside its mouth. The reptile began to blink its eyes, belched, and sunk below the surface of the water.

"What the hell was that?" Buddy said, staring at the air bubbles surfacing on the algae-ridden water.

"Crocodile repellent." Bantu pulled the pack onto his shoulders. "C'mon, let's go." He shook his head at both of his traveling companions and trudged forward down the sandy trail. "Outsiders. Unbelievable."

67

Doc and Bob Garbo followed Tuber as he led them across the village towards the shortcut that led back to Nirvana. Tuber, armed with several blowguns and a long wooden stick that was razor-sharp on one end, was setting a quick pace. Doc and Bob, both burdened with heavy backpacks and a SkyWriter, struggled to keep. Tuber, not breaking stride, glanced over his shoulder, snarled, and chattered sharply at them.

"He told us to pick up the pace," Bob said.

"Yeah, I got that," Doc said, wiping sweat from his forehead. "We could have used this guy back in Desert Storm."

"You were this guy back in Desert Storm," Bob said, laughing.

Bob stopped as they reached the entrance to the trail. "Damn. Look at this shit."

Doc stopped next to Bob and stared into the dense mangrove swamp that stretched before them. Above, the overhanging foliage, a collection of dense trees and climbing vines that co-mingled into an impenetrable web, hung low just above their heads. Parrots and monkeys greeted their arrival, and the amount of available light dropped precipitously.

"Garbo," Doc said. "I have a feeling were not in Kansas anymore."

"Indeed. Pay no attention to the cobra behind the curtain."

"Follow the yellow prick home, follow the yellow prick home."

They laughed until Tuber cut it short with an angry grunt. They fell silent and waited. Tuber pointed his stick at the narrow path that stretched out before them and shook his head. He then pointed the stick up at the sky and nodded yes.

"Any idea what he's talking about?" Doc said.

"Not a clue."

Bob chattered briefly in his new language and waited for Tuber's response. Bob nodded and looked at Doc with a confused expression.

"Ground, bad. Up, good."

"Well, that makes perfect sense. Anyone can see that." Doc swatted at an enormous spider that had dropped onto his shoulder. "Could you see if Daktari here could expand on that a bit?"

Bob chattered with Tuber whose voice became more animated as he continued to point upwards with the stick.

"He's talking about a shortcut," Bob said.

"I thought this was the shortcut."

"I can't quite understand what he's saying. I'm not so sure he knows the language that well."

"And you do?"

"Well, excuse me, Bwana. At least I'm making an effort," Bob said.

"I think I liked you better when you didn't talk," Doc said.

He moved closer to Tuber and watched the tribesman continue to wave his arms and point to the sky.

"How about that?" Doc chuckled when he comprehended what Tuber was telling them. "How are your climbing skills these days?"

Both men watched as Tuber stepped off the small pathway and began to climb a series of vines knotted together. Seconds later, Tuber was standing on a small platform nestled between two trees branches just above their heads. Although he was only four feet above them, Tuber had virtually disappeared.

Bob and Doc climbed the vines and stood next to Tuber. Stretching in front of them was a tunnel that had been cut through the foliage approximately ten feet in circumference. Underneath their feet were planks of wood and rocks that comprised walkways and steps as the tunnel bobbed up and down in concert with the overall terrain of the mangrove swamp.

"This is incredible." Doc peered down the vast stretch of tunnel until it veered right and disappeared.

Bob chattered with Tuber, who puffed with pride and beat his chest as he responded.

"He built it," Bob said, continuing to listen as he translated for Doc. "He says he got tired of getting chased by the crocodiles."

"And this thing leads all the way back to the beach?"

Bob chattered with Tuber, who nodded his head vigorously.

"Apparently so. He says we can travel six moons as fast as those below on the ground. Should I ask him how fast a moon is?"

285

"No, I think we get the point."

"Let's go, then," Bob said, gesturing for Tuber to lead the way.

"No crocodiles," Doc said. "Nice to catch a break. Hey, ask him if there are snakes up here."

Bob nodded and chattered with Tuber, who thrust the stick back and forth with his arm.

"He says that's what the stick is for."

"Yeah," Doc said, scanning the surrounding leaves and vines for signs of deadly asps. "I got that one."

68

    Freak and Sir Bentley both regained consciousness at the same time. A bolt of lightning flashing a few hundred feet directly in front of your hang glider tends to have the same effect on most people. Sir Bentley blinked, then remembered where he was. He wrapped both arms tighter around the metal control bar and elbowed his way towards a larger share of the John Deere lawn tractor seat he was sharing with Freak.

    "Knock it off," Freak said. "You're hogging the whole thing."

    "Don't snap at me, soldier. I'm still your Commander."

    "Not up here, you ain't." Freak stared down at the vast expanse of ocean that stretched below them. "It's every man for himself." Freak fought back the onset of vertigo and adjusted his goggles.

    Sir Bentley looked down and gasped.

    "How the hell did we get all the way up here?"

    "SkyWriter recoil, sir. I figured we'd get some lift, but this is nuts. We must have caught a thermal on our way up."

    "How far up do you think we are?"

    "Ten, maybe fifteen thousand feet?"

    "Isn't that a little high for a hang glider?"

    "Well, it's not the height that's the problem. It's the fact that we're up here holding on for dear life to a piece of metal in a lighting storm."

    "Then get us down. We're over the ocean so Nirvana must be somewhere down there."

    "I'm sure it is, sir."

    Freak attempted to pull the reluctant control bar into a controlled right turn.

    "Hmmm, that's not good."

    "What's not good?"

    "This thing won't turn."

    "What do you mean it won't turn?"

"For somebody who's supposed to be so smart, you sure do ask a lot of dumb questions. I said it won't turn."

"But aren't we headed straight out to sea?"

"There you go again with the dumb questions. Do you see any land underneath us?"

"No," Sir Bentley said, summoning the courage for a quick peek below.

"Then yes, we're headed out to sea."

Another bolt of lightning flashed in front of them, and both men screamed.

"But the wind is blowing onshore. Won't we eventually get blown back over land?"

"Probably," Freak said, pulling back on the control bar. "But we're starting to lose altitude again. We're carrying too much weight. Either we make it back to land before we run out of altitude or…"

"Or what?"

"Or I guess we'll see if this lawn tractor seat can actually be used as a floatation device in the event of a water landing."

Panic enveloped Sir Bentley. Not a panic like the time when his company's stock has dropped precipitously as rumors of a potential sell-off hit the street. Nor was it like the panic when he'd been discovered snorting coke off the ass of the sixteen-year-old daughter of the Duke. Nor was it even remotely like his recent bout of panic hiding behind the pineapples. This panic was all-consuming and driven by one simple fact; the self-controlled man who controlled industries, even entire economies, now found himself powerless to control anything.

The cobalt ocean beckoned and waved as he squinted down at his pending fate.

Sir Bentley Carruthers.

Shark Chum.

"Do something," Sir Bentley said. "I command you to do something."

"Command all you want, sir. Command until your ass puckers and your eyeballs bleed for all I care. I'm sorry, Commander, but I'm out of ideas."

"Useless. I should have let them hang you from the yardarm after you sunk my yacht."

"What is a yardarm anyways? I always wondered about that," Freak said, still struggling to get the hang glider to turn.

"I don't know," Sir Bentley said. "What's that?" he said, pointing at a canvas bag.

"Never mind what that is." Freak reached behind him and grabbed the bag.

Sir Bentley stared at Freak with a wild-eyed mixture of fear and fury and then remembered the nine-millimeter tucked inside his jacket pocket. He steadied himself with one hand as another bolt of lightning flashed directly in front of them and pulled the pistol. He pointed it at Freak's head.

"What's in the bag, soldier?" Sir Bentley said. He rested the pistol on the tip of Freak's nose.

"P-p-parachute."

"Parachute?" Sir Bentley eyes glistened with excitement. "Thought you were going to pull a fast one, huh?" Sir Bentley grabbed the parachute and pulled it over his arms and tied it securely.

"What about me?" Freak said.

"You? You're just one more casualty of war. Don't worry. I'll make sure you get a hero's funeral."

"You bastard. I should have sunk you along with that boat."

"It was a yacht, not a boat, moron. I'll see you in the obituaries."

Sir Bentley slid off the seat and dropped into free fall. Freak looked down and saw the parachute open. He watched Sir Bentley surge towards the heavens and then drift as the breeze began to carry the magnate safely back towards shore. Freak fought back a lump in his throat as the glider soared further out over endless cobalt sea.

69

Tuber clutched the vine, got a running start, and launched himself off the edge of the plank. Doc and Bob watched as he soared and landed effortlessly on the other side of the ten-foot gap. Tuber spun around, shoved the vine back, and waited with a smug expression.

"You first, Tarzan," Doc said, handing the vine to Bob Garbo.

"Piece of cake." Bob launched himself across the gap in the trees and landed next to Tuber.

Doc caught the vine from Bob, pushed off, and joined them on the other side. Tuber reluctantly grunted his approval and continued through the above-ground tunnel.

"How long do you think it took him to hack this out?" Doc said, admiring the neatly trimmed inside perimeter of the tunnel.

"What's that saying Bantu always uses? Go slow, but never stop?" Bob said. "I guess when you have no real sense of time, it doesn't matter how long something takes."

"I'm impressed, Bob Garbo. A very Buddhist concept indeed."

Tuber turned his head and snarled for them to be quiet. He pointed a finger through a small opening in the foliage and Doc and Bob silently peered through. A hundred feet ahead, they saw the back of Bantu who was slowly picking his way through a particularly thick section of mangrove.

**

"This sucks," Buddy said, swatting at a large spider that landed on his forearm. "And I'm not just saying that. This is the fucking suckiest situation I've ever been in."

"Suckiest?" Genevieve said, ducking her head under an overhanging mangrove branch. "Is that a legal term?"

"Yeah," Buddy said, banging his shin on a rock. "Ow. Shit. It comes from the Latin term, Suckadotious Momentus."

Genevieve managed a small laugh as she maneuvered her way around the rock that had just claimed Buddy as a victim.

"I can't wait to get on that Gulfstream and take a shower," Buddy said.

"Oh, a shower," Genevieve said. "Don't torture me."

"Maybe you and I can shower together. You wash my back and then I'll do you. But you'll have to wash your own back." He laughed, blew her a kiss and walked into a mangrove branch that opened a three-inch cut on his forehead.

"Sonofabitch, that hurts."

Sweat covered every inch of Buddy's body, and the bleeding mess that was the lower half of his body had turned his new Cloudlifters a squishy crimson. He blinked as blood dripped into his eyes and paused to wipe his face.

"It opens up a bit about a hundred yards ahead," Bantu said, stopping to catch his breath.

"C'mon," Buddy said, his nerves and patience frazzled by the hostile environment. "We're losing the light. And this is no place to be in the middle of the night."

"This is no place to be anytime," Genevieve said.

"I need a break." Bantu removed the heavy pack from his shoulders and sat down on it. "I've gotten soft while I was away. As a boy, I used to go exploring like this all day. It was one of my favorite things to do."

"One more reason your tribe is a bottom feeder on the food chain," Buddy said. "C'mon, let's go."

"No," Bantu said.

"A break's not a bad idea," Genevieve said.

"Give me the fucking pack. I'll carry it." Buddy removed his pack and tossed it at Bantu. "You can carry mine." Buddy pulled the pack on, staggered under the weight, then trudged forward. "Let's go. Follow me. Team FUBAR, moving out."

**

Doc stretched out on the plank and hooked his feet under a tree branch as he peered down through the large opening in the foliage. At this point in the tunnel, the ground was a mere six feet below, and Doc scanned the trail in both directions and climbed to his feet.

291

"Yeah, I think he's right," Doc said, nodding at Tuber.

Tuber grunted and chattered at Bob.

"He says he's done it many times before. Especially when he wants to frighten someone."

"Well, that would certainly do the trick," Doc said. "Okay, I think there's room for both of us to stretch out. I'd like to take care of this in one shot.

Bob nodded and stretched out on the plank. He looked down through the opening and then back up inside the tunnel.

"Yeah, I think there's room," Bob Garbo said.

"You take Bantu," Doc said. "I'll take care of her."

**

"So tell me, Buddy," Genevieve said, picking her way through the last stretch of mangrove before the trail opened up. "How much do we stand to make off this stuff?"

"More than enough to keep you in sarongs and champagnes. Millions, baby. We're gonna make millions. Maybe billions if we're lucky."

"So you're just going to steal from my tribe?"

"You had your chance, Jungle Boy. But I guess since you people have no use for money, I shouldn't be surprised. Of course, once we get to where we're going, if you decide to play nice, I'd be willing to cut you in on the deal."

"You didn't answer my question," Bantu said.

"What? About the stealing? The way I see it, Sir Bentley is only taking what is rightfully his in the first place. After all, he did buy the island."

"What happens to me if I help you?"

"That's up to you, Jungle Boy. We'll set you up in a house. You can come back for a visit when we're ready for another bagful of plant extracts. Who knows what else might happen? You might even start to like being an exploiter." Buddy laughed.

"You could do a lot worse, Bantu," Genevieve said.

"Traitor," Bantu said.

"Oh, grow up," she said. "This is how the world works, and the sooner you and your tribe learn that the better off you'll be."

"Ooh, stop it, baby," Buddy said. "You're making me hard."

292

"You just hold that chubby for a while," Genevieve said, scanning the stretch of sand in front of them. The overhead foliage was still thick and lush, but the mangrove swamp they'd been dealing with was rapidly receding and giving way to native grass and sand.

"How much further?" Buddy said, adjusting the heavy pack.

"It's not far," Bantu said.

The afternoon sun cut through the foliage and jagged streams of filtered light angled their way into view. Buddy seemed to find his second wind as their arduous journey appeared to be winding down. He stomped the excess blood and sweat out of his Cloudlifters, then waved Bantu and Genevieve forward with a newly discovered spring in his step.

They looked at each other and trudged after the lawyer.

**

"Get ready," Doc said.

Bob Garbo, stretched out prone next to Doc in the tunnel, stared down through the opening and nodded. They watched the top of Buddy's head pass directly underneath. Seconds later, Genevieve, then Bantu passed directly underneath the opening. Simultaneously, Doc and Bob reached down and grabbed their targets under the shoulders and jerked them skyward. Their frightened screams were cut short as they were gently placed down on the plank walkway inside the tunnel. Doc held a finger to his lips commanding silence as he smiled at the wide-eyed pair. Genevieve embraced him in a silent, bone-crushing hug. Bantu smiled and nodded at Tuber and Bob, then marveled at the inside of the tunnel. Tuber beamed with pride.

**

"What was that?" Buddy paused mid-step. "I thought I heard a scream. What is it, another snake?"

He turned and discovered he was alone. "Ha, ha. Very funny. Olly-Olly, oxen-free." Buddy glanced around and listened carefully to the jungle. "Okay, this isn't funny."

Buddy began slowly walking backward away from the direction of the scream.

"You know, Sir Bentley and I don't need your help. We can figure this shit out by ourselves. And there's a ton of scientists around the world who'd love to work on this project."

Buddy glanced up at the overhanging foliage that appeared to be closing in on him.

"So quit screwing around and get your asses out here."

Buddy stared down at the crimson footprints he was leaving in the sand.

"Genevieve? Jungle Boy? Anybody? Hello."

**

Doc pulled his head back from the opening and climbed to his feet. "Okay, he's out of range."

Genevieve grabbed Doc and kissed him long and deep. Tuber, very impressed by her efforts, grunted his approval. She pulled away and stared intensely at Doc.

"How on earth did you come up with this plan?"

She looked around the confines of the above ground tunnel.

"All the credit goes to our friend, Tuber."

Doc gently placed his hand on the man's shoulder.

Tuber smiled, bowed slightly and returned the gesture.

"Are we glad to see you," Bantu said, sitting down on the plank. "I didn't think I could keep up that act much longer."

"You did great," Genevieve said. "I was beginning to believe that you really did hate me."

"I loved the part when he came up with that horrible little poem," Bantu said, rolling his eyes. "How did it go?"

"Something about a case of Dom and hitting it till dawn," Genevieve said. "Jungle seduction. Just what every girl wants when she's stuck in the middle of a swamp. It was brutal."

Doc peered down through the opening.

"We should get going. I don't want to give him too much of a head start. Bantu, you and Tuber take Genevieve back to the village. Your father's worried and I think you should have enough light to make it back before dark."

"You're not coming?" Genevieve said.

"Bob and I have some unfinished business to take care of."

"Be careful. And hurry back."

Doc hugged her and waved at Bantu and Tuber to get going. He and Bob watched them work their way back through the tunnel towards the village and then headed off in pursuit of the lawyer.

70

Once his terror-riddled body stopped pumping adrenaline, Sir Bentley settled down and enjoyed his parachute ride back to solid ground. He gently kicked his legs back and forth as they dangled in mid-air. As he approached the beachfront that fronted his beloved resort, he began making plans for its immediate repair and expansion. From a thousand feet, he cast his eyes over a portion of the island he knew would be perfect for a world-class golf course. Further up into the island, he saw the tops of the jungle canopy that marked the boundary of the village where the burnout Doc was hopefully dead from the poison dart.

He chuckled as he imagined the folklore the natives were undoubtedly inventing to put into words the spectacle of Sir Bentley's recent ascent towards heaven.

He gently tugged one of the parachute straps and drifted in the direction of his Gulfstream. The huge green dollar sign on the tail beckoned. He hovered above the runway and scanned the horizon for signs of Buddy and Jungle Boy. Sir Bentley bent his knees to cushion the shock, hit the sand, and rolled. He stood, removed the parachute, and thrust both arms up in victory.

**

The sooner Buddy got out from underneath the overhanging foliage that had seemed to come to life, the better. Over the past several minutes, a plethora of spiders, bugs, monkey-droppings, and two ill-tempered snakes had dropped from above onto his head and shoulders. Beating them away with flailing arms had left him even further exhausted and on the verge of a nervous breakdown.

But now he was confronted with an even bigger challenge from a most unexpected source.

Buddy's prior experience with pigs had come entirely from the supermarket. Bacon, pork loin, and shoulder roasts wrapped and ready for the grill were sources of delicious delight. An enormous wild boar with twelve-inch tusks was something else altogether. The boar was pissed and blocked Buddy's path.

"What?" Buddy stopped in his tracks and threw his hands up in the air. "Man, I can't catch a break."

The boar remained silent and began to sniff the air.

Buddy looked down at his soggy crimson Cloudlifters.

"You smell the blood? Is that it?"

Buddy dropped the pack and knelt down to untie his sneakers. He waved one at the boar. It cocked its head and stared at the sneaker. Buddy heaved it as far as he could into the mangroves and waited. The massive beast stared at the remaining sneaker in Buddy's hand.

"Okay, here goes nothing," Buddy said, firing the second sneaker in the same direction.

The boar followed the sneaker's flight, took a final look at Buddy, and waddled off towards the Cloudlifters.

"Hah," Buddy said. "This jungle shit is a piece of cake."

Buddy pulled the pack on and continued down the pathway now transitioning from soft sand to jagged coral. Buddy's cries punctuated the breeze with each step as the bottoms of his feet were torn to shreds. A new trail of red marked his slow, painful progress.

**

Doc and Bob laughed as they watched Buddy's encounter with the boar and his tippy-toed march towards the Gulfstream. After running out of things to drop on his head, they had positioned themselves at the end of the tunnel that sat about ten feet above the ground and overlooked the runway. Doc removed his binoculars and peered through the light foliage.

Doc watched Sir Bentley inspect the outside of the aircraft and open the stairway. He watched Buddy continue to stagger towards the plane. His entire body was covered with blood. His eyes were dark and wild.

"He is tenacious."

Doc watched Bob prepare the SkyWriter.

"I'll give him that."

"He's a lawyer," Bob Garbo said.

297

Doc nodded as he scanned the skies through his binoculars.
"I don't believe it."
He handed Bob the binoculars and pointed to the sky.
"Talk about tenacious."
Bob took a quick look and handed the binoculars back to Doc.

**

Freak leaned as far right as possible and nodded in approval at the slow right turn his aircraft was making. He'd spent the past fifteen minutes moving everything on the craft to the right side. The two remaining rockets sat adjacent, precariously held together by duct tape that was rapidly losing its adhesive abilities. With all the weight on one side, the glider tilted at a forty-five-degree angle. Whether or not Freak would eventually hit land anywhere near the resort was irrelevant. Any direction he was heading other than further out to sea was a definite improvement as far as he was concerned.

Freak pulled his binoculars up and peered through his goggles that were saturated with sweat and condensation. He tugged at the salt-encrusted goggles and yelped like a puppy that had been stepped on. Several hours in the wind and sun, enhanced by the reflective abilities of the goggle's metal frames, had left Freak's upper cheeks and forehead severely sunburned and blistered. Confronted with the choice between poor visibility and multiple layers of skin being ripped off his face, Freak trained the binoculars over his goggles and scanned the shoreline.

A reflection from the foliage that ended about a hundred yards from one edge of the runway caught his attention. He recognized Doc staring back at him through binoculars with a look of concern. Freak waved and continued to scan the shoreline. He watched a bloodied and agitated Buddy tiptoe barefoot towards the plane. The lawyer was lumbering under the weight of a large backpack and Freak was impressed by his single-minded focus. Freak watched as Sir Bentley lowered the steps leading up into the aircraft. Freak felt anger surge as he cursed the magnate and reached down to remove his Cloudlifters. He hurled the sneakers downward in Sir Bentley's direction, but they merely splashed into the ocean several hundred feet below.

Freak felt a jolt of remorse for having doubted Doc's intentions and intuition. His brother-in-law had bailed him out of numerous jams in the past and continued to support him with encouragement as well as a generous paycheck long after everyone else had written Freak off as a waste of oxygen. His sister, a troubled soul throughout her entire life right up the point of her untimely death, had been right when she'd said that she saw something in Doc that gave her hope for humanity. The fact that he constantly strove to be a better person despite the demands of his chosen profession was, to her, a testament to Doc's true inner soul. More importantly to her was Doc's need to protect the weak and the damaged. To bring them into his fold and do his best to nurture them.

Freak thought about his sister, her intelligence crippled by paranoia, her sense of humor overridden by fear, and her ultimate inability to function outside her ever-dwindling environment until she had locked herself in a four by six closet and put herself, and she hoped the others in her life, out of pain. Tears mixed with the sweat trapped inside the foggy lenses and burned Freak's eyes as he completed another long 360-degree turn.

What had she said?

Freak forced himself to concentrate. And remember what she told him near the end.

Doc is a collector-protector of damaged souls.

Freak nodded at the memory and thought about Esmeralda, the crazy bitch that Doc had somehow hooked up with. To Freak, Esmeralda was his sister on tequila without the threat of razorblades and was someone to avoid. With the memory of his sister's words ringing in his ears, Doc's unwillingness to extract himself from such dysfunction finally made some sense.

Freak would have been long gone soon after consummation.

He trained his binoculars on Bob Garbo, sitting quietly on some form of platform hidden amid the foliage. Freak shook his head in amazement at the silent one. Armed with only snippets of the man's history Doc had reluctantly shared, he could only wonder at some of the horrors Garbo had witnessed and imparted on others throughout his career. What does it take, Freak wondered, to make one fall silent and go through life unwilling to offer an opinion, tell a joke, give directions, or yell and scream?

A collector-protector of damaged souls.

Freak glanced down at the rapidly approaching cobalt sea, buffeted by the breeze and topped with Cool Whip.

"Now I get it. I'm one of his damaged souls."

Freak stared back at Doc through the binoculars.

"I'm sorry I was such a fuck up, Doc."

Freak saw Doc nod his head. Freak frowned and shook his head.

"There's no way he heard that."

Doc nodded his head for a second time.

**

Buddy stepped past the last piece of coral and felt his feet buried to the ankles in the burning sand. The sand sucked at his legs, and he dropped face first. The weight of the backpack pinned him down and his ears filled with the hot grains. He rolled sideways and slid his arms free. He wiped his face with both hands to remove clumps of sand coagulated with blood and sweat. Struggling to his feet, he stumbled forward towards the Gulfstream and the smirking Sir Bentley who was sitting on the bottom step of the stairs. He dragged the backpack and limped his way forward. Approaching Sir Bentley, he placed the heavy pack at his feet and collapsed at the foot of the stairs.

"Where are they?"

Sir Bentley opened the backpack and examined the contents.

"You won't believe it," Buddy said, breathless. "They disappeared in the mangroves."

"You're right. I don't believe it."

"Honest, Bentley, one minute we're traipsing through the swamp, the next I'm out there all alone. I tell you, they just disappeared. I think a crocodile got them. Or maybe a snake."

"Hmmm. I see," Sir Bentley said. "So what do you propose we do now?"

"What do you mean?"

Buddy propped himself up on his elbows and surveyed the damage the jungle had inflicted.

"I mean, what do we do now? We have no indigenous expertise to explain how these various remedies are used."

"So what?"

"I will tell you so what, Captain Quizling. The whole point of this exercise was to not only obtain these remedies but to also acquire local expertise."

"Jesus, Bentley. I just risked my life getting this pack to you, and all you can do is criticize."

"Hmmm," Sir Bentley said. "I'm afraid this isn't your best work."

"Best work? Jesus, Bentley. I just hiked through a mangrove swamp and survived encounters with cobras and a crocodile that must have been fifteen feet long. Not my best work? Fuck you."

"This," Sir Bentley said, pointing at the backpack, "has limited utility. Without local expertise, I could be forced to spend years trying to crack the code."

"Well, send in another search party to capture the Chief or that little prick, Bantu. And use someone better than that burnout Doc and his gang. By the way, what happened to him?"

"I took care of him," Sir Bentley said. "Poison dart right between the shoulder blades."

Buddy laughed and winced from the pain in his ribs. He struggled to his feet and headed towards the stairs.

"Then we're done here. Let's the hell off this island and get this stuff to a lab."

"Where do you think you're going?" Sir Bentley said, holding his arms out to prevent the lawyer's passage.

"On the plane. Where do you think I'm going?"

"You're not getting on my plane looking like that. You're dripping blood everywhere, and I'm not going to have my carpet and leather seats ruined."

"Well," Buddy said, "I suppose I could take a shower at Nirvana, but you'd have to either carry me or go get one of the golf carts. I can't walk any further."

"No, we don't have time for that," Sir Bentley said.

"Well then, that's just too bad." Buddy stepped around Sir Bentley and headed up the stairs. "I'll pay for the cleaning out of my share of the profits."

Buddy paused when he heard the unmistakable click.

"I'm afraid, that since you failed to deliver on your part of our deal, you won't be getting any share, Captain Quizling."

Buddy turned around on the step to face Sir Bentley, who was pointing a pistol at his chest.

"Have you lost your mind? Have you forgotten about the sealed envelope?"

"You mean this?" Sir Bentley pulled out a document from inside the jacket pocket of his safari suit.

"Where did you get that?"

"From the guy in your office. Who else? About a month ago. He wasn't happy with the cut you offered and thought he could negotiate a better deal with me by giving you up."

"I guess he got what he wanted."

"Oh, most definitely." Sir Bentley laughed. "And then a week later, he got something else. Two hollow points in the back of the head."

"You can't just go around shooting people, Bentley."

"Sure I can. It happens all the time."

Sir Bentley waved Buddy down the stairs back onto the hot sand.

"It's not my favorite way to do business since it doesn't have the subtlety I'm famous for, but it is effective. Especially out here. No witnesses. And after the wild boar get through with you, no body."

"We had a deal, Bentley."

"Yes, we did, didn't we?" Sir Bentley pointed the pistol at Buddy's chest. "You know the drill, Buddy. It's not personal. It's just business."

"Bentley, for chrissakes. Has your brain been fried by the sun?"

Sir Bentley pulled the trigger and watched Buddy's body turn an even deeper shade of crimson as he staggered backward on the sand.

"It is hot out here," Sir Bentley said.

"You're going to rot in hell," Buddy said, staring up at Bentley.

"Yeah, I know. Save me a seat."

Sir Bentley pumped a second round into the lawyer's chest. He grabbed Buddy by the scruff of his neck and dragged him through the sand towards a nearby set of palms. Moments later, Sir Bentley made his way back to the Gulfstream. He carried the backpack up the stairs, wiped his feet, and sealed the plane shut.

**

"I can't believe it."

Bob Garbo peeled off a hundred dollar bill and handed it to Doc.

"How did you know he was going to do that?"

"We're talking about Sir Bentley Carruthers. Easy money."

"Damn it. I hate losing money. Especially to you."

"Double or nothing?"

"Absolutely."

Doc laughed and trained his binoculars on Freak, who continued his descent about a half mile offshore.

**

Through his binoculars, Freak watched Sir Bentley blow the lawyer backward into the sand and finish him off with a second shot to the chest. Freak watched as the Gulfstream slowly taxied to the end of the runway and prepared for takeoff. His vision permanently blurred and the blisters on his face beginning to pop and ooze, Freak took a deep breath and summoned his final vestige of strength.

He fixed his binoculars on Doc, who was staring back at him. Freak choked with emotion and waved at his brother in law. Doc lowered his binoculars, smiled, and then saluted. Freak, tears now filling his goggles, returned the salute, and turned his attention to the Gulfstream that was beginning to accelerate down the runway.

Freak repositioned himself inside the glider, and it increased its downward spiral. He clung precariously to the metal control bar. His fingers grasped the triggers of both remaining SkyWriters, and he stared through murky goggles as the Gulfstream took flight. It soared over the sea, its flight path directly underneath him.

Freak fell back on his years of small and large arms training and mentally calculated the speed at which he and the Gulfstream were traveling.

He began to calculate the potential effect of the wind.

He began to calculate.

Then Freak stopped and reviewed his track record.

He laughed and decided, for once in his life, just to wing it.

"Fuck it."

303

He fired both rockets straight down at a ninety-degree angle.

**

Sir Bentley saw the rockets raining down on him before he saw the hang glider. He screamed and throttled back. The jet rapidly decelerated, and both SkyWriters roared past the Gulfstream's windshield. Sir Bentley exhaled and grinned from ear to ear.

"I am indestructible."

Those were the last words Sir Bentley Carruthers ever uttered. The Gulfstream and Sir Bentley exploded into small pieces that scattered and dropped into the cobalt waters along the coast. Only Sir Bentley's pith helmet survived in one piece where it floated upside down.

The recoil from the launch of the SkyWriters propelled Freak skyward. Eventually, the glider stopped its ascent and collapsed into a pile of metal and canvas.

As he dropped from the sky, Freak watched the Gulfstream explode before his eyes and, momentarily, he completely forgot about his impending fate. The fireball burst below him, and it fell into the sea and continued to burn. As his speed increased, Freak got a close look at the giant green dollar sign as the tail floated momentarily on the surface, then sank and disappeared.

"I did it," Freak said. "I finally did it."

After completing a free fall of two thousand feet, Freak hit the water. From that height, even Cool Whip feels like cement. Fortunately, Freak had passed out before he hit the water. Upon impact, Freak's clothing was shredded, and his pulverized body floated naked for some time before the sharks drifted by for dinner.

The goggles, however, remained in place.

**

"Nice shot."

"Thanks," Bob Garbo said, disassembling the rocket launcher. "But I'm afraid Freak's not gonna make it."

"No. Poor bastard." Doc pulled the binoculars away from his eyes. "I can't watch it."

"Three people dead in the last half hour," Bob said, shaking his head. "It's been awhile since I've seen that."

"Yeah," Doc said. "Let's hope it's the last."

"Feel like heading back to the resort?"

Doc stared out to sea as the last piece of the burning Gulfstream sank below the surface. He nodded and climbed down off the tunnel and dropped into the soft sand. Bob tossed down his backpack and the case holding the SkyWriter. Doc caught both and waited until Bob brushed himself off. They slowly walked through the sand towards Nirvana.

"Now what?"

"That, my friend," Doc said, throwing an arm around Bob's shoulder, "is a very good question."

"Maybe we should go talk about it over a dozen cocktails."

"Absolutely. Let's just hope Esmeralda hasn't drained the place."

They trudged through the sand, both sneaking the occasional furtive glance out to sea.

71

Coco Puffs, the estranged wife and now widow of Sir Bentley Carruthers, picked at her food as she surveyed the damage to the bar and dining room.

"What is this?"

"Boar," Doc said.

"Wild?"

"Not anymore," Merlin said.

"And you are?" Coco said.

"Hungry," Merlin said. "But I'm afraid this isn't cooked."

"Merlin, if it were cooked any longer, it would be a Cloudlifter," Doc said.

Merlin scowled, nibbled on a crispy bit, and pushed his plate aside. He turned his chair and watched Summerman and Bob as they shared the piano and worked their way through an aggressive jazz improvisation.

"I still can't believe that's Summerman Lawless," Coco said. "I thought he was killed in the boating accident with the rest of his band."

Merlin glanced at Doc, who sipped his cocktail and shrugged his shoulders.

"No," Doc said. "Apparently, he was the sole survivor. Along with his dog."

"He's a massive beast," Coco said, staring at Murray stretched out under the piano with his head resting on Summerman's feet. "What is it?"

"A mix of Golden Retriever and Newfoundland," Doc said.

"He looks like a tiger."

"Yeah, he gets that a lot," Merlin said.

Genevieve approached, kissed Doc on the cheek, and sat down. She lighted a Gitanes and offered the pack to Coco.

"So Coco," Genevieve said, "Have you decided what you're going to do with this place?"

"It's a lot to digest." She blew a smoke ring towards what used to be the ceiling. "The stupid bastard never got around to changing his will. He was convinced he was indestructible."

"Not anymore he's not," Merlin said. He caught Genevieve's glare and shrugged his shoulders. He turned to Coco. "I'm sorry. But I hated the prick."

"Get in line," Coco said.

"I like this woman," Merlin said.

"All those millions for that jet and it explodes because of a leaky, ten dollar fuel line. Unbelievable," Coco said.

"Yeah," Merlin said, glancing at Doc, "I had a hard time believing it the first time I heard it."

"And then I get the news about the will and the money," Coco said. She tried, but couldn't keep the smile from returning. "Thirty billion. What does one do with thirty billion dollars?"

"Feed the poor. Heal the sick," Doc said.

"Clothe the naked," Genevieve said.

"Bite your tongue," Doc said.

Genevieve laughed and punched Doc on the arm.

"Don't mind them," Merlin said. "Hopefully, they'll leave before they start swapping spit."

"I think it's sweet," Coco said. "I could use a little affection myself."

"Maybe et ez I who could help you out with that."

Coco looked up at the scrawny man who'd approached the table. Next to him was a woman holding a bottle of tequila and swaying back and forth.

"And you are?"

"I am Piqûre. Ze lead singer and bass player for Les Gendarmes."

"Good for you," Coco said, returning to her drink and cigarette.

"Coco, it's so nice to meet you. I'm Esmeralda." She belched, grabbed Genevieve's pack of Gitanes and helped herself. "You don't mind, do you? Thanks."

"I'm so sorry your stay was interrupted by the tragic events," Coco said.

"Tragic? No, we're cool," Esmeralda said, waving her cigarette as she swayed. "I found a few more cases in one of the storerooms."

"Damn you, Esmeralda." Piqûre shoved her away and examined the fresh burn on his forearm. "You with ze cigarettes."

"Lighten up, Frenchie." Esmeralda turned to Coco. "What I was going to say before being so rudely interrupted was that, after having to go through what we did, I deserve a raise."

"A what?" Doc said.

"A raise. As head bartender, it was most traumatic. And, as you can imagine, my tips are way down."

"I'll have a double vodka, rocks," Doc said, holding up his empty glass. "Four ice cubes."

"Get it yourself," Esmeralda said. "So, what do you say about that raise, Coco? I think a woman of your means could swing a grand a week."

"I'll see what I can do." Coco dismissed them with a wave of her hand. She watched them stagger off and focused on Doc. "I need to ask you about something my lawyer said."

"Sure. Go ahead."

"She said that there's a rumor on the street that Bentley was the behind the scenes owner of some Italian weapons company. I remember him dabbling in that stuff when we were married, but nothing ever came out of it. Or so I thought."

Doc glanced at Merlin and then back at Coco. "Yeah, I've heard the rumors."

"Is there any truth to them?"

"I think there's probably a grain of truth in all rumors," Doc said. "But I don't think there's any actual company."

"Not anymore," Merlin said.

"What?" Coco said.

"Nothing."

Coco stared at Merlin and then refocused on Doc.

"My lawyer was asking because two days ago, she was reviewing Bentley's financial statements and saw an Italian account that had a couple of hundred million in it. But he never had any operations in Italy. And the next day, the two hundred million was gone. It just vanished. No, I take that back. The account still had one dollar in it."

"Probably just a rounding error," Merlin said.

"What?" Coco said.

308

"Well, you know, with thirty billion and all those zeroes. I imagine it's easy to lose track of a few million here and there."

Doc coughed and kicked Merlin under the table.

"Not that I give a shit about some weapons company," Coco said. "Still, two hundred million is a lot of money."

"And that dollar is nothing to sneeze at either," Merlin said.

Doc kicked Merlin again, but couldn't suppress a laugh.

"I'm sure it'll turn up," Coco said. "Genevieve, let's go for that walk now. I need to hear all about this tribe."

The women excused themselves from the table and wandered off in the direction of the beach. Doc watched them until they disappeared then turned to Merlin, who looked at him with an innocent smile.

"Two hundred million?" Doc said. "Are you out of your mind?"

"Why are you getting pissed at me? You're the one who says we need to be well paid for our services."

"Yeah, but Jesus, Merlin. Two hundred million?"

"Hey, I left them a dollar."

Doc rubbed his forehead and chewed an ice cube as he pondered the possibilities.

"And you're sure nobody will ever be able to trace it back to you?"

Merlin stared at Doc and waited.

"Sorry," Doc said. "It's just a lot of money."

"Don't worry about it. He made it selling that shit to people who had no business getting their hands on those things in the first place. And she'll never miss it."

"What are you going to do with your share?" Doc said.

"Sorry, Doc. That's none of your business."

"Excuse me, Mystery Man. Have you told Summerman and Gene yet?"

"No. I thought I should wait until the four of us do our wrap-up. But we need to do it soon. Summerman crosses back over in nine days, and he said he wants to spend some time with Mamo. He's planning on flying out tomorrow. And I think Gene is catching a ride with him."

"Okay, we'll do it in the morning over breakfast."

"You going to stick around and help Chief and Bantu with the transition?"

"Absolutely. For as long as I can."

"Genevieve?"

"She'll be leading it. And I finally convinced Bob to stay on as head of security."

"Interesting. I'm surprised."

"I had to agree that he could play piano in the lounge at night." Merlin laughed.

"Well, have fun in that jungle. I've had a dozen showers and am still finding cooties."

"Oh, don't worry," Doc said. "I plan on it." He looked down when he heard his phone chirp. He removed it from his pants pocket and looked at the number. "Shit."

"What?"

"Samuels."

72

"Fifty million?" Gene whistled and looked out at the ocean.

"Each share is around forty-eight and change. Doc's setting aside five million for Garbo," Merlin said. "I still think it should come out of your share."

"Well, it's time for you to readjust your thinking," Doc said.

"Who gives a shit?" Gene said. "Almost fifty million bucks for pretending to be that dickhead's lackey for nine months?"

"You were the dickhead's lackey," Merlin said.

"You know what I mean."

"I'm getting used to this," Summerman said. "The Posse strikes again."

"Well done, gentlemen," Doc said. "It was a bit unorthodox, but it seemed to work out. Now, it's on to new business."

Gene groaned.

"Jesus, Doc. I'm flying out today with Summerman and my plan is to take a month off."

"You can have a week," Doc said.

"Two weeks," Gene said.

"Five days," Doc said.

Gene shook his head. "Damn. All right. A week it is. Samuels?"

"Yeah. I'm not real happy about it either."

"You tell Genevieve yet?"

"I'll tell her later."

"Man, you two just can't catch a break," Gene said.

Doc shrugged his shoulders and turned to Summerman.

"While you're on the other side, I've got a list of people Samuels needs you to hover in on."

"You mean during those rare times when I'm not trying to find the Cave Dweller?"

"Exactly. And Gene?"

"Yeah."

"Pack some warm clothes."

311

"Where are we going?"

"Someplace cold."

"I'm going to need some clarification here, Doc."

Doc laughed.

"Northern Russia."

"Shit. For how long?"

"Hopefully only a couple weeks, but you never know. And you need to bone up on your art history."

"What?"

"Don't worry about it. You'll do just fine. But pay particular attention to European painters from the 18th century. After that, Prince Abbas needs our help."

"All right," Gene said. He nodded at Merlin. "What about him?"

"What about me?" Merlin said.

"Merlin can do what he needs to do from anywhere," Doc said.

Merlin beamed at Gene.

"You should have studied harder in school. Maybe you would have learned some skills that are useful. You know, after all this sun, I'm thinking about maybe Aspen. The fall is beautiful up there."

Summerman laughed and noticed a plane beginning its descent.

"There's our ride. You ready, Gene?"

"Yeah, let's get out of here."

"Murray. You ready?"

The dog bounced to his feet and said his goodbyes. Doc and Merlin rubbed his head and then hugged Summerman and Gene.

"Travel safe, guys," Doc said. "And remember to say hi to my folks on the other side, Summerman. And my brother."

"Will do. How about you, Merlin?"

"Just the usual. Thanks, Summerman."

Summerman and Murray, trailed by Gene, headed towards the jeep that would take them to the plane. Summerman stopped and turned.

"I just remembered. Any message for Sir Bentley if I happen to run into him on the other side?"

"No," Merlin said. "And don't tell him about the two hundred million. The last thing I want is that bastard haunting me."

73

Doc stood waiting in the light rain falling against the setting sun and studied the rainbow that seemed to begin where he was standing and end in the distance near the resort; now a GPS-measured distance of 4.2 miles. Isolated from the outside world for centuries, the tribe was down to a mere four mile trek that would soon seem even shorter as the Outsiders demanded accessibility and comfort.

The rain fell harder, and the birds began chattering amongst themselves. Doc looked through the rain and watched her climb from the water. Not bothering to dry off, she tied her sarong across her chest and smiled at him. Washed clean by her swim and the rain, her skin glistened in the disappearing sunlight. She kissed his cheek and hooked his arm as they strolled towards their hut.

"You're smiling," she said. "Must be the rainbow."

Doc reached down and squeezed.

"Yeah, that must be it."

She stroked the side of his face with the back of her hand.

"You need to go?"

"Yeah, I've got to get out of here tomorrow. Summerman's sending the jet back."

"Tell him I said hello when you see him."

"I won't be seeing him. Not for the next nine months."

"Will he be traveling?"

"Yeah, you could say that."

She looked at him quizzically, but let it go.

"Are you sure you wouldn't like to stay a few more days?"

"Are you kidding? I wish I could spend a year here. But duty calls."

"Maybe someday you'll explain to me exactly what that entails."

"Maybe." Doc held her hand as she worked her way across a small stream. "Are you sure you're going to be okay here?"

"Don't worry. I'll be fine. And Bob will take good care of me."

"That's what I'm afraid of."

Genevieve laughed and squeezed his arm. "We really can't catch a break, can we?"

They stopped to watch a group of children kicking and chasing the soccer ball Doc had given them.

"What's on your mind, Bodhisattva?"

"I was just thinking. Today, soccer. Tomorrow, it'll be beer commercials."

"It was Chief's decision, Doc. His and Bantu's. Our job is to help them manage the change, not control it."

"I know. I'm just afraid they're going to lose something in the process."

"Like their virginity?"

Doc considered the idea and nodded.

"Yeah, that's pretty close."

They resumed walking and soon reached the steps that led inside their hut.

"Well, if it's any consolation, thanks to you it's going to be consensual. And not rape."

"Speaking of consensual."

"Yes? Something on your mind, Doc?"

They effortlessly hopped up the two steps and, inside, she kissed him hard. He reluctantly broke away and tossed her a towel. She grabbed two beers from a cooler filled with ice, one of the few outside luxuries they'd allowed themselves. She took a long swallow as Doc approached from behind and untied her sarong. She smiled, squeezed rainwater out of her hair and patted her breasts dry. She turned and stared at him.

"I've been going nonstop all day and need to take the edge off," Genevieve said. "Momma needs a good workout tonight."

Doc moved behind her and dried her back with a fresh towel. The birds and animals fell silent as the rain intensified and Doc, also speechless, gently slid his hands down her back and sighed as he reached nirvana. He stared at her from behind, then inched closer and nuzzled the back of her neck

"And I'm talking about a real workout. We might even have to break out the white powder."

Doc sighed again.

"I seriously doubt that."

"So you think you can handle it, Bodhisattva?"

"Booga, wooga, nooga."

www.ingramcontent.com/pod-product-compliance
Lightning Source LLC
Chambersburg PA
CBHW060401260626
47160CB00006B/2395